Imperfect
Lives

Richard C Davis

Cover by Muarizio Marotta

ISBN-13:978-0692158708

DEDICATION

To my mother and father who brought me into being and lovingly cared for me. To my Brother David who always kept me on my toes and was an enormous help and comfort when my oldest son died. To my sister who was the smartest sweetest woman I've ever known. You are all gone from me, but we were a wonderful loving caring family. To my wife Catherine and grown children who have supported and encouraged me every way possible. Thank you

ACKNOWLEDGMENTS

I would like to thank my many great teachers for all their efforts on my behalf. From first grade on. You're scattered over five states, eight schools, and three universities, but you were marvelous, and I'll never forget any of you. Also, a grateful thank you to all the intelligent gracious people that I've worked with and learned so much from. Especially, Don Stoltz, Michael Bloom, Lyall Phillips, Kent Mount, and Peter Mrozinski.

ONE

It was early, eight o'clock. Another summer morning, but when still half-asleep Morris wandered into the kitchen and saw the mountain of food, his mother was pulling from the refrigerator, pantry, and grocery bags he remembered. Mom was putting on one of her events. It wasn't like going to the fireworks in the boat with his friends, but for a family obligation it was okay. Later in life, Morris would look back on this Fourth of July as the beginning of unimaginable changes.

He would meet Hanna today. She was the daughter of his mother and father's friends, Annette and Robert Williston. Beyond knowing of her, her name, and that she was an only child; she wasn't any part of Morris's circle. He knew Hanna's father, but only the name of the daughter. That all changed at their Fourth of July party. Hanna was fourteen; going into her first year of high school. The same high school Morris graduated from in June.

Morris's family moved here from New Jersey when he was fourteen, Hanna's age. His father was head of the engineering department at General Mills. His mother invited the senior staff and their families to join them at their lake home for what was to become a summer tradition. It would come to be known as, Fourth of July, at the Stevens.

The senior engineering staff was a close-knit group. Over the past three years, Morris, interacted with all the men at various times at the headquarters office, and during their visits to his home. He knew them well and, understood through the daily routine of relying on one another the men became friends.

The senior staff consisted of Morris's father, William Stevens, a civil engineer, and head of the engineering department. Craig Anderson, a structural engineer, George Costellano, an electrical engineer, and, Robert Williston, a mechanical engineer, each headed those specialty engineering departments. They were bringing their wives and children for a swimming, boating, lots of food, good old-fashioned fun Fourth of July. Morris's mother didn't do a lot of entertaining, rarely more than four times a year, however, when she did it was an event.

In ten weeks, Morris would be a freshman at Northwestern University four hundred miles away and was caught solidly between anticipation and apprehension. Most unsettling for Morris was not having any idea what he might want to do in life. In two days, he would turn eighteen, and his worldview was one of vast panoramas of possibilities and only that.

He had applied to Harvard because he believed it to be the best. But he didn't learn he was accepted there until almost five weeks after being accepted at Northwestern. Cautious about his future, Morris took Northwestern's offer. He justified not waiting for Harvard's response believing an actual offer was real and more valuable than all the wishes and hopes he might ever have.

His family concurred, reminding him, all the flying back and forth to Boston would end up being a considerable additional expense, not to mention a constant logistical bother. Second-guessing himself Morris was continually reminding himself Northwestern would be fine, he would do fine, and everything would work out fine. Nevertheless, his apprehension continued unabated as full-time background noise.

Would he fit in? Would he like it? Would they like him? Would he do well? He was leaving behind friends. Actually, just two close ones, but they were important to him and his well-being. His family moved a lot during his earlier years, and he knew in time things usually worked out. He wasn't terribly concerned about being alone in a new place. Still, this time, leaving home, being on his own was a major event in Morris's life.

It hadn't taken long for Morris to reach that place where he wanted to stop thinking about it and just get on with it. His close friend, Jerry Ransom, who enlisted in the Navy, would probably end up stationed overseas. Morris's other best friend; Michael Worthy, intent on becoming a priest, enrolled in a Catholic Seminary.

As was Michael's whimsical way, he referred to his Jesuit College as the priest factory. He was continually saying things like, "I can't wait. It's run by the same bunch that ran the Inquisition. They'll know every way there is to get you to pay attention." The three of them were close, steadfast friends from ninth grade and, by the end of August; all three would be starting new lives, far from each other. It was hard for him to imagine not having each other to rely on.

Morris's immediate family included his mother and father, a younger sister, Alice, who Morris thought to be both smart, and caught somewhere between adorable and pretty. She would turn sixteen in a few weeks. His baby brother, David, who in Morris's eyes was probably the brightest of them all, but more to the point was considered by Morris, because of his never-ending never reprimanded for shenanigans, to be a thoroughly spoiled eleven-year-old brat.

The three families coming to the party were bringing six children of which Hanna was, by four years, the oldest. At first glance, Hanna, was every bit the typical junior high student. Thin, with a boyish figure, her breasts were barely noticeable. She had almost no hips and appeared to be either very serious or shy. Her marvelously formed face like that of a European high fashion model came across a bit on the reserved haughty side.

She had long, almost white blonde hair, a pleasantly shaped mouth, and nicely proportioned teeth. Best of all, and as everyone soon discovered, when she smiled there was this incredible transformation. Her face would suddenly be unbelievably warm and friendly, an altogether welcoming sight.

In a few years, Hanna was going to be an unusually attractive woman. Her eyes like her mothers were stunning. The most unusual incredible shade of blue Morris ever remembered seeing. They looked like two perfectly matched, gleaming turquoise stones, sitting on blanched white bone and when people first met her, they couldn't help staring.

Morris immediately noticed Hanna being endlessly managed and fussed over by her mother. It was a constant ongoing stream of directives. "Hanna quit twisting your hair, sit up straight. Cross your legs you're wearing shorts. Hanna, help Alice keep an eye on the children and be sure to ask Morris about Northwestern. He's starting there in the fall."

Hanna soon moved taking a seat next to Morris's sister. Hanna was two years younger than Alice, but they seemed to share some commonality beyond being girls and having blue eyes. They ended up spending most of the afternoon in each other's company. When the time came, Hanna readily joined in helping Morris and Alice set out the food, plates, and cutlery.

Morris spent the afternoon in operational mode, grilling the hot dogs and hamburgers, helping set out the food, and later taking everyone out in the boat. He spoke with Hanna briefly. Just enough to determine she was bright, didn't like being noticed, and possessed the lowest, thick honey-like, but oddly cadenced throaty feminine voice he'd ever heard.

Three years younger than him, in the scheme of their teenage worlds, Hanna was a child. Nevertheless, her thick, wonderfully sensual voice ensnared him. That such an unintentional evocative womanly sound came from the mouth of a fourteen-year-old girl startled him and everyone else. The cadence and intonation were lusty, earthy, low, slow paced, and unforgettably sensual. It was a remarkable voice, and it belonged with someone much older.

Despite trying not to, Morris found himself aroused by that voice. It was way too captivating for someone so young. It stopped him cold and awakened him all at the same time. He was instantly attracted to her and found himself just wanting to listen to her. He began encouraging her, asking her all manner of things about what she liked to do, and what she was interested in.

Morris found it extremely difficult to listen to her voice and follow what she was saying. She told him she mainly liked to read and draw, and she was learning how to paint. He managed to track that much, and said, "Is that what you want Hanna, to be an artist?"

"Hopefully, someday, but so far, the painting part's been difficult, lots of trial and error, with not such good results. Getting it technically perfect's hard. When it's wrong, it ruins the whole thing. It's awfully frustrating, but I know it's the only way I'll learn."

"Don't tell me you expected to be perfect right out of the gate?"

"No, but it's not been easy. There's so much to learn. I get some of it right, then I try something, and ruin it. I get frustrated and disappointed, but I'm getting better."

"About working with the paint?"

"Yes, about color, and especially understanding and seeing light. Then there's learning the techniques to make it all work. It's a lot to know let alone master."

Their conversation was going along nicely when quite innocently, he said, "Speaking of color, your eyes are remarkable." She flushed and looked down. Morris instantly wished he hadn't said that and excusing herself Hanna abruptly moved off. At that moment, he had little time to worry further about Hanna's sudden discomfort or her abrupt departure. It was a hectic, busy afternoon. Nevertheless, Morris didn't forget about her, nor what drove her away.

***

Morris rarely thought about where he lived or how privileged he was, but he was. Their home was situated on one of the most spectacular vistas anyone could ever wish for. The house, a spacious five-bedroom home, looked out from on high over a large portion of a big renown freshwater lake twenty-five miles west of downtown Minneapolis.

The house was built in 1895 and framed on both sides and in front by mature elms. A person, sitting in one of the swings on the ten-foot-deep full-length screened-in porch, could see almost all the way to Wayzata, seven miles away. The house was a far cry from the modern, white brick, mahogany, and expansive glass home his father designed, built, and they left behind in New Jersey. But it was a grand old house on a great site on Lake Minnetonka, one of the most beautiful freshwater lakes in the country.

TWO

The spring after they moved here his father designed and added an addition to each side of the house. The additions, done in white brick, provided a large modern open kitchen and family room on one side. On the other side was a new master bedroom, incorporating a large full bathroom with access from both the new entryway and the new master bedroom.

Originally square with some gingerbread trim at the gables and about the cornices, the house was boxy and ordinary appearing from the street. Not so looking up at it from the lake. Sitting back from and up on the hill twenty-five feet above the lake with its full-length screen porch and second story sunroom the house was impressively grand looking.

His father's additions gave the house a much more expansive gracious look. The new front entrance in addition to providing two large coat closets and a much more spacious foyer greatly improved the house's overall street appearance. Nevertheless, Morris's favorite thing about their home remained the huge screened porch on the lakeside that ran the entire length of the original house.

From the screened porches double doors and broad steps, thirty-six four-foot-wide stone steps worked their way down to the expansive lawn. From the bottom step to the beach was about a hundred and fifty feet. There were two buildings on the furthest opposite sides of the property. To the left and at the water's edge was the boathouse. On the far right, set back thirty feet from the beach was what the Steven's called the barbecue house. Had the property been a hundred feet wider their home would've been considered an estate.

Both the boathouse and barbecue house were built like barns once were. Both buildings were pegged post and beam construction. Both were finished on the exterior with lap siding and gingerbread trim matching the house. Unlike the boathouse the side facing the lake of the barbecue house was screened almost the full width from the floor to the roof joists.

The back of the barbecue house had a fieldstone patio surrounded by Hosta's, Yews, and shaped Arborvitaes. Full Dutch half doors provided a serving opening. Inside on the end of the building facing away from the property, there was an impressive fieldstone open-hearth fireplace. It had a large opening and a substantial wrought iron swing out rack. The rack held several sturdy iron hangers which were once used to hold large cast iron pots. One of the big pots still hung there, but the others were long gone.

Built-in as part of the back wall just under the double-wide Dutch serving doors was a counter height stone and brick wood burning stove. It was fitted with a removable cast iron grate for grilling and with the double Dutch serving doors opened was where Morris grilled the hamburgers and hotdogs.

The interior wood was baby skin smooth with a lovely warm honey brown patina. Both buildings were built at the same time as the main house. The terracotta tiles and monstrous twenty-two-foot-long wide board table in the barbecue house were warm, not overused, and welcoming. The table was forty-two inches wide with three six-foot-long trestle benches on each side. There was plenty of space between them for easy access. It could seat twenty-four, more if stools were added.

From the outside, the buildings looked similar, but were built for entirely different purposes. That wonderful old boathouse contained an aroma which was unique and as distinctive as anything Morris ever encountered. It was a complex aroma made from mixing the smell of wood, varnish, water, hemp rope, canvas, oil, leather, caulking, and paint together for many summers. Now, after sixty-five years, that aroma was embedded in the wood forever.

It was an odor unique in the world. One Morris would never forget. Not only did it smell wonderful, but once inside you were enveloped not only in all those aromatic sensations but wrapped in the most beautiful soft light ever imagined. There were places in there where he swore you could hold the light in your hands. It worked its way in through the high clearstory windows. It spilled all over the smoothed now aged wood beams, trusses, work benches, and cabinets. It went everywhere reflecting gently off the water sending flashes dancing casually all around and up in amongst the beams and trusses.

Even on an overcast day, it was a magical place. It was Morris's special place, a remarkable gentle, aromatic, quiet chapel like place. They moved here over thanksgiving just in time for winter. That first summer he'd often go inside and just be there letting all those smells and that incredible light surround and hold him.

The posts and beams, the workbenches, shelves, everything in both buildings were made from hand-planed and smoothed unfinished hardwood, all of it sixty-five years old and aged to a luxurious soft brown perfection. In the middle of all that aged unfinished wood and those wonderful aromas in the channel leading to the lake sat a perfectly centered gleaming twenty-three-foot-long mahogany runabout.

Approaching Hanna and his sister who were sitting next to each another, Morris asked them to give him a hand getting the boat out. Hanna tried to beg off, but Morris insisted, "Hanna it takes three. I wouldn't ask, but we need you."

Somewhat reluctantly, Hanna followed them to the boathouse. As they were crossing the lawn, Morris said, "Hanna, you aren't going to believe this place. The first summer we lived here I'd come down and just stand inside. Being in there early in the morning or just before dark is otherworldly. If you find it as intriguing as I think you will and want to, you're welcomed to come back and visit it again. Have your dad bring you some Saturday when he has to stop by one of us will get you home."

When they first entered, it was quite dark compared to the bright July sunlight. It took their eyes a few moments to adjust, and seconds after passing through the doorway an odd little noise escaped Hanna's lips. Not a gasp or a sigh it was something else. Given her unusual voice, Morris took it as an utterance of surprised amazement. A few moments later she said, "What a wonderful place. The light's unreal. I could sit in here for hours learning it."

Morris said, "I thought you'd appreciate it."

Still trying to take it in, looking everywhere about her, Hanna said, "What was it you needed me to do?"

Hanna and Alice opened the doors to the lake. With Hanna on one side, Alice on the other and Morris in the boat the three of them carefully backed the boat out. It didn't take long to travel the twenty feet necessary to clear the decking and get to the lake. With the boat now out in open water, Morris stepped off the foredeck and onto the boathouse deck across from Hanna. He handed the line to Alice who walked the boat up and tied it off. Trapped on the other side Morris indicated to Hanna she'd have to get back to the yard through the boathouse, he said, "You can help me close the doors."

Back inside she said, "What an amazing place. They're places in here where I can hold the light in my hands."

"It's been special for me. One of my most favorite places, but it's also a down to earth practical building." He pointed out the overhead winches ready to lift the boat out of the water for storage. He showed her the workbenches and storage bins. He pointed to the canoe resting on the beams above their heads.

Listening to him she had grown quiet. He could tell she was somewhere else. Morris also silent and close almost touching her watched spellbound as her thin, delicate fingers traced their way across the silky-smooth wood of the workbench. In that light with her almost glowing blue eyes and white-blond hair, her face was as arresting as anything he'd ever seen.

The way he suddenly felt toward her took him by surprise. It was sensual, arousing, and given her age, he believed, completely inappropriate. But stepping out through the side door into the bright sunlight, and seeing all the people gathered on the lawn, brought an instant end to any further fanciful imaginings.

Much as he tried not to Morris found himself continuing to look over at her. Later, he asked Hanna to come along and help Alice, and he manage the younger children in the boat. What with the children's boisterous behavior, there was little opportunity for further discussion, and they spoke only sparingly the rest of the afternoon.

As the adults began rounding up their children and preparing to leave and say their goodbyes, Hanna made a point of seeking Morris out. She said, "I'm glad you asked me to help with the boat. I know it was your way of getting me to see the light in the boathouse. It's a wonderful place, Morris. Thank you." And putting her hand over her heart, she blessed him with her amazing warm smile and said, "I'll keep it right here."

THREE

Other than a visit later that summer with her father when Hanna spent the entire visit alone in the boathouse. Morris did not see or think about Hanna until he came home from Northwestern for Thanksgiving. When his mother informed him; the Costellano family, the Anderson's, and the Williston's along with one of his sister's teachers from the high school and one from his brother's grade school were all going to be at their house for Thanksgiving dinner did Morris know he would see Hanna again.

That his mother was putting on Thanksgiving for all these people did not surprise anyone in the Steven's household. They all knew their mother upon learning someone didn't have any family nearby and were going to be alone over the holidays she would invite them. She especially tried to make room for single people who were away from their families on Thanksgiving or Christmas.

These were most often teachers occasionally someone new from his father's office or possibly an older recently widowed person from church. She called them her holiday orphans saying to her children, "It's no fun to have Thanksgiving or Christmas dinner alone." She would insist, strangers or not they join them. This Thanksgiving there were two teachers and the three men and their families from his dad's office.

One of the holiday orphans was a young man born and raised in Rhode Island. The other from Brother David's elementary school was a young woman who grew up in a coastal town south of Portland, Oregon. Having strangers for Thanksgiving was fun and always made for an interesting table.

His mother would get the conversation started by asking the guest she felt was most at ease among all these strangers something such as, "Andy tell us about Thanksgivings at your house?" This got the conversation going and gave the others time to compose their thoughts and be prepared for when Claire came around to them.

Morris's mother, Clair Stevens, was black haired, bright blue-eyed and tiny. She was Southern, five feet two inches of old Charleston, South Carolina, Southern. She had impeccable manners, and so did her children. She was composed, pleasant, and as gracious as anyone who ever lived. She was a pretty, shapely, smart very feminine woman. Due to her even smaller size as a child, she grew up with the nickname Tadpole which became Tad at some point.

Tiny or not, Claire Stevens brooked no bigotry or intolerance of any kind, ever. He watched her on more than one occasion cause quite an understated, but well remembered openly public ruckus about it. As a first grader, it was the first thing Morris remembered learning that was terrifically important to his well-being.

He was to never ever use the word whop, chink, nigger, mick, or kike where his mother or father might hear or find out. He was told if he did he'd have to find a new family to live with. Denigrating people because of their color, dress, religion, language, or using racial slurs of any kind was forbidden. It was absolutely, and utterly unacceptable in the Steven's household.

It was the only rigid, inflexible rule his family ever had. Like every family, they had lots of other rules about right and wrong. Those were mostly learned by observation, assumption, and indirect and direct commentary, and they could occasionally be bent or outright broken. But not the bigotry rule, it was crystal clear and inviolate.

He thought maybe the bigotry rule was there because his parents grew up where racism and bigotry were practiced as an accepted way of life. Morris never learned why this was such an essential matter to his parents. In the end, it didn't matter why it just was. On these issues, Morris tried to never use such words or to allow himself that kind of thinking.

His mother's events at Thanksgiving and around Christmas and the Fourth of July were interesting to Morris. It was one of his unspoken family duties to pitch in and help with the guests, the food, and generally anything else. He supposed somewhere long ago there was some instruction or discussion concerning his duties, but he couldn't remember when. He'd been doing this since he could remember, and he accepted it and went along helping wherever needed.

He saw and spoke several times to Hanna over the next two years at what became his mother's annual Fourth of July, Thanksgiving, and Christmas parties. They talked to each other enough for her to learn she could trust him and for him to learn she felt she was getting somewhere with her painting. She told him she spent her childhood growing up in a small town called Hanes somewhere in Indiana. Hanes sounded safe and unique. Hanna told him there was a big park with a creek, next to a field with tall grass. On warm summer night's there were lots of kids and lots and lots of fireflies.

Hanna was a remarkable young woman, exceptionally intelligent; she easily kept up with him. He tried his best to figure her out. Reading people was something Morris was good at. Nevertheless, Hanna remained his enigma. She appeared shy, but he thought that to be a substitute for whatever was going on. She was cautious and kept a part of herself hidden from everyone. Morris was sure the root of her caution and hesitancy with him was all about him being male.

Regardless of her caution, her voice bonded him to her. He never failed to think of her as special. He knew it wasn't right, but he was tremendously attracted to her. Morris worked hard putting her at ease, just so he could draw her out and keep her talking. She always seemed pleased when they saw each other, and both enjoyed catching up on each other's lives. He was also keenly aware of the increasing tensions between Hanna and her mother.

FOUR

Morris came home from school for Thanksgiving at the beginning of his junior year fully expecting to once again be pressed into service. He smiled a smile of relief when he learned they wouldn't be hosting Thanksgiving. He could kick back, relax, and enjoy himself. Mrs. Williston took it on this year. She said, "Tad's hosted Thanksgiving for the past three years, and the Anderson family would be out of town. They'd have plenty of room at their house for the remaining families."

Morris off-handedly asked his mother how Hanna was getting along. She rolled her eyes, and said, "Hanna's changed. She's dressing oddly for a girl and doesn't have much to say to anybody. Try not to be overly surprised by Hanna."

"What's that mean? She get a big tattoo?"

"She took a scissors and cut off all that gorgeous long blond hair. Annett's quite upset about it. She told me Hanna used to be timid and shy, now she's sullen, preoccupied, and withdrawn."

Morris, searching his closet to find some things he needed back at school left for the Williston's after the rest of his family. He took a wrong turn arriving, much to his mother's consternation, just as they were all being seated at the dining table. Hanna answered the door saying, "They're waiting for you," and quickly hung up his jacket. Hanna was a shock. She cut her long white blond hair not just off, but short. The little left went everywhere, like a little boy's might. She was wearing men's clothes. Morris was dumbfounded.

When she first saw him she smiled automatically, her voice and that smile disarmed him. Surprisingly, without the long hair her face, with the high cheekbones, beautifully formed mouth, and almost perfect symmetry looked older and even more open and welcoming than he remembered. Hanna was a quite attractive young woman, especially so, when she smiled. Unfortunately, she did that sparingly. Morris concerned about the radical change almost asked her what was going on but thought better of it.

She was wearing a long sleeve, red, and gray plaid Pendleton shirt, with a tee shirt under it. The long sleeve shirt was too big for her, and if she had breast, they weren't evident. She had on boy's dungarees rolled up at the cuffs and black high-top sneakers. He followed her into the dining room fully aware from behind, in those baggy pants; she had no discernible hips and looked to be a boy. He wondered how she was keeping them up.

Without the absent Anderson family, there were twelve in all. The Steven's family, the Costellano's and their children, all happily seated in the dining room with the Williston's.

The teasing by Robert and George about Morris getting lost began the moment he entered the room. It entertained everyone, but Hanna who was seated across from him and stuck in her new, closed mouth, silent mode.

Morris liked all the men who worked with his father, but he was particularly fond of Hanna's father, Robert. He had short reddish blond hair and a quiet, careful, relaxed, thoughtful way about him. He always took time with Morris and asked, with genuine concern, about what he was doing and how he was getting along.

Morris didn't know the wives as well having only been together with them for the picnics, the Thanksgivings, and a few times at various Christmas gatherings. He'd little opportunity to get to know them. The times Morris did have a chance to speak with them consisted mostly of questions to him about his college courses and those sorts of niceties. But he was keenly aware the wives all seemed genuinely interested in the welfare of each other's children. Having interacted with the men in a much more personal direct way, many times over the years, at his home and his dad's office Morris felt considerably more at ease with the men.

FIVE

Morris no longer thought of himself as a child, although he carefully towed the line between being a man and when in the presence of older established men, maintaining his subordinate position as a young adult. Morris was observant, smart, nineteen years old and a junior at Northwestern. He was earning a double major in humanities and linguistics.

Morris worked hard these past two years taking the maximum credits allowed. He thought he'd like to be a writer, a serious one, and he already knew enough to keep that to himself. Mrs. Costellano said, "Morris are you planning on continuing on to graduate school? And if so, what have you decided to Study?"

He smiled, and said, "Dad thinks I'd make a good architect. Mom would like to have a Lawyer in the family."

Mrs. Costellano asked, "And what do you think Morris?"

"I'm still thinking about it. All of it, all the time."

Annett said, "Morris whatever you decide, do your parents a big favor, don't go off fancying yourself some beatnik artist character. Look at Hanna. She's a senior in high school, but now that she fancies herself an artist look what she's done to herself." Morris looked across at Hanna hearing Annett's words pouring out, "All that beautiful long hair, gone just like that. She'd wear those clothes to school, but they'd send her home. Why would any young woman want to dress like a boy? Can anyone tell me? I'd like to know."

Morris unsure about wading into this, but feeling awful for Hanna, decided to say something. Hanna, flushed, deeply hurt and, embarrassed her mother was doing this in front of all these people, spoke first. "Mother, really? Now, at the Thanksgiving table, in front of everyone, nobody cares what I wear? Well within reason, and this is certainly within reason."

"Why can't you wear something appropriate like Alice? She looks lovely, and nobody's going to wonder for a second if she's a boy."

Morris heard himself say, "Don't worry Mrs. Williston, you'd have to be half blind or drunk and see Hanna's face, and think even for a second, she was a boy."

Annett said, "She never does her eyes or wears makeup, not even lipstick. With that short hair, she looks like a boy to me."

Trying his best to defuse this, Morris said, "We all go through alternative clothing periods trying out different things. There are a few hilarious photos of me when I was seven or eight when the neighbor girls dressed me up in their mom's clothes. I remember when David was five. We were in a store getting him rain boots. He wouldn't have anything to do with those ugly green and black ones. David went right over to the girl's side and picked out a pair of bright pink ones and wore them until they no longer fit. I thought that was a pretty neat thing for him to do."

Annett said, "Well, Morris, Hanna's not five or seven or eight, she's a senior in high school."

Knowing better Morris kept talking, "We all try out different clothes trying to fit into our particular situation the best we can. All the men in dad's office know exactly what they're supposed to wear at work. They're all talented, highly accomplished engineers, and I'll bet not one of them gives a hoot about their clothing. They conform because it's expected and not to would be a distraction and bring lots of unwanted and unnecessary attention."

He heard his mother's soft southern voice, "Annett, Morris's right about that. Our husbands are engineers and, if we didn't give them our help, they'd show up looking more out of step than Hanna."

Morris Said, "Some of us do their rebelling through their clothes, but personally, I've found it's less complicated and easier to just go along. I wear my student uniform, it's always the same. Slacks, loafers, dress shirt, sweaters, maybe a blazer, and occasionally, a tie."

Annett's disapproval of his continued participation was clear when she said, "Morris what exactly are you inferring?"

He thought to himself, Jesus, Morris, you're in it. You've stepped right into the middle of it. Trying to defuse Annett's increasing acrimony and allow room for alternative possibilities. Morris said, "Hanna's a straight A student if she sees herself an artist what's the harm. She's just experimenting with different looks."

Annett like a dog being pestered and poked with a stick in a strident, rising voice, said, "She calls it art. But her room, excuse me, her studio is supposedly full of her paintings, but we've no idea if any art exists because she locks the door. We weren't allowed in when she was working! Now she keeps it locked all the time!" Silence descended over the table.

Four-year-old Ellen Costellano said, "Mom, I need to go to the bathroom."

Robert, embarrassed and unbelieving of Annett's going after Hanna in front of their friends, wasn't at all sure how to end this. But it needed to stop. The requested bathroom break was it. Exasperated, Robert said, "Hanna why don't you take Morris up to your room, ah, your studio, and show him your artwork?"

Getting up, Hanna said, "Right dad, I'm sure that's what Morris expected for Thanksgiving, to have to go see some teenage girl's artwork."

Morris heard his voice, "I'd like that." He knew the whole dinner was about to go up in flames. He needed to get Hanna out of there. He sensed she was moments from true nastiness. It hurt him to realize whatever was going on between Hanna and her mother had solidly taken root damaging both. "Lead the way," he said, following Hanna out of the dining room. They crossed the living room, up the stairs and down the hall to her room.

***

With watery eyes, Hanna unlocked the door and ushered him in, saying in a wavering, but still marvelously sensual voice, "You don't have to do this Morris. Dad knew I was about to say something unladylike and storm off. She won't leave me alone. It was all Dad could think of to end it as quickly as possible.

"When she first saw me after I cut off my hair she burst into tears saying, Hanna, what have you done? Why? I don't understand. She was crying the whole time she was talking. She stewed for two days and took me to a beauty shop and pleaded with them to do something with my hair. What a scene that was. Five beauticians gathered around me like I was a washed up dead creature. They trimmed up my more glaring hacks and gave me what they unanimously decided was a tussled boy look."

"Hanna, she loves you. You're her only child. All her eggs are in one basket. Your clothes, cutting your hair off, trying so hard to not look like a girl; you're scaring the crap out of her."

"I don't want to be all girly, get married, and make babies. I hate all that boy-girl stuff. The whole idea makes me sick. It's revolting and demeaning. I saw it coming a mile away my first day at the high school. I was minding my own business, walking down the hall, going past a bunch of senior boys not even looking at them. One of them said; look at all the white blond hair. I'll bet she'd really be something to roll in the hay. Even more touching, from one, I heard, I'll bet you ten bucks her snatch doesn't match. I didn't even know what that meant." She had tears in her eyes.

Glancing at Hanna from across the room, Morris continued moving from one drawing to the next. He said, "You know what the very first thing people notice when they see another person? The first thing is what sex they are. It's so automatic we don't even realize we've done it. We never even consciously think about doing it, but it sets the table for everything that follows, good and bad. Like that boy commenting about your pubic hair color. Most of us would keep that to ourselves, but he didn't and, that's different, that's a whole other kind of behavior problem."

"I can't be an object, Morris. I won't be."

Morris concentrating, moving from drawing to drawing said, "No Hanna you don't have to be anyone's object."

"How do you stop it?"

"Some women use razor-sharp humor, and are quite skilled at it, but most just keep their head up and ignore it. Hanna these drawings are outstanding, and the painted pieces are?"

"Experiments, I'm trying different techniques with paint."

"What an eye. Your lines are dead on, they're perfect. How long you been doing this?"

"Since we first moved here, when I was eleven. It was right after the school year ended I didn't have any friends, so I started drawing."

"Do you go to art classes or take instruction somewhere?"

"I taught myself."

"You taught yourself to draw like this?"

"I practice all the time. Mostly I learn from books and trying different things."

"Boy, Hanna, you must read a lot?"

"I do, but not for fun. I'm trying to figure out how to manage the paint the way the Renaissance painters did."

"You said you were learning how to paint, but everything here, these are all drawings, and I have to say they're amazing. I'm astonished. Wow! We have a star amongst us, but where are the paintings? I'd like to see some."

"If I show you will you promise not to tell?"

"Tell what?"

"What they're about."

"Sure, I'll keep that promise."

She went to her closet and wrestled a large folio out from behind some other folios. Morris put it on the bed, sat beside it, and opened it. The first image was a young woman imprisoned in vines. Her face was fiercely alive. She was looking directly at him. Her eyes commanded him to help her; she gazed out at him with such intensity it made him uneasy.

Morris was stunned by what he was seeing. Transported far away and in astonished silence, he paged through painting after painting of mostly female figures. Some enmeshed in foliage, some behind lace curtains so delicate he found his fingers touching them. Morris was overwhelmed at the ability and creativity of the young woman sitting across from him.

Dumbfounded, Morris sat there for many minutes looking at one painting. She gazed out at him from behind a delicate sheer black veil. She was engulfed in a misty ominous darkness and so sad he was choking up. Morris knew how to paint in oils and could draw and well, but not like this. Not anything like this. She could do a whole figure perfectly in a few strokes. Her lines were precise, unimaginably good. The colors were soft, warm, the flesh appeared alive. "These are acrylics?"

She nodded, and said, "I underlay the skin areas with translucent washes. I studied how the old masters did it with oils, I experimented a lot. I use acrylics because they dry faster. It's taken forever, but I'm beginning to get close."

Morris knew he was sitting across from someone extraordinary, a truly unbelievably gifted person. He set the painting down and looking directly at her said, "Hanna this is unbelievable. These are the most amazing paintings I've ever seen. Do your mom and dad know about them? Have they seen them?"

"God no! Dad's an engineer and mom doesn't think of art in any way beyond having something colorful to hang above the sofa. The only things they've seen are the sketches and color experiments pinned up on the walls."

"I think you're shortchanging them. I think they'll be even more impressed than I am."

"Why would you ever think that?"

"You're their daughter Hanna, and this is the finest most accomplished work I've ever seen."

"Morris, you're just saying that because of what happened at the table?"

"Really, that's what you think? I'm being nice to you? Hanna your drawings, the paintings, it's like being back hundreds of years in an old master's studio. This is the most astounding work I've ever seen. That girl behind the black lace veil is spectacular, unbelievable. I had to touch her veil, I wanted to lift it. Hanna, you've got to show your work."

"They're not that good, and neither am I. I'm nowhere near ready for anything like that."

"Hanna, these paintings are spectacular."

"Morris, you don't understand, I'm terrified of anyone seeing my paintings."

"You showed them to me."

She blushed and said, "You're different Morris. You understand me, but you're way overestimating my ability and the quality of my work. You're exaggerating Morris, and I don't know why."

"Hanna I'm not. I'm amazed, shocked at how good you are. There are four paintings in that folio that could hang in any major art museum in the country. That's the gospel truth."

"Morris, you're the only person I've ever let see my paintings."

"Why, Hanna? God above, if I could do this, I'd jump for joy and never come down. If you don't believe me, bring some over and show them to my mother. When we lived out east, she spent half her life in art museums with me. She might not entirely understand why you have these young women trapped in foliage or behind lace curtains and screens, but I'm betting she will. She knows fine art, and she'll be as surprised by your imagination and ability and what you've accomplished as I am."

"Do you really think she'd want to see them?"

"She likes you, Hanna. Call her and ask her. You need to do this."

"I don't know Morris even thinking about showing them to your mother is really scary for me."

"She doesn't bite, she's interested in you, and she'll love seeing your work. Trust me on this.

"I'll think about it."

"Hanna, my mother would never in a million years hurt you. She's a kind person, and she genuinely appreciates art."

"Morris, I said I'd try."

"Hanna, you've got to quit being such a fraidy cat."

"Do you really think of me as a fraidy cat?"

"Yes, I guess I do. It's mostly because you're an only child and never had to fight for the last pancake or for much of anything else."

"I know. I've always been pretty much sheltered and protected. Mom continually tells me what I should do. I didn't even understand about sex until this year. I've never done anything, but now at least I know about it. Mom would've never told me. I don't think I've ever heard the word spoken in our house."

"Crudeness and vulgarity in people surprises you and scares you, doesn't it?"

"Yes, and I don't like high school boys because of it. All they think about is sex, and all they want is to get with a girl, any girl. The girls all worry about their clothes, who's going out with who, and how big their breasts will be when they mature."

"Surely there are people at school deeper than that?"

"We should go down and join the others. If we're here much longer, they'll all start worrying about what we're doing."

"Do you have other folios?"

"Yes, but you can't see them, I'd have to put my brave on for that."

"Are some of them nudes?" She flushed scarlet right to her hairline and looked away from him. "When you've got your brave on I'd like to see them. I'll bet they're breathtaking."

SIX

Morris's mother set a time with Hanna to visit during Christmas vacation and bring some of her paintings. After driving Hanna to his house, Morris left the two of them sitting together in the living room. He proceeded to round up David and Alice to take them into town, to poke around, and not be underfoot during Hanna's visit.

As Morris was ushering Alice and David out and pulling the front door closed he heard his mother say, "Hanna, are you, all right? Your hands are trembling. Would you like some water?"

"No. But Thanks. I'm just nervous."

"Hanna, Morris was impressed with your paintings, and I've been anticipating the opportunity to see your work and visit with you. I appreciate your trusting me. This is very mature and generous of you. So please, sit back and relax. The worst that could happen is I might not understand what you're trying to express."

"Only Morris has seen my paintings, Mrs. Stevens. He was sincere about liking my work, but I'm positive Morris was so complimentary because he was trying to make me feel better about what happened between Mom and me at Thanksgiving."

"Hanna, Morris told me you swore him to secrecy about your painting's subject matter, but he was emphatic about me seeing them. He told me your paintings were the most accomplished unbelievable work he's ever seen."

"He's exaggerating Mrs. Stevens. I didn't believe him then, and I still don't."

"Hanna, I called you and was insistent about setting up this visit because it was important to Morris, and I believe him. Morris knows his art, and I've never seen him so delighted or surprised by what you showed him. He wouldn't mislead you about something as personally important as your art."

"I hope you're right, but I can't help it; I'm terrified of letting others see them. I'm not good enough yet. I'm just not ready, and I feel just like I would if I was in the auditorium, on stage, naked in front of the whole school."

"Hanna, you weren't afraid to show them to Morris."

"I was afraid. But Morris understands me and what I'm trying to do." Pointing to her heart, she said, "He knows what I am in here."

Claire smiled, and said, "Hanna I love art. But I'm not a critic. You're not naked, and I'm not your whole school, so please, trust me, you're safe here."

She opened the folio, and Hanna carefully observed Claire's eyes as she perused the paintings. Hanna's suspense and anxiety were close to overwhelming her. Claire said, "Morris is right Hanna. That you could be this accomplished is amazing. Your subjects are disturbing and exquisite. For you to have this ability, skill, and such a creative imagination at seventeen is astounding."

Hanna, much relieved, slumped back in her chair almost passed out and said, "Really, Mrs. Stevens? You like them?"

"Hanna these are marvelous. The subjects are alive. I can see the life in their skin and in their eyes. They're beautifully painted. Hanna this is an unbelievable accomplishment, and Morris told me your parents haven't seen any of them?"

"Mother would hate them, and they'll scare dad."

"Why would you think your mother would hate them?"

"They're meant to be serious. They're not for wall decoration."

"And why would they scare your dad?"

"They're mostly of young women trapped, imprisoned. In some cases, they're only half-formed, incomplete, and want desperately to be set free."

"Is that you Hanna?"

"Pretty much, that's my life."

"Hanna, part of that comes from being a teenage girl. Part of it comes from being a second-class citizen, which defines womanhood as we know it here in 1963. Women have a lot of rules and expectations placed on them men don't."

"I don't want any part of being a woman."

"Whether you like it, or want to be, or not, you're a woman. Don't try to hide it or run from it. There are so many wonderful things about being a woman. Women rarely show it, but we're incredibly powerful beings."

"I sure don't feel powerful."

"To put it bluntly Hanna, men want what you have. Just by being a woman you can be a safe place and add so much to others lives. Your loves and husbands may come and go, but you'll have your children for life."

"Mrs. Stevens, I've almost as much trouble with girls as I do with boys. The only difference is I believe girls would be less likely to physically hurt me."

"This is complicated and hard to talk about Hanna. But you must have some positive belief in the decency of others and don't be afraid to place trust in women, especially your mother. Believe it or not, we understand life, and we've all come close to or done just about anything you can imagine."

Tad went on, "We've all made mistakes, often given up what we dreamed, and made bad choices. But none of us want our children, especially our girls, to walk down a road or live a life that's any harder than it needs to be. There are enough things we do to ourselves, and unforeseen circumstances which put a woman in jeopardy, much more so than if she were a man.

"Very few know this, but I was married and divorced before I married Morris's father. Being a divorcee, I was considered a fallen woman; used goods was the most common label. Polite society used the term, experienced. Either way, those words all carried an unmistakable sexist judgement, a deplorable thing to do to a person. Few would dare make such a comment about a divorced man. But women have struggled with those kinds of dichotomies for centuries. A woman can get the most amazing labels and reputation just from their makeup and clothes never mind who they're seen with.

"There are hundreds of expectations spoken and unspoken placed on women that no man would ever tolerate. There's nothing fair about them. Men can have dozens of lovers, but if a woman tries that way of life, she'll find herself shunned, marked with a scarlet letter by proper society for life. An independent woman's reputation is in constant danger. No matter where she goes or what line of work she pursues, she will constantly struggle to overcome gossip and suppression by the prejudicial old boys' club."

"You sound like you're speaking from experience?"

"Who's ever met a woman loan officer? I had men refuse to work with me because I was a woman. That sort of thing doesn't mean I'm saying you shouldn't try and follow your dreams. There's a social revolution going on out there. Things are getting better for women, and I believe it'll continue, at least I hope so."

Hanna said, "I hate being objectified and I hate all the judgmental comparisons. It's all so self-righteous and for what? Just to one-up one another. My shoes are better than yours, my boyfriend has his own car, my dress cost a bazillion dollars, it's all so mundane."

"Hanna this goes much deeper with you than catty gossip."

"The boys at school talk about me sexually, sometimes openly, like I'm not there or just a thing."

"High school boys have one thing on their minds, especially their master brain, the one between their legs. You know it, we all know it, and even they know it. They have trouble concealing it, and some of them don't even try."

"Mrs. Stevens is that really what my world's going to be? To be stared at, hustled, and lusted after? I'm not a person to the boys at school. I'm a piece of meat."

"Hanna you're in a world of raging hormones trying to be controlled by immature teenage brains. It comes out open, raw, and sometimes not very pretty."

"Morris isn't like that."

"He's more under control and refined than your classmates, but he's also older. Nevertheless, if you weren't the daughter of his parent's best friends, you encouraged him, and if he liked you that way, I'm pretty sure you'd find him wanting to make love to you."

"Really, Morris?"

"Yes, my dear, really. It's the natural way of men and women. Hanna, even if you don't believe it, and this was true before you showed me your folio. You're an enchanting young woman. You have the most remarkable captivating voice I've ever heard. You've been blessed in so many ways. You have a fresh, lively open face, the most amazing blue eyes, and a wonderful endearing welcoming smile; when you turn that smile on it makes all of us want to hug you."

"On top of that, you're a straight-A student, and you're well read. You've worked hard, developed your gifts, and Morris didn't exaggerate in any way. You're a highly creative and wonderfully imaginative person. Those two things also make you different. So here are three things I believe you can do to make your situation more bearable.

Claire pulled two paintings from the folio, and said, "I want you to show these to your mom and dad. They deserve to know of the amazing young woman living in their house. This one is stunning. It's arresting, very warm and delicate. Simply put, it's exquisite. This one is the opposite. It's sublimely beautiful and profoundly disturbing all at the same time. They're going to leave your mom and dad as speechless as they did Morris and me.

"Secondly stop fighting your situation. Get through high school as best you can, if possible do so with a knowing smile. Move on to a College or a University where you can meet and be with other creative, imaginative people. You have a God-given gift, Hanna. It's spiritual, and it's going to show the world a whole new way to see. It's unmistakably powerful and remarkably feminine. You're only seventeen, but your ability is that of someone who's thirty years older. You won't believe me, but what you've already accomplished is an absolute wonder."

"Third, and most important, get rid of the clothes. You aren't fooling anyone. As much as you might want to, you can't be sexless. You can forego the makeup, eyeshadow, lipstick, and skip the fingernail polish and jewelry. But as Morris said at Thanksgiving, it won't matter what clothes you wear, you're still going to be a lovely young woman. Trust me about this Hanna. Later in life, you'll welcome knowing you're still pleasing to the eyes of others."

Trying her hardest and using the best of what she was capable of, Hanna only managed to complete the first of Tad's three suggestions. She got a start on the second. It was a beginning.

SEVEN

He heard somebody downstairs yell, "Morris phone!" He hustled down the stairs to the small study and picked up the receiver and said, "Morris Stevens here."

"Morris, I wish you'd just say hello like most people."

"Mom, there's four of us living here. Yes, mom, you've told me my voice is distinctive many times. Okay, okay, for you I'll say hello first. So, what's going on? Is everything all right?"

"Yes, but I need a favor."

"And what would that be mom?"

"I want you to take Hanna Williston to her senior prom."

"God above mom! You just up and volunteered me?"

"Don't be short with me Morris."

"When is it?"

"May first, it's a Saturday night."

"Mom, it's an eight-hour drive each way. I'll have to drive all day Saturday and then all-day Sunday to get back here. What's this about? What's so important that I need to take her? She's pretty, surely she'll be asked by someone."

"That seems to be the problem. She doesn't want to be asked by anyone at that school."

"Well, we all know she's not much of a fan of boys, but you're asking a lot mom. It's an eight-hundred-mile round trip."

"Morris this is important. You know I don't stick my nose in where it doesn't belong, but I like Hanna. She's special, and I swear Annett and Hanna almost came to blows over this. Annett's given her no choice about going.

"Hanna went on a rant about being a piece of meat and having to accept a date and go with someone she disliked. Then she said I'm sorry mom, but none of those boys care a thing about me, they just want to have sex with me. Her mother pooh-poohed that remark and went on and on about whether Hanna wanted to or not, she was going to the prom. Annett said no daughter of hers would miss out on her senior prom. It wasn't up for discussion."

"Why was Annett so insistent? I thought things were better after you talked her into showing them her artwork."

"It's a lot of things. Hanna's never been on a date, she keeps to herself. Her mother just doesn't understand why she won't participate in any of the high school activities. Things got better after she showed them those two paintings, but Annett's on a tear about the prom. She went on and on saying things like if you don't go, you'll regret it forever. Every girl wants to go to their senior prom. It's a rite of passage. My prom was a fun time, one I'll always remember and cherish.

"Then Hanna said why mom, what was so memorable, was it the first time you did it? Well, that set Annett's jaw, and she went on, saying, you're going, Hanna. For once you're going to do something normal. Accept it. I know you were asked and turned down Mrs. Johnson's son Carl. There'll be no more of that. Hanna said, mother, he's a horrible person he's always making suggestive comments about me. He just wants to fuck me. I couldn't believe Hanna used that word."

"Hanna said that, right in front of you?"

"Yes, and it took the conversation about as low as it could go. Hanna looked awful, just beat up, Annett looked shocked and worried to death, and I wanted to be back in New Jersey. I swear almost every time I've been there in the last few months those two get into it over something. Hanna usually slinks off to her room, but not this time. I felt terrible for them.

"I said, Hanna would you consider going with Morris? Her eyes lit up, she smiled. She looked like a drowning person who was just thrown a life ring. Hanna's such a sweet girl. She said Morris would do that, drive all the way back here just to make mom happy and be my date for the prom? I said something about having to talk with you, and I'm sorry Morris, but I threw in something about you taking your sister to the prom and both of you having a great time."

"Geez mom, you've left me no way out of this, have you?"

"Morris I'm sorry to put you in this situation, but that family needs help. Besides, even with that boy haircut, she's a lovely young woman. She won't be an embarrassment. Just do it for me, for the Williston's. They need peace in that household. Poor Robert, he hasn't a clue about how to go about rectifying any of this."

"Can you help me out with the gas and the tux rental? I don't have extra money or time to spare."

"Of course, you've been very good about managing the money and getting that Job's made a big difference; it's really helped. Is everything going well?"

"Yes, mom. What about the corsage?"

"I'll take care of the flowers."

"Good, because it's a nine-hour drive, I'll have just enough time to eat something, get dressed, and pick her up."

"Thank you, Morris, and please try not to look at this as an obligation. You can smile; you're doing a good deed."

"Yes mom, I know how to smile."

Tad said, "I don't understand why those two can't make more of an effort to get along. I don't understand Annett. She's fed up with Hanna's not wanting to partake or participate in the same things she did in high school. She recognizes Hanna's abilities. Annett knows she's gifted, special. But she can't understand her disdain for everything Annett thinks of as typical for young women."

"Mother I'm pretty sure deep-down Annett's worried sick Hanna's a lesbian."

"Honestly, you think that's what all the turmoil and hurt feelings are about?"

"I'm almost positive that's what's going on."

"It never occurred to me, but I'll talk to Annett. Something's got to change between them. It breaks my heart to see them going at each other the way they do."

"Mom I don't think you should say anything to Annett about Hanna's sexuality. That's the very last thing Annett wants to face, and I'm positive to even acknowledge the possibility of Hanna being homosexual will be the end of Annett's world. I don't think she has any way to even consider such a thing much less have a way to deal with a lesbian daughter."

"You think Annett's in that kind of denial."

"Mom it's not denial. Annett's terrified. If you think my taking Hanna to the prom will help, I'll do it, but I think it's like putting a bandage on a severed artery."

"You'll have to call and formally ask her."

"What if she says no thanks?"

"She's going to the prom Annett's given her no choice."

"She could run away."

"If she doesn't go with you I'd bet on it."

"Things are that bad?"

"Over the prom, yes, and thank you, Morris, for doing this. Call her tonight if you can. She needs all the help she can get. She's afraid of her own shadow and smart as she is she wouldn't have any idea of how to go about running away. Even with that boy haircut, Hanna's a beautiful, intelligent, well-mannered young woman. She's not going to embarrass you."

He made the call, and that remarkable, unmistakable, earthy sensual voice of Hanna's said, "Hello, Williston's residence."

"Hanna it's Morris."

Hanna's sultry magical voice crawled its way right into his brain, "Morris, I know what this is about, and you don't have to do this. I mean it.

"Hanna, I wish you wouldn't say that to me. That's the second time."

"Sorry, I remember, last Thanksgiving when dad asked you to go with me to see my artwork."

"So, will you stop saying that?"

"Morris, I mean it; you don't have to do this."

"Hanna Williston, would you do me the honor of being my date for the senior prom?"

A few seconds went by, and she said, "Yes, and Morris, I think you've saved my life. Thank you!"

"Glad to be so useful, especially over the phone."

"We won't have to stay for the whole thing. We can leave early if it's boring for you."

"Hanna, I'm not driving four hundred miles to leave early."

"I meant if it turns out to be no fun we don't have to stay. We can leave early."

"It will be fun Hanna. Have your dad show you some dance steps, and I'll see you May first." He hung up and started up the stairs not even trying to get that sultry, sensual voice out of his head. Morris vividly remembered thinking the first time he heard it no fourteen-year-old girl should have a voice like that. It stopped him cold then and left him wanting more just as it did tonight.

EIGHT

They left the prom early, just after ten. In the car, Hanna said, "Thanks for getting me out of there. That was dreadful. No one said a word, not one. They just kept staring at us. It was creepy. I don't think I could've stood another minute."

"Why are you so surprised? You're always telling me you don't have any friends there."

"I don't. Not any close ones. Not like you and Jerry and Michael were, but there are people I talk to."

"Then I guess it was odd."

"Odd? Morris it was God awful. It was downright creepy." A few moments went by, and she said, "Where are we going?"

"Like I said to see something special, something you'll appreciate. It's a clear night and almost a full moon. This should be just about perfect."

"Is it much further? Mom will be worrying herself sick."

"We can find a pay phone and call her."

"That'll make it worse."

"Why? Did you forget to tell me when you were expected home? The dance doesn't end until midnight. It's only ten-twenty."

"She knows I despise those kinds of things. I don't date. I keep to myself, and the only reason I'm doing any of this is that she threw a complete fit and gave me no choice. If it weren't for mom's insistence and the fact you're taking me out of the kindness of yours and your mother's hearts, I wouldn't have gone in a million years. I'm sure mom expected me to have talked you into bringing me home by now."

"And then there's always the possibility you're having the time of your life."

"You could bet everything you'll ever have against that, you'd be as safe as betting on Budinsky reciting poetry."

"Who's Budinsky?"

"Our cat."

"You know miraculous things happen. The Civil Rights Act has been signed into law. We've put men in space. Stop worrying. I'll have you home before midnight."

"Morris there's pictures of you in the high school trophy case in the lobby. I've been told you were a big deal athlete throughout high school, even as a ninth grader?"

"Who told you that?"

"Alice. She told me you were an outstanding baseball and hockey player. You were fun to watch, and she told me you were offered scholarships to play hockey and baseball at lots of colleges including Dartmouth, but you turned them down. Is that true?"

"You sound surprised?"

"I can't picture you being a jock. I've tried, but you're not anything like those guys."

"Well, I played lots of sports over the years. Hockey was fun, but to be successful, you had to be disciplined and not retaliate when you got checked or messed about. It's hard physical work, but it's a fun way to blow off steam."

"Alice said she loved watching you play. She told me you were unbelievably quick. That you scored lots of goals, but she didn't like watching baseball as much. She said when you pitched your team always won, but it wasn't fun like hockey because nothing ever happened. You struck out almost every batter."

"I did my best. I enjoyed playing. My coaches liked me. I could pitch and hit and handle the puck, and yes I scored a lot of goals and struck out a lot of batters."

"But why would you turn down a scholarship from Dartmouth? That's a very prestigious school?"

"It's more complicated than you might think. I got good grades. But I'm not some super smart person. Even though I applied to Harvard because I figured it was the best and it would be neat to go there, I hadn't heard from them. So, when Northwestern accepted me, I took their offer."

"Why didn't you accept the scholarship to Dartmouth it's about even with Harvard?"

"Dartmouth's a small, moneyed Ivy League, elitist all male no women school and I like women. I wanted an education not to be a baseball player or hockey player. I didn't want to waste my educational opportunities doing sports. I'm not very big, and I don't have the drive and passion you need to be a great baseball or hockey player.

"When I met with their representatives, I didn't feel I'd fit in. Dartmouth doesn't give athletic scholarships it was an academic scholarship, but they made it clear I was to play both hockey and baseball. They left me feeling like the hired help and should be grateful for receiving their offer.

"I talked to my dad about it because the scholarship would've saved our family a lot of money. Dad said Morris, I've put aside money for your education, go to school where you want to, and don't play sports unless you want to. When

I was accepted by Northwestern on my academic record and said no thank you to Dartmouth, they couldn't believe it. Four other schools offered me athletic scholarships, and I turned them down because I didn't want to be a collegiate athlete. Just from the way, the representatives from Dartmouth reacted I knew I made the right decision."

"Morris, there's no way I can picture you in that kind of physical rough and tumble world. You're kind and always such a gentleman. You don't swagger about, or boast, or even talk about it. You've never even mentioned playing sports."

"Well thank you, but don't let my appearance fool you under this tux lives a real live male animal."

"You don't act anything like the jocks I know. You never talk about women in inappropriate or disparaging ways like the guys at school do."

"I try not to think those kinds of thoughts, and when I do, I keep them to myself."

"I'm surprised."

"Hanna I'm human we all think those kinds of thoughts."

He slowed and turned off the highway onto a service road running alongside a stretch of woods. Less than a mile later he stopped and turned the car around. "Sorry, I missed the turnoff."

Coming back to it he drove into the woods on a narrow, obviously to Hanna, rarely used road. The trees and branches were close, and with the tall grass growing on either side there was a powerful illusion from the headlights of a long narrow tunnel. He was going too fast; it was rough and bounced them all over the place. He braked and slowed way down. He watched as she let go of the armrest and took her hand from the dashboard. "Sorry about that. I forgot how rough this road is."

With a real edge in her voice, Hanna said, "Morris, what's going on? Are you going to try something with me?"

"Don't be silly. It's something you have to see."

In a clearing in front of an old barn, he swung the car around facing back the way they came and said, "We're here."

"Honest to God Morris! You scared the life out of me to show me an old barn in the middle of nowhere?"

Getting out of the car he said, "Come on, you won't believe this." In the light of the almost full moon, they made their way to a small side door. He wrestled it open and taking her hand, he walked her some thirty feet toward the center and stopped. She hadn't said a word since they went through the door. Hanna raised her face and eyes up looking all around her. Staring at the hundreds of iridescent streams of bluish opalescent light pouring in everywhere he could tell Hanna was speechless. It was even more spectacular than Morris dared hope.

Like a small child, Hanna put her arms straight out and moved them about watching the light ripple across her arms and upturned palms. She cupped her hands together like she could catch the light like water in her hands. She knelt cupping her hands watching the light pierce the room falling peacefully, delicately, everywhere on and around them and into her cupped hands.

Enchanted, she stood and began turning around and around. Surprising Morris, she threw her arms around him and said, "Thank you! Thank you, Morris, it's the most amazingly beautiful thing I've ever seen, what a wonderful night and to think I almost feigned being sick."

"Why would you ever do that? What was so hard about going to a prom?"

"Lots of things, everything."

"Like?"

"Girls at that school are a commodity, just something the boys want to have sex with and if you're asked by someone you don't want to go with, and turn them down, even if you don't like them, you've hurt someone's feelings. If you don't get asked by one of the popular boys, you're thought of as second best or worse not being worth anything.

"Worse yet they'll say, have you heard? I can't believe who Jane's going to the prom with? All the girls have their hair done. And meanest of all is the whole bevy of catty unmerciful hair, clothes, and appearance critics. It's all pretend and phony. The way everyone was staring at us not even saying hi or hello or anything was making you as uncomfortable as me."

"Hanna none of them know who I am. They were all surprised at how beautiful you look. They were speechless and couldn't believe how fantastic you look. They didn't know what to say, so they didn't say anything."

"You're kind Morris, but they all think I'm different, strange, especially the boys and I'm sorry, but I distrust everything about that place."

"Come on Hanna I bet lots of fellows asked you."

"Some, and thanks to you I could tell them thanks, but I already have a date. Mom told me I had to go. I didn't have a choice. So, you saved me. What could be better than having my one true friend take me? So, thank you, Morris; you took all the heat off me."

"Hanna if you'd faked being sick tonight I don't know if I would've ever been able to trust you again. I also think I would've been a little heartbroken. What happened? Why were you toying with getting sick at the last minute?"

"The whole idea of it, of being there in front of all those people was overwhelming. I knew everyone would judge me, make derogatory comments about me, my shoes, my dress, and my hair."

"Hanna, you don't strike me as someone having much truck with that kind of stuff."

"I don't, but the whole school does. My mother does, I can't escape it. She reminds me every single day, Hanna what will people say? I swear it's her new job. You heard her at the table at Thanksgiving. She's unmerciful, she's worried to death there's something wrong with me. Mom's petrified I'm one of those people."

"So, if you are, tell her, and if not do some things to set her mind at ease?"

"You mean like ditch my north woods outfits and let my hair grow out?"

"It would be a start."

"My mother's a smart, complicated woman, she thinks way too much, and it makes her life hard. Ever since dad took the job in Minneapolis and started making so much more money, mom began worrying about her social position, what people say, and all those kinds of things. Back home in Hanes nobody gave a tinker's damn about any of that stuff."

"That's a whole day's conversation Hanna, but I should get you home."

"This is so incredibly beautiful can we stay a little longer, just a few more minutes?" Gladly, he stayed.

The ride home was mostly silent with Morris wondering how Robert and Annett produced someone like Hanna. Then wondering even more why she was so threatened by and fixed in her views of her peers. Mostly he thoroughly considered the all too real possibility Hanna might be one of those people. Guided by his suspicions and over thinking things he said, "Hanna, I want you to know, I meant what I said about you being beautiful. When you want to, you can look very feminine, and when you bless us with that smile of yours, you're terrifically becoming.

"Put it together with the stockings, heels, and that gorgeous dress, you're as lovely and feminine as anyone could be. Your classmates were shocked that's why they didn't say anything to us."

"You know Morris nylons are the strangest things. Have you ever touched someone wearing them?"

"No. I don't think so."

"Then you haven't. Believe me, you'd remember. Give me your hand." The next thing he knew she'd taken his offered hand and put it under her dress on the top of her thigh.

"Isn't that the weirdest feeling ever?"

"Yes. It sure is."

She slid his hand further up, past the top of her nylons beside her garter strap where his fingers met the soft bare skin of her inner thigh. Hanna said, "See how much different my skin feels."

"Hanna! Geez!" He pulled his hand away.

"Sorry. I just wanted you to know how weird it feels."

"It's not weird it's sensual, and you of all people know it. Some of your paintings are the most sensual things I've ever seen. I saw your face and your eyes in the barn. You were completely enchanted by the light, weren't you?"

"I was trying to see it. To know it."

"Did you?"

"I think so, a little. I got a start."

"Good. So, Hanna's prom night was a roaring success?"

"Morris how many girls have you brought out there?"

"Not another soul."

"How did you know about it?"

"Jerry and I were prowling around between the woods and the fields looking for a safe place to target shoot when we stumbled on it. It was nestled back in the woods behind the field. We checked it out. It was an amazing sight with all the dust and the sunlight shining through the cracks and holes in the roof, but nothing like tonight in the moonlight."

"What did Jerry say?"

"Wouldn't be much help in a downpour."

"I wanted you to see it because it could be gone any day. You of all people needed to see it, especially in the moonlight." He walked her to her front door and paused in the light from the carriage lamps, "Hanna you've got some bits of straw on your shoes and your dress."

"Don't worry, if mom asks me where did that come from? I'll smile sweetly and tell her, strolling in the hay mom."

"Hanna! For crying out loud, don't you dare take your mom down that road? Why would you want her to think you were rolling in the hay, especially with me? That would-be God awful for everybody."

"Relax Mr. Stevens or are you wishing like all the other boys were tonight? Were you hoping to get a roll in the hay?"

"Come on Hanna, what are you doing? That's so unlike you. I think the world of you; you're the most creative accomplished person I've ever known. I think you're lovely. You're seventeen and the daughter of my parent's best friends. I would never do anything like that, not without your wholehearted approval, and even then, I'd think long and hard about it."

"I know that Morris and thank you for taking me to the prom and showing me your barn, it was even more enchanting than your boathouse. Seriously, Morris tonight was the nicest thing anyone's ever given me."

"Glad you liked it. I was pretty sure you would."

"I did, and I have one last thing to ask before you run back to your college life."

"And that is?"

"I need a kiss."

"Hanna?"

She turned toward the door, "I'm sorry Morris. I don't know what's gotten into me. I knew that was too much."

He put his hand on her shoulder, stopped her, and turned her back toward him. Gently cupping the back of her head, he kissed her slightly open mouth. It was a wonderful kiss. It went on and on until they were both light headed.

Shocked, and more surprised than either had ever been, neither spoke. They stood hands at their side's inches apart looking at each other. Many seconds later he said, "Goodnight Hanna," and turned toward his car.

"Thank you, Morris, it was wonderful."

Morris drove back to his parent's house stunned. It was to be a quick little kiss, and they would say goodnight and carry on as before. The kiss affected him like he never expected. He couldn't imagine what happened, nor could he understand the warm pleasure or the light-headed sweet ecstasy that swept through him. The kiss completely befuddled him.

He floated back to his car confused wondering when? Where did Hanna ever learn about that? What he did know was it was a thousand miles from anything he ever imagined or expected. Morris kissed a few girls, three passionately and tonight, the very first time they kissed, Hanna took him somewhere he never experienced with any of those other girls. He never felt anything like that warmth.

It was just a simple kiss with slightly open mouths. No making out with passionate tongues. No trying to make love with their mouths, it was a simple kiss. He puzzled over it all the long drive back to Evanston. Nevertheless, with school and work, it eventually left him. He would see Hanna at his mother's annual Fourth of July shindig and not again for seven months.

NINE

It was a Wednesday, two weeks before spring break. His mother called, "Morris, I need a big favor."

"What now mom?"

"Hanna's in the University Hospital, and she's asked to see you."

"What's happened?"

"I believe I've got the story straight. She was walking back to the dorm from the library last night with a young man, and three men who were harassing them earlier followed them and attacked them. They beat them up. The young man, his name is Frank Sweet, is in a coma in critical condition. Do you know him, Morris?"

"No mom, I don't. What were they doing? Why did they get beat up?"

"I don't know for sure. The police caught the men. They were drinking in the library and being obnoxious. Apparently, they thought Hanna and the Sweet boy were a homosexual couple. They followed them and attacked them."

"I'll bet she still has that boy haircut and was wearing one of those lumberjack outfits of hers."

"I don't know about any of the particulars, but Robert and Annett are awfully worried about her. She's been seriously injured. She's not having visitors, but she asked for you. Morris, they'd be eternally grateful if you could come. It would mean a lot to them."

"Couldn't I just call her?"

"Annett said Hanna begged her to get you to come in person."

"Are Hanna and Annett getting along any better?"

"Hanna's living on campus, she's hardly ever home. From what Annett's told me she hasn't been on any dates, she likes college better than high school. But Annett said she wasn't showing much enthusiasm for her classes."

"Is she still getting A's?"

"Yes, but she's been disappointed in her courses."

"Freshman year isn't always the greatest. Is she taking art classes?"

"I believe that's where the problems are. She's taking two studio art classes. I think she was expecting something much different from what she's getting."

"When are visiting hours?"

"One to four."

"I don't have classes Friday. I'll leave early so I can see her Friday afternoon."

"Morris, when you see Hanna tell her when she's up to it, I'd like to visit her."

"I'll tell her mom, and I should be home Friday around five."

"We're all looking forward to seeing you and do give Hanna my love and my wishes for a speedy recovery."

Morris thought he should get her some flowers but decided to stop at the campus bookstore and see if he could find something more lasting. The girl at the bookstore was a little surprised when he asked if she could wrap it. She said, "It's a college bookstore we aren't set up for that."

He said. "I'm stuck, and I wouldn't ask, but this is important." People instinctively liked Morris, and she smiled and managed it. He thanked her and left a little pile of dollars on the counter for her.

He was nervous about seeing Hanna, and he wasn't sure why. When he entered her room, she was in bed propped up, lying back motionless. She was unrecognizable. Her head looked misshapen and her face, her whole head was a horrifying purple-black. Her neck, shoulders, and arms were bandaged in gauze. The skin showing was dark purple and yellow. She didn't look human. He gagged and almost threw up, but continued in, "Hanna its Morris."

Her head turned, and as Morris caught sight of those magnificent blue eyes, he saw water streaming out of them. He took a tissue and gently mopped up the tears. "Hanna I'm so sorry this happened to you."

"Oh God, Morris, I've never been so scared. They had a bat and kept hitting and kicking us. They kicked me so hard they broke my arm, three ribs, and my pubic bone. I'm going to have to have screws put in it. Those men walked away laughing and left us in the street like trash. Thank God that older woman walking her dog found us or God knows what would've happened. The detective who caught them told me, they were real proud of themselves right up until I told them the white haired one was an eighteen-year-old girl."

Shocked and frightened by her injuries Morris was at a loss for what to do or say. Wondering more than anything why it was so crucial for her to see him in person. He said, "Mom said you really needed to see me."

"I want another kiss, Morris."

"Jesus Hanna your mouth, your whole face is covered in stitches."

"Morris you're the only person that's ever understood me. I don't know another living soul who'd say in the middle of a girl's prom night right out on the dance floor; I can see this is all very trying. Would you like to go see something extraordinary?"

"Hanna you're the only girl I know who would've left her prom to go somewhere completely unknown with a man she hardly knows. Since I can't kiss you, could I hug you?"

"I don't think so."

"How about holding your hand?"

Pulling the heavily wrapped hand from under the covers she said, "My left one got smashed when I tried to protect myself, but my right one's okay."

"Jesus Hanna, that's your drawing hand."

"Doctor Sanderson said, it'll take more than this operation, but he was sure he'll be able to make it good as new."

Bringing the chair, he moved around the bed to her right. Hanna slid over toward him placing her good hand where he could cover it with his. As she repositioned her hips and legs, she displaced the covers. It was only seconds, but long enough.

He saw the curve of her hip, her leg, a deep purple bruise, and an amazing dainty patch of white blonde hair. A tube running toward that spot was taped to the inside of her thigh. Those very private sights stumbled into his brain, and he instantly averted his eyes. Everything jumbled together and then came apart. In that instant, Hanna became someone she never was before. She had stark white pubic hair, and she was all grown up, suddenly a woman.

Part of him liked her as a grown-up, but most of him didn't. He wished he hadn't seen her like that, but he did. It was terribly unfair. She was his friend, badly hurt, and now he could, but sit holding her hand, and hope this unfortunate visual disruption would pass, and quickly.

Hanna said, "Morris I've made an awful mess of things. I hate my studio art classes. I swear if I ever again hear, Hanna I don't care about you being creative just show me you can draw the model as she is. I swear Morris, I'll never stop screaming. They're prerequisite courses I have to take them."

"Hanna, who in the world could teach you much of anything about drawing? You draw with the grace of Arthur Rackham, the sureness of Andrew Wyeth, and you paint with all the magical sense of Turner. Throw in the brilliant coloration of Van Gogh, and you just might get close to Hanna Williston's work and, I'm not kidding, not one little bit."

"Morris, I can draw the model just as she looks, but why? Where's the joy in that?"

"It's a beginning class Hanna. They just want to see that you can draw what's there."

"I thought I'd come here and find an enchanting world full of brilliant creative people and never stop smiling. But so far this is so much like high school and nobody understands me, not one of them."

"I don't believe that's true. It's your first year. You haven't found your place yet."

"I wanted to drop out. Maybe go to New York or LA, but my parents will have a fit, especially after this."

"With good reason, what was this about, anyway?"

"I don't know. Those men were half drunk. They were drinking right there in the library. I don't have any idea how they got in or why they were there, but they started harassing us.

They got it in their heads we were a gay couple. One thing led to another, and they started saying some nasty things. I wouldn't even look at them. Frank told them they didn't know what they were talking about and to grow up. I never said a word to them. It got so bad we left. It never crossed my mind they might be dangerous."

"I'm sure being drunk, and because of your attire they couldn't make out your breast or see that shapely little fanny of yours. What with your Marine Corps haircut it wasn't much of a hop skip and a jump for them to get to a little girly queer guy."

"I'm not a homosexual Morris!"

"I know you're not and even if you were what they did is atrocious, despicable, and unbelievably cruel."

"Why are you so sure I'm not a lesbian? You suspected I was? I know you did?"

"You kissed me, Hanna like no one ever has."

"Ah, yes, Morris, the very reason I wanted you to come see me. What a beautiful night that was and what a glorious end. I floated around the house for days afterward then I tried my very best to paint the moonlight in the barn. After almost thirty tries I finally did it."

"That light was so fragile and beautiful. I held it in my hands. It's still here in my heart. I know it's just romantic claptrap, but I wanted you to come and see me, ugly, and scary as I look, and kiss me again. So, I could feel like I did that night and not like this. I hurt everywhere. I can't move my hand without crying. And I don't think I'll ever get over this and don't worry from now on I'll be wearing clothes that show my fanny and my breast."

"Hanna I'm so sorry this happened to you. This should never happen to anyone. That it happened to someone as gentle as you is heartbreaking and unforgivable."

"It was a shock. It's certainly going to make me pay more attention to who's around me and the tone and what's being said. And it's sure made me think about men in a whole different way."

"How long can I stay Hanna?"

"Don't worry they'll come by and kick you out. I haven't had any visitors, but they're very efficient about visiting hours. Dad always comes by after work and cries and feeds me and cries some more, but he's family, they let him and mom in any time."

"How's he doing with all this?"

"He can't stop crying. I think his heart's been broken."

"Hanna, you asked me for a kiss prom night, and I'm glad you did. It was a magical thank you, and now I'm going to ask you for something. I want a promise you'll go back spring quarter, if you're able, and do a little nosing around."

"About what? Where?"

"I don't know. Try the clubs. Film, books, flying, poetry, just get out there and talk to some people. Find out what they're doing and what they're excited about. You're the most creative imaginative person I've ever known, and even you know you're not ready to be on your own in LA let alone New York."

"Okay older, wise man Morris I'll make that commitment I'll do another quarter, just for you."

"Hanna, do it for you. Sit in on some classes, architecture, Renaissance painting, anything that sounds interesting. Astronomy, botany, how about paleontology, you've got a great mind. Spend the time and find something you like. Something interesting you could see yourself doing for a long time."

There was a knock, and a nurse stuck her head in and said, "Just letting you know visiting hours are over."

Hanna said, "Give us a few minutes."

"A minute my dear, we've got to change some of your dressings, and the doctor needs to do a checkup."

"I need two minutes! Morris, you've brought me something."

"Yes, I was going to bring flowers, but I thought why not something that would last a little longer? It's Jo Mielziner's book on designing for the theater. I read it about a year ago. When I saw it on the shelf I thought of you, so it's yours, and even if all you like is the dust jacket, it'll be enough."

"You've wrapped it and everything how special. Thank you, Morris, thank you for coming; it was an awful long way to come to see someone as messed up as I am. I know how awful I look. They let me see myself for the first time this morning. I didn't recognize myself. I'm damn scary looking."

"You still have those incredible eyes, and even with all those stitches I'll bet that lovely smile is still there."

"Can you come back?"

"I planned on driving back Sunday; I'll have tomorrow to visit with you. Your dad can help you open the present tonight. You can page through it before you go to sleep."

"Promise, you'll come tomorrow?" He nodded.

***

Carrying an empty mason jar and a handful of yellow daffodils, the stems wrapped in a dampened paper towel. Morris arrived at the third floor waiting area to see Robert and Annett seated on a sofa toward the back holding each other. He didn't like the way they looked and went straight to them. Sitting across from them he asked, "Has something happened?"

Robert said, "Hanna went into convulsions. She's in surgery. They're trying to relieve the pressure on her brain."

Annett with a hanky dabbing at her eyes said, "She was doing so well, really happy. Jabbering on and on about that wonderful book you brought her. She was relaxed, seemed stronger, and sounded so much better. She asked me how Frank was doing if he was conscious. I hesitated about what to say and thought I can't lie to her she'll hate me forever, so I told her. Frank died last night.

"She started crying and then sobbing. I got a nurse to come help. Hanna started convulsing. The next thing I knew the room's full of nurses and doctors. They ushered me out, and Hanna was whisked off to surgery."

Unaware the flowers left his hand Morris's brain blanked. His stomach was in his mouth. For God's sake, he thought; don't let anything more go wrong. Please don't let anything more happen to that wonderful girl.

Trying hard to gather himself he bent over and began gathering up the flowers. Thinking, what are you doing Morris, nobody cares about the fucking flowers? Then he heard himself say, "I'm supposed to drive back to school tomorrow." He couldn't think right. All he could think about was, Hanna's dying, you're picking flowers up off the floor, and you just said I've got to drive back to school.

The hell with school, screw the flowers; you're staying until you know if she's going to be all right. You're afraid for her, of her, that you'll never see her again. Stop it, Morris, put your brave on. Morris heard his voice say, "School can wait," and he heard more words, "She'll be all right. She'll recover don't worry. She's such a talented creative person nothing will stop her, not for long."

Robert looked at him and said, "Morris she was going on, and on, and on, about the book you brought her. She kept saying, Morris always understands me, he knows what I am, and where I belong. So, I must ask, have you and Hanna been seeing each other on the quiet, are you more than friends?"

58

"No secrets. And yes, we're more than friends, but not in a boy-girl way. It's a mutual admiration help each other the best we can kind of thing."

Annett said, "She doesn't like men Morris, not at all. You and Frank Sweet are the only two she's ever had anything to do with."

Robert said, "The happiest I've seen her in the last four years was after she was with you. The first time I was aware of it was Thanksgiving when you went to her room to see her artwork. She was almost human all the next week.

"Then there was the prom. The pleasantness lasted for two solid weeks. When I asked her about the prom, she said, it was heavenly dad, truly divine, I learned so much. Yesterday at dinner time when I came to see her, she was so delighted you'd come all this way to be here for her. So please Morris, stay in touch with her. You make a remarkable difference in her well-being. That book you brought gave her more hope than I ever have. This morning she told me, Dad, I know what I want to do."

They brought her to the recovery room, and Morris took one look, and his heart sank. She looked awful. She wasn't conscious. The vibrant dark deep purple-black he saw yesterday was now a washed out muddy gray. She appeared to him as though death was already holding her hand. He silently said, Oh God, and prayed she'd somehow be okay.

He had to leave. He couldn't stand to see her like this. He hugged Robert and Annett, and said, "I'll come tomorrow when she's awake. I promised her I'd come today. So, if she wakes and asks, tell her I was here, and not to worry. I'll come tomorrow in the afternoon when she's awake. Tell her I'll bring her kiss. It's a code between us. She'll understand."

He walked into Hanna's room with Annett holding onto his arm completely unbelieving of just how much trouble Hanna was in. Not quite so washed out gray, she still looked pathetic. He was shocked and sat beside her and took her good hand in his saying, "Hanna its Morris."

"I know. I can see you."

Late Sunday after Hanna convinced him the Mielziner book had given her renewed hope about everything and she was on the mend. She told him not to worry she would recover. Not until then did he drive back to Northwestern. The four hundred miles took seven hours and a year and a day. When he finally arrived, Morris knew where he was, but wasn't at all sure it was where he belonged.

Morris called every few days to check on Hanna. It was always the same, aftercare for her craniotomy, plastic surgery for her face, multiple operations to reconstruct her hand. Two planned operation's one to reset her forearm and a second to repair and stabilize her pubic bone. She told him there might have to be another to fix two ribs which hadn't healed properly. She was going to put it off, maybe until summer. Through it all, she kept going to classes working around the surgeries.

She told him the only things that bothered her was being perpetually and continually tired, always in pain, somewhere, and being unable to draw or use a paintbrush. She knew those things wouldn't be forever but were a challenge. Morris knew Hanna wouldn't have told him about any of it if he hadn't insisted she be honest with him. He was amazed at her unflagging spirit, but he felt awful about what she was going through.

TEN

The beginning of Morris's senior year was his crossroads, his start on the passage to another level of being. He met Diane toward the end of his junior year, during spring quarter, and they started seeing each other. That summer he moved into a small house with Michael Bloom, a doctoral candidate, and four years older than him. When Morris first met with Michael about becoming his housemate Michael's girlfriend, Elaine, was there visiting. It was because of her and their obvious affection for each other he became Michael's housemate.

Was it not for that chance encounter with Elaine being there, he would've met with Michael, left assuming Michael was homosexual and passed on being his housemate? Morris spent the rest of that summer checking on Hanna, working, spending time with Diane, and learning everything his roommate Michael could cram into his head.

Michael was an amazing man. Brilliant and fuller of intellectual understanding and passion than anyone Morris ever met. He loved music with a passion you could feel. Especially opera, and not so currently popular musicians as Edith Piaf, the German performer Anita Berber, the American cabaret performer Josephine Baker, and many of the now forgotten performers who appeared in the Berlin Cabarets in the 1920s and 30s.

Michael wasn't shy about sharing his knowledge or his understanding. He had Morris listening to his opera records and cabaret singers while he explained the phrasing and one voice nuance after another. He had this amazing ability to get Morris involved, and to a degree, his unwitting student could scarcely believe.

Michael was singularly focused on completing his doctorate degree and did so with so much energy it was almost frightening. He was exceptionally thorough spending considerable amounts of effort to get his research right. He quickly made Morris part and party to his thesis having him read, review, and discuss with him every detail and scrap of research.

Along with Michael Morris also had the good fortune to come to know two professors his junior year who actively encouraged him to continue to graduate school. John Stanton who was chairman of the humanities department and Robert James, John's second in command, who all the other professors affectionately called Robbie. Both men took an interest in Morris.

Morris's girlfriend Diane was supportive, and he believed she liked him a lot, a whole lot. She was knowledgeable in the ways of men and women. Morris was not. She thrilled him and patiently and lovingly taught him of the many wonders to be shared between men and women.

Toward the middle of August with no prior hint or warning she told him on the phone on a Thursday night she was leaving. She was transferring to Berkeley for her senior year. It was where she needed to go to graduate school. Without further words, or seeing him, or even a handshake she drove away early the next morning. He was stunned.

When fall quarter started, he was way over on the sad side of things, very much missing his lover. Michael gave Morris little time for moping pressing him into service to help him prepare for his orals and organize his thesis research. Between Michael's continual requests for help, his own coursework, and his part-time job there was little left for dwelling on the missing Dianne. Nevertheless, she stayed on living in his head.

Michael worked tirelessly, but always made time to drag them off to every theatrical, musical, or opera production he could find. He was indiscriminate. They went to Northwestern productions, and nearby colleges, to high schools, and community theaters, and Michael always went with the highest of hopes. He said, "Morris, never pass up a Shakespeare production. The man wrote thirty-seven plays, and hardly more than ten are ever produced. So, if you get a chance to see one go! And go they did.

With Michael's extraordinary critical observations and incisive commentary, Morris was getting a tremendous education. Michael criticized the productions in the way criticism was meant to be used. At every performance, he always found something new, original, and well done. He would comment on and tuck these finds away for future use. He called these nuggets of originality his pearl collection.

They were going at this eighteen and twenty hours a day, especially Michael who was spending a tremendous amount of time finalizing his research. It was tedious and complicated. He often had multiple translations done of the same passages by different translators.

Michael began spending ever-increasing amounts of time with the language professors having them help him compare and understand the subtleties of the different translations. He believed he was wearing his welcome thin. But Michael's professorial cohorts seemed to be enjoying this as much as Morris was. Michael took copious notes always insisting Morris read and go over them with him. Hectic as this was they were thoroughly enjoying each other's company, and both felt their lives were moving along in the proper direction.

***

Michael came home on a Monday afternoon in early November and calmly said, "Morris, I'm sorry about this, but you're going to have to start looking for a roommate. I'm leaving the university. I'm packing up and driving home at the end of the week, Thursday probably."

"Has something happen at home?"

"No, not exactly."

"What Then?"

"Elaine's pregnant. We're getting married Saturday."

"Jesus Michael! I know you've been talking to her a lot, but you've only gone home to see her once all term."

"She's pregnant Morris."

"Okay, she's pregnant. You're the father. What's the big rush to get married? You can still finish your Ph.D. You've finished your orals completing the dissertation would only take you maybe another two months."

"Four if I'm fortunate."

"You're just walking away?"

"It's a doctorate in theater. I don't need it."

"You've worked so hard. My God, Michael, it's all just sitting there, ready to be put together."

"It's just a pile of research. I wanted to write an important book, not just the dissertation. A book is entirely different from a dissertation, and it's going to take a lot of planning and craftsmanship to make it into a book."

"Surely Elaine understands how much work you've put in. How close to finishing you are. What's the sudden rush to get married all about?"

"Morris I'm done. None of it matters anymore. I've got somebody I love, and she's in trouble. She's a junior high teacher. There are reputations at stake and things, and nuances to our lives I couldn't explain to you if I had ten years."

"For Christ's sake Michael, even kids can count to nine."

"That's part of the problem. I'm sure lies will be told, and truths stretched. What matters right now is for us to marry, to be husband and wife, living together, and the sooner, the better."

"So, you're having a small family wedding on Saturday."

"We're going to a justice of the peace in Canton. We're the only two people beside you who'll ever know. There won't be a living soul in her hometown who will ever know. She told her parents we secretly married in August and she wouldn't be telling them now if she hadn't gotten pregnant."

"Jesus Michael, I can't believe this, all that work, and you're just walking away."

"I have a job teaching at the high school waiting for me starting after Christmas. And right now, as a soon to be high school teacher having a doctorate in theater seems pointless."

"I can't believe this, all that time, the documentation, the research?"

"Morris if my walking away bothers you all that much why don't you take it over and finish it. Make it into a book. You know as much about it as I do."

"Michael that's just wrong."

"Morris, my uncut diamond, if you somehow found the time, and a way to pull it off, I'd be quite surprised, actually amazed; but neither I nor anyone else would ever consider using my research wrong. You still have to graduate, you have a job, and you're starting graduate school next fall. Should you somehow manage to pull off the miracle of all times; I'll be satisfied with credit as a researcher, and a mention as a friend."

"You really wouldn't mind if I tried?"

"Absolutely not, trust me Morris; trying to weave that mess into a readable, coherent work, is going to take some serious skill and more work than you can imagine. Just thinking about the amount of time and work is overwhelming. I don't even want to try; it's simply too damn much work. It would be unimaginably time-consuming; especially knowing I need to be with Elaine putting our lives together.

"Living together isn't going to be easy for either of us. But being separated from each other now would be intolerable. We have a million practical things to do, but mostly we need to be together learning how to live with each other. We've only got about eight months before there'll be three of us."

"I hope you're not doing this out of some idealistic sense of doing the right thing by her. You really love each other?"

"Since ninth grade, it's the only thing in my whole life I've been absolutely sure of. I'm just sorry I got her pregnant. It's screwed up everything for her, and it's going to make her life hard. She might have to give up a lot of her hopes and dreams."

"You both are! Jesus, Michael, I can't believe this. I'm really going to miss you. Is there anything I can do?"

"Help me load the car Wednesday night and wish us well. Finish that damn project if you can. I know you're smart enough, but you're still a kid. My rough-cut diamond. So, don't just jump into it. Spend some time thinking it through. Try to figure out how to weave it together. If you do manage to pull it off, I'll be thankful not to have to feel like it was such a wasted effort."

Morris spent a month mulling over and reviewing the material. He wrote out countless outlines hoping to find some way to organize the material. But nothing came. He was on the verge of giving up. On a Sunday morning absently staring into the pan while scrambling eggs the way to structure the book popped complete in his head. Amazed, Morris finished his breakfast, thanked the eggs, and started in on it. It took nine months of night and day effort to get it ready for submission. He spent most of the last quarter of his senior year working on the book.

The bulk of the writing he completed during the following summer. But getting it revised, corrected, and ready to be published kept him working on it right through the fall quarter of his master's program. During fall quarter, the manuscript made at least three trips back and forth between the humanities department and his publisher. He was sleeping maybe four hours a night sometimes not at all. Somehow with Professor's Stanton's encouragement and Robbie's help he finished it.

The only break he took was when he came home over the Fourth of July holiday. As expected Morris helped with his mother's annual Fourth of July event. He grilled the burgers and hot dogs and took the younger children and the adults out in the boat. Morris tried to talk to everybody but found himself so preoccupied with the book he barely remembered talking with Hanna.

They talked because he remembered that unimaginably incredible voice of hers, how frail she looked, and how much he wanted to hug her. Taking her in his arms was awkward. Hanna made an awful sound and said, "Sorry about that I should've said something. I'm still recovering from that last surgery, the one on my ribs I put off."

She told him despite everything she continued going to classes. She was planning on returning full-time in the fall and thanks to him she was on her way. He remembered her face covered in long thin red lines and hundreds of tiny red dots from stitches so small you had to look carefully to see them. He remembered her beautiful smile and her voice.

She said, "I was lucky I didn't lose any teeth, and Doctor Sanderson saved my hand. It took him three surgeries and nine weeks of physical therapy, but it works just fine."

He left three days later. Right after his birthday and returned to Evanston. On the eight-hour drive, he figured out how to write the concluding chapter, how to do it had been driving him crazy for weeks. Morris found writing not in any way easy, it was a tremendously frustrating struggle, but when he got it where he wanted it, there was such a sense of satisfaction.

But that happened so infrequently he continually struggled. He found himself questioning everything, his inability to say what he needed to sensibly, or correctly, his inability to understand and use words succinctly, properly, and with clarity. He was continually bone tired, overwhelmed, and close to tears. He wanted to give up, but the thought of that was unthinkable.

Mostly Morris began questioning himself, his intelligence his abilities or lack thereof. He would go back to something he thought was fine, completed only to realize it wasn't and would have to be rewritten. There were many such times when he threw his hands up in disgust and knowing he was awful at this deciding it was time to face he wasn't and never would be a writer.

But this writing thing had taken hold of him with a dogged ferocity. This wasn't something he could just stop doing or put aside. It kept a tight grip on him. He couldn't and didn't stop, not for anything. He would wake realizing he had fallen asleep at his desk mid-sentence, the thought and phrasing gone. He would be so tired and frustrated he was close to despondent.

When Morris looked back on this time, he wondered what drove him and kept him going. He had no one prodding him or encouraging him, the whole time Morris felt overwhelmed and wondered what he thought he was doing. Morris decided his dedication had all come from Michael. He so imbued Morris with the importance of the information and what he was trying to accomplish Morris felt it had to be completed.

Michael was a force, one of those rare people who know how to help others without doing anything more than just mentioning something. He pointed the way to an answer without ever raising his arm. Morris, alone in a very quiet house found himself missing Michael terribly. Michael's energy and passion for theater, music, and especially opera was contagious. It didn't merely rub off. Morris felt compelled to devour every crumb offered.

Sharing his love of theater, and especially of music and opera, Michael explained in detail every facet of each production they attended. Using every nuanced piece of knowledge at his command, Michael did it with such enthusiasm and love he easily held Morris's attention. It was like getting a second master's degree.

Morris's senior year, the following summer and the first quarter of grad school was a hazy impenetrable fog of obscure mystery. The book and his coursework were done and done exceptionally well. However, it was completed in such a whirlwind of herculean effort and with such unbelievable speed he all but missed it.

Morris was now enmeshed in much more advanced and sophisticated strivings. But he had no understanding of how he got here, or of how changed he was. He did it living two sometimes three lives and hardly sleeping. He survived and welcomed coming home for Christmas where he could finally relax and enjoy what he thought of as normal times.

ELEVEN

Hanna recovered, as did Morris. He was two-quarters and a term from completing his masters and already accepted into a doctorate program. Morris hadn't made his plans for getting a doctorate degree known, but he planned on telling Hanna. Except for his phone calls and briefly seeing Hanna at his parent's Fourth of July doings last summer Morris hadn't been home or talked in person with Hanna.

Morris opened the front door, and there stood Annett, Robert, and Hanna. Morris was so unprepared to see those three standing together he forgot himself. He left them there in the cold staring at him. Recovering he said, "Come in, come in. How nice to see everyone well and all together and we're nowhere near a hospital." Taking their coats, Morris saved Hanna's for last. His mother appeared and escorted Robert and Annett into the living room. Grinning at Hanna, he said, "Can I hug you without hurting you?"

"Sure, I'm all better now." And at the sound of that low melodious magical voice, he melted. He held her close, but not firmly. Talking in her ear, he said, "Hanna you look terrific. You look happy and just plain wonderful."

"I am."

He was overjoyed to see her looking healthy and vibrant. Still holding each other, she whispered in his ear, "I still want my kiss, Morris. You promised."

"A promise is a promise Hanna, but this time it doesn't look like you need it."

"Morris, I'll always want that kiss, but we can save it until I really need it."

She changed almost everything. She wasn't a shy timid teenage girl. Hanna didn't look frail or sickly. Her hair was still cropped short, but it looked intentional and shaped. Her blouse and slacks allowed all to know she had a figure. Best of all she was wearing the nicest warmest most effervescent smile you could ever want to see. It lit up her face almost commanding him to hug her. He said, "Let's go somewhere after this, and catch up?"

"I'd like that."

Hanna and Morris wound their way through the evening both wanting only to run off and talk with each other. By the time they managed their escape, the party had become painfully tedious, but they soon found themselves seated at a local restaurant in a booth relaxing and talking

"Hanna it's hard to believe, but you look like it never happened."

"They did a fantastic job of putting my face back together. You need to look close to see Doctor Meyer's sewing. She used dozens and dozens of tiny stitches instead of big clunky ones. She's a plastic surgeon, and I was lucky she was on call the night it happened. Doctor Meyer spent hours sewing me up. There are still things wrong that don't show, but they're getting better.

I told you I didn't think I'd ever get over what happened, and I don't think I ever will. But Morris that Mielziner book you brought changed my life.

"I read some that night after dad left. I knew what I needed to do and where to look. I was so lost, and that book gave me so much hope and a path. The next morning when mom told me Frank died my heart just broke. I've never felt so awful. I hurt everywhere. Much worse than the beating or anything I've ever known. Frank was like you, gentle and kind, a true gentleman. He went to the library with me just to keep me company. Because of how I looked he got beat to death. If I'd just looked like a girl, he'd be alive."

"Hanna, you don't know that. You're not responsible for what happened that night."

"He wasn't any taller than me Morris, but he had this huge sense of humor; I don't care what the situation was. There we were, lying in the street, five feet apart, neither of us able to move. Barely conscious, hurt everywhere, absolutely beat to shit. The last words I heard before I passed out were Hanna girl, what should we talk about while we're lying here in the street?"

"Hanna, you weren't responsible for what happened. You did nothing and those men, Jesus Hanna I can't even begin to understand what kind of fear and loathing was behind what they did."

"Because of how I looked we were attacked, punched, hit with a bat, and kicked into senselessness. Because of what happened you came four hundred miles and brought a lost soul Jo Mielziner's book. I ended up with a life to look forward to, and Frank died. God above Morris it's just not right. Not in any way."

"Hanna those men were the twisted sick ones. They made it all up in their drunken heads. To be so afraid of something that has nothing to do with you that you beat someone to death? God above it's beyond me."

"If I were dressed like I am tonight, it would've never happened."

"Hanna, you don't know that. You have no way of knowing what was going through their minds. All anyone knows is they were drinking and intent on causing trouble. Where did the baseball bat come from? One of them brought it. Who does something like that? They were looking to hurt someone. If they'd known you were a girl, they would have most likely beat Frank up and raped you, probably killed you both. God above Hanna, you weren't responsible for what happened. You've got to stop blaming yourself for what those sick people did."

Hanna half smiled and said, "So what about you Morris? How are you? You got anyone special in your life?"

He looked across at her and said, "Just you Hanna."

"It's so good to see you, Morris. When I don't, I do so miss your older man wisdom."

"Looks like you've got yourself pretty well figured out. Except for your hair, you look."

"Normal? It's a costume Morris it keeps the peace at home. The boys can all see I'm a girl. But I refuse to use makeup or any of that to make myself all sexy and alluring."

"You are alluring Hanna, very much so."

"Sorry Morris, but I want nothing to do with that kind of alluring."

"Too much reality for you to acknowledge a man might consider you appealing, be attracted to you, and want to get to know you?"

"You mean he might want to fuck me?"

"Hanna that's not at all what I meant. I shouldn't have gone down that road. I see it's still way too complicated. Anyway, before people fuck, they usually get to know each other, and then decide if they might enjoy doing that."

"Sorry, Morris it's not for me. Way too complicated, but don't worry I get pulled back into the real world now and then. Especially when one of my professors leans over one of my renderings and says, Hanna don't forget someone has to figure out how to build all that fairy dust you're having so much fun sprinkling all over that drawing."

"You're really enjoying yourself, aren't you?"

"Yes, I am, and with no male complications. How about you Morris, what are you enjoying?"

"I've some big news! I submitted a book and surprise of all surprises its being published."

She practically came up out of the booth and across the table saying, "Morris why didn't you say something. That's terrific. What's it about?"

"It's academic. Textbook stuff, but I tried my best to make it a good read."

"Come on Morris, tell me."

"It's about language and translations. How the mistranslation of as little as a single sentence, a few words can alter or change the meaning of an entire work."

"Examples."

"There are too many you'll have to read the book."

"I will, especially if you send me a signed copy."

"Hanna it's so good to see you all okay and happy. You look terrific."

"It took a while, but I'm finally enjoying myself."

"A career in the world of theater, you are a brave soul."

"I love it. I must've read two hundred and fifty plays while I was first recuperating. It drove mom and dad nuts. I was sending them to the library every few days. I read every play dad and mom could get."

"According to Morris Steven's new book, plays, and poetry are particularly prone to problems with mistranslation."

"Which plays Morris?"

He cocked his head, and she smiled and said, "Okay, okay. I can't wait to read your book."

"So how are mom and dad doing with your career choice?"

"I think they'll adjust, maybe even get over it. My friends scare mom to death, Dad just says, well, I was young once too, whatever that means."

"Hanna, it would be nice if we could see each other more."

"You mean like date or get on a path to somewhere or something?"

"That sounded strange. Like we'd be reorganizing our worlds or breaking a rule."

"It's not a rule Morris. I don't date, I don't get married, and I don't do that thing that makes babies."

"You sure kiss amazingly well, at least I thought so."

"I draw, paint, and design even better."

"So, you don't want to consider dating a guy who's on his way to be a professor?"

"Morris what we have is special. We aren't that way with each other. It's way more and better than dating or anything like that. You already know who, and what I am and better than anyone else ever has, or ever will. We're four hundred miles apart. It would be impossible to manage. It wouldn't be any different from now."

"You're right, still?"

"Don't worry; there'll come a time when I'll call. I'll be in a place once again when I really need that kiss and all that warm reassuring comfort. Now, enough with the boy-girl stuff. It's your turn. Catch me up on grad school and what you're doing."

"So far so good, but I'm looking forward to summer and having time that's not so all-consuming. Writing that book my senior year and all last summer took every bit of me. I worked on it night and day all summer long, and I couldn't stop or put it down. I just kept at it until it was done. Somehow after three revisions, it's being published and hard as it is for me to believe, I'm on my way to life in academia."

"It will suit you well Morris. You're sincere and charming, the students will love you. You enjoy everything about the world even economics. You sure understand me and always know what I need. There were so many things you've done that made it come out right for me.

"It started when I was fourteen when you insisted I go with you and Alice to the boathouse to help. Then there was the day in my room when you first saw my paintings. Praising them and me to the heavens, insisting I show them to your mother. Prom night when you took me to that barn, I understood light. I saw it. How it looks and feels. I learned more that night than I have in all my years in school and, Morris, the warmth when we kissed? I know I'm going to need that again.

"When I was in the hospital, and completely lost, you brought Mielziner's book, and it showed me the way. I don't understand how you know what I need, but you do. Every time it's the perfect thing for me. Morris, you've been an absolute godsend. I can't think about my life without thinking of you."

"Hanna, whatever do you think we might someday do about us?"

"Let's just let whatever it is between us grow wild. I know we've got to stay in touch, at least with words. We'll need to check on it every so often and see how we're doing. What with all the surgeries I've got at least four more years of school. That'll include summer sessions before I'll graduate, but meantime I'll be working, getting paid actual real money.

"I'm designing some shows here in town, and two of the local galleries are scheduling shows for me. Let's let whatever we have between us grow on its own. And one more thing

Morris, I don't care about anything else, but promise me you'll come to my graduation party."

"I will Hanna, and I'll bet you I'll have my doctorate by then."

"I mean it, Morris. Promise me you'll come for my graduation. I've tried to keep my requests reasonable only asking when it was important when I needed to be saved, and I've never cried wolf. Your help is something I rely on. You know I don't do well at celebratory things, especially one that will be dedicated to just me. Mark my words, mom, and dad will invite everyone they know."

"You have my word, Hanna. Shakespeare's furies couldn't keep me away."

TWELVE

Morris's life was in Evanston. He had a girlfriend for three months between his junior and senior year, and they grew close. He was very fond of her, and she brought something he'd never experienced. Dianne was quite the accomplished sexual partner. He missed her and those lovely random afternoons, mornings, and nights they enjoyed together. When she left Michael stuck Morris's nose to the grindstone and gave him no time to pine over his loss. For the past two years, busy as he was when he thought about women he thought of Hanna and her unbelievable ability and talent.

Occasionally Morris would try to think of Hanna as his partner. He thought of her voice, that wonderful smile, her amazing white blonde hair, and of making love to her. But given Hanna's penchant for eschewing anything and everything to do with men, it was a difficult thing to imagine. Last Christmas he hinted around about something more with her and without a moment's hesitation she brushed it aside. Morris was more than aware they meant something important and necessary to each other, he just didn't understand it, nor did he know what it was.

When he returned to Evanston after Christmas vacation, everything went back to normal. He was no longer spending every moment struggling with the writing. Michael was married and teaching. Diane was long gone. Morris was working on his master's degree and only on what that involved. He took classes all summer and didn't return home until Thanksgiving when he came to help his parents pack up the house for their move. His father had taken a job with Bechtel, an extensive worldwide engineering, and construction firm. That Christmas, he flew to San Francisco to spend it with his family at their new home.

He called Hanna every so often, and they spoke to each other about their lives and how things were going. She reminded him more than once of his promise to attend her graduation. The school year flew by; he received his master's degree, and his advisor and mentor, the head of the humanities department, John Stanton, kept him busy all that following spring and summer. He helped Morris in every way he could to prepare for his doctorate program.

Once his parents sold their lake home and moved to San Francisco Morris began thinking of Evanston as home and lived in the house he and Michael rented. He had two housemates and a teaching assistant's position which made it all doable. Morris spent the summer after he completed his master's degree with John going around Evanston to informal gatherings at John's fellow professor's homes.

The visits were enjoyable and always entertaining. Not writing and studying twenty hours a day Morris relaxed and was enjoying meeting all these new people. John was giving Morris a window on understanding what life as an academic would be. Spring turned to summer and Morris met more and more of the faculty. He was overwhelmed and unprepared for what publishing such a scholarly work at his young age and station had on these well-established professors.

The continual outpouring of praise and compliments was unnerving and left Morris struggling to accept that these scholarly learned professors not only read his book but were impressed.

Morris also learned his book was enjoying wide circulation amongst academics all over the country. At a luncheon, Margret Bergstrom, a middle-aged sociology professor, when introduced to him, blurted out, "Good heavens! You're just a boy." John later explained what Morris accomplished was close to unbelievable to all of them.

In fairness, the note he received from Michael just before the book's publication gave Morris confidence in his writing ability and some insight into the magnitude of his accomplishment. But Morris didn't take Michael's words overly to heart believing him to be quite biased where he was concerned.

Yet, Morris trusted Michael implicitly, and when he sent Michael, one of the pre-release copies of the book, he knew he'd respond. He also knew his assessment would be honest to a fault. So much so Morris grew apprehensive about what Michael would say. Michael not only surprised him but gave him confidence in his abilities. Michael also gave Morris some awareness of the scope and actual dimensions of what writing the book might mean for him.

Dear Morris,

"What a student, it's a stunning achievement, unbelievable, you've done it. You've amazed me. The book's a jewel, Morris. It's a no kidding sparkling showpiece. You're no longer my diamond in the rough; you're beautifully cut, superbly faceted, and brilliantly polished. You're all grown up kid.

I would like to think I could have done as well, but in my heart, I don't believe I would've. It's masterfully written, scholarly, and ever so readable. I couldn't be more pleased for you. Thanks ever so much for the credit and your exceedingly kind words in the foreword. It meant a lot to me. Thank you. You're a true friend Morris and one hell-of-a-student. My best so far!

We have a girl, Marla! Everything's great, better than I ever expected.

All my Love, Michael

THIRTEEN

Morris's second book, a novel, came about because of his relationship with his mentor and advisor John Stanton. John's mission of introducing and making sure Morris met everybody at Northwestern who might be of any conceivable help to him inevitably brought Morris and John to the home of John's lifelong friends, professors Albert, and Marion Hendry.

Explaining to Morris while walking from John's office to their house, John said, "Albert and Marion taught here for more than fifty years. They retired about eight years ago, but they were participating and active in student's lives right up until the end of this spring quarter."

Morris said, "How were you involved with them?"

"Albert was Chairman of the humanities department before me. When I was a graduate student he was my advisor and mentor. He's the reason I'm the present Chairman."

Shortly after they arrived Morris became aware, Marion wasn't doing well, and they were preparing for Marion's move into a nursing home. Morris could tell Marion was struggling with rheumatoid arthritis in her hips and knees. Her breathing was labored and just getting around appeared to be difficult.

Albert was eighty-six, and Marion was eighty-eight. Surprising, to Morris, they were both interested in him.

He could tell this went much further than just being pleasant. They wanted to know him and everything about him. They completely disarmed Morris when they started behaving toward him as if he were a visiting grandson or some other significant member of their family. Morris, like most young people, didn't spend much time with seniors. It wasn't what his life was about, but having spent many summers at his grandparent's home, he held clear memories of both his grandmother and grandfather. He remembered he'd never thought of them as old.

His grandfather taught Morris how to drive when he was ten and was out every day inspecting the fields and managing the crops on their substantial land holdings. Before the Civil War, it was a thriving plantation. The main house, all the barns, the stables, and outbuildings, everything, but the slave quarters, were burned to the ground by Sherman's troops on their march to Columbia. It was never rebuilt.

The land came to Morris's grandfather through his mother who, at the end of the Civil War, was the sole surviving member of her family. Elizabeth Fail was quite a story herself. Her mother died earlier that year of pneumonia her father unknown to her froze to death in a prisoner of war camp just outside of Chicago.

When the family's plantation was burned, she had just turned fourteen and was living there by herself. It left her homeless. She moved into the slave quarters with the remaining slaves and after the war, she and those now freed slaves, continued together, managing to make a living from the land. His grandfather still pretty much ran the place the way his mother set it up back in 1865.

Having taught Morris to drive on his tenth birthday, Morris, from then, drove his grandfather and his friend Amos around to inspect and decide on the harvest schedule for the different fields. Morris got to listen to that marvelous white-haired black man and his grandfather, laugh, and laugh as they sat in the back telling stories and reminiscing about their many years of working together.

On every visit, Morris, and his grandfather went fishing, and his grandfather managed the boat, motor, and their gear without effort. His grandmother would be up early and working in her amazing flower garden. She taught Morris about flowers, hummingbirds, chickens, the peacock and the ornery Guinea hens. She taught him to set a formal place setting using the proper silverware, four knives, four forks, and six spoons.

More importantly, she showed him how to make a pie crust and biscuits from scratch. Both had white hair, but he didn't remember ever thinking of them as old. But just after Morris turned thirteen his grandfather died and his grandmother a few months later. His mother said she died of a broken heart. It was a big shock. He hadn't thought of either as old.

Marion, even at eighty-eight, was a remarkable looking woman. Morris could see she was a stunning beauty when younger. She still exhibited some of the vestiges of her earlier life. She had a lovely, remarkably pleasant face. A body that was once limber and shaped, and even today with her arthritis, still appeared to be ruled by the elegant posture of a trained dancer.

Constant pain does something to a person, and Morris was aware she was uncomfortable just sitting in the chair. Nevertheless, her eyes sparkled and flashed when she was talking with him. Marion was as gracious, as his mom, and her interest in Morris was as genuine as his mothers. He wanted to know all about her, especially what she taught. She told him classical literature. He couldn't help but wonder if her classes were filled to overflowing with young men. Watching the two of them, Morris became very much aware there was a lot to master regarding the social graces of a nuanced academic life.

Albert and Marion traveled the academic road for over fifty years. Under similar circumstances in other such professors company, Morris was more circumspect and reserved with his ideas, answers, and thoughts. He was enjoying Marion and Albert and found himself very much at ease and attracted to these two uncommonly gracious people. Thoroughly enjoying his present company, Morris, already about as without pretense as a twenty-four-year-old could be, relaxed, and set any remaining defenses and cautions aside.

Later in the afternoon John thoroughly embarrassed Morris. He went on much too long, explaining Morris having just this spring finishing his master's program, had written this brilliant scholarly book on problems inherent in translations. Explaining further that Morris wrote the book while an undergraduate.

He went on and on about how surprised Robbie James was when Morris brought his manuscript to him and asked for his opinion. John said, "Morris is very capable. I'm just as pleased as I can be to have him with us at Northwestern. He's going to make an exceptional addition to the department. Both Robbie and I believe his doctoral thesis will also become another important academic work."

Marion said, "So Morris tell us what your thesis intends to shed light on."

"I'm still working out the details, but it'll center on language, specifically words, how we use them, and how others misinterpret them."

Albert said. "Sounds like you're planning to expand on Ludwig Wittgenstein's work?"

Morris said, "Wittgenstein's basic premise that many of our philosophical confusions derive from the vocabulary we use and how those words are interpreted has generated a great deal of academic interest. I believe he's right. There's a measurable correlation between the vocabulary we use as part of the language we speak and how those words directly affect and add to the philosophical confusions we try so hard to formulate and live by.

"I'm interested in exploring if there is the same degree of confusion and misunderstanding between the literary forms, which use only written vocabulary, and film or theater, which rely on combinations of speech, gesture, music, dance, mime, sound, art, and spectacle to deliver their message."

"I've been digging into seeing if there've been any studies about perceivable differences and so far, what I've managed to turn up hasn't been much help."

Marion said, "You've found nothing out there in the literature?"

Morris said, "A few things, but most of its unusable."

Marion said, "Why's that?"

"Unsupported supposition and speculation, I was surprised."

Albert said, "It's an intriguing idea. You'll need a method to accurately measure the results of the levels of understanding between reading the written word and watching a film or live performance?"

"I'm working on some ways to do that, but I'm even more interested in the causes of the confusion and why misunderstandings even come about. A word has distinct meanings especially in carefully thought out usage, yet when used in texts they're often misinterpreted. I want to determine if the same concepts and ideas presented theatrically or through a film might result in the understanding being perceived differently. Possibly more accurately and comprehensively understood than from a written or spoken text."

Albert smiling, said, "Sounds ambitious and you're crossing quite a few areas of study. So far, I heard linguistics, philosophy, psychology, humanities, and probably statistics. I like it, its original, but awfully ambitious it could turn on you and leave you in a quagmire. It could be frustrating."

Smiling Morris said, "I played Hockey all through high school that's about as frustrating as anything ever gets. But writing that book on translations was the hardest most difficult thing I ever tried to do. Believe me, I know about frustration. But I'm confident I'll be able to put together a meaningful thesis."

Almost grinning, Marion said, "Oh, for the certainty of youth, especially in the face of adversity, it's so refreshing."

John said, "I'm putting my faith in Morris. I'm going to turn him loose with this, just like you did with me, Albert. I'll ask him to come by every couple of months and tell me how he's doing. His book on translation errors was not only fascinating, but it was well written. The premises and proofs are outlined in clear, concise, unambiguous terms, and it's wonderfully readable. The young man has a gift."

"John, please. If my head gets any bigger, I won't be able to stay upright, and I still need to walk through doorways, and fit in cars."

"Morris I'm teasing, but it's all to do with how pleased I am you're here working towards becoming part of our humanities department."

John knowing full well neither Albert nor Marion were up for cooking for themselves much less for company suggested he go get a couple of pizzas and some salads. This was agreed by all to be the dining plan. Leaving to take care of it, John left Morris behind with Albert and Marion.

FOURTEEN

Albert said, "So Morris what do your parents do? Where did you grow up?" Morris explained his father was a civil engineer, a very experienced prominent one. Before she married, his mother worked as a loan officer at a bank, and his parents met when his father was a student at the University of South Carolina.

He told them how his father spent four years in the South Pacific during WWII as the commanding officer of a CB battalion. Like Marion and Albert, his mother was older than his father. His dad worked for Sears when they lived out east and just left General Mills having taken a position with Bechtel Corporation. He'll be overseeing, the designing, and implementing of one-half of a massive rapid transit system connecting San Francisco and Oakland.

Albert said, "So Morris what sort of activities did you enjoy growing up?"

"My parents are both from South Carolina. I was born during World War II in Boston. I'm the only child in our entire extended family born above the Mason-Dixon Line. So, I have the dubious distinction of being the only Yankee in the family."

Marion, laughing, said, "Me too, and my great aunts never let me forget it, or stopped talking about it."

"Most of what I remember was growing up in New Jersey on the Delaware River. I spent a large part of my summers sailing, playing baseball, and visiting my grandparent's in South Carolina. I went to an excellent private Quaker school right up until we moved to Minnesota. I took classes at the Franklin Institute, the Philadelphia Museum of Art and the Pennsylvania Academy of Fine Arts on Broad Street and I've been thoroughly spoiled. I had the best childhood anyone could ask for.

"We moved to Minnesota when I was fourteen and again thanks to mom and dad we ended up living on this beautiful huge freshwater lake just west of Minneapolis. The house was built in 1895 and dad added on to it. It was the most wonderful place a teenager could ever want to be. The house sat up high looking out over seven miles of lake, and there was this amazing boat house built right down on the water. We had a beautiful Chris Craft speedboat I used all summer long.

"When you went into that boathouse it was like going into a wondrous little chapel. The light coming in was the most unbelievable sight you could ever imagine. On the other side of the property set back about thirty feet from the shore was what we called the barbecue house. It was also a unique space.

"Both the boathouse and the barbecue house were pegged post and beam construction like barns use to be built. The wood was all hand hewn, finished with draw knives, and hand planes. It was like baby's hair to the touch and after sixty-five years everything inside had aged to a beautiful warm almond brown. They were incredible places.

"The barbecue house was screened from floor to the beams on the lakeside. It had a monstrous table inside that easily sat twenty-four. At one end was a huge fieldstone open-hearth fireplace. Built into the back wall was a wood burning oven and grill. The fireplace had a rack with long sliding iron hooks used to hang big cast iron pots from.

"Every Fourth of July Mom and Dad would invite their friends, and they'd bring their kids. It was really something. I got to grill the burgers and hot dogs and take everybody out in the boat. With all the youngsters, it was rowdy, but always an entertaining, enjoyable afternoon."

Marion said, "You sound more than a little nostalgic about living there?"

"It's where I went to high school. I still have friends there and lots of great memories. But now if I go back I don't have a home, family, or a place. I'll end up in a motel. It'll never be the same. I'll be a stranger in my own land."

Albert said, "So you're feeling displaced? That everything's suddenly different, almost like it never was?"

"Mostly I'm mourning. That life's gone, and I'll never be able to be there again. It feels very much the same as when my girlfriend left to go to school at Berkeley. I knew we'd never see each other again. I sure didn't want that, not at all. It stung."

Marion said, "Losing the place where you grew up might even be more traumatic than losing a love."

Morris said, "Leaving people and things behind wasn't new to me. Our family moved many times. But for some reason I haven't figured out losing our family home on that beautiful lake has been terribly disconcerting. I had two close friends who lived nearby. I loved my family and that home, especially the boathouse. I spent a lot of time there working on the boat. The whole time I was there working I was enveloped in a spiritual world of smell and light. I never realized what I had."

Marion said, "So you took it for granted?"

"Worse, I'm sorry to say. I never thought about it. It was simply where we lived."

Albert said, "Morris you'll have to find your way and make a new home, your own home, and place."

"I'm starting to believe I'm going to have a life at Northwestern as a professor. I've been working as a TA, and

I like it. More importantly, the students seem to have taken to me. Maybe someday I'll have a home as lovely as this and a family who'll appreciate it. But right now, I'm struggling with how much I miss our lake home."

"Morris, I think that's exactly how Marion and I will feel when we leave here. We've lived in this place since we first married. We raised our children here. The place was full of life and noisy love. I know it isn't true, but it seems as if we sell it, and no longer live here, and like you, we can't come back. It all becomes as though it never was."

Morris said, "You can carry the memories with you, and your children and grandchildren can come and be a part of your new place. It won't be the same as being here, but the love and caring between you will all be there."

Everything stopped. Silence engulfed them. It descended all around and over them. It was the most unbearable quiet Morris ever heard. Marion looked away from him, and Albert looked down.

Looking from one to the other Morris didn't know what happened or what to do. Albert said, "Morris, John didn't tell you, and I'm sorry you had to put your foot in it to find out. But all of our children are dead."

Morris felt awful. Struggling, he finally said, "I didn't know. I'm truly sorry."

Albert said, "Ann was the oldest she graduated here in 1936. The boys graduated in 1939 and 41. They enlisted right after they graduated. Mark the oldest boy, our track star, went to England through Canada. He was an RAF pilot. He died in July 1942 in a crash while attempting to land his damaged Spitfire.

"James joined the Navy. He was killed in November 1942 during the battle of Guadalcanal. Ann was struck by a car in January two months after James died. Within six months they were all gone. We have no children to come visit. This place, this house, has kept them with us. I'm afraid of what it will be like to be in a different place. I'm not sure at all about what it will be like."

Marion said, "Morris you can have an exceptional life and career here at Northwestern. You're nice looking and likable. You've been blessed with quite an endearing little boy smile, and better yet, you've already established you're bright and hard working. You just need to find that right person and start loving and making babies. Trust me it'll all work out. And Morris, please stop looking like you tracked dog poo across the living room carpet. It happened twenty-five years ago. We've learned to live with it."

Morris said, "I'm sorry about the way it came up. I feel awful about what just happened. What I said, my words were terribly hurtful. You've both been so warm and gracious to me, you've been as welcoming as my own family."

John came through the front door carrying the food. He was a welcome sight. He swept the awkwardness and all that darkness right out of the room. They quickly busied themselves going about setting the table and preparing to eat.

John said, "So what did you talk about in my absence?"

Marion said, "Morris explained no boy could have grown up in a better way and places than him. He told us he was blessed and privileged to live where he did. You're right John. Morris's an interesting, modest, and refreshingly straightforward young man. The University's will be lucky to have him."

FIFTEEN

Such was Morris's beginning with Albert and Marion. Over the next three weeks, at Albert's direction, he cleaned out their attic and basement. During the second week of his helping, Marion moved into the nursing home, and Albert was on the waiting list for an opening in the assisted living section.

The third afternoon of it being the two of them as Morris was carrying out the last of the basement Albert up and said, "Morris I'll sell you the house at a great price. But you must take it as is."

Morris put his hand on Albert's shoulder, and said, "Albert you're just feeling overwhelmed. Once I'm finished with the cleanup, you can get the estate sale people in, and they'll take care of everything. Albert, it'll be okay."

"This is our life Morris. Everything's here, our books, the china, our art, the furniture. It's where we lived with our family. This is it, all of us, every drop of our lives. Marion bought the furniture pieces and carpets a little at a time. She was particular and never afraid of paying too much, but she always wanted the nicest."

"It's a beautiful home, Albert. You've made a lovely home here. If this is too much for you John and I can meet with the estate sale people and work out the details."

"No, no, you don't understand Morris. All our children are dead. I want this to all stay together, right here, where Marion worked so hard and carefully to get it the way we all wanted it. Breaking it up is almost unthinkable."

***

Sitting in John's office late on a Friday afternoon Morris was telling him he was almost finished helping Albert get the house ready for the estate sale people. Once he finished, the house could be put up for sale.

Morris said, "All that's left is to go through the upstairs bedrooms and then try to figure out what to do with the books. There must be 2500 books in the study. They take up two twelve-foot walls floor to ceiling. The whole fifty years of their academic lives are in that study."

John said, "I'd take them if I had anywhere to put them."

"Maybe it's time to work on getting you a bigger office."

"Fat chance of that."

Morris said, "Maybe the university library would want them. It's an outstanding collection."

John said, "How's Marion doing?"

"Albert told me she's dying of congestive heart failure."

"Is he coping okay?"

"He said Marion's been better since she's no longer trying to care for the house and fix meals. All Albert cares about is being with her. He doesn't believe she has much time left. I see him every day, and I'm worried about him. Albert's preoccupied. He needs to be in that assisted care facility. He's not doing a good job of taking care of himself. If he's there, it'll be a lot more convenient for them to be with each other."

John said, "I've talked with the director, and she assured me she would get Albert in within the next two weeks."

"He'll be pleased about that."

During one of Morris's working visits, Albert followed him around talking, and said, "Although I was liked as a professor Marion was beloved. She was glorious, a stunning, elegant woman, and she was every bit the accomplished professor I was.

"She chose me, Morris. Why I never understood? Women do that you know. Men chase after the woman, and the woman decides whether she wants to be caught. Marion was twenty-eight, a brilliant sparkling woman with a dozen suitors. I was twenty-six and not even close to handsome, but she let me catch her. She's spent her life with me, and she's loved me all these years. Every time I see her I know I'm the luckiest man on this earth.

"Marion taught with such passion and feeling it was a glorious thing to witness. Her students loved her, especially her graduate students. She had a gift for teaching. I know you saw it, Morris. It's in her eyes, and it's still there, even after all these years. Her classes had no shortage of students they were always popular."

Albert continued, "She's always been such a positive soul. Even through that awful, horrible time, she managed it with remarkable grace and humility, so much better than I did. She refused to let the deaths of our children destroy our marriage, and it came close.

"I was struggling with the deaths of our boys. The night of that final blow when Anne was hit by the car, we got the call and rushed out of the house to the hospital only to find she died before we got there. I wasn't dealing well with the deaths of our boys. I was already struggling with my grief.

"When Anne died, I refused to believe it. Its what intellectuals suffer when a sudden tragedy strikes. We try to think those sorts of things through believing we'll be able to understand it. The rationale is if we figure it out, and make sense of it, it'll somehow be all right. It's a senseless undertaking, Morris. There's nothing to comprehend, or to understand. Death is instantaneous, final, and forever. It's one of the real horrors of being alive. It leaves the loved ones in pure unadulterated endless pain, and it stays and stays, for as long as it wants. There wasn't anything left in me the night Anne died. I felt as dead as my children.

"Sitting on a sofa together in the hospital lounge we were too stunned to move, cry, or do anything. Marion saw I was undone. On a slippery slope sliding away, minutes from being swept into a permanent unholy state. She took my hand and said, Albert! Look at me. You can't leave me. I need you more than I ever have. We must be here to help each other with this. Thank God for that woman, for I'm sure I would've either stumbled in front of a bus or ended up committed somewhere for a long time."

Albert told Morris he taught five undergraduate classes a quarter, and they averaged about twenty students a class. He figured in forty-six years of teaching he taught fifteen thousand students. Marion did a third less going to a part-time when the children were young.

Albert said, "What I came to enjoy most was working with my graduate students. Working with them gave both Marion and me years of pleasure. It was a pure joy to be with them. They both felt to be part of their graduate student's lives after losing all three of their children was a life healing elixir for them.

"It is so miraculous to sit with a young man or woman and realize this person is exceptional. There right in front of you is a talent and ability that is so large as to be almost incomprehensible. I relished those moments and even though all the students who come here are uniformly able. Finding one of those unique young people was like finding a perfect ten karat emerald in amongst a pile of two karat diamonds.

"It would just take my breath away. When you teach, you'll every so often meet such a person. It might be years from now, but when it happens, that moment will refresh you and make you smile from ear to ear. You'll want to help and encourage them in every way you can."

Morris said, "I've had that experience twice."

"That's rather unusual for someone as young as you. You're lucky to be so fortunate Morris."

Morris Said, "The first was instant compared to the second. It took a little time for me to realize I was rooming with an extraordinarily creative person. My senior year I was sharing a house with Michael Bloom. He was four years older than me and working on a Ph.D. in the theater department. Michael went about finishing his doctorate with so much energy it was close to frightening. He was beyond thorough and spent considerable amounts of time getting his research right.

"Michael made me part and party of his thesis having me review his research and read, reread, and go over every detail and piece of information. We'd sit at the kitchen table for hours sorting, analyzing, and discussing it. For weeks before he took his oral exams I sat in a chair opposite him for hours and hours asking questions and rehearsing the answers with him.

"The whole time we lived together he was dragging me off to every play within a hundred fifty miles he could find for us to go see. He loved opera and spent hours playing his vast record collection explaining every subtle nuance of the music and voices. Where he got all those records or learned what he knew I don't know. He came home one Monday in early November and said, sorry about this Morris, but you'll have to find a new roommate. I'm leaving the university Thursday.

"I couldn't believe it and said why what happened? He said I'm getting married Saturday and I have much more important things to take care of than getting a Ph.D. His girlfriend was pregnant. Michael wanted to marry and get on with making a life with her. He said it would take ten years to explain it, but it had to happen now. I said, Michael, you can still finish your doctorate. You've completed the orals finishing the dissertation would only take two months. He laughed and said, four if I'm lucky. I argued with him about walking away. I kept saying, all your work, it's just sitting there, waiting.

"Michael said Morris if you believe it's that important you do it. I said, get real Michael. He said, Morris, you know the material as well as I do, and we argued about his doctorates importance and all his time and effort, and how he should finish it. He said, Morris take it, it's yours, make it a book if you can.

"I kept looking at him. He said Morris; you're as much a part of it as I am. You know just as much about it as I do. I said, Michael, that's because you insisted on me being part of it. You never gave me a choice. It doesn't seem fair let alone proper for me to even consider trying to do something with your research.

"Smiling away, he said, Morris, if you somehow find the time and a way to pull it off, and I will be more than a little surprised if you do. Neither I nor anyone else would ever consider it wrong. Trust me, Morris; you've no idea what you're getting into. Trying to weave that pile of research into a readable, coherent work will be one hell of a lot of hard work. That's the real reason I can't do it. I can't be in two places at once. Not when I know, in my heart, Elaine and I need to be together working out our life. I'd never be able to focus or be single purposed enough to do it justice.

"He was a brilliant, overpowering personality, but always in a wonderfully creative way. He was one of those rare people who know how to help by just mentioning something. Somehow what he said was always the right thing. He overwhelmed me with his love and enthusiasm for theater and music

"He made it ever so fascinating. I couldn't wait to learn more. He continuously opened my eyes to new worlds. Without thinking about it, he provided me with an incomparable education.

It came from his unwavering, unthinking, spontaneous, exuberant passion for the subject. He loved it, all of it.

"We'd be riding home in the car from one of our theatrical outings, and he'd start. He'd review, critique, explain, and pound into my head every aspect of the production. The sets, the lighting, the acting, the direction, every little nuance of it, and he always found something he thought was inventive or well done. It was an amazing experience. I learned enough for a master's degree just by living with him. Most of all, he could, with just a few words send me in the right direction to an answer without ever conspicuously pointing the way."

Albert said, "Michael was like Marion. Just by being in the room with him you soaked it up. He understood his subject completely, intellectually, and intuitively. He loved it. People like Marion and Michael make it simple. It's so much fun learning from them. It's so easy it's embarrassing. Who was your other gem?"

"A young girl named Hanna Williston. She was the daughter of my mother and father's best friends and a senior in high school. We'd known each other since she was fourteen and I was seventeen. I would see her at my parent's holiday parties. She was exceptionally bright and well read. We enjoyed talking about things. When I came home my junior year at Thanksgiving, we ended up at her parent's house for Thanksgiving dinner.

"Hanna was struggling with her identity and just about everything else including her parents. In the middle of dinner, there was an awkwardly uncomfortable dust-up between Hanna and her mother. It happened right in front of the other families and the children."

"It was about the way she was dressing and Hanna cutting off her striking white-blond hair. Her father, to save the day, and get Hanna away from the table before she and her mother destroyed the Thanksgiving dinner, suggested Hanna take me to her studio and show me her art. I found myself in her room looking at the most amazing collection of drawings I've ever seen. The lines were perfect. Her drawing ability was masterful, years beyond her age. She was as skilled as Andrew Wyeth or Gibson."

"There were no actual paintings on her walls just her color experiments. I asked her where her paintings were and after haggling about not telling anyone about them, she pulled out a folio from the back of her closet. I put it on the bed and opened it. Three paintings in I was speechless. I couldn't believe what I was seeing. The brushwork and color choice took my breath away. The flesh of her subjects looked like it was alive.

"Painting after painting, her work was unbelievably sophisticated, accomplished, and original. I have formal training in both drawing and oil painting. She didn't. She taught herself from reading how the old masters did it and experimenting. I was dumbfounded. I couldn't get over what I was seeing."

"That's it, Morris. That's what I'm talking about. It doesn't happen often, but when it does, it takes your breath away, leaves you awestruck. You can't stop smiling. That's what it was like when I first met with John to go over his thesis project. I sat listening to him tell me about what he wanted to accomplish. What he explained was so brilliant and astounding it took my breath away. It made me smile, and I couldn't stop. When Robbie James showed your manuscript to John, that's what John and Robbie felt about you."

Albert's comment surprised him. Morris was amazed by Hanna's creative and technical ability and Morris never got over the depth of Michaels intellectual comprehension or his enthusiasm. He knew they were both extraordinary special people. But Morris didn't think of himself that way, even more so after he struggled so writing the book. Morris got A's in school, but the only thing he ever felt he excelled at was baseball, and that was limited to excelling at a high school level. Morris believed he only excelled at that level on his best days. Morris was both an outstanding hockey player and a superb pitcher.

He was no fun to bat against, and he continuously put pucks in the back of the net. Dartmouth and four other schools wanted him in their sports programs. Even though he was blind to his abilities, Morris understood, he knew how to, and did very much enjoy learning. Math, science, history, the arts, it all came to him easily. He never thought about it. He enjoyed satisfying his curiosity. But being special was beyond him. He knew he was athletic and could read and understand people; everyone except Diane and Hanna, but what Albert suggested startled him.

"Morris, you look surprised?"

"I am I don't know how to think of myself that way. I don't think I can."

"Don't try Morris. Just keep doing what you're doing. Michael was like Marion they understood and loved what they were teaching. They comprehended it with every fiber of their being; their hearts and souls were in it. They loved it and imparted it to their students with all the joy and pleasure of serving ice cream Sundays.

"That young woman, your artist friend, she doesn't think about being special. She's like you; she works on getting better and doing the work. For people like you and Hanna, the vision the ideas are in your head full blown. You barely have the means or patience to get them down, to make them real. You're so focused you make the people around you crazy with your unyielding ability to concentrate."

Morris said, "That's pretty much Hanna. She keeps working and experimenting, trying to get better."

"That's pretty much you Morris."

Albert said, "When you have children there's a sense of them continuing on with at least your genes. Hopefully, it's with all of what you lovingly taught them and worked so hard to prepare them. Unfortunately, at Marion's and my age having lost our children, there isn't any sense of us or anything about our family continuing. Not much of anything tangible for the future. Without our children to carry on, our lives are just coming to a quiet, empty end.

"Most young people don't understand what they have when they have it. Good health, looks, hopes and dreams, and bodies that work. Bodies designed and made for loving one another for hours and hours. Morris, make use of every advantage afforded you. We tried to with our children, our marriage, and our academic life. But now we're fast approaching the end it doesn't seem like much. There's no one to carry us forward."

"Albert, you and Marion have launched thousands and thousands of young people. You've shaped and formed so many lives. You must see the enormous mountain of work you've accomplished?"

Albert smiled at him and said, "What are you going to work on today Morris?"

"I'll finish the upstairs rooms, and then I'll start on the study and the books." Morris saw Albert wince and said, "Don't worry Albert, I'll find a proper home for your books."

Morris was dreading starting on the three upstairs bedrooms. He looked in all the rooms when he first helped. The children's bedrooms were just sitting there at the ready waiting for the return of whoever they belonged to. Beds were made and ready for use. The rooms with all their lovely furnishings were intact. Dressers, side tables, lamps, chests, and a wonderful hand painted hope chest in Anne's room. Everything was at the ready, waiting. In each room, there were a few well-used books and curios, but that was all that was visible.

Morris supposed these were their personal favorites: "Grapes of Wrath," a Shakespeare anthology, "War and Peace," two poetry collections, and a few framed sports posters in the boy's rooms. Some photographs and small odd mementos on the dressers, a necklace and a ring in the daughter's room, a little wooden carving of a bear, and a dog-eared baseball card stuck in the mirror frame. It was all so typical of young people.

Morris's trepidation was focused on the wall length closets and five pull-out bins built in below. He'd already cleaned out the upstairs study which was a larger fourth bedroom with the same closet and bin layout. It also had a full bath. That took two days. The closet and pull-out bins in the study were overflowing with the children's things. There were track shoes, tennis rackets, ice skates, children's drawings, the odd child's Christmas construction, cards, trophies, and a lifetime of their things.

There were many framed academic awards and lots of first, second and third place ribbons proclaiming various track victories. One son was a track star, the other played hockey. They were both Eagle scouts. The daughter had dozens of ribbons and awards for her figure skating triumphs. All three were gifted.

As he sorted through the records of their childhood, high school, and college awards and achievements, he found himself very much wanting to meet and know them. When he finished, he had a clear sense of them and what they were about. That all three were dead made his heart heavy. He carried the boxes downstairs, and Albert wouldn't look at any of it. He said, "Please Morris, just get rid of it."

The big five-door closet above the pull-out bins overflowed with winter coats, sports attire, ski equipment, both downhill, and cross country. Any attire one might need for almost any physical activity imaginable was in that closet. There were hockey sticks and gloves, figure skates, three backpacks, two sleeping bags, a tent, and other assorted camping equipment, all of it at least thirty years old.

But it was going into the children's rooms and cleaning out their individual closets and dressers that spooked Morris. The thought of handling their clothes, their intimate personal items made him sad, deeply and terribly sad. Morris approached

Anne's room first because he thought it would be the most difficult for him.

With great trepidation, he pulled the middle closet door open. The closet was empty, just a few wood coat hangers waiting on the closet rod. He pulled the bins open one after another. They were all clean and empty. He crossed the room to her dresser and one by one he pulled open the drawers. They were also empty and clean.

Morris found he was relieved, but disappointed because he'd learn no more of them. There would be no more sense of them, their lives. There was nothing left, no clothes, or papers, just the mementos on the dressers. All three of the children's rooms were emptied long ago.

Over the past few weeks, Morris came to understand the emotional devastation of someone losing a child let alone all of them. Thinking about them hurt terribly, and he didn't personally know them. Albert's and Marion's whole family everything they loved and worked so hard to guide shape, and form, all their care and efforts were extinguished, taken from them within six months. He could palpably feel the loss in every room in the house, but Morris felt it most when he discovered the children's closets and dressers empty.

Such a loss was a nightmare, a horror, and Morris had a small sense of it. He remembered years ago he and his friend Jerry hunting pheasants one lovely fall morning. They were fifteen and they had a pheasant apiece. As noon approached they looked about for a place where they could relax and eat the lunches they packed. They decided on the highest bit of land around. A little hill top sheltered by a group of mature red oaks still holding their leaves. It sat above a dirt road that led to a nearby wind break of red pine and spruce that once sheltered a farmhouse now long gone.

When they arrived, they were greeted by seven square upright stones laid out in a semi-circle. It wasn't until they crossed to face them they realized what they were. Lenora

15, Henry 13, Sam 10, Mary 7, John 5, Ann 2. In the middle a slightly larger seventh stone said, RIP, in the year of our lord, 1919. The stones were crude, so hastily carved Morris could see the tears. It took his breath away. It was the emptiest, saddest place he'd ever been. They stood there looking at each other. Jerry said, "Jesus," and they left. But Morris never forgot them or that place.

But this was different. Not such a shock nor a mystical thing, not like he believed there were spirits or ghosts of perpetual sadness lurking about in their rooms. It was the feeling one gets early in the morning, mid-week, standing alone in the center of an empty two-hundred-year-old church. Morris was in one like that in Charleston and another in Philadelphia. There's a powerful sense of lives lived in such places. A quiet spiritual glory to lives and relationships built over many years and generations. All of it made with loving effort, year upon year of Easters, Christmases, weddings, christenings, and funerals.

Like those sanctuaries, Marion, and Albert's home was a place full to the brim with striving for spiritual completion, knowledge, and being well loved. Within months, it was ended. It was just unfathomable to him. From discovering the graves of six children who died in the great flu epidemic he understood the shock of such an event. But Morris struggled to have a realistic understanding of the enormity of the emotional loss of a single child, let alone all of them. Try as he might he couldn't conceive of the emptiness, the silence.

Albert approached Morris again about buying the house just the way it was. With all the furnishings, books, the artwork, and ceramics, two sets of china, the everyday dishes, the silverware, cutlery, the pots, and pans. The closets full of towels, blankets, and linens, all the things of their everyday lives. He wanted Morris to have it all.

Morris and Albert talked further, and Morris soon understood all Albert cared about was being with Marion. He realized the only thing of importance to Albert was the house stay intact with someone who would care for it and appreciate it. At least until they were both gone. Morris understood Albert and Marion both liked him. That passing their home on intact to someone like him who understood them, their lives, and who they were was everything to them. Initially, it made Morris uneasy. He was wondering if they saw him as some sort of a stand-in for their children.

He talked to John about his concern and told him Albert again offered him the house and everything in it at a ridiculously low price. A few days later John assured Morris such was not the case at all. Albert and Marion had no need of money and would be donating their money to a university scholarship fund. They felt they might as well begin their giving with someone they already knew, liked, and felt was soon to be a big asset to the university.

Morris never understood the attraction between people, where it came from, or why or how it worked. But he was drawn instantly to both Albert and Marion, particularly to Marion that first day. This wasn't sexual or anything of that nature. It was a tremendous attraction coupled with curiosity and wanting to know all about these people.

It was like finding a long ago put away, lost, but never forgotten box full of personal childhood treasures, and was in every way a warm, pleasant thing. He recognized he and Hanna also experienced a peculiar bond he didn't understand on any level. Morris knew, as unexplainable and unknowable as it remained his relationship with Hanna was enormously important to them both.

Hanna was always with him. He thought of her all the time. Even during the time, he was sure he loved Diane and thought Diane felt the same. The way Diane left devastated, Morris. She spoke to him on the phone Thursday night telling him she was transferring to UC Berkeley. When he arrived at her place before eight the following morning to say goodbye, she was gone. That was it. No words, no note, not even a simple thank you. No tears, hugs, kisses, nor even a handshake.

Morris was left standing in her doorway listening to her roommate's sincere, but useless condolences. All Morris ever managed was to try to understand what attracted them to each other and why his feelings for her took forever to subside? Morris never figured out any of it. He thought of Hanna and their relationship, but he never figured it out either.

Morris was similarly surprised about his feelings when Michael left. Michael was a man and, yet he felt almost the same way he felt when Diane left. Morris was aware in just a few weeks he'd become a big part of Albert's and Marion's lives, and that too was about to end. They both liked him, and he knew passing their home on to someone like him who would care about it was important. It was what they most wanted, and Albert and Marion encouraged him to buy it. When Morris said, he would find a way they were overjoyed.

Morris's father flew in from California and met with Albert, and the three of them went through the house together. Thankfully, the two men enjoyed each other. After a meeting between Morris, his dad, and a local banker, his father met with both Albert and Marion and asked once more if they were certain about this. Albert and Marion assured Morris's father this was what they desired, and it was settled. Morris's father agreed to help Morris buy it. After an enormous hassle, over where the closing would take place, it was decided to do it at the nursing home.

For two hours, there were all kinds of strangers in Marion's room pushing about large quantities of documents. Morris felt awful for Marion. She was struggling to breathe. Having all these strangers whose only concern was crossing T's and dotting, I's in her private space was disconcerting to both Morris and Albert. It was especially trying for Marion. With the business concluded, her room once again empty. The first thing Morris did was make sure Albert, and Marion knew they were welcome any time they wanted to come by.

A few days short of a month later Albert asked, and Morris said, "Of course." Marion came home in an ambulance to die in her home of fifty-eight years. Morris had left their bedroom untouched, choosing to sleep upstairs, while he was going about figuring out how he would manage owning the place.

It was a day that would be with Morris the rest of his. Sitting in the big quiet downstairs bedroom with Albert, John, and John's wife Dee as Marion slipped away; Morris tried with everything at his command to understand what Albert was feeling.

SIXTEEN

Three days after Marion's funeral Morris started cleaning out their downstairs bedroom. The dressers were empty. Their clothing went with them to the nursing home. There were just a few things left. Albert told him to dispose of them. Marion's closet was empty except for a few blankets up on the topmost shelves. Pushed to the back behind the quilts he discovered two shoe boxes full of letters. He pulled them down and put them on the bed. The letters were correspondence between Marion, Albert, Anne, and their boys when they were overseas during the war.

Morris sat between the boxes pulling the bundled letters out. He counted eighty-four letters, and he began looking through them. There were letters returned to Albert and Marion they'd written to their boys which came back to them when their boy's personal effects were sent home. Also, among these were the many letters Anne wrote to her brothers which were also returned with their belongings.

There was a series of letters Anne received from a Captain Henry stationed in North Africa. One of them was uncommonly poignant. It was the last one he sent. When he wrote and posted it, he was unaware Anne had been struck by a car and killed. Along with the letters sent home to Albert and Marion and Sister Anne from the boys were several letters from the men who served with them offering their condolences. Morris couldn't stop himself from reading the letters.

They were full to overflowing with their lives and love and concern for one another. He knew this wasn't any of his business. But he already had a sense of the children. The letters put their place and importance as once living breathing people squarely in concrete reality to what he already knew of Albert and Marion.

It took three days for Morris to read them all. He was overwhelmed by the goodness that flowed through their words to one another. Full of care and concern for each other it left him joyous and in tears. Those letters threw open the doors to their characters. After reading through them, Morris felt he knew them better than he knew his own sister and brother.

He struggled, continually to remind himself all, but one was no longer living. There were amongst all those letters four he would carry with him the rest of his days. Morris found himself wishing with all his heart he'd been able to write to someone he loved and cared about with the strength and concern they did. Inside one written to Anne by her fiancé was a letter sent by Anne he was returning to her.

Those two letters bothered him tremendously. Both died long ago, but their words were alive and so full of life. When Morris asked about his daughter, Albert told him her fiancé died less than a year after she did during the invasion of Sicily. Anne was the oldest of the children and a brilliant young woman. She was as fit as she could be. A gorgeous woman, appearing every bit to be the elegant dancer her mother did. Anne was engaged to Augustus Andrew Henry, a Captain in the US Army serving in North Africa.

Anne was to begin her doctorate program winter quarter and was working as a research assistant at a prominent Chicago law firm. She was living with two other young working women in a nice apartment on shoreline drive. From the letters sent from him to her and the letters, she sent to her brothers Morris concluded Anne was a proper, honorable, confident, but modest young woman.

She was living a remarkably unexciting life. There was little drinking and only sporadic going out dancing or attending the cinema with her roommates. There was no partying except at her parent's home when they entertained. When Morris read this one letter from her fiancé, he was amazed it still existed.

He supposed the only plausible reason it was there was when Marion found or was given Anne's cache of letters from Captain Henry she didn't read them. She placed them in the box with all the others. Neatly bundled and bound with a lovely pale-yellow ribbon they appeared undisturbed.

Dearest Anne,

I am well, but still losing weight. I'll be getting a little more money I've been promoted to Major. I wish I could say it was because of my outstanding leadership abilities. But my promotion has more to do with the sudden and never-ending depletion of our ranks. After only four months of service here I'm referred to as the old man. But please try not to fret about me. I'm careful about advertising my rank or whereabouts, and I know perfectly well to keep low.

I'm returning a letter. The one I received three weeks back. It's such a loving and private collection of your thoughts. It would break my heart if something thing happened, and it fell into the hands of a stranger. I knew after reading it I should have destroyed it, but I couldn't bring myself to do it. Your words made this place and being here almost bearable and that my love was a monumental accomplishment on your part.

Thank you for your honesty and unexpected direct manner of explaining your feelings for me. I was surprised by the frankness of your words. But I've never felt so honored or blessed. Anne, you are fearless and the most decent, honorable, and loving woman I've ever known. My love for you couldn't be made any stronger. Your words meant more than you can imagine. Reading it, I could feel your presence right here with me.

Your letter's been with me on my person inside my shirt. I've read those words over and over, so many times, I've memorized them. I can repeat your letter word for word. Your sentiments are dear to me, and I would like very much to revisit them. So, if you have a place where the letter won't be discovered, please keep it for me.

I've kept all your letters and every time I open and reread one it allows me to touch a part of you. With your loving words written in your hand, you're real, but the letter you're getting back was the most wonderful thing you could have ever given me. I'll treasure you and those words forever.

I've read it so many times it's become quite tattered. It's made being here so far away from you almost bearable. For a letter that's really saying something. Thank you, Anne, for your love and keep you and your special words safe. I miss you terribly and can't wait to once again be with you.

Give my best to everyone and may God watch over all of you. I'm thinking of you always.

All my Love, Augustus

He gently unfolded Anne's letter and started reading:

Hello, my Captain,

I hope you're safe and well. As we can do nothing more than write to one another, I sincerely feel bad about doing this to you. But I need to express my feelings to you about the last time we saw each other.

You need to know our time together wasn't anywhere near enough. Until we can once again be together, it never will be. So, my wonderful, beautiful Augustus you better come back to me. I know neither of us has much control over that, but I pray to God every day for his help with your safety. I will be forever grateful to you, August, if you would humbly do the same.

You know only too well I'm a proper prude, always coming down on the correct, reserved, and acceptable side of social behavior. As my parents are both well-known university professors, I'll lay all my hesitancy and propriety off on them. That said, I didn't have the chance to say any of what I'm about to tell you.

So here it is as straightforward as I can be. I want you to have my words and know my heart and all of what I felt about our glorious last time together. I know you struggled with all the rights and wrongs of going to a hotel with your virgin fiancé. I very much appreciated your hesitation and all your concerns about the two of us doing such a scandalous thing. You are a wonderful, honorable man Augustus.

I now know, and quite shamelessly, that I like you even more naked and I'm sure you feel the same toward me. I know speaking so directly of such things is shocking but remember August all we presently have between us is the truth of our feelings. My life has been blessed, and I've had many moments of great joy, and a few spectacular ones. Winning two meets in a row and then going on to win the regional junior figure skating championship was truly splendid. At that moment, at fourteen, I felt darn powerful, on top of the world and overjoyed.

Graduating Suma Cum Laude from Northwestern and looking out at mom and dad, Mark, and James at the graduation ceremonies, seeing their ear to ear smiles. I don't think I could've been any happier or felt any greater sense of accomplishment. I was truly elated. However, dearest August, compared to my night with you all those moments are only little bitty blips in the road.

I've never in my life been so surprised or experienced such joy as I did with you. Those feelings were so powerful I could barely speak. You were so sweet asking me several times how I was doing or something of that nature. I remember saying, please Augustus stop talking. This is so heavenly, please; just keep doing what you're doing. I'll admit I was unbelievably wanton, but it was pure ecstasy. I would give anything and everything to have you inside me and be able to repeat those words. So now you know. I'm yours and will be forever more.

I went about deciding to have sex with you, so pragmatically and unemotionally I'm almost ashamed to tell you of it. But once I put aside my fears about getting pregnant, and being such a naughty, very bad girl, I became quite brave. I wholeheartedly and lovingly wanted to send you off properly (and I'm going to skip the mental gymnastics necessary for me to make that permissible). Being the first child of not one but two Ph.D.'s I read everything I could find about sex.

I tried to prepare myself as best I could. It was all for naught. Nothing prepared me for being with you. Not my intelligence, nor anything I researched and read, nor did my rather vivid imagination even come close to conjuring up what happened between us.

I could scream it from the highest building, write a million words, win a hundred skating championships, and never be able to get out how wonderful I felt. I thank you with everything in me, heart and soul, from the top of my head to the very ends of my toes for loving me as you do.

Augustus, I know what we have between us. I understand completely what we gave to each other, and it's a deep, very much alive source of everlasting joy. It was the most delicious, unbelievably uplifting experience I've ever had. You almost missed the train. Neither of us wanted to leave that hotel room and my darling I can't wait to welcome you home.

I skipped bathing for almost a week, so I could keep you with me. I don't regret many things in my life. But if I had even the remotest inkling of what being with you would be like, I would have joyously been in your bed months earlier. I'm apologizing for not coming to you sooner. My prudish ever proper ways prevented us from experiencing a lot of joyous moments together. I cannot wait to be Mrs. Augustus Henry, and I'm warning you. I'm planning on keeping your evenings as full of joy as I can.

Please, please keep safe, Augustus, and do your best to come home to me soon.

I hold you in my thoughts every moment of every day.

Love, Anne

Later that day Morris found a letter from Master Chief Petty Officer Hoshea Love House:

Dear Mr. and Mrs. Hendry,

My name is Hoshea Love House. I'm a U. S. Navy Master Chief Petty Officer. Your son James was my commanding officer. I've been in the Navy for twenty-one years, and I'm nicknamed Lovey the Lifer. I seen maybe a dozen 90 day wonders like your son come and go, but none like our Lt. James L. Hendry. He was our ships Damage Control officer. A really good one. He was an exceptional naval officer and always a gentleman.

His damage control team was me and eighteen other seaman and petty officers. We spent most of our days training the rest of the ship's crew in proper firefighting, flooding, and battle damage control. I asked him once. So, James (I was supposed to call him sir, but he looked younger than my son). Anyway, I asked him what he studied in college that would help us win the war. He said not a thing that'll help in any way. I said so what were your studies about. He said humanities. I said what's that?

He said chief it's just like it sounds. It's about humans, and all the great things they've done and achieved and this war sure isn't gonna be one of them. I said, okay Jimmy what've you got, what are you bringing to the party? He said not a lot. I played hockey in high school all four years and know about getting roughed up cheap shots and being perpetually frustrated. I also know how to score goals and how to win. I told him I thought that would be enough for me and the navy.

They are going to give your son a medal, the Navy Cross. We all think it should be the Congressional Medal of Honor. But that really doesn't matter. What matters is if it wasn't for his complete disregard of his own self, me and sixteen other guys wouldn't be here today. I could not have done what he did. I don't have that much courage. I could never be that unafraid, and I can't thank him for my life, none of us can. So, me and the others in this letter would like to thank you and tell you we are eternally grateful to him and miss him. Your son was one giant of a man, and each one of us is gonna carry him right along with us for as long as we live.

Respectfully, Joshua Love House and Seaman, Roger Olson.

PS. Roger helped me getting this right for you, especially spelling humanities. He went two years at Rutgers.

It was neatly signed by seventeen men.

A third letter he discovered the second day came from a Group Captain, Sir Nigel Workman, their oldest boy's squadron commander:

Dear Mr. and Mrs. Hendry,

Mark was one of many fine pilots we've lost. Every single one of them right to their core was an outstanding brave man. Your son Mark was a special one. Not only did he remind me in a hundred ways of my son, but he kept the whole squadron's spirits high. He was a tremendously positive force in what the whole world now knows was a desperate situation. They've named it the Battle of Brittan, but we fought it one nameless day at a time, over fifty-seven days. Bluntly put, it was a slog.

We were facing an almost insurmountable task. Every one of those lads was asked over and over to continue going up. Mark made it through the dark hours of 1940 always doing his job. Continuously emphasizing and reminding his fellow pilots with his enviable humorous way they were to go after the German bombers and avoid fighter-to-fighter combat. That wasn't easy for any of them. Going after an enemy fighter had all the allure and fear of attempting to rescue a beautiful woman from an enemy in a sword fight.

Mark was a remarkably dedicated fellow. On his first combat mission, he fired all two thousand rounds from his guns and never once hit the Messerschmitt he was pursuing. The Spitfire's guns are correlated out to four hundred fifty yards, but Mark felt this was too far away. He spent all that night working with the flight mechanics to reset his guns at two hundred and fifty yards, and thereafter he had one success after another.

Trimming his guns to two hundred and fifty yards was not an easy thing, but it was effective, and daring. His Spitfire was traveling at over three hundred and fifty mph. Two hundred and fifty yards would be covered in less than three seconds. Mark became the most fearsome shot in the squadron.

After downing his seventh enemy plane I told Mark at dinner, I was putting him forward in my postings for the Distinguished Flying Cross. He came to me later that evening and said Nigel you can't do that. I asked why, and he said I'm not here for medals or any of that.

I'm an American. I'm here illegally, with forged Canadian papers. No one can know about me because if discovered it would cost me my citizenship. It might even put my parent's positions and careers at risk. We said no more about it, and I did not put him forward for the DFC. Mark was an exceptional flight leader, and the whole squadron enjoyed what they thought was his offbeat, unusual Canadian sense of humor. Knowing him as I did I'm confident he never told you any of what it was like here. But I'll try to convey a sense of it.

Life isn't easy for a fighter pilot; every day's a long one. Up at five to prepare for the day ahead, a pilot's day was a strain on both mind and body. He had to contend with squadron mates who failed to return, maybe missing in action or as was usual, killed in the line of duty.

None knew what the next day was to bring, although most talked bravely of claiming a victory over an enemy, they were just fighting for survival. They toasted lost friends then prayed for their own safety. This was done day after day for over fifty days in a row. Mark died saving the lives of twenty airmen. They belonged to an American bomber squadron all unknown to him. Both bomber crews recorded his plane's number and told everyone what this unbelievably brazen Spitfire pilot did to save them.

Out of ammunition, he flew right into a group of three attacking 109's surprising them. He broke their formation and disrupted them allowing the two badly damaged bombers to duck into the clouds and escape. He brought one of the 109's down using his wing tip to clip the enemy's propeller as he dove through their formation. His aircraft was damaged in the incident and knowing we were short of aircraft instead of bailing out he tried to bring his Spit back to base.

Because I'm the squadron commander, I was required to investigate and interview the aircrews involved and verify what occurred. I also had to deflect their wanting to go through their command structure to be sure Mark's skill and bravery was acknowledged. I'll say no more to you other than it was a remarkable bit of flying and a selfless, courageous thing. Two B-17's and their crews, twenty men, would have been lost that day if it hadn't been for Mark's courage and skill.

Mark maintained to the squadron he had no immediate family, only an aunt, and uncle, a cousin, and a niece who lived in America. But because Mark wrote and received a continuous stream of letters from his American relatives most of us suspected this not to be true. As I was the only one, who knew he was American and his Canadian papers listed his American cousins as distant kinships, so, to not give away his family and country of origin I made the final arrangements for his burial here in England.

Three days after the crash, on twenty-eight, July, his fellow pilots and his plane's crewmen accompanied Mark to his final resting place. His coffin was draped in the Canadian Royal Union Flag. It was important to me so unbeknown to the others I obtained a small America Stars and Stripes which I placed with him.

Mark is buried at Boxgrove Priory Church, a lovely peaceful, serene place. It's eight hundred and fifty years old and sits in a delightful village in West Sussex, three miles from the Cathedral City of Chichester. It was a simple ceremony. The RAF Buglers sounded a farewell. The rifle squad cracked the silence with a salute and brave as the men gathered there are there were tears.

Rank and decorations are important to the British, so I have included Mark's two Distinguished Flying Crosses he asked never to be awarded. They are mine, but of all my pilots Mark most certainly deserves them. The DFC is the single silver cross and light blue ribbon with bars. The bars indicate the recipient was awarded the DFC twice for two separate actions. I have also included the Battle of Britain clasp which is attached to the ribbon of the star medal. The only higher military service medal Britain has is the Victoria Cross.

I lost my son at Dunkirk. His body was never recovered, so I know none of this is going to help in coming to terms with the loss of your son. It's important to all of us for you to know Mark was a courageous, wonderful young man, and our nation owes him everything.

I have included my wife's name along with our home address. So, in the future, when this unfortunate business is suitably concluded, and you should wish to visit your son's final resting place. One or the other, or both of us would be more than honored to accompany you. My son is buried somewhere in France probably in a mass grave. At present, I have no idea where. I've taken consolation from a Rupert Brooke poem, and I hope you might also take some small comfort from his words. I have altered it slightly substituting America for England:

> *If I should die, think only this of me:*
> *That there's some corner of a foreign*
> *field that is forever American.*
> *There shall be in that rich earth a*
> *richer dust concealed; a dust whom America*
> *bore, shaped, made aware, gave, once,*
> *her flowers to love, her ways to roam a body*
> *washed by the rivers, blest by suns of home.*
> *And think, this heart, all evil shed away,*
> *a pulse in the eternal mind, no less*
> *gives back somewhere the thoughts by*
> *America given; her sights and sounds; dreams*
> *happy as her day; and laughter, learnt*
> *in hearts at peace, under an American heaven.*

Respectfully,
Group Commander, Major Sir Nigel R. Workman, KCMG

After stopping for lunch, Morris started writing about Albert and Marion, their children, and their long shared academic life. Working with great speed, Morris managed to get down most of the words he overheard spoken between Albert and Marian. Morris jotted down all the things Albert told him about teaching and their efforts with their graduate students. He wrote out their recollections of their children when young.

Before he recognized it, the book was blocked out. Through the letters, he understood their characters, their lives, and he didn't stop or go to bed until eight the next morning. The book was alive in his mind, a living thing. Morris woke a few hours later ate something and went to it. He found he couldn't stop writing. He quickly wrote out whole sections. Afterwards, he found himself continually going back, pouring over every sentence.

Morris didn't care about the perfect word only a proper one. The one which made the thought or passage he was trying to convey come alive. Within days the story took on a life of its own. The words became as precious to Morris as Albert and Marion, and their three children.

He might be working on the house, making lunch, or shopping, and a piece of the story would crawl into his head. He'd drop everything and get back to it. He was the caretaker of their lives, and he wanted this right for them. He felt compelled the same way he did writing his first book. He fought hard to get Albert and Marion's story down in the most caring meaningful way he could. Morris found this to be an even greater more frustrating struggle than writing his first book.

This was different because the first book was about ideas and concepts and this was about people he loved and admired. They were in his book walking about and taking part in life. They needed to be clothed appropriately to succeed. Morris struggled to always be sure Marion, Albert, and their family was at the ready, presented consistently, and properly spoken on every occasion.

It was no easy task. Marion and Albert were from another time, educated, and had years of experience that Morris was nowhere near, but trying to impart. He was putting words in their mouths trying with everything at his disposal to bring them to life. It was the most trying frustrating thing Morris ever attempted. But as before he refused to give up and kept working. Morris wanted this to be right.

Eleven weeks later Morris approached John and told him he'd written a story about Albert and Marion, their children, and what they faced at the end of their lives. He wanted to know if John knew of someone on campus he could use to edit the raw manuscript. Furthermore, once the editing was completed did John know of a publisher other than the departments he could submit it to?

Surprised John said, "I've been wondering why I've seen so little of you. I thought maybe it was the house, or you met someone."

"It was their story. They were terrific people. I had to write it."

"So, you've written a novel?"

"I didn't think of it that way, but yes, I've written a novel."

"Morris most professors believe writing for the public is not what academic scholars were put on earth to do. They tend to question those who do. I'm both older and old school, and to be honest I still hold to those traditional beliefs. Being an academic scholar means complete dedication to the intellectual life, the pursuit of knowledge, and staying true to those ideals. But I'll talk with my friend Marcus at the department's publishing house and ask the question. I don't think it would be wise to have someone here on campus edit your book. I'll have to see what I can find out about that for you."

"John, I sense you're concerned about this. Is my writing and possibly publishing this going to cause problems for you?"

"Morris, you aren't close to completing your Ph.D. You aren't a professor, and there are some older, traditional, very conservative people at the university who might see you as dancing on two sides of the room, and not at all ready to assume the mantle of an academic scholar."

"Sorry John, I never thought of it as anything more than Albert's and Marion's story. The more I got to know them the more extraordinary they became. I think everybody should know about their lives, their dedication, and their collective mountain of accomplishments. They had such love for family and their students. Within just a few months all three of their children died. They somehow kept going. Both continued long and fruitful academic careers. It's important for people to know about them, about their goodness.

"May I read it, Morris?

"Of course."

"Let me do that. Then we'll talk."

"John, I can put it in a drawer and wait. I don't have to try to publish it now; especially if you feel doing so is going to bring your choice about sponsoring me into question. I know the book on translations gave me a leg up academically and won me favor within the department."

"Not just our department Morris all over the country. It was well written, infinitely readable, and understandable, it was brilliant. It was a much-needed work that made everyone keenly aware of language and the problems and dangers inherent in translations. Truly, it was an outstanding achievement especially so for someone as young as you."

"So, you don't want me to undermine what I've accomplished by publishing a novel?"

"That's about the gist of it but let me read it then we'll talk further."

Four days later John met with Morris in his office and told him he talked extensively with the humanities department's publisher about Morris's book. John's friend Marcus offered to forward the manuscript on to a close friend of his at a publishing house he felt was better equipped to publish a first novel.

"Wow, this is a surprise. I was pretty sure you were going to ask me to hold off until I finished up everything and had a position here secured."

"I read it, Morris. It's a marvelous story; it made me smile and feel more wonderful about their lives and about my own academic life than I ever believed possible. I cried my heart out at the end. It's quite a meaningful moving story. It's beautifully written Morris, and you're right. Everybody should know about the lives of Marion and Albert Hendry and their children. Morris, you never cease to surprise me. Your book is awe-inspiring, and every academic I know is going to read it and smile."

"Does that mean you're no longer concerned about it causing a problem for you and our Northwestern academic community?"

"Should the rest of the old boys take the time to read it they will like me feel better about their own lives and the choices they've made. Maybe even hope someday you'll write about them. Mostly they'll be envious and jealous of you. Morris, you truly are our boy wonder."

"You're kind and very lavish with your praise John, but I'm not a boy wonder. I'm just me."

"Morris, you've earned every ounce of my praise. You continually amaze me. Albert and Marion surely deserved to have their lives told, and you've done it in a spiritual, wonderfully told and beautifully crafted story. It's going to be well received."

"Exemplary Lives," was well received. It spent five months on the best seller list and complicated Morris's life considerably. There were calls from almost every member of his extended family. He spent a lot of time on the phone, mostly talking with his extended and immediate family. There were two special letters, one from his high school friend, Michael Worthy, and a letter all the way from the Philippines from his not forgotten high school friend Jerry Ramson.

Just before fall quarter started his publisher flew him to New York. He put in a lot of appearances. They included three formal parties, a half-dozen informal dinners, several cocktail gatherings, and a reading and Q&A for more than a hundred. Morris found himself amid a world of literary aficionados, connoisseurs, and a few quite knowledgeable and sophisticated enthusiasts from the publishing world.

Morris quickly realized some of these people did not have his best interest at heart. A few went out of their way to try to embarrass him. He was keenly aware he was seen by most to be an outsider and not part of their highly polished literary world. A few took delight in doing what they could to expose his educational deficiencies about the world of letters. They made sure he clearly understood he was considered at best a plucky upstart. He quickly learned to nod and say little.

He left New York thinking for all his assailant's collective literary knowledge and brilliance they didn't understand the language, ideas, and history preserved in the world's literature were priceless. They literally meant everything. Unfortunately, those same self-styled connoisseurs didn't understand the literature forms themselves represented only a small area of importance to any given era. This was especially so for the present one.

When he arrived home, he was deluged with phone calls. Interspersed with the appreciated calls from friends and acquaintances came every manner of salesman and hustler with offers and schemes galore to say no thank you too. On the positive side, the book earned him a lot of money which was welcome. John was right there being more than a little envy and jealousy from both his peers and superiors. Thankfully, unlike New York, most of the jabs and sneering was hidden, and outside of the many phone calls, nothing interrupted his progress toward completing his Ph.D.

There was a welcome note from Hanna.

"You've done another book and what an uplifting story, you're such an extraordinary man Morris. You understood

Marion and Albert just like you somehow know me. What an amazing ability. What makes it possible for you to always understand and know how to help me and others? What is that?

And their children Morris, all three had such a sense of family and what outstanding, courageous, loving people they were. I understand what it means to do your best and to keep trying to get even better. That I know of, but Morris I can't imagine going through or being able to do what any of their children did.

Where does one get the courage it takes to give up your life, so others get to live? Where did that come from? Both of their boys did it. Anne did it too. She knowingly and fearlessly went to that older woman's aid. She surrendered her life to save an old woman who slipped and fell in the street. How does a person do that? Everybody else just watched.

You showed us how hard Marion and Albert struggled. How they clawed and fought with everything, they had to get through losing all three children. I would like to think I could be like them. That I wouldn't give up and would continue as they did. What a gift you have and what a terrific enlightening story. I cried my heart out for them, and I know Albert's old, but I do hope he's all right.

Miss you, Morris; hope we'll get to see each other soon. But if we don't, don't you dare forget you've crossed your heart and promised me you'll come to my graduation party?

Love, Hanna

Less than a week after Morris signed off on the final manuscript John called to tell him Albert died in his sleep. "He played bridge with the other residents, went off to his room apparently in good spirits, and passed away during the night. They found him this morning in bed."

Morris remembered hanging up the phone knowing Albert died of a broken heart. Morris knew his death was the direct result of his being bound ever so tightly by his love of Marion. Morris clearly remembered just before she went into the nursing home Marion said, "Albert I told you someday you'd regret marrying a gal who was older than you."

Even though Morris and John and Robbie and their wives made a point of stopping by and spending time with Albert Morris knew full well, Albert was just going through the motions. Albert was no longer present or interested in being here. He had nothing. All that was left was to surrender, and Marion was no longer there to pull him back. Morris fought it, but he saw the water hit the table. He was crying.

SEVENTEEN

The bedside phone rang several times before Morris answered. Half asleep, he said, "Hello."

"Morris?"

He said, "Yes." And Hanna's unmistakable earthy voice had him sitting up straight wide awake.

"It's Hanna. Have you got a minute?"

"Sure, I've got the rest of the night. What's up?"

"First off, I'm sorry your parents moved, and we haven't been seeing each other at their parties."

"Hanna, you're calling at three in the morning to say you're missing my mom's parties?"

"Sorry Morris, but it's been a long time since we've seen each other in person. Anyway, I knew it was late, but I know you stay up all hours when you're writing. I thought I'd take a chance."

"What's going on Hanna? Is something wrong?"

"No, everybody's fine, but I'm stuck. You're the only person I know who might be able to help me. Promise, I'll only take up a few minutes."

"I've got time Hanna. What's going on?"

"The faculty dumped this set design project on me, and it's an absolute nightmare. It's my final project for my MFA and like a doctorate thesis; it has to be right, my best work."

"Hanna, you didn't tell me you were in a master's program."

"Well, I am. It's an MFA. It's a terminal degree. That's as high as I can go in theater set design. There aren't any doctorate degrees in set design, but they're making such a gigantic fuss about this I know something else is going on."

"I've no idea where the money came from, but they hired an alumnus as a guest director. She's coming in from New York. Her name is Maria Carlson, and she's a genuine big deal. She's already won two Tony awards for best director, and she's nominated for another. I'm doing the set design and the lighting for the show."

"Wow! Hanna that's terrific. You'll be working with a proven professional. You'll know all about the big time. What could possibly be better?"

"She's going to think I'm a child and have no business designing a show for her."

"Hanna, you're the most extraordinary creative person I've ever known. She'll admire your work and fall in love with you like I did."

"I don't think so. We're doing Bernard Shaw's, Saint Joan. It has four acts an epilog, six different sets, and multiple scene changes. I can't see a way to do it that isn't complicated and awkward or has any hope of a pleasing uninterrupted flow. Maria will be here next week to meet with me, and I've got nothing to show her."

"Hanna, what's going on? You sound scared."

"I'm stuck, I've never been stumped, but I am now. I'm nowhere with this, and I've read it five times. There's nothing in my head, but clunky realism. When the show first ran in New York, there was so much scenery they went to four intermissions. It ran over four hours, and everybody knows that won't work.

The department heads are already looking at where they might cut the script and some of the scene changes."

"Michael took me to see that play at a small college in Wisconsin."

"And?"

"It's a great story, but the production wasn't all that good. It was too long. But we both liked the acting and what the designer tried to do for the settings. Unfortunately, it didn't work all that well. The lighting never came off the way we thought it was supposed to. We talked a lot about it on the way home."

"For crying out loud Morris, talk to me."

"How about I just tell you what Michael said. The set was three large platforms like pancakes overlapping each other. Michael said if the platforms had been wider and looked like they were floating it might have worked."

"He said something about pulling the first platform out over the front of the stage and raking all three. The river scene and some of the others didn't work because all they used to suggest the location were fancy colored lighting patterns. From our seats, we could barely see or make out the patterns."

"The rest of the scenes had set pieces which rolled in and out. I remember some gothic arches, a gothic window or two, and the rest was basically a nice try at period furniture."

"Morris, you marvelous, wonderful man, you are so amazing. I'll never know how you do it. You always, always show me the way when I get lost."

"I did? That helped?"

"Yes, my dear sweet man. I can see the whole thing clear as can be. You're amazing Morris. Go back to bed. I'm going to hang up and draw up Saint Joan."

"Hanna?"

"Yes."

He almost said I love you, but instead said, "Take care of yourself."

"I am, and I will, and Morris, thank you! You've saved me yet again."

Morris said, "Goodnight," to the rude buzz of the disconnected phone.

EIGHTEEN

When Morris once again saw Hanna in the flesh almost four years had flown by. It was, as he promised, at her graduation party. The party was at her parent's house on a perfect spring Saturday afternoon.

The Williston's could not have asked for a more pleasant day. The air was warm, soft, and combined with the seventy-two-degree temperature it gently held the fragrant sweetness of lilac. It gently surrounded and followed him as he walked from his car to their house. Morris arrived at the Williston's front door with a nicely wrapped, oversized, heavy, and expensive book. It contained several hundred color plates of the best of European set design.

Four years ago, his parents sold their lake home and moved to San Francisco, and Morris no longer had a home here or a family to come home to. He stopped just outside of Minneapolis at a truck stop, shaved, and changed his clothes. He was feeling uncertain, alone, and in unfamiliar surroundings. Very much like the proverbial angel cast from heaven.

As he looked back from the Williston's front steps surveying the long line of cars on both sides of the street, he found himself uneasy. He hadn't seen Hanna or her parents in four years. There were way too many cars, and he was stressed and uncomfortable. He came because he promised, and he wanted to see Hanna. He wanted to know how she was and to find out how her project with the Tony award-winning director turned out.

When Hanna saw Morris in the doorway, she came running throwing her arms around him saying, "Morris, I'm so glad you came. Wow! This is just outstanding."

Hanna so surprised him every one of those uneasy thoughts racing around in his brain left. Relaxing, grinning, Morris said, "I told you not even Shakespeare's furies would keep me away."

Joyously Hanna said, "This is perfect, Morris, just perfect. I've some big plans I need to talk over with you." She was so effervescent and full of joy. She grabbed his hand saying, "Come meet everyone." Everything was happening fast. She was dragging him toward the crowd with him still clutching her present.

"Hanna hold on. Where can I put this?"

She took it from him saying, "Goodness, it weighs a ton. What is it? Should I open it?"

"It can wait. It's not candy or gold, it's for your thinking time."

Taking his hand and struggling to hold the present against her chest she started off pulling him along after her. She went straight to her dad, and when Robert saw Morris, he hugged him. Robert said, "Morris, how wonderful, it's just not the same without your mom and dad and family. We've sorely missed them. I'm so glad you could come."

"I promised."

"Your Mom and Dad, Alice, even David called to congratulate Hanna. They all asked us to tell you they missed you and would be thinking of you today. They went on and on about how proud and pleased they were for Hanna."

Hanna handed the book over to her Dad and said, "Dad can you put this somewhere for me."

Robert said, "Goodness Morris! Is it a boat anchor?"

Morris smiling said, "Just a big picture book."

Morris was lost. Everything was different. Robert hugged him like he was his missing son. Hanna was just glorious. He couldn't take his eyes from her. She was glowing. She kept introducing him as her professor friend from Northwestern University, Doctor Morris Stevens.

Morris was thinking, "True I was awarded my doctorate, but the tenured professorship wouldn't be official for another week. But Morris let her run with it. She seemed to enjoy saying it so much, but it only contributed to his bewilderment. He was amazed. Morris met directors, art gallery owners, managing directors, actors, and technical people. Several of her professors were there, all of whom he could tell were delighted to know and be part of Hanna receiving her MFA.

He was having real difficulty imagining this Hanna her open joy and her associations and friendships with all these different people. Morris was very much aware in four years Hanna seemed to have changed everything he remembered about her. He hoped with all his heart it was as it appeared, all for the better.

Three of the men made quite an impression on Morris, but for different reasons. One was a gallery owner from New York, Henric Olbermann, who was dressed considerably better than anyone else. He was maybe forty and spoke with a not overly apparent Swedish accent. He was distinguished in every sense of the word.

With him was an elegant also particularly well dressed attractive raven-haired woman, she was introduced as Erica, his wife, and business partner. He soon realized as gallery owners representing many well-known contemporary artists they were well to do, full-fledged members of that urbane rarified Manhattan world of fine art. Morris wondered why they were here.

The second was Hanna's kindly appearing, but reserved gray haired lighting professor, Dr. Ralph Eriksson. He was in his dignified way, as pleased with Hanna's abilities as Morris. Professor Eriksson was warm and complimentary toward Hanna and her amazing creative insight and understanding of light. He said, "Hanna has amazing eyes, and I don't mean their color. She sees and understands light better than anyone I've ever known or taught. She amazes me."

The third, Lyles Engels, was five or six years older than Morris. Just over thirty and was introduced to him as the technical director of the civic opera company. Even though Lyles was here with his wife right beside him, Morris could see the poor man was completely taken with Hanna.

The first thing Lyles told Morris was Hanna was the most brilliant creative designer he'd ever worked with. He couldn't emphasize enough how Hanna understood and used the technical and construction end to her advantage, "She's unbelievable. She really gets it. Hanna's such a pleasure to work with. She can be offered ten ways to do something and she always, always chooses the simplest most elegant one."

As the afternoon wore on, he became more and more amazed at Hanna's transformation. She'd evolved into a just out of the cocoon, pristine, radiant Monarch. Her colors crisp and vivid, her wings just this minute pumped out to perfection and ready for flight. Amazingly fresh, Hanna was as vibrant as could be.

Morris was pleased for her and continually smiling from ear to ear. About five she found him out on the patio and pulled him a little away from the others. She said, "Some of us are going to meet up at eight in the lobby of the St. James hotel downtown. We're discussing my future, and I want you to be there. This is important Morris. Will you come?"

"Who could say no to you, especially today?" Once again, she was hugging him. He said, "Is what I'm wearing all right?"

"You look terrific. Come just like that."

Morris parked his car in the hotel ramp and ate across the street. A little before eight he took a seat in the hotel lobby. A few minutes later distinguished looking Henric Olbermann with his elegant wife Erica at his side came through the front doors. They turned every head in the lobby. And even though Morris added a very appealing tie to the gray slacks and black blazer he was wearing he felt woefully underdressed. He was somewhat saved by being young and having the physical grace of an athlete. It helped his appearance significantly. Still, he wasn't wearing a suit much less a tailor-made one.

Seconds later Hanna stepped out of the elevator once again surprising him, this time completely taking his breath away. She was gorgeous. Willowy and elegant in a long-sleeved fitted black dress with a hem just a few inches above her knees. She was wearing nylons, black four-inch heels, red lipstick and of all things, a pearl necklace. Together with the matching pearl earrings and tousled short, brilliant white-blond hair, Hanna looked incredibly posh.

Hanna gathered them together just as a very attractive older woman came through the hotel entrance doors. Hanna turned toward her waved and said, "Over here Maria." They went into the cocktail lounge and took over a back corner of the room. The high heels and overall look gave Hanna the appearance of a remarkably powerful grown-up woman. All of which was a shock to Morris. She was no longer his girlish appearing gentle, timid little friend. It was unsettling.

Morris's sense of Hanna was altered, and he struggled to try to come to grips with the changes. But soon enough everyone was seated with their drink of choice. After a brief, understated explanation by Morris to the others of their teenage and young adulthood connection and why he was here, Morris retreated into the background and listened.

Morris liked Maria very much. She was in her thirties maybe thirty-seven with a lively attractive face, a nice trim shape, and she understood humor. She used it well and wisely. Morris felt Henric, who was reserved and less humorous, looked on him as a potential meddler in Hanna's affairs, or perhaps worse, a suitor. Henric's reserved manner was off-putting making unlikely the possibility of Morris forming anything, but a rudimentary relationship with him.

His wife, Erica was warm to Maria and Hanna, but politely ignored Morris and said little to him. She continually glanced over his way looking at him as if he were hors-d'oeuvres she didn't recognize and was trying to decide whether to take a chance on having one. Morris was sure she was observing him that way because she was trying to understand what he might be to Hanna. Morris felt he was pretty much irrelevant to the others and their concerns and hopes for Hanna. He arrived at this conclusion within minutes of sitting.

Morris did not assume these people knew anything about him, nor were they aware of the strength of his and Hanna's bond. Morris asked a few questions, but only when he sensed Hanna might need further clarification. But for Hanna's sake, he listened carefully to everything discussed.

It soon became clear they were deliberating how high and far they thought Hanna would soar. The discussion centered on the best and fastest way to get her there. He was a little taken aback at what they thought Hanna was capable of. Morris found himself afraid for her. He didn't see Hanna being as strong or mature as they did, but then he'd known Hanna when she wasn't even close to any of those things.

When deciding on a life in academia Morris received strong support and guidance from two older professors. They both went far, far out of their way to help him. But from most of the other mid-career professors, he experienced both envy and sniping about his being both wet behind the ears and damn lucky.

The lucky part surprised him and was disheartening. Wet behind the ears he accepted. It was true. The ink wasn't even dry on his doctorate, but lucky hurt. He knew he was fortunate to fall in with Michael, but lucky, no! For sure no! He worked night and day and put every ounce of his energy, everything he was capable of into writing his three books and dissertation.

He didn't cut a single corner or hold back anything. Morris understood he was both new to the world of academia and naïve. He didn't have a firm understanding of the hierarchy and importance of not just being published but being lauded by others from other notable highly respected institutions. He found the hierarchy; the pecking order like the social positions and standing of the lords and ladies of English Victorian times. The only difference was the Victorian lords and ladies were born to it. An academic had to produce to gain his standing.

Morris earned his place fast and well. He worked twice as many hours as any of the others, sixteen and twenty hours a day for more than five years. He also learned to do your best and do it exceptionally could bring out the sharp fangs of envy and jealousy. This was especially true in a place like New York.

He thought someone as naive, young, and creative as Hanna was walking into a viper's nest. Morris lived in the Northwestern academic world of refined words and polite manners. They were talking about Hanna moving to and working in a place where the theater and art critics had advanced degrees in pure unadulterated crystal clear witty meanness. The food critics often used their words to figuratively devourer the chef.

Listening to the three of them Morris was very much thinking regardless of how grown up Hanna appeared she had neither the armor nor the emotional skills needed to withstand the sharks, charlatans, or the snide envious people she was sure to encounter. New York, he knew from his experience publishing his novel, could be an exacting heartless place.

The fact that his first book was a success by academic standards, his second, the novel had become a bestseller combined to put him on an enviable fast track to a full professorship. His third book derived from his Ph.D. research was even more favorably received by academia. His well acknowledged successes brought the harpies out in force. Morris had, as they say, earned his stars and bars. Both of Morris's academic books were being lauded from such places as Columbia, Penn, Princeton, and yes even Yale and Harvard

Northwestern wasn't taking any chances on him being poached by one of those Ivy League schools. The powers that be with John Stanton's and Robbie's encouragement made him an offer. It included tenure even before he had completed his doctorate.

He was seen by the university powers as the fair-haired boy, and he was fully aware of the envy of many of his fellow professors. His friend, mentor, and chairman of the humanities department, John Stanton did everything he could to help Morris. But John couldn't resist flaunting his great find by never tiring of introducing Morris at every opportunity as the department's boy wonder.

Sitting here with Hanna in silence Morris's take on the hour and a half with Henric, Erica, and Maria was they saw Hanna as a young person with unlimited ability and artistic possibilities. They all recognized her as having a creative mind and skills the potential of which were unfathomable. Henric, he thought saw Hanna, if she could fulfill her promise, as an unending treasure trove.

Erica seemed content to enjoy listening to Hanna's remarkable voice. Maria, with no apparent monetary reasons or ulterior motives other than wanting to collaborate with her, seemed to not only respect Hanna's abilities, but was going to help her in any way she could.

Morris never for a moment felt there was anything sinister going on. The indecision and waffling came from the lack of a solid goal or any of them knowing the best direction or how hard to push Hanna toward it. He could tell none of them wanted to lose her. They all wanted to work with her.

These three, ten and twelve or more years older than Morris and Hanna, were renown and well established in their respective professional worlds. Maria's was theater. Henric's was fine art and Erica he abruptly learned was a much sought after well-known translator of French and Italian plays, and poetry.

Morris learned of Erica' profession toward the end of the evening when she leaned toward him and said, "Morris, you used a few passages from my translation of Giraudoux's, "Ondine" as examples in your book. You made my heart go pitter patter when you picked passages you felt were particularly tricky but demonstrated the best of a translator's thoughtful and careful efforts."

Realizing who she was, but not showing any of the total surprise almost shock her words gave him, Morris casually said, "I believe that would make you Erica Morningside."

"That I am. Mrs. Erica Morningside Olbermann, and you weren't nearly so charitable to many of my rivals."

"I did get some pretty irate letters from three who felt I was overly critical of their work.

Smiling at him Erica said, "And I bet I could name each of them. I don't believe they work as carefully or thoughtfully as most translators."

Erica's revelation was the first any of them let on they knew anything about him other than he was Hanna's friend and a brand-new professor. Winding up the meeting Erica reminded

Hanna New York City was the hub, the very center of the arts and theater world. It would be the natural place of choice to launch either her fine art or theatrical career. Reaffirming Morris's belief, he was a man of considerable means Henric reiterated he and Erica would be delighted to sponsor Hanna and get her established in New York.

The three of them left it at talking further in a week giving Hanna time to think this through and decide when and how to proceed. As they stood, Maria said, "Morris I thoroughly enjoyed "Exemplary Lives." It was a wonderfully written, uplifting, and heartbreaking read. Such gracious honorable people, I couldn't put it down."

Again, showing no surprise at Maria's sudden and unexpected acknowledgment of knowing about him Morris said, "Thank you, Maria. I'm glad you enjoyed it."

They stood there in silence for a few seconds. Erica said, "It's been a genuine pleasure to meet you Morris, and Hanna take the week to think carefully about all of this."

Looking at Hanna and Morris standing next to each other Maria pleased said, "You're so young, both of you. The gods have blessed you both. All that creativity and ability, it's an amazing thing to be with in the flesh." The women hugged and exchanged pleasantries, while Morris shook hands with them. They departed leaving Hanna and Morris standing next to each other.

Bewildered Morris just stood there. They knew about him, of his work, but didn't let on until the meeting was almost over. Maria not until she was preparing to leave. Feeling puzzled, somewhat deceived, and no part of this new world of Hanna's, Morris said, "You've had a big day Hanna. I should be getting on my way."

"Where are you staying?"

"It's only nine thirty if I start home now I'll be in Evanston before morning."

"Morris the only place you're going is upstairs to my room. It's quiet, and we need to talk. I don't want to sit down here and drink. You owe me four years of catching up. I've got a million questions, and as always I need your help."

"You've got a room here?"

"Yes, it's a suite. Dad insisted. He didn't want me out alone, drinking, and driving."

NINETEEN

A few moments later he was in Hanna's very nice suite still wondering how she went so far so fast. She was, he realized, all grown up.

Wearing her warm, enchanting smile, Hanna said, "There's a bar over there if you want to fix a drink."

"I could go for some water, how about you?"

"Please."

"Those are some interesting friends you have. I'd no idea. You've sure grown up a lot, especially the way you look, the dress, the heels, red lipstick. Wow! I'm impressed."

"It's a costume, Morris. I'm still little Hanna with my flannel shirt and dungarees just like at Thanksgiving."

"You were just as lovely that day, but you're not little Hanna from Thanksgiving. You're a thousand miles from there. Those people aren't fooling around. Henric's deadly serious about your future. He was almost drooling thinking about what you can accomplish as a fine artist. So was Maria about working with her as a set designer."

"Henric put five of my paintings in his spring show. All five sold the opening night. He wants more. He says there's no limit to what I can do. They flew me out to New York for the show. They showed me a studio space he wants to set me up in. He bought the building.

It's an old warehouse with eighteen-foot-high ceilings and the most amazing end block wood floors. It looks right out across the river at Manhattan. It's three stories, and the top floor has dozens of skylights. It'll make a fantastic studio. He wants to remodel the second floor for my living quarters."

"Slow down Hanna this is a lot to digest. He wants to set you up in New York in your own place, and you've sold five paintings. How much did you get for the paintings?"

"Two sold for six each, one at nine, another at eight and the big one went for twenty-three.

"Fifty-two hundred dollars? That's spectacular Hanna."

"Thousand dollars Morris."

"My God Hanna, that's a fortune?"

"Well not quite. The gallery gets thirty-five percent for marketing, showing, framing, delivering, and sponsoring me. Most charge fifty."

"Still Hanna, that's amazing, your first show, looks like you're all set.

"I was surprised and thrilled

"So that's why Henric's so keen on you. You're a gold mine. What about the theater design?"

"I could make six to eight thousand a show. Lots more once I'm in the Scenic Artist Union and lucky enough to get to design the sets for a successful Broadway show.

"Why not do both."

"I'm thinking about it. I really get along with Maria. She's already offered me two jobs, but I've got to decide about that quickly."

"Where are they?

"She directs for regional repertory theaters. Like the new Guthrie, here in Minneapolis. One will be at the Long Warf, in

New Haven, Connecticut, and the others at the Arena Stage in DC."

"How did all this come about? There must've been sixty people at your house. It was an incredible mixture, and they were all so pleased about knowing you and working with you."

"Theater's different from anything I've ever known. Nobody gives a care how old you are or if you're a man or woman, married, gay, single, celibate, crippled, white, black, or yellow. All they care about is how good you are and what you can do. It's so different from high school or college it's almost unbelievable. The faculty went out of their way, and I mean way out of their way to have Maria be our guest director.

I know they did it because they all believed in me and wanted to give me and a few others career's a flying start. Nobody said anything, but I'm not stupid I knew it was important, particularly to some of the actors and me. That's why I called you at three in the morning. I was so lost. I was petrified about messing up."

"You didn't. Maria told me your design for St. Joan was astounding, an amazing combination of simplicity and unbelievably clever sophistication. She also said the lighting was breathtaking and emotionally powerful. From where I sat they all think you're special."

"You know I'm not special Morris, you know me. You understand how it works with me. I love doing it, working it out. Getting what I see it in my head to be real."

"You are special Hanna. You're just going to have to accept you're different, a rare mix of amazing abilities. God above Hanna when you and Erica went to the lady's room Maria couldn't say enough about you. She told me you were the most creative, easiest, most fun designer she's ever worked with. Henric said Hanna's the youngest most remarkable talent I've ever encountered. It was genuine Hanna. They meant what they said. They both think you're brilliant."

"If I am it's because of you Morris. The moment I heard you say three overlapping platforms the whole set and all those scenes and how to get back and forth between them was there in my head. It was instant. I saw it all, the mood, and the places, how to move between them, how to light it. It was wonderful. You opened the door to a whole world for me."

"I'm pleased for you, Hanna that this has worked out well. So, who's helping you with this? Are your mom and dad supporting you?"

"Reluctantly, but you will Morris. Basically, dad's afraid for me, and mom's so terrified about my being taken advantage of she just tears up. I swear to God they both see me as fifteen going off to live in the den of iniquity. But you're going to help me, Morris. You always have, and I hope you always will. I'm a big girl Morris. I can figure things out, and make decisions on my own, but you've always given me the right direction. Speaking of direction that three-ton book you gave me is breathtaking. It must have cost a fortune. Its scope is incredible. It sure whet my appetite."

"I was worried it wouldn't get here in time. It didn't show up until Thursday."

"Morris right now I want to stop talking about this."

"How come?"

"I told you someday I'd ask you for my kiss and I need it tonight more than ever."

That threw him. He didn't know what to do or say. He was barely able to assimilate seeing Hanna so grown up in all these wondrous ways and right out of the blue, she wanted her kiss. Morris was baffled. Hanna was having a terrific day, and he thought of the kiss as a stand-in for a shoulder to lean on, a much-needed hug, as comfort during a time of trouble.

He didn't understand what she was asking of him. Given their circumstances and remembering what happened so long-ago prom night, he had little doubt about where her kiss could lead. Knowing full well such a thing would change everything between them Morris stood there in expressionless silence looking upon all grown up Hanna.

She said, "Give me a minute," and left him standing in the middle of the room. She disappeared into the bathroom. Her sudden departure gave him time to think. When she came back into the room barefoot carrying her heels and nylons, he noticed she was no longer wearing the earrings, necklace, or red lipstick. She dropped the heels and nylons on a chair, gathered him in her arms, and kissed him until they were so lightheaded they almost tipped over. Holding him, she said in that marvelous low thick syrupy voice, "I've never made love to anyone, but I've done my homework. I know how it works."

Morris was as aroused as he could possibly be and as lost as he could possibly be. Hanna was a beautiful, powerful being. All that creative talent was in his arms big as life, vibrant, womanly, ready, and telling him she was willing. For the first time in his almost twenty-six years, he was afraid. Hanna was no longer a scared, timid teenager. She was a remarkable, brimming with life, and unbelievably beautiful woman. He wanted her, but, was hesitant, wary. Deep within Morris knew this was fraught with danger.

He didn't understand what the danger was, but he sensed it in every part of his being. In the few minutes Hanna left him there alone, he'd reconciled nothing, concluding only this was incredibly complicated. He somehow understood making love to Hanna no matter how much he wanted to would create a huge dilemma. "Hanna are you sure about this. Our lives, the way we are, where you're going. Where I am, this won't go where it should."

"Stop worrying. It'll be like before. We can just let it grow wild and check in on it occasionally."

"Hanna whatever happened to, I don't date, I don't get married, and I don't do that thing that makes babies."

"Trust me about this. We'll be okay."

"Hanna, you said we weren't that way with each other, and you're smart, you're brilliant, and you know full well doing this will change everything."

"No Morris it'll add to everything. And hush! You're hurting my feelings. I'm not a child. I know what I'm doing."

"Hanna?"

"Morris, I need to know. I want this, and it must be you. Please, just get in bed with me."

Morris had been with three women in his almost twenty-six years. The first, Jan, was a sort of, okay, sure, let's try it. The second, Allison, was sweeter, but almost as straightforward a trial and error coming together as with Jan. But with Allison, it was repeated a few times before they thanked each other and discontinued.

Diane, a young woman with considerable experience in such matters, was the third. They grew sweet on each other before they became lovers. As they continued spending time together, Diane taught him of the many pleasurable ways between men and women. Morris thoroughly enjoyed making love to Diane and looked forward to doing so whenever they could. But for all her winsome ways and experience Diane in no way prepared Morris for being with Hanna.

Hanna brought every bit of her creative being to this. She welcomed him and responded to his touch in ways he could not imagine. It was pure pleasure to her. She was joyously pleased with him. She showed her pleasure like she did in her art, without reservation, openly, and fearlessly. In his most creative, wildest, most romantic fantasy Morris could not have created Hanna. They were perfectly and lovingly matched.

Savoring every second of every moment from the first touch forward Morris felt her very being and all her living power right through her skin, lips, and fingertips. Being inside her, holding her was even more remarkable. Hanna was the other, and somehow, she was one with him. It was the most heavenly, mystically sensuous thing he ever experienced.

They never said a word. They couldn't. This wasn't any kind of a time for words. The love flowed between them smoothly, naturally, and softly like warmed honey. It alternated throughout the night between a spiritual, dreamy, relaxing, ever so quiet slow-moving stream and a ferociously swelling, wild, scary, and uncontrollable thing. It left them panting, glowing with excitement, breathless, and even more speechless. Many hours later they drifted off to sleep enshrined in the mystery of this wonderful powerful thing they'd done with each other.

***

He woke in the morning with her leaning over him her face mere inches from his she said, "We need to talk Professor Stevens."

Quickly sitting up, he said, "Is something wrong?"

"Nothing you can't fix but get dressed. Breakfast is on the way. I ordered you a cheese omelet, toast, sausage, and coffee.

"Geez Hanna all my stuff, my razor, my toothbrush, my clean clothes everything's in my car."

"Use my toothbrush and put on what you wore last night and be quick the foods on its way. We've lots to talk about."

Morris was in and out of the bathroom fast. Dressed and almost awake he sat across from Hanna at the little two-person table in a spellbound fog. The room appeared frozen in time and not in any way like a hotel room. Morning light poured into the room through the big windows behind her. It was clean, warm, and so soft and dreamy he almost cried.

Remembering it later he was sure he was in a fantasy. The furnishings were copies, but first rate and the drapes and carpet left him with an impression of a long-ago French sunroom. The light was unworldly, lovely, and so was Hanna. He tried hard to gather himself to come to terms with where he was and who he was with, but most of all with what transpired last night. He was wholly undone.

"Morris, are you, all right? You look like you're going to cry."

Like a five-year-old, he buried his face in his hands. Morris knew at this moment he would happily and without further thought give away his soul and everything he possessed to stay here forever. He had to say something. This was too good, too wonderful. He wanted to cry his heart out with joy. "Hanna?"

"No Morris, not yet. First things first. Eat, then we'll talk, and after that, we can try to talk about last night.

TWENTY

"Okay, Hanna, your way, and don't start with what should I do?"

"What did you think of Henric and Erica?"

"I think they both admire you and he's got an eye for talent which comes in a form he believes he can manage. I also believe you're a diamond mine to him."

"They've offered me a lot of support, and they've been very generous. When they came to my first gallery show in Minneapolis and saw my paintings, he took three for his spring show. He gave me an idea for a fourth and then he handed me a clipping of a group of young girls. He said, Hanna, I want you to take this and make it four feet by six feet. I said I don't plagiarize. He said, Hanna, that's not what I want. Capture their emotion, use the feeling, make it yours."

"I'm sure you came up with something brilliant."

"I did a few preliminaries and sent them. He sent them back with some suggestions and a check for a thousand dollars for the canvass, paint, packing, and shipping."

"Wow, he has faith in you."

"It came with no strings. Henric's not pushy Morris. He's been very generous with the money and looking after me. Both he and Erica have."

Morris said, "I think Henric saw me as a potential problem; perhaps one that might sidetrack you or impede your development."

"He would, he views Maria the same. We're young, and he knows you're important. Maria has design work for me. He's worried about me being in love with you and becoming a professor's wife or going over to life in the theater. But I don't believe he has anything, but my best interests at heart."

"Neither do I. All three of them see you as amazing, unique. So, what would working with Maria include?"

"Meetings with the director to come up with a set design, Maria in this case. Then meeting with the managing director about my fees, the budgets, and then doing the technical drawings for the sets and props. Meeting with the technical director to go over all of it; they'll all want me to be on site for the build. Depending on the situation I could just come back the last week to paint everything. But I'd need to be there for the setup and right through to opening night."

"That sounds doable."

"Not entirely, because doing the lighting adds a lot of time and complexity to my responsibilities during the setup. Maria advised until I get my feet wet I not do the lights, but I'm struggling with it. The lighting is a huge part of my designs. Thanks to you and Jo Meliziner I design with light as much or more than I do with painting and set pieces.

"Maria says I'll burn out trying to do both. She told me she has a great lighting designer named Pat Simmons. She told me I would not only enjoy working with her but could learn a lot from her. So, if I did stay on site I'd be there for a month solid and two weeks before getting the drawings and renderings completed."

"How did you come by all the technical know-how?"

"They teach it at the university. I've been there for five years, and I'm not slow that way. Dad's a mechanical engineer, a good one. I'm sure I got some of his genes."

"And what did you get from your mom?"

"Stubbornness, white blond hair, some extra smarts, and my baby blues all came from mom."

"Your mom has red hair."

"She's dyed it since before she met dad."

"I'll be, I would've never guessed. Where did the other thing come from?"

"What other thing?"

"Your uniqueness, the creativity, your amazing drawing ability, your sense of color, your skill at painting, where in heaven's name did it all come from?

"Dad's a good draftsman, and my grandmother made a living as a calligrapher. I practiced sketching for years and years. Morris, I worked long and hard learning all those techniques I use working with paint."

"Hanna, you see things so differently. Someone says paint me a girl in a chair, and you make her so appealing and alive I want to get to know her. Your subjects have such a presence I see all the mysteries of life in them. Same with your theater design.

"Mention seventeenth century ballroom I see tall windows with opulent drapery, inlaid parquet floors, and ornate panels. I see miles of sumptuous flowery gold decoration, crystal chandeliers, and big oil paintings. You see the essence. You use just enough detail to tell everyone where they are."

"I don't know how to explain it. I think about the emotion I'm trying to get across, and I mess the ideas, situations, and subjects around in my head. Then I try to come up with what would best show it to an onlooker. However, in all seriousness, the result originates from a kind of moonstruck insane distillation process."

"The set design works pretty much the same as the painting except it's three dimensional and is all about the playwright's words. Because the ideas are presented through actors, a play is alive in real time. I start with light, from a space in total darkness. Then I add only the kind, amount, and quality of light needed. I'm sort of playing God

"I see the whole show right there in light first. It's full-blown, in my head. Sometimes I sleep on it, but it always comes. Ever since the night, you talked about Saint Joan I've imagined locations and places in remarkably different ways. It's obvious how to best convey a setting. What it should be, what to draw, and how to paint it. I bring my thoughts to the director as renderings, and we mull them over. With sets and with my paintings I use the light to steer an audience to how I want them to feel.

"With a play or painting after I have the lighting down, I try for the essence, reducing everything to the barest essentials. What's necessary for an onlooker to understand where they are and what's going on. I could talk about this for hours. I try to help the playwright, the director, and the actors with all my heart and soul and everything I put on that stage."

"Hanna, I think you should talk with Henric and Erica and tell them you'd like to try both venues and see how it goes. I think the fine art and the theater will feed each other and make you even more able and creative than if you held yourself to just one. I believe they'll both see it working well for you if you don't overextend yourself. And one other thing and this is important. You need to get the money thing straight with Henric. Specifically, the costs per month of the studio and your living quarters.

"You need to know what he'll be expecting you to produce yearly, and you need a formal written agreement between you. I think it would be helpful to both of you. An agreement will give you boundaries and keep the expectations for both of you in the healthy zone. You've never been very careful about some important things and Hanna that's an important thing.

"I also think you need to sit down with your mom and dad and walk them through your plans. You've never been any good at that either. But now you're twenty-three and all grown up it's time to start. They can help you. No matter what happens, they'll be there for you. Hanna, they love you more than you might imagine. They'll be there if you need them."

"Morris. Come with me."

He sat there in silence that lasted so long she finally said, "Morris?"

"Hanna, I don't understand last night. I didn't know anything like that existed, it was from another world. I can't believe what happened or how I felt.

"Morris, I want more than anything in this world for you come with me?"

He groaned and said, "How Hanna? We both need to keep going down our own paths, at least until we have a better idea of where we're going, and how to get there."

"I know you're right Morris but being with you last night was unbelievable. I've never felt so wonderful or alive and close to someone. We were one."

"Hanna, I was inside you. That's what being one with another means."

"Morris, it was more than physical, much more, a whole great big unbelievable world more."

"Believe me, Hanna, I know."

"Could you stay one more day? We could stay here."

"Hanna, we can't stay here. Your mom and dad would have a fit. Besides, I've faculty meetings for the next two weeks starting Monday. I've got outlines I haven't finished due for all of them. I haven't officially gotten my professorship, and I'm supposed to start teaching summer term."

"Was that no, Morris?"

"Jesus, Hanna this is hard! Last night was the most incredible, wondrous and glorious unexplainable thing I've ever experienced! God above it was unbelievably beautiful, but please Hanna, hear me out."

"I'm listening."

"I'm living in a house which I own just getting by and can't afford. Thank God, I have a bunch of guys paying me rent. I need that professorship. The royalties helped. I paid my dad back and paid off most of the mortgage, but I need that professorship. My family's gone, our home here is gone, and they're living in California. I've no money to spare." She sat expressionless listening. He continued, "Where would I live in New York Hanna? Would we live together? And what would I do? I'd have to find work and start making a living right away."

"Morris, you could apply to Columbia I'm sure they'll offer you a professorship."

"Maybe, but from what I know to be offered a tenured professor's position you need to be near to famous. At the very least have a mentor, a sponsor, someone who sees you as special and wants to help. Like Henric, Erica and Maria can help you. The first question they'd ask would be why did you give up tenure and leave Northwestern. I think they would see me as an ungracious spoiled brat. I've taken on a house Hanna. I own it. John and Robbie moved heaven and earth to get me a tenured position. I'm just starting out. I owe people big time. After all their help, work, and backing they'll be terribly hurt if I up and leave."

"Morris people do it all the time."

"Not this people. Not a twenty-six-year-old just tenured professor."

"I know you feel obligated, but I think they'd understand."

"Hanna you're just starting out. You need to jump in and see what this will be like. You'll probably love it, but you could end up hating it. It's a long way from here, and you'll be doing the equivalent of your final MFA project on every show."

"You're right. I need to get on with my work, and you'd be the most gigantic impossible distraction ever."

"Hanna as much as I want to it makes little sense for me to come to New York with you. It would be counterproductive to everything we're trying to do. Especially for you, we're both at the beginning of everything."

"Morris please think about it. Will you at least say you'll think about being with me?"

"Hanna believe me, I'll never be able to stop thinking about being with you."

"Morris, I think we can find a way.

"Hanna, our parents, are best friends, where would our running away to New York leave them? What would they say to each other?"

"I hadn't given that part much thought. I was so surprised about how I felt last night. I didn't know making love to you would be anything like that. Is that what it's like for every couple?"

"I don't believe so, Hanna. Nobody would ever get anything done."

"Morris last night changed everything. It swept me right off my feet, it was heavenly, spiritual. I've never been so close to another. I couldn't imagine that. What it was"

"I know Hanna; it was, well, I'm speechless."

"So, what are we going to do about it?"

"Hanna, your mom, and dad see me as your guide, a mentor maybe, but not your lover. My mother looks on you as some remarkably talented, gentle, female Vermeer who needs all the help, encouragement, and protection she can send your way. They don't think of us as a couple or anything like that. In their eyes, we're their first born, their babies just starting out."

"Morris, my mom's been trying to push me into the arms of a boy for years, and just about any boy would've done. She likes you, and if you come with me, she'll know I'm normal. At least she'd know for sure I'm not a lesbian."

"I'm sure she knows you're not."

"No Morris she's still plenty worried about it because I've never dated or shown any interest in men. God almighty if I even suspected anything like last night I would've been in your bed every chance I had. Morris, that was absolutely positively unbelievably wonderful."

"Hanna, our living together unmarried would be nothing, but a huge betrayal of everything our parents hoped and dreamed for us. They'd be shocked and feel deceived. If they even suspected I stayed with you last night they would be mortified, crushed. I know my father would think I lost my mind if I gave up my home, my education, and my future to run away with you. I know he was disappointed in my career choice, but he's never messed with me about my life choices. However, I think he'd see me running away to New York as insanity and would feel obligated to bring me to my senses.

She left her chair and sat on his lap. She put her arms around his neck and said, "Now that I know about this I'm not going to just let it go. You've always been there and kept me going in the right direction and last night. Well, Morris, I don't believe I could paint the way I felt if I had ten years."

"Hanna, I think down the road we can figure out a way to be together." With her arms around him hugging him he kissed her cheek and whispered in her ear, "One nice thing Hanna, we sure have something wonderful to look forward too."

***

They made love all morning and afternoon and hard as it was for either of them to believe, it kept getting better. Starting to leave the bed, Morris said, "Hanna, I've got to get going."

"Stay, just a little longer."

"Hanna, I can't it's already four o'clock, and it'll be at least another hour before I'll be able to do anything. It's an eight-hour drive, and I have a big deal faculty meeting at nine in the morning."

"I'll call room service and get us some food. Then you can go. Please?"

Three hours later, spent as he could be, they kissed and held one another at the door. Walking away and leaving Hanna standing in that doorway was the hardest most gut-wrenching thing he'd ever done.

TWENTY ONE

Morris was teaching by day and up late every night preparing, reviewing, and mastering his course material. Trying to stay on top and ahead of his classes was work. Hanna was up to her ears in moving in, setting up her studio, hiring people and embroiled in all manner of theater and painting projects. They talked on the phone of seeing one another, but neither had a plan or any idea how to manage it. About five months after her graduation over Thanksgiving he was in New York for a mandatory meeting with his publisher.

Morris spent Thursday, all of Saturday, and Sunday morning at her place in bed with her. It was the most wonderful unforgettable experience either ever dreamed of. Neither knew what to say to the other beyond thank you, thank you, and ask, when will we see each other again?

He saw her again during spring break, and they spent four days together, most of them in bed together. Morris couldn't believe the enormous amount of work she was embroiled in. Her studio was huge, and there were paintings everywhere. They were on easels, leaning against the workbenches, and stacked against walls. There were sketches, set designs, and light plots on every flat surface.

They parted late Sunday afternoon exhausted. Neither slept a wink, or spoke about what they were doing with each other, nor did they speak of anything further between them. They were burning the candle at both ends, she even more so than him.

He saw Hanna again early that summer. The studio was overflowing with her work, and she now had a second assistant and a new apprentice. Morris was amazed at all of what she was involved in. Their being together was better than ever, but as his stay went on he was aware his presence was adding a lot of pressure to what he could see was a staggering workload. Without ever saying, so Hanna and Morris understood living together was out of the question. Without ever talking beyond that simple unspoken acknowledgment they accepted and assumed this would be what it was between them. They would be together when they could.

He hated leaving her. Trying to ease his sorrow and emptiness he reminded himself on the flight home of the many times she reiterated she had no interest in dating or being married much less in doing that thing that makes babies with any man other than him. Their relationship seemed to him a paradoxical dilemma. They were on the most fantastic, amazing, and magical, but unworkable road to nowhere imaginable. So, Morris tried to not think about it.

TWENTY TWO

Morris met Annie at one of those mandatory fall faculty dinners which Professor Atkins's and the other department heads and their wives so relished putting on. The dinners were commonplace proceeding and during the first quarter of each new school year. Their stated purpose was to introduce new faculty members, encourage friendships, and the exchange of ideas and information across departments.

Morris, considered a must-have participant by the wives, was invited to every one of these dinners. He was young, a new professor, unattached, and an acclaimed author of two well-received academic works and a best seller. He was twenty-six. Nice looking, modest, well mannered, fit, and could not yet afford to say no.

Morris's dissertation research was planned from the start to be a book. The book was published before he submitted his revised proof-laden edition in dissertation form. His second academic book was a textbook in use all over the country in graduate courses. His earlier book on translations was enjoying the same use and both were considered an academic must read.

Both works were well received by the academic world and Morris was fortunate to be young and healthy because he came close to a breakdown getting the first book completed and published. The second academic work based on his dissertation research was completed and published before he had either his doctorate or teaching position.

Morris put in twice the time of the other Doctoral candidates. He worked to near exhaustion several times during those years. It was a long hard trying road to get where he was. Ironically, it was his novel, the best-seller about Marion and Albert that John was so afraid of and not the academic works which produced his campus celebrity status. It was what made him a must-have addition to the faculty dinners.

People read novels for pleasure not textbooks. They read Morris's and were always delighted to talk with him. He enjoyed it at first, but the questions soon became predictable. Morris very much-loved Albert and Marion and not wanting to diminish their lives or what they stood for in any way he held up his end always with a smile and care.

Morris had a lean, taut face and depending on his attire he became almost anything an observer might wish to imagine; race car driver, detective, cowboy, hoodlum, pilot, athlete, lawyer or FBI agent they all looked to be a possibility, almost anything, but a university professor. John's wife Dee suggested he might wear suspenders along with bow ties instead of belts and ties. The bow ties and suspenders helped, but not his lean hard athletic physique. Morris couldn't abide Dee's last suggestion to get some turtlenecks and tweed jackets.

Morris wasn't big, five-ten, but no one ever took him for granted or tried to mess him about, not even in high school. He looked like he could take care of himself and would if he had to and not just a little. His fellow students, especially the women's first impressions, where Morris was most likely one of those bad boy types. He had quiet, steady sapphire blue eyes, a deep slow paced distinctive voice and quite the disarming little boy smile.

However, even with his unreadable face, his demeanor worked well. From his appearance, it wasn't apparent, but Morris was a decent kind person. When people bothered to get to know him, it didn't take them long to come to realize it. He was single, nice looking, and whether a bad boy or not the faculty wives, both young and old, just plain liked him.

Not by accident Morris figured. Professor Annie Taylor ended up seated across from him and hard as Morris tried he could not stop looking at her face. He picked her out the minute she arrived. Noting right away she was tall, five feet seven or eight; slender, curvaceous, with long legs, and silky coal black hair. She wore no makeup on her unusual, intriguing face. Her lips were defined, full, and they often worked their way into a playful, honest, and appealing girlish smile.

She had dark brown almost black eyes. With her rather long slender nose and straight coal black eyebrows, the pieces came together completing a face of enchanting complexity. Her cheekbones were high, but not defining. She had freckles, lots of them. Morris thought her appearance was priceless. The freckles gave her face an incredible mix of sultry mystery and childlike innocence. Without saying a single word to him, Professor Annie Taylor was already unforgettable.

He was always careful at these dinners. With just the merest use of a few too many innocently spoken words, one could light up the gossip machine. If one were to pay a little too much attention to someone, to one of the younger wives, it often became the speculation of the week. It was a delicate rope to walk. Morris remained quiet and let the people seated all around them do the heavy lifting. Male or female it didn't matter the regulars would always grill any new face. Morris sat silently and let the others carry out the Inquisition.

Not wanting to tip his hand to her or the others about how interested in her he was he remained the silent not interested observer. He knew the others would ask all the usual questions about her marital or friend status. Her shoe size, favorite color, academic situation, her educational background, blood type, and what her long-term plans for making her way in the world might be.

It was always the same, but tonight it seemed to take forever to get to the important things. Morris was considering trying to go about asking her to come home with him. Nothing like this had happened to him in years. Not since Diane. He was surprised to be thinking about this woman in that way. He lost track of the conversation while he busied himself coming to grips with his attraction to her.

Morris had been terrifically spoiled by Hanna. He always felt no one could ever match what he and Hanna shared. He believed it would be monstrously unfair to ask or expect someone to even try. Morris knew if there were ever to be someone it would have to be something else even more potent that carried the relationship. At this point in his life, he couldn't imagine how or what that might be, but he was open to the possibility.

Noticing he wasn't part of the cross-examining team and seemed to pay little attention to her or the process Annie turned to him during a lull and said, "And who might the quiet one be?"

Morris said, "Will a name do?"

"That'd be a start."

"Morris Stevens at your service, ma'am."

"The Humanities department's boy wonder? They told me you'd be here. You're much younger than I thought you'd be."

"Shucks, I was hoping I'd be nicer looking."

"Oh my, clever too."

Knowing the table was all ears and listening to everything being said Morris suspected he and Professor Taylor had already gone too far. He knew to be careful about flirting. But there was something about her, her manner, about that face, her smile which allowed him to say to himself, go for it. Give it a shot

Morris. Not being at all prudent, he came right out and said, "Would Professor Taylor date a man she's just met?"

"I like to go for walks and talk."

"That appears both appropriate and workable. Do you do that by yourself or do you like to have someone along capable of answering when you talk?

Speaking in general, but to him, she said, "My goodness? An interesting man, we should definitely walk and talk."

"By chance would there be a time and place, where this walking and talking begins?"

"I'll be taking my daily walk around campus tomorrow starting at three thirty. I start from the steps of Lutkin Memorial Hall."

Having gotten what he wanted, Morris moved on to all those many other things professors and academics talk about at dinner parties. Those seated nearby were aware Annie and Morris were more than a little interested in each other. Without hesitation and right in front of them they had negotiated a date.

***

Not taking any chances or having any fear of her knowing this was important to him Morris was there early sitting on the Library steps. They set off together walking and talking. She was twenty-seven a year older than him and grew up in Philadelphia earning her undergrad degree at Bryn Mawr.

She explained she did her graduate work at Penn and got her doctorate in social anthropology there. Annie was newly employed at Northwestern as a full-time professor and was enjoying settling into her new life. She told him she was divorced, that the marriage lasted less than sixteen months. She stopped and looking both puzzled and surprised, said, "I can't believe I just told you I was divorced. That's something I very

166

much intended to keep to myself. It's not something I want known."

"Don't worry about it. It'll be our secret. I've never had any interest in gossiping about other people's lives. But I'm pleased you felt I was someone you could trust not to blab it all about.

"You didn't seem at all surprised or put off."

"Why would I?"

"A marriage lasting less than sixteen months could be an indicator of poor decision making or serious character flaws."

"My mother was a divorcee. I never thought any of those things about her, and I never questioned her character.

"A son wouldn't."

"My Mom's first marriage didn't work out. We talked about it once. She was heartbroken. Mom told me the only real downfall to being a divorcee, back in the day when a divorce was unheard of was being thought of as a fallen woman. Men looked upon her as being used goods and easy. She said in more gentile society a divorced woman was spoken of as experienced."

"Is that how you see me?"

"Get serious professor. I just met you. For all, I know the marriage might've never been consummated."

"Whoa. I'm not a complete prude."

"Seriously Annie, the most I'd venture to speculate on about your having been married would be to surmise you've had more chance to practice than single woman."

"Practice? That's an interesting way to think of sex."

"Annie, I meant practice as in Law or medicine, what married people do." Feeling this was all about to go off the tracks, he said, "It's none of my business. I can see you're a smart, thoughtful person. I assume you married with all the hopes and dreams of most couples. I'm sorry it didn't work out. It must've been a wrenching disappointment?

"It was."

"So, Professor Annie Taylor, do you have men friends?"

"No, haven't had time, I'm new here, how about you?"

"Neither a man nor woman."

"Oh, that's cute."

"Until I got the professorship, I didn't have the time. Not a spare minute. Between my class work and the writing, I've been putting in twenty-hour days for the last six years."

"That doesn't sound like much of a life."

"I got to go to New York a few times to see my publisher. It was a nice break. I have a family friend there I've known since high school. She's a fine artist and a professional theatrical set and lighting designer."

"Now that sounds interesting. Do you stay in touch?"

"She summons me on occasion when she gets in trouble or needs help to find her way."

"So, the boy wonder has no ongoing female interests or obligations."

"Not since I was an undergrad, and that was a while back."

"Those kinds of relationships usually end in marriage or a broken heart.

"Is that what happened to you, Annie?"

"Pretty much? What about yours?"

"Diane was smart and sweet. She taught me a lot, and I think I was in love with her. One night about eight Diane called me and announced she was transferring to Berkeley. She went on explaining how it was a better fit for her graduate work. With not so much as a goodbye, a kiss on the cheek, or even a handshake she drove away early the next morning. She took a sizeable chunk of my heart along with her."

"You survived?"

"It took a while, but I don't think I had anywhere near as much invested as you did in a marriage."

"Morris, I think that would be a hard thing for anyone, but you to determine."

"So, Annie from Philadelphia, will you have dinner with me tonight?"

"Depends."

"On?

"Where, when, that kind of thing."

"At my house, tonight."

"You have a house?"

"Yes, it's big and gracious. It's been good to me. I have three graduate students living upstairs and have the downstairs pretty much to myself. We share the kitchen and occasionally the living and dining rooms. I wrote the novel about the couple I bought the house from."

"That also sounds interesting."

"It is, and now that we have all these interesting things to talk over how about it? Will you come for dinner?"

"This is for Dinner? Nothing more."

"I was hoping you'd stay after dinner and we could talk some."

"And then?

He thought that would be up to you Annie, but said, "I assume at some point you'd get tired and want to go home.

"What time should I be there?

"It's almost five how about six thirty?" Morris walked away saying, "I've some shopping to do. I'll see you at six thirty?"

As he moved off, she called out, "Morris?" He stopped and turned back toward her

"Not unless you tell me how to get there."

"Damn, and here I thought I was so smooth."

***

Annie arrived right at six thirty looking very nice. He wondered if she would go all out or keep things more reserved. She dressed about the same as she did for the dinner party when they first met. She wore no makeup or jewelry and was not trying to be suggestive or alluring or make this seem overly significant. Annie didn't need to do any of the things women do to be attractive. Annie in her natural state was plenty intriguing.

He liked her and hadn't stopped thinking about her since they parted earlier. She was reserved, but straightforward, proper, but not prudish. With her pleasant, quick sense of humor, she was easy to like, and he could tell she was as interested in him as he was in her. He went all out for her preparing a summer squash dish he'd always been successful with. A mixture of fresh onions, zucchini, yellow summer squash, and tomatoes all sliced and stirred together. He also mixed in a handful of square cut green and red peppers. He seasoned it with an assortment of spices and served it over linguini

During dinner, she said, "I must ask Morris. How could you afford to buy this house while you were going to school? And where did all the beautiful furnishings come from? How did you ever find the time? Did you have someone decorate it? I know you're the grandson of a robber baron.

"Whoa! That's about as bad as being vilified for being a divorcee."

"Okay, fair enough. Are you independently wealthy?"

"I wish. But no, Annie. No such luck. I couldn't afford this place not until I got my position. The book royalties made it possible. This house belonged to an older couple, and the wife was going to a nursing home. The poor man was heartbroken that he and his wife had to leave. They both taught here at Northwestern, and they lived in this house for almost sixty years. John Stanton asked me if I would help him help them get it straightened up and ready to sell."

"The Chairman of the humanities department? That John Stanton?"

"Yes. I owe John big time. He and Robbie James are why I'm here. Those two have supported me in every way they could. Especially with getting the books published. Professor Albert Hendry the man who owned this house was the Chairman of the Humanities Department and John Stanton's advisor and mentor when he was a young doctoral candidate.

"John told me he owed Marion and Albert Hendry for everything he had or would ever be. He said, I'll never be able to repay them, and I'm not a spring chicken anymore. But Morris you could come along and do some of the heavy lifting. At least you won't have to worry about not being able to move the next day

"John brought me along. They were just as welcoming and gracious as could be. After our first meeting, I came back to help get the house cleaned out, and ready to sell. Albert liked me. More so after he found out, I played hockey in high school. One of his sons played.

She said, "It's an impressive home.

"It's big. There's a sizable study and three bedrooms upstairs along with three bathrooms. The bedrooms each belonged to one of their children. When I started helping, the upstairs bedrooms were just the way they were when the children left home. They weren't done up like a shrine they looked like the room of somebody away at college, but it startled me.

"I learned all three of their children died within six months of each other. I understood some of the sadness I felt coming from Marion about having to leave and go into a nursing home. Marion was eighty-eight, frail, and dying. But she still exhibited the sense of a woman caring for a home and a loving family with purpose and a nod to the future. Their home, this place was keeping those feelings alive for them. How about if I stop talking about this and give you a copy of the book? They were remarkable people. You can read it when you get bored."

"I've read it, Morris. My mother insisted. She said, Annie, if you're going to be a professor you need to read this book."

"Wow! I hope you enjoyed it."

"I did Morris, very much."

"Anyway, long story short. After Marion went to the nursing home, Albert was living here alone. He convinced me the only thing that mattered to them was for their home to stay intact with someone who'd care for it and appreciate it. At least until they were both gone. I finally understood it was all that mattered to them. It was what they both wanted. So here I am living in a kind of testament to someone else's life.

"You're a lucky man Morris. It's a beautiful home. Was Marion an artist?"

"I don't think so. Why?"

"The furnishings are simple, but elegant; she had an eye."

TWENTY THREE

Smiling Morris said, "So Annie tell me how you ended up at Northwestern?"

"After my divorce, the gossip started making the rounds. It wasn't pleasant. The things being said were disturbing. It all came to a head one afternoon when I overheard one of my professors say to another, Annie's a striking young woman, and she's brilliant, but not about men. Once it gets around, she's a divorcee she'll only attract men looking for an easy piece. None of them will ever be serious about her. She'll always be just a nice-looking woman to enjoy

"I couldn't believe that was what men thought about me. It was shocking. I thought God above that's not me and I knew if I would ever have a life I had to get far away from being any part of that thinking. That's why I was so surprised when I up and told you I was a divorcee. Anyway, I was lucky. I applied here, flew out met with the search committee and some of the faculty. They offered me the position at the end of that day."

"You must've made quite an impression."

"It was an interesting meeting. At lunch one of the search committee members told me everybody including the chairman was impressed with my Doctoral Thesis. It all felt right, and I could tell we liked each other right off."

Fascinated and watching her face he couldn't stop himself and said, "Annie I'm sure you've heard this a dozen times, but you have the most remarkable amazing face. It's so different. It's mesmerizing, fascinating, especially with your freckles. I'm sorry, but I can't stop looking at you." Every bit of color left her face. She turned away. He saw tears starting down her cheeks. "Annie what, what's wrong?"

"I'm sorry Morris. Do you have a hanky?" He brought her a box of tissues and sat across from her. He watched as she dabbed her cheeks and eyes putting that enchanting face back together.

"Morris please don't stare."

"Sorry. I was trying to figure out what I did."

"It was what you said."

"I said you have the most remarkable amazing face, it's so different. It's mesmerizing, fascinating, especially with your freckles.

"It's word for fucking word what Don said on our second date!"

Surprised at the language, her intensity, and already unnerved about her tears, several extra seconds floated by. Morris found his voice and said, "I assume Don was the man you married, and my words just opened a lot of unpleasantness?"

She slid her chair back and said, "You meant well. I apologize for my language and thanks for feeding me. It was very nice of you, but you needn't get embroiled in my baggage. It's unfair, and apparently, it's all come along with me to Northwestern.

"Annie I'm sorry my words triggered such a painful memory; I just wanted you to know I like you, your face, how interesting you look."

"Hearing those words in that order took me by surprise. I was right back there. I guess some things just stick. Anyway, it's already eight thirty, I should get along.

Seeing her getting up, sensing a sizeable impenetrable door about to close, Morris stood saying, "But I don't, Annie!"

"You don't what Morris?"

"I don't mind your baggage. Not in the slightest! Please, stay and talk to me, tell me about Annie Taylor.

She struck a chord somewhere deep inside him. There was so much going on with her. He was hooked. He didn't know why, but he wanted her to stay and talk and let him absorb everything about her. She experienced something he never did. She thought she found it all, a life of promise, the hope of a family, and a snug loving secure future with another. Suddenly, it was vapor, gone forever. All her hopes and dreams ended badly, painfully, and the memory of it would remain always and be forever that way. She tried to live a life he also wanted but could barely imagine.

Sitting she said, "So you like spending your time with damaged people?"

"I don't think you're damaged Annie. Maybe a little dented because to have and hold until death do you part was short and didn't end in death."

"All I know Morris is you can't make someone love you any more than you can make a silk purse out of a sow's ear."

"Don wasn't what you expected?"

"I didn't have a clue about his true nature. I woke up one morning in a hospital trying to face some ugly truths. The person I loved, the man I married, hurt me and put me there. I couldn't understand any of it. I thought I'd been blinded or put under some spell that kept me from seeing what was right in front of me.

"It was a terrific shock. I always fancied myself observant, careful about people, and a decent judge of character. I couldn't believe I married such a sadistic uncaring person. The whole time he spent with me before our marriage and for some time after was a monstrous lie."

"So, you either missed something, he was skilled at hiding, or maybe somewhere along the way he traded in his spots for stripes."

"I felt like an idiot for not seeing what he was. Worse, I stayed because we married and made promises. I didn't take my vows lightly, but I haven't been able to trust my judgment since."

"Annie, we all misread people or get mistaken feelings about them."

"True, but most women, especially intelligent women don't marry them and stay, even though they're being mistreated. This was like believing the Pacific Ocean is a pond."

"Does it help to talk about it?"

"I don't know? I've never talked about it.

"Not even with your parents?"

"Not with anyone. My dad was heartbroken when he realized I was leaving Don. The one time I tried was with my mom. I asked her if she was ever forced to have sex. She sat there looking at me with the most horrified blank look on her face. I cried. Mom tried to get me to explain myself. I begged off, and that was the extent of my talking about it."

"And you talked no further to your mother?"

"My mom couldn't conceive of being forced by her husband. She would've been no help. So, no, I haven't talked to anyone."

"You know the University Health Services have counselors for just this kind of thing."

"Morris I'm not comfortable thinking about it let alone going through with talking about what happened to a stranger."

"Annie, we're talking."

"You appear to be a caring soul Morris, a kind, very discreet, and considerate person. Even with my inability to read my ex-husband's true nature, I think even I can tell that much about you."

"Talk about it, Annie. Go ahead, say it out loud. I won't tell anyone or get embarrassed. I might cry for you, but that'll be the worse you'll get from me, promise."

"What the heck? I've already told you I was divorced. I'll take a chance, but Morris this can't come back on me. You've got to promise me!"

"I promise. It's our secret, and Annie, I keep my word."

"Okay then, here goes. Don, my husband, like my dad, was a tall, nice-looking man. He spent a lot of time courting me; Don came across in every way as attentive, caring, and loving. After quite some time we became lovers. He was the first and only man I've ever been with. It all seemed to be working out great.

But sometimes when we were making love, he'd just stop. He'd get dressed, go sit in his chair and read or he'd leave. I thought he needed to be by himself. If I asked why he'd say I don't feel up to it. That should have been something I paid attention to, but I didn't. I didn't know squat about lovemaking, or sex, or anything about those kinds of things. I was stupid innocent, I still am.

"The sex wasn't magical and not in any way earth shaking. In the beginning, he was considerate, but it seemed odd he never talked to or kissed me. The sex was nothing like I'd been led to believe or read about. It wasn't much of anything. I wondered what all the consternation and fuss was about.

"When we first dated two of my classmates suggested I not pin my hopes and dreams on Don. They judged him to be a player a Lothario, but I had no sense of being two-timed or anything like that. I paid no attention to their warnings. We weren't living together, but we'd see each other two or three times a week. Everything was good. He asked me to marry. It all seemed close to perfect

"I loved him and felt loved by him, and I believed we could make a great life together. I was about fourteen months away from completing my doctorate. Don had an excellent job with an insurance company, but he supported me in achieving my doctorate and teaching if I wanted to. That was important because while I was pursuing my graduate education, dad would teasingly suggest I was educating myself right out of the marriage market. Because of Don's support in that regard, he appeared the ideal man. Everything seemed about as good as it could be.

"I found out after the divorce by accident he spent the night before our wedding with another woman. Don had serious problems with the ladies. He wanted sex with all of them all the time. When he couldn't get what he needed outside our marriage, he'd turn to me.

"Within three months of our marriage, all the tenderness evaporated. He stopped being considerate and just climbed on. Don expected me to be ready and willing anytime he wanted. This didn't happen all at once it occurred over many months. We never talked about it. When I protested, he told me it was my duty. I was to obey. When I tried to refuse, he took me anyway. That's what my life became.

"I don't like admitting this, but I got used to it. If Don didn't hurt me too much, I could take it. It became my normal. It wasn't until later when he tried it three and four times a day on the weekends I suspected one of us was crazy.

"Jesus Annie, why didn't you leave? Why didn't you pack up and get out of there?"

"Pride, I couldn't face the failure. I've always tried my best. I only came in second once about something that mattered, I've worked hard ever since to never fail at anything. So, I was determined not to fail at something as crucial as my marriage. Not after all those hopes, dreams, and promises. I was also sure the whole mess was my fault. I thought maybe this is the way things work in a marriage. I couldn't understand what was going on or why everything was different or why he'd get home late or why he was so callous.

"I couldn't understand any of it. As time went on, it became more and more disturbing. I tried just lying there and let Don do whatever he wanted. That made him angry, and he did awful things. I realized his pleasure wasn't from the sex he was getting his pleasure from hurting me. Worst of all and unbelievably I loved him and just wanted things back the way they were in the beginning."

"What broke through the delusion?"

"In desperation, I tried my meek let him do whatever he wanted to act. Don got angry and did some awful things. I tried to fight him off. He beat me up and sodomized me. He tore my rectum so badly I ended up having emergency surgery and was hospitalized for eight days.

Annie's revelation floored him. She wasn't used goods as her professors thought, she was horribly damaged goods. He didn't twitch, blink, or say a word afraid anything he might do or say would frighten her away. Morris could barely hold his thoughts and his tongue while reorganizing his feelings.

Annie continued, saying, "At the hospital, there was this caring older night nurse who was concerned about me. One night while she was sitting on the bed taking my blood pressure she forced me to face my situation. I've never heard anyone talk about sex or relations the way she did. She said Annie, I heard from Shirley your day nurse you have a Ph.D. and teach at Penn.

You're an exceptionally attractive woman, so I'm surprised; I'm shocked you're in my ward in the condition you're in.

"She said, I enjoy men and I love good sex. I've worked here in this ward for twenty-five years. I've never married. But over the years I've had more than one romantic partner, and I can assure you there's no place for your kind of pain in lovemaking. You're a mess girl.

"She saw I was about to say something and she said, Missy, I don't want to hear any more shit about it being a sex experiment that went wrong. Was that tall handsome very contrite man with all the flowers the one who did this? I was afraid to say yes. I sat there looking at her. She said, well if it was him, flowers, tall and handsome or not he belongs in jail. Either that or you're some peculiar young woman, enjoying getting beaten black and blue and having your rectum stretched by him until it tears

"Besides lifting you by your nipples, did he force his hand in you? Is that what happened? I looked at her wondering how she could know any of these things. Then she said I don't get the sense from you any of that's your cup of tea. I sat there with tears pouring down my face. She said, and you know missy worst of all there'll be a next time. Then another next time, and one of those next times he's going to hurt you so bad he'll have to kill you."

"I heard her and knew she was right. I had to leave Don, and sobbing my heart out I said, but he's my husband. She said all the more reason you must leave. If you weren't married to him, this would be easy. I'd call the cops and have him arrested for assaulting and raping you. She held me while I cried my heart out. She said tell me who to call because you're not going back there. You'll end this and if there's no one to call I know people who will help.

"I knew it was over. We were done. My marriage was finished. It came down to being repeatedly raped, the shame of it, and at the end being badly beaten and hospitalized. I was left dealing with the loss of all my hopes and dreams, some paperwork, and trying to understand what happened. One day I was happily married with a whole life in front of me the next it was gone. Recognizing the situation, I was in, was unbelievable. Confronting it, seeing it, shattered my belief in myself and others. It almost destroyed me."

Finally daring to speak Morris said, "I'm so sorry that happened to you. I can't imagine such a thing. I got angry with Diane more than once, but I can't imagine hitting her much less raping her."

"It took almost four months before I stopped thinking what happened was my fault, that I caused it and brought it on myself. I came to realized Don was having sex his way, and it didn't matter whether I wanted it or not. He enjoyed hurting me sexually. He no longer cared about me. I was his property, his cunt. He said it so many times I believed it.

"The last few weeks before I ended up in the hospital he forced me repeatedly. He was sadistic. The last time was disgusting, demeaning, and the most embarrassing painful day of my life. He knocked me unconscious. When I woke up he was gone. I could barely walk let alone drive myself to the hospital. Trying to make up some plausible explanation for my condition, being examined by a young male doctor in front of two nurses was almost unbearable. It was demeaning, it hurt, and I cried through the whole exam. Don was my husband, and I couldn't understand why this happened, what changed. Everything was so different."

"It looks as though you've put most of that turmoil aside and managed to get back out and take your place in the world. You're a full professor at Northwestern, and that's not too shabby." The very moment shabby left Morris's lips he wished with all his heart he'd never used the word. He was already struggling to get past the sudden revulsion sweeping through him as he pictured Don forcing his hand into her. He did not want to imagine or see this lovely woman that way.

"I think working so hard to finish my Ph.D. kept me from taking a good long hard look at what was going on in my marriage. But I no longer have any illusions about a women's place in the world. We're supposed to be pure and innocent, virgins when we marry. Most of us aren't. We marry, support our husbands, have children, make a home, and try to live happily ever after.

"Most women fall in love with; wait, hold it. Without ever saying so or being consciously aware of it, they settle on a man who they believe will be the best they can ever get. Most women believe in their hearts they're in love. Like me, they're naïve and in for a shock. As young women, we're fed all this cultural hoopla about marriage as the Holy Grail. We're supposed to be overjoyed to love, honor, and obey. What a load of claptrap. I found the keyword for men is to obey."

"You don't believe that, do you?"

"I'm afraid I do."

"All the women I've cared about obeyed about as well as cats."

She laughed and said, "And who were they?"

"Six so far, my mother, my sister, my friend Hanna, Jan, Allison the first girl I was ever with, and Diane, the girl who took my heart to Berkeley with her."

TWENTY FOUR

That first month they walked together almost every day. She came for dinner twice more. He hugged her at the front door one of those times when she first arrived, but he never tried to kiss her. As much as he wanted to the night they met, he never asked her to stay overnight. They spent two months getting to know one another. The nights he wasn't working on his teaching he spent putting together the beginnings of a story. It was about a remarkable young woman who had her hopes and dreams dashed into a million pieces.

There came a Saturday late in October when she spent the day at the house helping him rake leaves, and later that afternoon, about four while sitting in the kitchen enjoying a mug of hot cider she said, "Morris do you want to be intimate with me?"

"Yes."

"You've never kissed me or even hinted at such a thing. Have I once again misunderstood and misread the situation? Is it me?"

"Annie, we were total strangers. We had no history. When I learned about what happened in your marriage and afterward, I knew you'd need time to get to know me before you could trust me. I wanted you to feel comfortable about giving a relationship with me a go, and I'm stuck Annie, I'm in love with you. I know after Don and your subsequent dating experiences you were, to put it mildly, more than disenchanted with men. So, I didn't want to rush anything. You've had more than your share of male disappointments."

"Morris you've been the most gentlemanly gentleman I've ever encountered.

"Am I being too gentlemanly?"

"Unless I'm dead wrong Morris, I feel you care about me a lot, and I just heard you say you love me. I'm not very experienced about this, but at some point, I was sure such feelings would lead to intimacy. Have you not asked because you know I was repeatedly forced and you don't know how to go about loving me? Do you think I wouldn't want to?"

"Geez Annie. Why would you think something like that?"

"Because I would if I were you."

"Okay, it's a concern. I very much want to hold you and kiss you. And yes, I do very much want to make love to you, but it means we'd be doing the same kinds of physical things as when you were married. I don't know how to even begin."

"You could've asked.

"I was afraid I'd scare you off and never see you again."

"Morris we've been seeing each other almost every day for over two months. The three guys I dated after Don had their hands all over me on the second date. All three tried for all they were worth to get me in bed. They'd say things like you've been married why wouldn't you want to enjoy yourself."

"And how did you tell me you dealt with that?"

"I told you sex was never enjoyable, and I didn't want to have sex with those men or anyone else. Just the thought of being used that way upset me to the point I gave up on dating and moved here."

"Annie, you told me you didn't want to be intimate with anyone. I understand why. I wanted you to get to know me and for me to know you without all that steamy stuff getting in the way."

"Have we?"

"Yes, and having the opportunity to just get to know each other was a good thing, an excellent thing. It gave us a chance. I think you're a lovely, intelligent, gorgeous, amazing woman, and I'm in love with you. I believe the feelings mutual. The first night I met you at Professor Atkins's dinner party I was totally enamored with you. That kind of thing just doesn't happen."

"Surely, you've met women who interested you, Morris?"

"A few, but no one like you Annie, you were vivacious, lovely, obviously smart, and enchanting. So much so I wanted to just up and ask you to come home with me. So, knowing how attracted to you I was from the moment I first met you, I was reluctant to let my lusty heart grab the reins and start at a gallop.

"After learning of all, you went through I'm very pleased I made that choice. I thought getting to know me without being pressured with intimacy was the only way you'd ever feel safe. I guess I was hoping at some point we'd maybe do a little hugging and kissing and if it got awkward, we'd talk it through."

"You know I felt the same way about you Morris and right from our first walk. I appreciate not being pushed, but it's time; we're way past a little hugging and kissing. We need to move this along. I need to stay the night."

"Annie is it really okay with you?

She nodded, and he said, "Annie I couldn't think of anything nicer. Just tell me you're sure."

"I'm sure Morris, but I need to go home and grab a few things."

"Come back about six-thirty, I'll fix us dinner and sometime Sunday morning I'll serve you breakfast. Oh, and bring a toothbrush and your pajamas."

Smiling she said, "Morris I sleep in my birthday suit."

"Of course, you do. But in the morning, try to remember the three young men living upstairs will be prowling about the kitchen. I don't want you giving them a heart attack."

"I don't think that's what I'd be giving them.

"We don't want any of that either."

Morris met Annie at the door hung her coat in the closet took her in his arms and kissed her. They spent several moments in the entryway kissing. They didn't break until Anthony, one of his graduate student roomers, pushed open the front door. Scooting past them heading for the stairs, he said, "How's everything, Annie?"

"Terrific Tony, great."

"Glad to hear it."

***

Later lying next to one another naked under the covers Morris said, "Is there anything I should know."

"I might need some lubricant. I put some in the top drawer of the nightstand on your side. And Morris, please don't get all worked up about trying to make this the greatest ever?"

"Can I at least give it a shot?"

"I guess so, as long as it doesn't hurt too much."

"Geez, Annie, I thought you told me pain has no part in making love.

"Morris, sometimes you amaze me."

"What I'd do now?"

"Sometimes you act so naive; you've got to know there's such a thing as rough sex. I was told by my girlfriends there are lots of guys who do it that way."

"Geez, Annie I thought that would be the last. Is that what you're expecting?"

"Oh, God No! Heavens no."

"Why did you think for me to make our first time the greatest it would hurt or be rough? I'm serious Annie how does me hurting you work in your head with us making love?"

"I think I know you Morris, but I've no idea what you'll do or what this might be like. I'm the woman, the receptive, you're going to touch me and do things, and I've no idea what it will be like."

"Annie, we don't have to do anything. Honest to God I'll be happy holding you."

"Morris, I want to make love, but just the thought of being hurt scares me to death."

"Annie, I won't hurt you."

"I don't believe you would, but Morris you look like one of those men who's been with lots of women. You're handsome; and graceful, likable and athletic. There's no fat on you, you're strong, and you come across as sensual. I've no idea what to expect."

"Annie, what's going on? You must know by now what kind of person I am. The last thing I'd ever do is hurt you."

"Morris we've never kissed until today let alone gone all the way. I've been told some men like it rough, or they don't know any other way. It's how they have sex."

"Annie, quit it. Just stop talking."

"I was married Morris, but I have no other experience. I think none of the sex Don and I had was normal and I've no idea what normal is or what this will be like. But being roughed up or hurt will be the end. I want that clear."

"You could've said it straight out.

"I just did.

"Annie, I know you're scared. What can I do to reassure you? How about you take a hot bath and I give you a nice gentle, back rub? Would that help?"

"Morris, right now I don't think either would help. I've been raised to be agreeable and accepting. That included being submissive to my husband, but I can't talk about this. I don't know how." She paused and said, "Could we start over? I want to be with you, and I'm doing my best not to be afraid.

"Sorry," he said, "I let us dig a hole and fall in. I've kind of lost the mood. Maybe if we backed up and just snuggled and kissed for a while, we'd both be able to relax?"

"Morris you're such a liar. You're as hard as a rock." She rolled half on him kissing him and said, "Don't tell me you're worried about being compared to my former husband?"

"A little, will you be grading this professor?"

"What about you Morris, who're you going to be comparing me to?"

"I'll try not to, but I will. So, will you? We've both been with other people it's unavoidable."

"Stop talking Morris and don't explain or ask any more questions. Please, just hush up and make love. I'll not be thinking of anyone else and neither will you. Besides, if we don't get it right, I'm willing to work on it."

TWENTY FIVE

After ten weeks of walking dates, thousands of words, five dinners, seven nights of gentle, careful, loving sexual trials and tribulations, all of it capped by several soul-searching discussions Annie moved in. They'd been living together for about three weeks, and at the end of fall quarter, she asked him to come home with her for Christmas and meet her family.

Annie was his everything and Morris was beginning to feel her out about how long and what would need to take place between them for her to say yes to a second marriage. She acknowledged she felt both loved and safe. But she reminded him, "This isn't the same Morris, but my first marriage started out pretty much this way. I've got to be sure this time, absolutely, positively sure."

After their first night of lovemaking, Morris knew sex with Annie would take all the kindness, gentleness, and patience he could muster. Within minutes of their first time, Morris knew the sum of Annie's sexual knowledge and experiences was at the hands of a person who was misguided, misused sex, and was likely severely disturbed.

Morris was surprised someone as well read, intelligent, and educated as Annie didn't have grave concerns about what was taking place in her marriage. He thought she would've at the least asked a more experienced friend if what was happening was even close to normal. Morris quickly came to understand as Don's wife Annie didn't believe she had any right to question her husband's sexual practices.

She came to Don unaware, unknowing, and willing to accept. Before being initiated Annie, both believed and welcomed the notion sex between a husband and wife would be a thing of joy. When it turned out not to be Annie quietly, unquestioningly accepted it.

Annie's and Morris's first time was quite the learning experience for both. Fortunately, they talked. She was surprised at how much time Morris devoted to stroking, touching, and kissing her. She was even more surprised, but delighted, when he caressed her nipples with his mouth and tongue. Annie told him Don never did anything like that, but she welcomed it and thought it immensely pleasurable.

But when Morris worked his head between her thighs, she pushed him away shocked. She couldn't believe he would use his mouth down there. Morris stopped and explained it was a gratifying activity, particularly pleasurable for the woman, Annie said, "I've heard of it, but I couldn't imagine it. But she let him. Later she told him even though she thought it shocking she enjoyed it.

As their relationship progressed, Morris learned Annie's sex life was awkward and joyless from the beginning. Don did nothing lightly. He never kissed or caressed her gently. Sex for Don was all about using his hands and fingers too, probe, and stretch and to tug on her breasts and nipples. From the start sex with Don was more like an uncomfortable medical exam than anything most people would think of as sex with a person you love

Don was a big man and easily controlled Annie. He could toss her around and did. Sex became an unwelcome, unwanted, very unpleasant part of her marriage. But she was continually told being available for her husband's sexual need was her sacred duty. Their intimate relations devolved into a dark, painful, and degrading thing. It was something she wanted nothing to do with and yet was continuously required to do so. She tried her best to get through it.

Not knowing and only able to guess about her feelings about sex with him. Morris did his best to take his time and make sure she was comfortable with everything. He talked with her about it hoping to gauge her response to what she was experiencing. It was a delicate undertaking. Too much talking killed both the spontaneity and the moment. He knew Annie was struggling to accept lovemaking as a natural, healthy, and enjoyable loving activity.

She was a willing, wonderful responsive kisser, and seemed to grow to be comfortable with him sexually. Morris was careful about where and how he touched her or even about moving quickly. He knew Annie was struggling with the ugliness of her earlier sexual experiences. But he found Annie to be sincere, willing, reciprocal, and most of all she always made him feel welcome. She was that way in their everyday walking around life and in their bed.

Morris believed Annie was enjoying her sex life with him. She came to him an easy, pleasant, and ever so comfortable lover. Far more important to Morris than having the joy he experienced with Hanna was the sense of completion Annie brought to his life

Their reasons for living together had been thoroughly discussed. It was Annie's only viable path to certainty; it had to be this way. She was not about to get trapped in another untenable, unlivable marriage. Morris didn't fight it. He knew this was the only way she'd ever come to trust him. Far more important to Morris than the overwhelming sexual joy he experienced with Hanna was the unbelievable goodness and well-being Annie brought into his life.

Annie helped him be a better person in every way and thing he did. He didn't understand how it worked or how she did it, but he found this ability of hers to be the most remarkable thing about her. She wanted children, to be a family, and so did he. They shared an impressive number of likes and dislikes. Their cares and concerns matched. Just being around her brought him joy and made his life so much more pleasurable. She was a mystery and a wonder and everything he ever hoped for.

His three graduate students couldn't get enough of her. Annie was their combination big sister, friend, professor and mother. Within a few days of moving in Annie laid down the law bringing order to their lives and the household. She made them accountable for keeping the kitchen shipshape, their rooms neat; the bathrooms clean, and themselves trimmed and tidy.

Annie managed this in such a way her gentlemen, as she called them, just wanted to hug her. But Annie wasn't any old cook and bottle washer. Using her unusual, appealing, and all-encompassing way they joined her. They gladly and willingly participated in preparing the dinners and the cleanup. Dinner became a much looked forward to pleasurable time for everyone in the house. She had such an enjoyable fun way of making the whole thing a pleasant, easy thing to do the household soon became a family.

A few days before the campus shut down for the Christmas holidays Morris sitting in John's office was talking to him about their planned trip to Philadelphia and his concerns about staying with Annie's family. John smiled and said, "There's an old saying Morris, visiting with relatives is the art of mastering both surprise and disappointment." Morris wasn't disappointed, but the visit became one surprise after another. Their stay wasn't in any way a culminating success. The family's rules of right and wrong along with the heavy hand of moral correctness surfaced almost the moment they cleared the doorway.

Morris learned upon arriving Annie's family came from a long line of Quakers including William Penn himself. The family lived in Chestnut Hill in what appeared to him to be close to a Mansion built in the latter part of the last century. "Completed in 1884," Mrs. Taylor told him. "My grandfather built it, and forty-nine years ago, I was born in the room you're staying in."

Other than describing her relationship with her parents and them as pleasant, loving, and straight-forward, Annie hadn't spoken at any length about her family. The only thing Annie made a point of telling him was her parents believed in the importance of education. She said they were supportive, providing help, money, and encouragement.

She told him her parents were modest and conservative about most things, but also liberal and accepting about most social issues. Morris made one too many assumptions when he took their liberalism to mean they backed the civil rights movement. Supported the anti-war movement and he assumed they acknowledged the unprecedented, sexual revolution, and were in favor of the burgeoning women's rights movement.

At different times Annie gave Morris brief descriptions of her three brothers and three sisters who were all younger than her. She told him it was a disciplined, but warm, and loving house. With seven children, it had to be. Annie expressed her feelings of gratitude about growing up in a home with parents and brothers and sisters who were all lovingly wonderful but, each in their own individual way at times annoyingly different. Morris's take on her family was it sounded as if it were pretty much a larger version of his.

Her father and youngest brother met them at the airport. While Annie went about greeting them and introducing her father, Morris couldn't help, but notice the youngster next to him anxiously waiting his turn to speak. Obadiah Taylor was eleven, polite, but insistently inquisitive. When he got his chance, he threw questions at Morris one after another, "Was the airplane you came in a jet? How many engines did it have?"

"Yes, it was a 707. It had four engines."

"Can you hear the engines inside the plane? Are they loud? Do you really write school books? How do you know what to write? Are you my sister's boyfriend?"

Dad reined him in at the boyfriend question saying, "Obadiah, Professor Morris and Annie had to get up early. I'm sure they're tired from the trip. There'll be plenty of time for questions once they're settled in at the house."

When they arrived at the house, there wasn't a nice neat proper line of children. It was a great cluster of bodies all waiting in the warmth of the spacious foyer to greet Annie and meet her friend. Once through the door, Morris and Annie put their bags down and were instantly engulfed. Annie was surrounded. Watching Annie being welcomed while he was simultaneously being introduced left Morris hopelessly trying to keep up and put names with faces.

Her dad grabbed one of their bags and said, "Come along Morris I'll show thee to your room." Using thee in place of you was a practice Morris hadn't heard since he left New Jersey. Morris knew the second he heard it he was in a Quaker household. He'd suspected as much when he first heard Obadiah's name.

The two of them went upstairs leaving all that joyous noise trailing off behind. Walking down a wide hall, one ample enough to be more in keeping with a hotel, Morris couldn't help but be impressed with the style Annie grew up in. It was a lovely imposing grand old house. Simple in its day it was now craftsmanship preserved.

Mr. Taylor pushed through a door saying, "This is the guest room it has its own bath. You'll have your privacy, and I apologize, Morris, if what I'm about to say makes thee uncomfortable. But Mrs. Taylor and I can't have you and Annie rooming together, so this is where you'll be. Annie has three younger sisters. I'm trying my best to discourage them from thinking living with a man unmarried is acceptable, or that such a thing would ever be condoned by us."

The sudden revelation of the strength of his disapproval was like a glass of ice water right to the face. Morris felt denigrated, shamed, and altogether in the wrong place. He almost blurted out; do you not want me here, should I leave? Morris feeling not only reprimanded, but also the awkwardness of the man having to say this to him tried to ease the tension. Morris said, "We better switch bags, Annie won't look good in my clothes."

As Mr. Taylor took the proffered bag, Morris saw a hint of a smile cross his face. When Nathan turned to leave Morris said, "Mr. Taylor I care a great deal about your daughter. We're working hard to change our status to get to a marriage. But given what Annie's been through she's being cautious. She wants to be confident about the relationship, but mostly sure about me."

Nathan Taylor said nothing barely nodding, but at least the nod acknowledged he'd heard his words. Morris continued, "Annie said nothing about it, but I was expecting to be bunking with one of her brothers, so thank you. This is a lovely room."

"Get unpacked Morris, freshen up if you need to and come downstairs and meet the family. I'll put on a pot of coffee."

When Morris came into the family room, everyone stopped talking. They all turned and looked at him. Aware of being the item of the day and feeling unsure and awkward after learning their living together was a big problem for her parents. Morris considered the silent staring faces and said, "What? Oh my! Don't tell me I forget my pants."

There were giggles both male and female then silence. Annie broke it asking, "Are we all settled?"

"I am I'm in the guest room. Your dad took care of your bag. I don't know where you are."

He could tell from the sudden apprehensive look on Annie's face she was concerned about what might have transpired between her father and Morris. She knew she left Morris completely unaware of how much her parents disapproved of her living with him. She knew full well she'd been much too blasé, saying to him when he asked, "Don't worry, they'll love you."

Now she wished more than anything she'd been forthcoming and talked about this with him. During her last phone call home, her mother made her feelings crystal clear, saying, "Of course we want you here. We want to meet Morris. Don't worry Annie your professor friend, will be treated respectfully, but I want this understood Annie. Under no circumstance will you be rooming together while you're here. We would never allow such a thing. It would be the same as giving our approval to what you're doing.

"You know how we feel about your living with a man outside of marriage. It's wrong Annie, and you know better." Annie was sick to her stomach about doing this to him. But she was so afraid if Morris suspected her parents were that disapproving of her living with him he would've never come. She kept looking at Morris trying to determine if he was upset.

Morris was almost impossible to read, and she got nothing. He had a charming little boy smile which endeared him to nearly everyone, but he didn't wear his emotions on his sleeve. Morris kept them close and never looked perturbed. She also knew Morris would not let her get away with this. He worked hard with her encouraging her to be straightforward about her feelings, especially the difficult things. Those powerful hard to acknowledge one's wrapped around money, sex, and what she most wanted or feared.

Annie found it difficult, sometimes impossible to talk about some of these things. However, she recognized by not doing so she'd put him in an incredibly awkward position. Having Morris come here to meet her parents and family was one of the biggest kinds of those things. In hindsight, she knew both her parents had reservations about Don before they married. They never voiced them, but she knew by the way her dad behaved when he was around Don he questioned something about the man.

But she ignored her father's unvoiced trepidation. She also remembered how vehemently they rejected her wanting to move in with Don before the marriage. Here she was, against their wishes, living with a man they never met and knew nothing of.

Annie wanted more than anything for her parents to like and be comfortable with Morris. She knew as much as she could allow herself she was in love with him. Annie wanted to let herself once again believe she could have it all. Annie wanted the things she grew up with; a loving enduring marriage, stability, a home, and children. So far, she had no reservations about Morris, well a tiny one. His eyes lit up whenever he talked about his high school family friend in New York. Annie never said anything or asked about her, but she suspected there was more to Hanna Williston than he let on.

Morris thought Annie's assessment of her brothers and sisters was accurate to a fault. Each was unique in their individual way, and as Morris was introduced to them, he quickly got them identified in his mind. Annie was the oldest at twenty-seven, a graduate of Bryn Mawr and the University of Pennsylvania where she earned a Ph.D. in Social Anthropology. Franklin was twenty-four a graduate of Princeton and now in his second year of graduate school. He was in a master's program in economics at Princeton. Not as tall as his father he was a friendly earnest young man.

Teresa twenty-one, in her senior year at Bryn Mawr, and already accepted into medical school at Columbia was a little too precise. All that precision made her come across as prickly, and it made Morris wonder what she might be like to live with. Hester eighteen, in her freshman year at Bryn Mawr, was an exact duplicate of Annie. They could've been identical twins. The only noticeable physical difference was Annie's being a little taller. He thought, thank God, their voices were unmistakably different. He was puzzled why Annie neglected to tell him they were so alike they were continually mistaken for one another.

Pearce sixteen and a junior in high school looked like a younger version of his father. He played lacrosse and was both sweet and trying his best to be a sincerely considerate young man. Temperance at thirteen was an amazing copy of her mother. She was both precocious and bold. Obadiah the youngest was a curious, delightfully earnest young man.

Her Father, Nathan, a tall man, was somewhere around fifty, He was genuine, but serious. He seemed a thoughtful, protective man and had a gentle kindly appearing face. Morris hoped this was the case. He was a banker and quite a tall imposing, but approachable appearing figure. It wasn't apparent until he used it, but Annie's father possessed quite the welcoming smile. Annie's mother Constance, Connie, was forty-nine, petite and a lovely woman. Like Annie, she had an extraordinarily gracious childlike smile.

Connie was to Morris a surprisingly well put together warm, friendly woman. She ran the household firmly, but graciously and with her years of experience an ease and effortlessness. He understood where Annie gleaned her expertise and remarkable manner over household matters.

TWENTY SIX

Teresa and Hester shooed Temperance off the sofa to make room between them for Morris. Thirteen-year-old Temperance not to be so easily excluded pulled the armchair across from them closer and sat. Having surrounded him, they all at the same time threw half a dozen questions at Morris. "What's it like to be famous for writing a best-selling book? How did you meet my sister? Did it take long to write it? Do you enjoy being a professor? Is it hard work? What subjects do you teach?"

After the initial onslaught Temperance, the most vocal questioner with eyes wide asked, "Did Annie tell you her real name? Did you know Annie was a great tennis player in high school? At the state finals, even though she was having an awful monthly and was sick with the flu, she still came in second."

Connie smiling enjoying the opportunity to see Morris deal with her daughter's onslaught, said, "Enough ladies. For goodness sakes, give him a chance and Temperance you know better than to talk out of turn about your brothers and sister's personal lives."

"But she did mom. Even though everyone could plain see she was sick, she almost won."

Smiling at them Morris said, "Ladies. I wrote a novel. It took five months, and people liked it. But I'm not famous, and

I don't want to be. Annie and I first met at one of Professor Atkins's annual fall faculty introductory dinner parties. I teach humanities, undergraduate courses on the Renaissance period and graduate courses on language how it's used and how people interpret and misinterpret it. I love teaching, and yes, it's sometimes hard. But it's also a great pleasure. Annie told me she played tennis in high school, but I didn't know she almost won the state championship. I also didn't know Annie wasn't her name. Did I answer everything?"

"It's Annabelle." Temperance blurted out.

"Like yours Temperance, Annabelle's a lovely name, but I prefer Annie even more."

Mrs. Taylor said, "Annabelle was Nathan's mother's name. Annie was our first."

Mr. Taylor rescued him saying, "Morris let's get thee that cup of coffee I promised." Franklin, the oldest boy, tagged along saying, "I could use one too."

***

It was a big kitchen, and Morris noted it had been renovated more than once. The three double-hung windows above the sinks were large and looked out onto a spacious backyard. Despite the snow, Morris could make out the gardens and a series of thirty-foot spruce trees seventy yards away at the far end of the yard.

In the middle of the kitchen was a large center unit about six by nine feet. It was the focal point of the room. There were ten stools stationed around it. This was a gracious home. More significant than the one he lived in on Lake Minnetonka, but it had the same old-world workmanship and character. He pulled out a stool and sat at the end of the long side of the big center unit with the sink and windows to his left. Franklin sat across from him, and Mr. Taylor poured three cups of coffee and put out three spoons a creamer and sugar bowl.

Franklin said, "When you write a novel do you plan the whole of it out before you start? How do you go about it? I'd like to understand how you organize that kind of writing."

Mrs. Taylor came in with Teresa and Hester and before Morris could answer Franklin Connie said to her husband, "Nathan you can't just whisk Morris away like that. We've all got questions for him."

Franklin said, "Not to be selfish, but how about if we let Morris finish mine?"

"Franklin trying to explain how I organized the novel will be difficult. It was an intuitive process, not a logical one. The story came intact, full-blown. I arranged the book more by my feelings toward the main characters and their lives than anything approaching a formal plan.

"I'll think it through and come back to you and try to explain it. On a simple level, I organized the book around their teaching careers. I broke it into their lives before the deaths of their children and what happened after. Albert and Marion taught somewhere around twenty-five thousand undergraduate students. I've no idea how many hundreds of graduate and doctoral students they counseled, guided, mentored and supported. But I included sections using specific incidents to show their kindness and their overriding care and concern for their students.

"Also included were sections organized around the lives of their children. Those sections conveyed how impressive, accomplished, and courageous all three of the children were. The last part of the book spoke to Albert and Marion's lives just before their deaths, and those themes all centered on showing how Marion and Albert in the face of overwhelming loss never faltered. They continued right up to their deaths to lead lives of loving service dedicated to the university, to their students, to each other, and to enhancing academic knowledge.

"They were modest, gracious and remarkable right to the end. I felt blessed to have the pleasure of knowing and helping

Albert and Marion at the end of their lives. They were the most genuine, loveliest people I've ever met. I will consider myself very fortunate to live a life as full of loving care and dedication as Marion and Albert Hendry did."

The kitchen was alive with voices coming at him from everywhere. Morris wasn't used to the sounds of so many conversations going on all at once. It was loud, all mixed, He tuned it out and drifted off staring out the window at the snow-covered backyard.

He was thinking of being at Marion's bedside with Albert, John, and Dee as Marion slipped away. Morris kept looking across at Albert trying to understand what this could be like for him. Four months later there was a morning call from John. He told Morris Albert played bridge with his friends last night, was his usual charming self, and went off to bed and died in his sleep.

Morris remembered sitting at the kitchen table by himself and realizing Albert died from a broken heart. He'd lost all his children, he lost Marion, and he had no one left to love or love him. He was alone, and without Marion to pull him back, Albert succumbed. And alone in that morning quiet Morris remembered crying his own heart out for the end of Marion and Albert and their three long-dead children. They had become his family and their end hit him hard.

Slipping back to the present, seeing everyone looking at him, Morris, with eyes full of water, turned away from them toward the windows. Wiping his watery eyes, he said, "Sorry, every time I think of sitting with Albert watching Marion slipping away it gets me."

Connie said, "I read your book Morris, and I agree. I enjoyed knowing them and reading about their lives." Handing him a box of tissues she said, "And just like you, it brought me to tears."

Franklin asked, "But how did you write that story? You only knew them for a few months. You never knew their children; they died when you were a baby. Did you make it all up?"

Trying to get back to normal and deal with his present circumstances Morris said, "I cleaned out their house. The upstairs study closet was full of the children's awards, papers, trophies, camping equipment, sports paraphernalia and letters. By the time I finished, I had a solid understanding of their lives and their accomplishments.

"I've never known or met anyone like Marion and Albert; I was with them at the end. Their children were long dead. No hope of their work, or principled goodness, or of all their loving, caring kindness being passed on. None of the children married, there were no grandchildren. Their working lives were over. One afternoon Albert rather bluntly said. It all ends here, with us.

"I jotted down some immediate remembrances and began writing their story. It went where it needed to. All I was trying to do was get across the enormity of Albert's words. He said, Morris all we've tried to do ends here with us. When we sell our home, and we're not able to come back, this life, our lives will be no more. I've no idea what that will be like or how we'll manage it."

Breaking the sudden quiet Mr. Taylor asked, "Morris has Annie told you how we celebrate Christmas?"

"No sir, she said I won't need to worry about presents. She told me Christmas was a special time for her and got better and better as the family grew in numbers."

"Being Quakers, as in everything, we keep Christmas simple. We don't give traditional gifts. We each draw a name from a hat and find some quiet time and write how that person affects us and what that person means to us. Christmas morning, we bring our missives and draw from the hat, numbers this time, to determine the order of the readings. We gather in front of the tree and read them out loud. At noon, it's off to meeting and later around four; we all sit down to Christmas dinner. We do the same at Thanksgiving, but we change it up a little and write about what we're thankful for. If you're willing Morris, we'd like thee to take part."

"I'd like to, but I think I would be hard-pressed to be anything more than superficial writing about any of you."

Smiling, Mrs. Taylor asked, "How about Annie? Could you write about Annie?"

"I'd stand a chance at that?"

Mr. Taylor said, "Good, it's settled. Morris writes about Annie and Annie will write something about Morris."

Theresa Said, "Boy oh boy will this ever be interesting."

"Why's that," Morris asked.

Hester jumped in saying, "You have no history. You don't know the kinds of things we say about each other or how we say them or anything. We've all grown up doing it. You have no context to draw on."

"I'll come up with something and hope it fits in with everyone else's efforts."

"Well it should," Theresa said, "After all you've written two important textbooks and a best seller. We know you know of Annie. But I don't know what you could say that would be very nice. We all know Annie's living with you. The whole family knows you're living and sinning together.

There was absolute quiet. Not a breath was heard although several deep ones were taken. Learning the whole family knew and disapproved of their living together was a shock.

Franklin said, "For crying out loud Theresa we're home for the holidays. Did you really need to throw that into the middle of Christmas?"

Theresa said, "Sorry, but everybody in the house knows, and it's a huge problem. Even Temperance and Obadiah know of their sinning."

Connie said, "Ladies, be it good or bad, right or wrong, we've talked many times about talking out of turn about each other's personal lives. Annie knows our feelings on the matter; I've made them clear."

Teresa said, "Why are they here? If I did what Annie's doing, you wouldn't allow me back in the house. I'd be banned, and you know it.

Hester chimed in, "She's right mom. You and dad would never get over either of us doing something like that. I'd be so ashamed I wouldn't be able to face you or anyone else here."

Theresa said, "Annie's parading around here like it's okay, like she's doing nothing wrong."

Mr. Taylor said, "Theresa, that's enough! Annie's private life is not our business.

Angry Theresa said, "But they're not married!"

Hester said, "She's our sister. It doesn't matter if she lives far away the shame of it's on all of us."

Nathan raising his voice said, "Enough! You both know better! Your mother and I invited Morris, he's our guest. I know Annie's behavior is shocking and disgraceful to you, but this is rude. It's not the time or place. I'm surprised at you both. Especially the way you've brought this up."

Mrs. Taylor said, "Teresa, Hester and you too Franklin you know full well your father and I believe the actions we choose gives direct evidence of our soul's condition. Our bodies contain the Light, it's part of you, and given to every one of us by God. Annie's your sister and is part of God. She's entitled to our patience and our forgiveness."

"Mom!" Theresa was angry, "What Annie's doing is appalling! You've taught us all our lives having part of Him in us means we're bound to honor his loving gift by not misusing our bodies. You've said it hundreds of times."

Hester said, "I know it by heart. All the other sins a person commits are outside their body, but whoever sins sexually, sins against their own body, their inner light. Being chaste is the only way to keep our soul safe."

Nathan said, "Nothing's changed. We believe living together outside of marriage is wrong. There's no commitment, and no promises made freely and sanctified by God. If there are children from such a union, they're at risk. At any time either party can discard the other."

Connie said, "Teresa, Hester, and you to Franklin, all my children, I will love thee no matter what you do until the day I die. But I will appreciate thee much more if you abide by my words."

Standing behind his stool, Morris appeared calm, but was undone. Her sisters had held back nothing. Never in his life had Morris felt more hopeless or unwelcome. He wondered to no avail what could ever make his being here right and to his dismay, he knew nothing would.

Mr. Taylor said, "Annie's in a different situation than any of you. She married. She kept her vows, but her husband didn't. Annie divorced, and it broke her heart. I don't believe living with Morris is the proper thing for her to be doing for her or Morris and I don't condone it. But I accept it. With forgiveness, we all need to." There was silence in the room the six of them and Mr. Taylor himself all thinking, good lord! Now what

TWENTY SEVEN

It didn't matter all that much how he was informed Morris saw it for what it was. He was in a gigantic, unredeemable situation. He had never been in a predicament like this. It sickened him, and there was nothing Morris could say or do. Morris was repugnant to these people. He couldn't be here. The only thing left was to go. He looked at his watch and said, "Excuse me; I need to take care of some things."

He left the kitchen going through the family room past Annie, Pierce, Obadiah, and Temperance, across the living room and up the stairs. He made three phone calls, threw his things into his bag, and wrote a note. Twenty minutes later Morris came down the stairs and without a word to anyone, took his overcoat from the hall closet, and went out the front door. Morris walked to the end of the drive and waited in the snow and cold for the cab.

Pierce seeing Morris from the living room standing at the end of the drive returned to the family room and said to Annie, "Where's Morris going?"

"Going? What are you talking about?"

"He's standing at the end of the drive with his bag."

Annie ran into the living room just in time to see a cab drive off. She went into the kitchen. "What happened with Morris?"

Mom and dad, Franklin, Hester, and Teresa all looked at one another. Hester said "Why? He said excuse me I need to take care of some things and left."

"And he wasn't upset?"

Teresa said, "He didn't look upset."

Hester said, "Why? Has he said something?"

Annie said, "No, but something happened he left."

Connie said, "Teresa said something about you living with Morris and Hester, they both voiced their shock over your doing such a thing."

Annie said, "That's my business, not yours. I don't care how wrong-headed you think I am. It's my choice. If you think I'm wrong say it to me, not to Morris."

Teresa blurted out, "But you're not married!"

At the same moment, Hester said, "It's a mortal sin, Annie!"

Annie said, "How've you come to think I don't know what I'm doing?" They stood in a silence of a hundred unsaid things looking at one another. With tears streaming down her face Annie said, "Next to Dad Morris is the kindest most loving man I've ever known. And you've made sure he knows because we're living together he's not welcome here. I guess I'm not either." Annie ran to the guest room to see if Morris left a note:

"Sorry Annie, but I had to leave. I was just made aware your whole family knows and believes by living together we are committing the worst most shameful, mortal sin imaginable. You should've told me how strongly your family disapproved of our living together. I would've been more prepared. We know why we're living together, but no one in your family knows why.

Your sisters are ashamed of us. None of them knows what happened in your marriage. There's precious little room if any for understanding your demons even less for how you've chosen to overcome them. We've been judged and harshly. I don't see what could ever make me acceptable or our living together forgivable.

I tried to catch a flight home, but there isn't a seat available. I'll get a room at one of the downtown hotels. I've left your ticket on the bed. Put it somewhere safe. I'll meet you Sunday at the airport for the flight back. Once I get a room, I'll call and let you know where I'm staying.

Annie, I didn't expect your mom and dad to approve of our living together any more than my parents did, nor did I expect to be rooming with you. But I thought like my parents, knowing we're both adults, they would voice their concerns to us in private. I hoped through a conversation they would come to see why we're doing this. When I learned all your brothers and sisters knew we are living together and saw how shocked, ashamed, and disapproving Hester and Teresa where I no longer felt I should stay.

I know how important your family is to you. I understand being without your family's love and support will add an enormous burden to what you're struggling with. You're everything Annie, all I'll ever need or want. I love you, and I hope you can enjoy Christmas with your family. I'm not walking away from you or giving up. But I'll be damned if I'll put up with anyone who throws dirt, guilt, shame, or anything like that on you or our relationship. I'd never be able to keep quiet.

That said if you feel the best thing for you is to end our relationship I promise I'll do my best to accept your decision. However, if like me you want to see this through, we have a mess on our hands. The deed is done and can't be taken back. Maybe, with me not there as a reminder, your family will accept you sins and all. I hope they'll forgive you; however, the real question is whether you can accept being judged immoral?

I can't, and I won't. I love you with all my heart and soul and every good thing in me. God above Annie I want us to marry *and love each other for the rest of our lives. I would give up everything I have including my life before I'd ever do anything to hurt you. When we get home, we can talk about our options, and if there's a way to rectify this. We have our work cut out for us.*

Love you, Morris

Annie went downstairs and approached her mother saying. "Mom I want you to read this, and you should know I tricked Morris into coming here. I never told him we were Quakers or how opposed you and Dad were to our living together." Annie biting her lower lip while she watched her mother read Morris's letter could barely allow her to finish before jumping in. "I didn't tell him we were Quakers or how opposed to us living together you were because I didn't believe he'd come. I didn't know the whole family knew. Mom, I wanted my family to meet and get to know the man I hope to marry.

"I knew you were upset about us living together, but you told me you wanted to meet him. You said Morris would be welcome and treated respectfully. I don't know what happened or what was said, but he doesn't feel welcome here. And I'm sorry mom, but if Morris doesn't, neither do I. I'm not about to leave him stuck here alone in Philadelphia over Christmas. When I know where he's staying I'm leaving to be with him and Mom, I'm not coming back."

"Annie I'm just as sorry as I can be about this. Neither I nor your father, neither of us meant for anything like this to happen."

"But it has mom, and it's a horrible thing. To be estranged from my family is just the most awful feeling. It's the last thing I ever expected could happen."

"Annie when Morris calls I'd like to speak with him."

"Mom, what can you say that will ever make this right?"

"I don't know, but I need to try. I like Morris, and I love you. God above Annie you're my first born I love you more than life itself. I can't let this stand."

***

"Morris its Connie, may I speak with thee, is that acceptable?"

"Yes Ma'am."

"I need to apologize for what happened in the kitchen. I told Annie Mr. Taylor, and I wanted to meet you and would be pleased to have you with us for Christmas. Knowing my feelings about your living together Annie was concerned about how you might be received by us. I assured her you were welcome and would be treated respectfully. We've failed thee. I can't take back what was said. It's two days before Christmas, and I know how hard this will be for thee. But Morris it would be the nicest gift you could give me if you can find it in your heart to stay with us as planned."

"Mrs. Taylor, I love your daughter, but learning the whole family believes we're unprincipled, immoral libertines was devastating. None of you know why we've chosen to live together, but it's because of what happened in her marriage. It left her fearful of ever being able to trust in herself or another man. It's taken every ounce of courage she has to try again."

"Morris, I know what I'm asking and how hard it will be. I've grown fond of you, and I love Annie more than you can know, I'm pleading with you to return. I won't have my family torn apart over this, not when I know you love each other and hope to marry. You not being with us is just plain wrong. Try to find it in your heart to overcome our words and put aside your feelings and stay with us?"

There was silence on Morris's end. Afraid, hurt, and overwhelmed, Morris wanted to lash out, to hurt back. To scream, fuck you! Fuck all you self-righteous prigs! Knowing if he were to have a life with Annie such a thing would be the last straw, Morris swallowed his anger. He knew the Taylors were good people. Did not his mother question the wisdom of their living together? Morris said, "Thank you for reaffirming your invitation Mrs. Taylor and please, let Annie know I'll be back in the morning."

Morris Arrived about ten and spent most of the day in his room writing his Christmas missive. Dinner that night was subdued except for Pierce, Temperance and Obadiah none of whom had any knowledge of what had occurred. The three of them carried on asking questions about what kinds of things Morris did as a boy. Morris had fun with them telling them of some of his adventures as a youngster in New Jersey and with his grandparents in South Carolina.

His stories and misadventures had everyone in the family including Annie smiling if not laughing. After dinner, he tried to help with clearing the table and doing the dishes but was shooed away by the women. He gave Annie a kiss on the cheek and said he didn't sleep much last night and would be turning in early.

TWENTY EIGHT

By nine Christmas morning, the family was gathered in the living room preparing to draw from the hat. When Morris's turn came, he drew number one and could barely conceal his disappointment. He hoped to hear some of the other's efforts before reading his. Hiding his discomfort, he said, "This is about Annie, but it's also about us.

"I'm a full-fledged tenured university professor. Professors are all about words, ideas, and thoroughness so bear with me. Annie and I are living together, and our behavior is embarrassing and a major concern to all of you. Telling you why is essential. Hopefully, it will help you understand our situation.

"Despite being aware we're going against everything we've been taught about right and wrong and knowing our choice is in direct conflict with both yours and my family's values, we are living together. I met Annie at a faculty dinner party four months ago. I've never understood attraction or why it happens, but I was instantly drawn to Annie. She had this warm, friendly smile which I've since discovered is just like her mothers. I couldn't stop looking at her or listening to what she was saying. I'd never seen Annie before and knew nothing about her other than she was a new faculty member.

"As was standard for anyone new the people seated nearby spent the dinner finding out everything they could about her.

Among many other things Annie revealed, she was single, and I could see she wasn't wearing an engagement ring. I worked up my courage and asked if she might consider a date with a man she'd just met. Annie said I prefer to go for walks and talk. I asked her if she walked and talked alone or if she might consider having someone along to hear what she was saying?

"She smiled her mother's charming smile and encouraged I asked where and when her next walk was scheduled. I met her the following afternoon. For the next hour and a half, we walked and talked our way around the campus. I asked her if she would come to my house that night for dinner and she did. After the meal, we sat at the table and talked. Amazingly we trusted one another to what I now know was a remarkable degree.

"I learned Annie did her graduate work at Penn and her family and roots were in Philadelphia. I was curious how and why she was at Northwestern. She told me about wanting almost desperately to get a fresh start in a place where her personal history and status as a divorcee were not general knowledge. This elicited a string of questions on my part. Openly and honestly, Annie told me of her failed marriage and what it did to her spiritually, physically, and emotionally. Sitting there listening to her speak of it was one of the most amazing experiences I've ever had.

"Annie told me of openly and wholeheartedly making promises in front of her community, her family and God to share her heart, soul, and life with another. She did so with love expecting to be husband and wife for a lifetime. She never considered for a second such a commitment would or could end by anything other than death. For unknown reasons, the other half of their union did no such thing. Don chose instead to return her affection and commitment with unfaithfulness, practiced deceit, dishonesty, degradation, and ultimately barbarism. The opposite of what a loving God intended marriage to be.

"This left Annie trying to understand what was happening, what changed and worst of all, what she did to contribute to her situation. Not knowing about marriage outside of the family I grew up in and having no experience with a commitment until death do us part made in front of God and everybody, I said, for heaven's sake Annie why did you stay. Why didn't you leave? She gave me many practical and spiritual reasons for staying. The last one was the surprising one. She said, Morris, I loved him. I gave my word.

"Surprised, I said, after all that, you still loved him? She said I was sure right up to ending up in the hospital we could put it back the way it was in the beginning, that we could make everything right. I said do you still love him? Annie said, no and I don't understand what happened to it or where it went, but my love for him has gone from me

"Later while I was tidying up the kitchen and putting everything away after Annie left I spent the time thinking about Annie. About her love for Don, and what love was. I decided love was of the moment and then at that solemn moment of commitment in front of God and each other, it becomes forever.

"I marveled at the power of Annie's love. A love capable of withstanding all the emotional turmoil and heartbreak she was caught in. She didn't run. She stayed and hung on with everything she had to preserve the marriage. The whole time we were talking I kept looking at her wondering how she came to have such inner strength, such a commitment to the importance of her vows. Despite everything that was happening she maintained her belief in the ultimate good in people. As I came to know Annie, I wanted her to be part of my life under whatever circumstances she would be comfortable with.

"After Annie's deplorable experience in her marriage, I understood her caution and hesitancy about dating much less becoming involved with another man. She was understandably hesitant and cautious. We got to know each other over the next couple of months by walking and talking our way around the campus and through occasional dinners at my house.

"Annie's a remarkably capable and caring woman. I found myself wanting and willing to walk anywhere with her for a very long time. I discovered even after living through the heartbreak, pain, and dread of her first marriage Annie still possessed a charming sense of humor. She had unshakable faith things would come out right. Annie has the courage of a mother lion defending her cubs, and she's shown it through her willingness to try again with me. She's never lost her belief in the good in others, not even Don.

"You all know Annie, and I are living together. We are aware this came as a shock and an embarrassment to you. We know what we're doing flies in the face of both of our family's values and we acknowledge doing so has led to your embarrassment, indignation, and disappointment. Annie knows I want to marry and have a family. Annie also wants to marry and have a family. But after her unfortunate experiences in her marriage caution and prudence and the need to be sure of her judgments about what and who I am needs to be certain.

"This wasn't a choice made without a considerable amount of discussion about doing it this way. We both understand right and wrong, but we also know what needs to happen for us to go any further in our relationship. We're working hard on being honest and trying our best to be truthful to one another. It's hard, scary work because behind being honest with the person you love lurks that constant fear. What if I let them see who I really am, and they stop loving me? But more than anything Annie cannot find herself married to another Dr. Jekyll and Mr. Hyde. When Annie married, she was sure of Don. But she missed something big. Annie doesn't want to ever again get something that important so wrong.

"When two people live together, there's nowhere to hide. Unexpected differences flaws we conceal or minimize in public, everything about us becomes known to the other. Even something as trivial but irritating as leaving the cap off the toothpaste can be an issue. He heard Teresa, Hester, and Connie chuckle.

Morris smiled and continued. "We all put on our best faces in public and especially when we want to impress others, but when you live together, that becomes impossible. You become real to one another sometimes frighteningly so. That's what Annie needs. It's the only way she will be sure of me and what I am. So, we are living together, unmarried, and will until such time Annie is positive what she sees in Morris Stevens is what she'll get.

"Marriages are sacred, personal, and private. In a marriage couples at one time or another share every human emotion they're capable of, everything from the highest heights of ecstasy and joy to the blackest depths of hopelessness and despair. Couples stay together through ups and downs and tumultuous times because they love each other, because they promised, and with all their hearts want to.

"I'm going to ask you to listen to your parents about your personal conduct. The reasons behind their words are time-tested and genuine. When I told my mother we were living together, she hesitated not a moment saying, you're a grown man Morris, but I taught you better. There are compelling and important reasons why you don't cohabit outside of marriage.

"My mother is a wise woman. She knows about heartbreak and broken marriages. The concern behind her words was her not wanting either of us to end up heartbroken. To ease her discomfort over my news, I had to explain why to her much the same as I'm doing here. I know well of your concerns so learn from us. Use your friends and family to help you when you're choosing a partner for life. That goes double for the family. Especially about expressing in unequivocal terms even the slightest reservations about your loved one's other. Love has a way of leaving any of us blinded.

"Bringing me here to be with you was Annie's Christmas gift. You have a wonderful home and family something you can all draw on and share as you grow and move out into the world. Her family, from all of you is where Annie gets her humor and her strength. I know it's Christmas and not Thanksgiving. But I'm both grateful and thankful for having Annie in my life and to be here with you."

There was a long silence and smiling at him Mrs. Taylor said, "Thank you, Morris. That was frank and honest and as you'll soon see long." Morris glanced at Mr. Taylor and saw him head and eyes down looking at the floor thinking. Annie was wiping her eyes.

TWENTY NINE

After dinner with everyone gathered around the big island Annie's brothers, sisters, parents, and Morris were all engaged in multiple conversations. Annie excused herself saying she had a headache and was going to turn in. Mom followed her upstairs a few minutes later and came into her room asking if she was all right. Annie in bed with a book said, "Yes, I just needed some quiet time." Mom asked a second time if there was something wrong.

Annie said, "I'm okay mom, I'm just not used to my brothers and sisters all talking at once. I've forgotten what it's like. It's a little overwhelming when you haven't been around it for a while."

Mom sitting on the bed asked a few questions about teaching and how Annie liked her students and Northwestern. Aware her mother was not to obviously beating around the bush, but a little, Annie said, "Mom what's going on? Is there something you want to ask?"

Her mother looking at Annie as seriously as Annie had ever seen her, said, "Annie, "What happened between Don and you?"

"He hurt me mom, but it's over its history."

Connie pivoted more toward her and took hold of Annie's chin. She looked her in the eye and said, "Annie this is important. I need to know what happened. All of it."

It was like a dike giving way. Annie didn't hold back mince words or leave out any of it. Connie heard it, and in much greater graphic detail than Morris did. This was the second time she told someone about what her life with her husband became. It was getting easier. It was definitely easier than it was that night with Morris.

No one had ever spoken to Connie about being treated like Annie was. Connie was shocked. She couldn't conceive of being treated like Annie was. What her daughter went through with Don was horrifying to Connie

Several times, while she was speaking Annie, stopped because she thought her mother would be sick. When Annie finished, tears were running down Connie's face, she was holding Annie saying, "Never again will I hold my tongue and remain silent. I never felt comfortable with Don, and I never said a word. The morning of your wedding your father said I hope this will be all right."

"He's never said anything about his sense of Don or his misgivings. But I know he didn't believe Don was right for you. This is criminal Annie. I'm so sorry we let you down. We were all about not interfering, propriety, and modesty. Morris was right we very much needed to say something."

"Mother I was so sure of Don I doubt I would have heard you. The marriage became a nightmare, it's over, and I'm glad. I just wish I could've seen what was happening. It didn't happen in a day. It got worse and worse, and then it would be better. Then it would start all over again, and each cycle became more violent."

"Annie, why didn't you come to me?"

"I was ashamed, and I didn't understand or know how to speak about it. Nor did I believe I had any right to talk about my husband's sexual practices. I stayed trying my best to hold on right until I ended up in the hospital. That was the most painful degrading humiliating experience of my life. That older nurse just forced me to see my situation and under no conditions was she going to allow me to go back to Don.

"Does your father know of this?"

"My night nurse pulled him aside and talked to him. She was frank and straightforward with me, so yes, I think he knows of some of it. He came back to the hospital two days later and brought me home. Dad wouldn't let me get my things from our apartment without him being with me. I'm sure he knows some of what happened. We've never spoken of it. I was too ashamed to talk with you about it. I could never bring myself to speak to dad about it."

"Well, he and I will speak on this; I'm not having any more reserved silence in this house, not when it leads to one of my children being mistreated. I'm so sorry I wasn't of any help to thee. You asked me if I had ever been forced to have sex and I couldn't imagine such a thing with my husband. I thought something happened outside of your marriage. Annie, I have no sexual experience outside of our marriage, but you can infer from our seven children we've enjoyed each other that way. It's always been a joy and with love. Does Morris know of this, of what happened?"

"Yes, but I spared him most of the disgusting details. He knows toward the end I was repeatedly forced and beaten. He knows why I was hospitalized."

"I like Morris Annie he's a good man. I remembered thinking at the time I was reading Exemplary Lives this author understands what it is to be a loving person. That's why I asked you and Franklin to read it, you both wanted to be professors. I thought to see what such a life could be would be welcomed. The older couples love for one another was such a pleasure to read about. They shared their love with each other gave it to their children and their students with such understanding. I knew they had to be real. No one could just make them up."

"Mom that was mostly Morris he knows how to tell a story. He loved Marion and Albert, but he made up the personal moments between Albert and Marion and their children. He read a lot of letters written between them when their boys were overseas during the war. But he didn't meet Marion and Albert until a few months before they passed away."

Connie said, "He knew how to let me see them as extraordinary loving people. They led fearless lives letting their light shine on everyone. I wondered if they were Quakers."

"We're living in their house. It's a beautiful home right on Lake Michigan. Albert and Marion sold it to Morris for a quarter of what it's worth. We're very fortunate to be so young and have such a wonderful home."

"You sound like you're planning on making it your home?"

"I hope so. I want to, but I have to be certain this time."

"Annie if you weren't nervous about that kind of commitment after going through what you have you wouldn't be human."

"I'm not worried about the commitment mom. That's not it. I was certain of Don and that he was a loving, caring man and look what happened. I need to live with Morris to be sure. He's asked me to marry, and I said not yet not until I'm sure. He's so patient and understanding sometimes I think he's a wise old person in disguise. He keeps telling me, Annie you'll never be happy living in fear, and you'll never be able to love fully until you can without reservation. So, take your time you're living with me, and I'm not going anywhere. You'll come to it."

"Are you able to share intimacy?"

"Ah Mom please, I can't talk about that."

"Sure, you can. Annie, it's important you know you can talk to me, about anything."

"We make love and Morris is wonderful about it. He knows how I was treated, that I was forced and how hard it is for me sometimes too, too."

"What Annie? Don't be afraid, say it.

"To enjoy being touched and sometimes I struggle with having him inside me. I fake, and I don't like myself when I do it. It's so dishonest."

"Annie, what you went through is horrific, convoluted, and life-changing. I know you're a self-contained very private person, but there are counselors for rape victims. I'm sure Northwestern's health service can set you up with someone."

"Mom I couldn't talk about it with you. I don't know to this day how I spoke of it with Morris. I'd just met him and yet there was something between us that made me feel safe enough to tell him about what happened."

"You love him don't you Annie?"

"Yes, and I want to believe it's real with all my heart. But I'm terrified it'll happen again just like it did with Don. I was in love with Don, and I had no idea of him, what he was. I married the man. I still can't believe I was so mistaken about him. It's messing up my ability to have a trusting, loving relationship with Morris or anyone else for that matter."

"Annie, I can assure you Morris is not Don."

"I want to believe it, but I can't stop myself from holding back. It's not a conscious thing. I know way deep inside I did it once and I could be doing it again. It's terrifying."

"Annie when you get back promise me you'll go to the health services and arrange to see a counselor."

"I don't know if I can."

"Annie you're the best educated most widely read woman I know. Surely thee understands and knows there are trained professionals who know how to help women who've suffered traumas like yours. This isn't going to resolve itself without some help, and you just told me it's still affecting you. Promise me you'll see someone. Do it for both of you."

"I'll try mom. I promise."

"Don't put it off because without the loving commitment of marriage the relationship will come undone. You're both so bright; you scrutinize things, especially your own lives and thinking. There'll come a time when living together won't be enough. There won't be any sense of belonging to each other of being one. You won't be planning a future or wanting children or thinking as a family.

"Trust me on this Annie, Morris's mother was right. Without the commitment and promises made to each other in marriage no matter how much you love each other the relationship will remain without its true deep meaning. Sooner or later it'll come through. The relationship might survive out of habit, but I believe it'll just sputter out."

"Mom what do you think of him?"

"He's not a Quaker."

"Why is that so important?"

"It's the foundation of our lives, our marriage, and our family."

"Don's a Quaker and look how that worked out."

"Annie, I don't know what Don is. He's lost his way. Deriving pleasure from hurting another couldn't put him any further away from his Quaker upbringing."

"Morris understands what Friends are, what it means to be a Quaker. He went to a Quaker school until he was thirteen He knows our ways our beliefs."

"His words are clear and sincere, his light is self-evident, but he's not a Quaker."

"Mom can we try and get past the Quaker thing. Just tell me what you see?"

"I've grown fond of Morris. He's bright, unafraid, and appears at ease with himself. He's forthcoming and modest; however, unless he tells you what he feels you'll never know him. He hides behind those impeccable manners of his. He can conceal his emotions better than anyone I've ever known. When Hester and Teresa dropped their bombshell in the kitchen, most men would have shown something. Fear, anger, embarrassment, at least turned red, something. Not Morris. He stood there as calm and unaffected as anyone could ever be.

"You and I know he was horribly upset, but he hid it. I think I would've run out of the room. I almost did. When the dust settled, he said excuse me I need to take care of some things. I don't know if appearing that calm is a good thing or not, but I'll bet Morris's a cool customer in an emergency. I know he loves you Annie, and he's trying with the rest of us. He came back despite our shaming. He stood by you."

"So, you like him?"

"Yes, I do, very much and he certainly likes me."

"What does that mean?"

"He likes women. It's apparent he likes me as a woman."

"Mom I can't believe you're suggesting such a thing."

"Annie, you opened the door. You told me you spent eight days in the hospital after emergency surgery to repair your bottom. You spoke in the frankest grizzliest terms imaginable how Don tore you shoving his hand in you."

"Okay, okay, I got it mom, but what are you implying about Morris?"

"He's pictured me like a flesh and blood woman. Not just some proper Quaker wife and not as your mother. I know you see me as this mature, correct, moral woman and I am. But I was young once. I paid close attention to everything about the differences between the men I was attracted to and all the things concerning attraction between men and women. Morris's imagined me. What I'd be like as a partner."

"God above mom I don't believe this, Morris would never, not in a million years."

"Yes, dear he would. He's done it with me, Teresa, Hester, and maybe even Temperance. She looks just like me, and she's physically a woman.

"I'm sorry, but I don't believe for one second Morris would have a dalliance with my sisters or even flirt with them. Especially not Temperance, and surely not my mother."

"Annie, I didn't say he would ever do anything. I don't believe that at all. I'm saying he's looked upon us and imagined all the women in this house that way.

"God above mom what's Morris done to suggest such an improper thing."

"Annie it's a human thing. He's a man, a young very sensual one. You live with him surely; you've noticed how sensual he is? I didn't mean to suggest he's been anything, but polite and well mannered. He likes me and proper Quaker wife or not it's renewing to be admired that way by someone so young and handsome, especially after seven children."

"Mom you're scaring me. I can't believe we're even talking about this. You honestly think he would have sex with you, with my mother?"

"Annie when you get home ask him to be honest about imagining the women of the house. I think his answers will surprise you. Unlike a lot of men who just use women, Morris likes and admires women as equals, it's obvious. I believe he's had experiences with a woman who's special to him. I'm assuming that would be you, Annie."

"Mom what you're suggesting is shocking. Morris is the kindest most caring man I've ever met. He doesn't have a secret agenda. And unlike Don, the only gossip I've ever heard was wonderment amongst the women in my department and the faculty wives about why someone as appealing as Morris didn't have a string of girlfriends a mile long.

"I asked him why once. He looked at me with that smile of his and said you're my girl, Annie. I said, Morris, the gossip is that all during your years here after Diane left you were never seen in the company of a woman. Not one. He said, Annie, I'm seeing you. I said that's now what about before? He said I wrote two dissertations, three books, close to a million words in less than six years. I completed two undergraduate degrees in two majors, a master's degree and a Ph.D. With the three hours a day left do you see where I had any time for dating or developing a relationship?

"I said, well, I guess, no. I didn't. For two months the only thing I allowed was walking around campus. I went to dinner five times those first months, and there was always at least one graduate student upstairs capable of rescuing me if things went wrong. He was such a gentleman. He never tried to instigate anything or kiss me let alone make out with me. Morris hugged me twice, and unlike my other dates, he never asked me to sleep with him. It was all so proper I wondered if I'd fallen into a Victorian time warp."

"How nice for you Annie he passed on the affection of the moment and spent the time getting to know thee."

"After the divorce, I went out with a few men here in Philadelphia. By the second date, they couldn't keep their hands off me. They all tried their best to talk me into going to bed. I was so disappointed I stopped dating."

"Annie, how did it come to pass thee are living with Morris?"

"I was at his house one Saturday in late October helping him rake leaves. After we finished up, we were sitting in the kitchen having some hot apple cider. I was fed up, I liked him a lot, and I thought the feeling was mutual. I couldn't understand why he didn't kiss me or want to be intimate with me.

"I asked if I'd gotten this wrong between us. Morris said, heavens no, I just wanted you to be sure of me, for us to have time to get to know each other without all the steamy stuff. He told me his mother taught him to never even consider making love to a woman he wouldn't be willing to marry. I said Morris where does that leave me? You've never even tried to kiss me. He said, Annie, I'm in love with you."

Connie said, "Annie are you sure I need to know about this."

"You asked, and yes, you do mom. You very much do. I said, Morris if that be true why wouldn't you ask me to be intimate? He said he was afraid it would scare me away. I asked, is it because I was repeatedly sexually abused? He said he didn't know how to love me without it reminding me of what happened with Don. I told him I wanted to spend the night.

"He said only if you're sure Annie and bring your sense of humor. I said I'm sure Morris, but it was a lie. I was scared to death. The only man I'd been with was Don. I knew that wasn't love, but I'd no idea what being with Morris would be like. When we got to the moment, I was holding my breath pretending I was okay."

"Annie, why did you, you know better?"

"Mom I wanted desperately to know what it would be like to be with someone gentle and kind, someone who would love me and not hurt me. Almost no one thinks about sexual matters like we Quakers do. Ask Teresa and Hester. Sex between couples is taken for granted. It's everywhere and commonplace among singles."

"Not for my children."

"Mom as much as I'm able to, I love Morris. I'm not a virgin, and I've nothing to protect. I protected myself from getting pregnant, but I wanted to find out if it was even possible for me to love him or be loved that way. Sex with Don was never good, but for the last seven months of my marriage it was an unwanted painful thing, but something I believed I had to do. Sex was disgusting, and I was always afraid. I wanted to know if it would be different with Morris."

"Annie sex outside of marriage is not appropriate. There's no commitment, and yet there is. You're sharing your light, that most sacred part of you; your soul, the most intimate essence of yourself. Such a coming together without the commitment and blessings of your maker is just improper."

"Mom, Don was a sadist, and he was the only partner I've ever had. I didn't think things were right, but we were married I made promises. Morris was so different, so gentle and caring. It took all my courage to get in that bed, but I had to know."

"Do you know?"

"He's gentle and kind and patient, but I'm struggling. Everything around me differs from what I was taught. All the old rules about sexual matters have been thrown out. The rules for single women are upside down. All the couples I know are thoroughly and unashamedly enjoying each other.

Women can go to a clinic and get reliable birth control, sometimes for free. A woman can be with as many partners as she desires. Men have always operated with that freedom. Men could be promiscuous with almost no consequences. Now if she chooses a woman can do the same. The whole equation's been rewritten.

"Granted, it's still unbalanced for women, but it's an entirely new, disturbing, and unsettling development, before everything was black and white. A woman dealt with three basics: Any man alive would have sex with her. It was up to her to say no. She was terrified of getting pregnant, and she was chaste or not. Now women can set aside those enormous responsibilities and see themselves as freed, a sexual being equal to any man. She can explore her feelings and what it's like to love another as an equal.

"Most of our upbringing about men and sex was centered on keeping us safe, which was to say we were morally obligated to be virginal before marriage. It served two purposes, we wouldn't get pregnant before our wedding and once married a woman could be kept away from other men. This meant a man could have some hope of knowing he was the father of his children

"I also believe virginity is a cockamamie idea perpetuated by men to keep women as ignorant and hostage to them as possible. Although most women don't know it, we're powerful beings. We care for the man's home, make it a safe, pleasant place. We provide warmth, pleasure, and children to our husbands; we cook, clean, and raise those children. We do all of this in exchange for a few words said at a meeting.

"Annie, you know your father, and I taught you to be chaste to protect your inner light, your soul. Of course, we didn't want you getting pregnant and all the heartbreak and recrimination that would bring. But our real concern for our children centers on our Quaker way of keeping you from damaging your spiritual being. We put the Quaker ways of loving God above all else."

"I hate saying this mom, but I've tried hard to love God above all else, but he stood by and let me marry Don. That man did enough spiritual damage to last my lifetime. It took everything I have, all my composure, all my prayers, and all my inner strength to be with Morris. He's a gentle, loving man and still, I struggle with my sexuality. I believe I love him, but I'm afraid I could be making it up, doing the same thing all over again. All around me young women are enjoying their sexuality, their freedom and I'm scared to death.

Connie looked surprised. "Mother the dorms on almost every college and University campus are coed. Women are more equal in their status and rights. They can say yes if they choose.

With conscientious management and reliable birth control the big consequence, getting pregnant has been removed. Things differ from even three years ago; women have an enormous amount of freedom to make choices. Unfortunately, there's no guidebook, and the rules of propriety are in flux. Everyone's kind of searching and going in different directions.

"Women can only try to do what's right for them, but now at least we have choices. Granted the social pressure to enjoy sex with a person you like is everywhere. What's going on is a million miles from what you brought us up to think and believe. Young people all over the country are choosing to be sexually active, to live together. It's so commonplace it's rarely commented on."

"Annie, neither my daughters nor my sons can go out into the world believing sex is entertainment. That it doesn't matter, or it can be done with anyone without consequences. That kind of behavior and thinking corrupts the soul. It pushes the person's inner light aside."

"Mom, I agree, but just saying no is not a solution. It's not what's sweeping the land, nor will it keep my sisters safe. We all come to wanting to hold and be intimate with that other. I'm not saying it should be done carelessly or without sincerity. But it's being done more than ever before. I've thought long and hard about this, and I know regardless of what might come to pass between Morris and me I'll never forget him. Nor will I be ashamed of sharing myself with him. I will always love him. I know he is the same with me. Right now, Morris's love for me is more grounded, open, and realistic than mine."

"Annie I'm sorry, but right now what you have is nothing more than air. Maybe if hoping and dreaming count you have something, but that's the sum of it."

"No mom even if we part I'll have lived on equal terms with a man who loves me. I'll know about sex with someone who loves me, and I'll know what that can and can't be. Best of all I'll know what it's like to have a complete and loving relationship with someone who deeply, truly cares about me."

"Annie it's difficult for me to see and accept you're doing this is the right thing, but I hope you know I'll try. I love you with all my being, but I'll hold on to my hope you and Morris find your way to marriage. You are both such remarkable bright people."

THIRTY

While at her parent's house Morris and Annie had precious little opportunity to speak privately to each other. Annie knew Morris would not let her get away with not telling him about her parent's position on living together. She used most of the flight back considering how to apologize and ways to minimize the damage. Annie's suitcase was on their bed and opened for mere seconds when Morris started. He wanted to know why she failed to tell him beforehand how adamantly opposed to their living together her parents were.

Annie knew, but her mother told her Morris would be treated well, and she believed it. Even so, Annie didn't know how they might react to Morris, and she was unaware the whole family knew of their living together. Annie said, "Morris, I'm sorry I ducked. I was positive if you knew the strength of my parent's beliefs you wouldn't come."

"Annie why didn't you at least tell me your family was Quaker. I would've been a little better prepared."

"This is embarrassing, but I didn't want you to know I was a Quaker."

"Why Annie, for heaven's sake what's that about?"

"Most people know nothing about Quakers, and if they do, it's wrong. Most think we're a pacifist cult that uses old English idioms. One that holds their worship service in silence, without a minister, without readings from scripture, no organ or hymns, in a building we don't even call a church. It goes downhill from there."

"Annie you've got to stop assuming things. What did you think would happen when we got there? I knew your family was Quaker when your dad said Obadiah's name at the airport."

"I thought you'd realize even though we're Quakers we're normal just like other people, other families."

"Annie we've known each other four months. I expected to be served up surprises when we moved in together. But not things like you were raised Quaker, or your family's views on us living together. I love you, Annie. You need to have faith and try to remember how much you mean to me. But mostly you need to level with me.

"Morris I've been trying my best, but surely you can understand some of this is difficult for me."

"Annie the hard stuff's what matters the most."

"I'm trying Morris, I've gotten better. Surely you recognize that.

"Annie, you trusted me enough to tell me your husband beat you, raped you, and tore you open with his hand. That had to be the hardest most embarrassing thing you've ever told anyone. A lot harder than telling me you're a Quaker?"

"You're right. Telling you about being abused was difficult. Even harder telling you I was divorced. I couldn't believe or understand why I told you any of those things, but I did."

"Annie, we saw something in each other. Something that said we need to be as honest as we can right from the start. We fell for each other and trusted it would be okay."

"For some bizarre reason Morris, I believed I could trust you."

"Annie whether you're willing to admit it or not it was right from Kahlil Gibran for both of us. It only takes a minute to get a crush on someone, an hour to really like someone and a day to love someone, but a lifetime to forget someone."

"What I told you that night was about what someone did. The other thing, being a Quaker, is different. It's about me, what I am, and my way of thinking about the world around me. There's a huge difference."

"Annie, you knew I went to Southfield Friends School from first grade until eighth. For all intents and purposes, I was raised Quaker."

"Morris, you saw my being beaten and misused by my husband as a tragedy but the second, being Quaker, is inescapable, that's what I am. The one thing throughout my teenage and undergraduate years that made almost every young man I met have second thoughts. Most of them backed away, made an excuse, and bolted never to be seen again."

"Annie, you should've told me so when your dad escorted me into that big bedroom and said this is the guest room and has its own bathroom. This is where you'll be staying. I wouldn't have been so surprised at what followed. Your dad can be quite intimidating. He just up and told me in no uncertain terms how he felt about us living together.

"He said we don't approve of such behavior and wouldn't have their daughter doing so under their roof. Then he said, Morris, I hope I'm not making you uncomfortable, but Annie has three younger sisters. I'm doing my best to discourage them from thinking doing that kind of thing is acceptable or would be condoned by us. I felt more than scolded by his words."

"Dad said that to you? I can't believe it, how awkward. What did you do?"

"I said we better switch bags because Annie won't look good in my clothes. He smiled for part of a second. I barged ahead telling him I really cared about you. That given what you went through in your marriage it was vital for you to know who and what I am. That living together was the only way to be certain."

"I can't believe my dad put you in that position, that's so unlike him. He's such a gentle soul."

"My first instinct was to say; do you not want me here? Should I leave? But I held my tongue. His words, knowing the strength of your parent's disapproval hurt. I wouldn't dream of harming you, and his words made me feel shabby and demeaned both our relationship and how much you mean. I was mad at you for not telling me about their feelings. You took away all my choices. Once the exchange took place, and he left I stood there wondering how being in your home for Christmas knowing how your parents felt if I would ever be welcome."

"Morris, I talked with my mother often. She knew I was seeing you almost every day, and when she asked about my new address and phone number, I couldn't lie. I hemmed and hawed and admitted I'd moved in with you. Mom was distraught, really upset. Trying to calm her I said, mom Morris's the nicest man I've ever met, and before I moved in we thoughtfully and conscientiously talked it over.

"I said it's not some romantic schoolgirl affair. This is about getting some important things straight. I thought she understood. My parents talk with each other. And I didn't expect to be allowed to room with you. But Morris, I never dreamed my father would confront you about our living together."

"Annie, you keep forgetting neither your parents nor anyone else knows what you went through with Don. They saw this as their daughter, the oldest, their pride and joy, discarding her propriety and every shred of decency. She was doing so with complete disregard for her family and everything they brought you up to be. It had to be a shock."

"Morris I'm an adult. It's my life, my choice."

"And loving you as they do, it was impossible for them to see you hurt yourself in that way."

"It's what I need to do to get past what happened in my Marriage. I need to be certain.

"You should've explained what happened to you."

"I know that now. But you don't understand the shame of it, how improper and disgusting it was to be used like that by my husband.

"Annie I'm just as sorry as I can be you were treated that way."

"Well, he did those awful things. What I don't understand is how living with a man who was abusing me in every way imaginable is okay and proper because we said words to each other at a wedding. And because we haven't, living with you, a man who's gentle and kind and loving is something I'm supposed to be ashamed of, and believe is immoral. It doesn't work in my head. I guess I really do need to think about getting some help with this."

"I told your dad we were doing what was needed to get to a marriage. I also told him we hadn't talked about it, but I had assumed I'd be bunking with your brothers. Then I said it was a very nice room and thanked him for it. So, it ended a little more upbeat, but I still felt mighty uncomfortable. I could see and feel his disappointment in me, in us. He all, but said I wasn't caring for you properly."

"Morris I'm so sorry I wasn't honest with you. When you told me, Dad took care of my bag? I felt awful because I knew I'd left you blindsided, but I never dreamed he'd say anything to you.

"Oh, it got better. Not an hour later Hester and Theresa let me know in front of your mom and dad and Franklin in no uncertain terms how appalling our living together was. To them, it was the worst most sinful abomination imaginable. I couldn't believe how shocked, ashamed and furious they were. They couldn't believe you could come home much less to bring me."

"Morris, I don't know how Hester and Theresa found out about us. They've called and talked with me twice, but neither has ever asked me anything about my living arrangements. I did tell them I met someone I was growing fond of. I suppose because of the new address, and phone number one or the other questioned mom about it. Bless her heart if they confronted mom as much as she might have wanted to mom wouldn't lie to them. Once either of those two knew it was inevitable, it would get around to the rest."

"I'm sure looking up to you the way they do and seeing the transformation of Annie must have been unbelievable. Not only did you get divorced, but you moved away. You were the oldest, the brilliant, talented professor, their amazing shining example of propriety, and all things good. Learning you were living with a man must've been the biggest shock, the most embarrassing, scandalous revelation they've ever faced, particularly so for your mom and dad."

"Mom told me they wanted to meet you and you would be treated respectfully. I brought you to my family as the man I hoped to marry. Thank God my parents read your book. But they saw you as my illicit lover me as your mistress. To them, it was their properly raised Quaker daughter, their morally correct sister moving away where she could be promiscuous, outrageously sinful, and completely inappropriate. I wanted with all my heart for them to know what a lovely man you are. To see what we meant to each other. Instead, my parents saw me as being immoral, and all my oldest sisters could see where you and me naked having sex.

"Thank god you said those words Christmas morning. I felt so relieved. I didn't know of what took place between dad and you until just now, and I didn't know the full extent of the scene in the kitchen until two days after Christmas when Franklin told me. There was so much tension in the house those days before Christmas I could hardly breathe. When Pearce asked me where you were going, and I saw the cab drive off, I knew something awful happened.

"I went to the kitchen and asked them what. I didn't get much of an answer, and I got upset. So, I went to your room and found your note. When I finished reading, I handed it to mom. I told her when you called I was going to you, leaving, and I wasn't coming back. I think it was then when she realized what you meant to me. She knew I wasn't going to let my family come between us. It shook her up."

"You're their first-born Annie. That carries a mountain of baggage. The firstborn comes with the parent's learner permits. By the time they're ten, firstborn children have been subjected to everything their parents ever dreamed about, read about, heard about, or thought about child rearing.

"Most parents are so invested it's almost impossible for them to see their child as distinct from themselves. Firstborn's also gets to have the mistakes of their parent's, parent's fall on their shoulders. If you're fortunate and all those first-time child-rearing experts do a decent job, you're blessed."

"Morris, both the family's actual standards and our imagined standards and expectations of good and proper behavior were high. Living up to them was important to us, especially the girls. I'm sure Teresa wanted to know why I wasn't openly reprimanded."

"There was a lot more to it than that. They were shocked, hurt, and plenty angry. They acted like you'd betrayed them. They were amazed you could come home, much less to bring me. I was even more surprised by Hester's comment when she said, mom if I did what Annie did I'd never be able to face my family again."

"I'm really sorry; it must have been awful for you. I would've left the kitchen crying my heart out. Seeing us and having to think about sex that way must have been a gigantic struggle for them. It would've made me uncomfortable at that age. If I'd known they all knew about us, I wouldn't have brought you.

"And just so you know Morris, I doubt if Teresa's ever been kissed much less experienced feelings for another. She's an unusual combination of being smart, holding strong beliefs, and being unafraid to speak on them. I'm sure Teresa feels I've betrayed the whole family. She's a little prickly, but she'll be a terrific doctor. I just hope she isn't as blind as me and ends up being prey. If she finds a man like dad or you who can love her right forever, she'll be one of the lucky ones. It won't be because she has any skills or even basic understanding about the ways of men and women."

"Maybe she'll be like my friend Hanna and put her work, her creativity first. She won't allow, or ever want a man or family to come between all that creative drive and the work."

"Teresa could be like that, although I know she's curious about sex. But because of how she's been raised and our family's beliefs, she'll be like me. She won't fall in love and surrender her virginity until she's found the one to marry, but those beliefs will blind her just like mine did me."

"I don't know Annie. Maybe it'll work like your mother said it's supposed to. Teresa will stay chaste bring herself to her marriage with no prior sexual knowledge or expectations, but unlike yours, her man won't turn out to be a flawed brute. They'll bring their two pieces of inner light together and like your mother said, unite, and wondrously become one."

"Morris, when a young woman raised like me comes to a marriage innocent with no experience or knowledge sex is a complete shock. Other than knowing our bodies are made to fit together and touching specific areas of our bodies may be pleasurable the actual business of mating is a scary proposition. I was starting from letting anyone see me naked as being improper. The idea I would let another touch me in my private places was unthinkable.

"Well, my brilliant one you should have either let your curiosity loose and done your homework or at the very least talked with your mother.

"I didn't know how to ask my mother. Mom's beliefs are ingrained, very much part of her. They've worked well for her. But neither of us knew how to talk about sex in any helpful, specific way. Bless her heart she's working on accepting what we're doing as the right thing. But I know she's praying every day we'll marry."

Smiling his special smile, Morris said, "Me too."

"Morris, please don't push. You know I'm trying to get there."

"Between your fathers making his and your mom's position known and that lovely scene with Hester and Teresa in the kitchen I couldn't have been more surprised or felt any worse. I could've come as your boyfriend, and your brothers and sisters might've wondered if we were lovers. But unless one of us told them, they would've been guessing.

"The scene in the kitchen was as embarrassing and awkward as having the whole family walk in on us going at it. The hurt and revulsion in their eyes were as strong as could be. We were the wickedest thing they'd ever encountered, and there was nothing I could do. I couldn't take it back and I wouldn't if I could. Nothing like that's ever happened to me, I've never felt so unwanted, shamed, and out of place as I felt that morning. All I could do was feel awful and leave."

***

"I never realized how much time we spend getting things straight between us. I was so glad you came back. I didn't want to leave, but I would've. Not being able to talk with each other was the hardest part about being there. But you were remarkably composed about everything. It was Christmas morning when you were reading to my family before I fully realized what a mess we were in."

"Annie, when I passed you and the kids in the family room I've never felt so uncomfortable or out of place. Not since some of the literary aristocracy, I met in New York let me know what they thought of me. They used their sugary sarcastic asides to make it clear to everyone within earshot they considered me an unschooled very lucky upstart. It wasn't pleasant, but nowhere near as upsetting as hearing what your sisters thought of us. In their eyes, we were dirty, an unclean immoral embarrassment bringing permanent, irreversible shame on the whole family.

"They believed we were endangering our souls. I lay awake in bed in that hotel room feeling this was the most hopeless situation I was ever involved in. I had no idea what to do or say, and I felt awful. There was no way I could see to ever rectify the situation. When I came back, everyone was polite, but God above Annie it was though they looked on me as a known child molester. Those were some ugly feelings. I wasn't at all prepared for it, and I wanted with all my being not have to spend another minute there."

"Morris you're talented, modest, and educated. Those people in New York were just envious. You did what all of them wish they could've, and you're not selfish. You have impeccable manners, and you treated my family with dignity and kindness. You stayed above all of it. Regardless of what you felt you were charming and considerate to everyone. I was tremendously proud of you."

Morris said, "Once I realized Hester and Theresa were so hurt about our living together I understood why it came out so ugly. Understanding their point of view took most of the sting out of it."

"In the eyes of my family, I've taken leave of my senses. The idea I would go against theirs and my own beliefs horrified them. Apparently, they needed to let you know they weren't pleased with either of us.

"Annie, didn't you talk to your mom about our decision to move in together?"

"I did, but I was mostly trying to calm her down. I realize now all she heard was I didn't want to make the same mistake twice. Until mom came in my room the day after Christmas, you were the only person I've ever told what happened in my marriage. It didn't matter anyway once the whole family knew we were living together the die was cast."

He said, "I'd say given everything Christmas at the Taylors was an interesting experience. We made it through it."

Annie said, "As much as they didn't want to, I believe they all came around to liking you. For sure mom and dad did. As far as I could tell they all did."

"I hope that's not a lot of wishful thinking on your part."

"Franklin was genuinely interested in you particularly in trying to understand what you do. He's always been our curious trying to understand person. Besides Temperance and Obadiah Franklin was the only one who put aside their judging. He was impressed with the way you handled yourself that morning in the kitchen. Pearce is a teenage boy he's just trying to grow up as fast as he can, and you and I are old. We aren't big on his radar screen. But bless his heart he was sweet giving me several hugs. If he was upset with me, he didn't show it. He was certainly circumspect."

"And Theresa and Hester?"

"Hester was afraid of you. She looks just like me and spent her time imagining you being as attracted to her as you were to me. She was wondering the whole time what that might be like. By the time we left Hester was trying to imagine being with you. So was Teresa, but she was subtler trying to divert my seeing those feelings in her by pointing me to Hester's continual looking at you."

"Oh, come on Annie, your sweet moral Quaker sisters?

"They were both attracted to you Morris. You're the virile, handsome man screwing their naughty, wicked older sister. It was a mountain of carnal thoughts, images, and imaginings. I'm sure it put both through a host of grueling situational, moral, and ethical conflicts."

"You really believe that was what was going on with Teresa and Hester? I was aware when I came back they were tippy-toeing around me?"

"I didn't learn the full extent of the scene in the kitchen until two days after Christmas when Franklin pulled me aside and told me what happened. Bless his heart he said, Morris's such a nice, polite man he stood there and took it. Franklin was shocked that Teresa just up and threw the thing about us living together right out on the table in front of everyone. He couldn't believe the looks on mom and dad's faces. He said it was awful, and Mom and Dad reiterated their beliefs trying to placate and reassure Hester and Theresa, but Franklin thought that just made it even worse for you.

Morris said, "I suspect they both realized afterward that calling out our behavior in that manner didn't endear them. They probably concluded I might be upset and angry about it."

"Were you?"

"Yes, but I felt sorry they were so hurt and shocked about us that it came out the way it did. I believe they were both trying to like me, but they couldn't get past the depravity of us being unmarried and living together."

"Teresa sure thought Hester had a thing for you. She said you could see it every time Hester was around you. It was disturbing to Teresa. But the way she talked about it, I knew she was struggling with the same thoughts and feelings."

"Annie, I think Hester and Theresa are both dealing with some powerful sexual issues."

"They know we're living together, sleeping together. Neither has ever had a boyfriend. They're trying to imagine what it's like. All the Taylor girls have gone to Bryn Mawr, even mom, but being a girl only college it doesn't afford much interaction with the opposite sex. It's an alphabet soup of unvoiced sexual unknowns and wonderment."

Smiling Morris said, "I knew coming home with you would put me under the microscope, but I had no idea I was going to be deemed an immoral ingrate. They were so ashamed of what we were doing and hurt by it, I still feel indecent when I think about it."

"You hid it well besides their outrage was on general principles not much on our reality. You're brave Morris, and you came back. Your Christmas reading pretty much straightened them out at least about what we were trying to accomplish."

"Annie, if my missive accomplished that, it would be a miracle."

THIRTY ONE

It was late, but Annie kept talking. Morris sensed Annie felt she'd put some of her issues to rest. Annie said, "The day after Christmas, the night I turned in early, mom came up to my room. She was beating around the bush, and I finally said, mom, is there something you want to ask me? Mom looked at me as seriously as I've ever seen her and said Annie, what did Don do to you? I said it's the past mom.

"She insisted, so I told her in all its disgusting, ugly detail. She sat there transfixed not moving a muscle. What Don did was horrifying to her. I stopped talking several times because she looked like she would be sick. The tears were running down her face, and she said, Annie, my precious girl why didn't you come to me? I said Mom I didn't understand any of it. He was my husband, and I didn't know what sex was supposed to be, and I didn't think it proper to talk to others about such things. She said Annie I'm so sorry I felt something wasn't right about Don when we first met. I didn't speak up, but never again will I remain silent."

"Annie, your mother's such a decent woman I hope you used some discretion in how you told her."

"I didn't. None! I was angry and awful. I blame her for bringing me up to be so fucking accepting and submissive that I let Don keep doing all those horrible things. I accepted it, went along thinking it was my lot, God's will for me. I was awful. I told her how he'd strip me naked push me down on the bed. How He'd force my legs open, spit on my parts, grab me by the throat and hump me like a rag doll. How he'd grab me by my hair and ejaculate all over my face and smear it in my hair and walk away."

"Jesus Annie, did you have to?

"I told her how sometimes when he forced me to suck him he'd twist my arm, or my hair, or both, and push into my mouth as far as he could; how I'd be gagging and throwing up while he was coming in my mouth. I was even worse telling her about the last couple of weeks when he would carry on all weekend long. When I told her about our last afternoon, I was unmerciful. I wanted her to feel it. To know every sordid detail of what it's like to have that happen to you.

"I told her how I scratched, kicked, and hit him in the face as hard as I could. How he tried to pull my nipples off, beat me nearly unconscious, and did what he wanted. What it felt like when he forced his hand into me. How it hurt so much, I passed out. How when I couldn't stop crying he hit me so hard he knocked me out.

"About coming to alone barely being able to walk, getting blood all over my car, and being questioned at the hospital. Crying my way through a very painful exam, having the operation, and being surrounded by all those people who knew what happened. How I couldn't have anything, but liquids and having all those embarrassing and uncomfortable exams and tubes, I told her everything.

"She asked if dad knew about any of this. I said we'd never spoken of it. She said we will speak of it. I'm not having any more reserved modest, none of my business silence, in this house, not when it leads to my child being brutally mistreated.

"I'm glad you could talk to your mother, but I sure wish you hadn't been so hard on her."

"There was no nice way to say it."

"I got what happened to you without you being that graphic with me.

"You're young Morris, sexual. I could tell you understood what I was saying. I didn't have to spell it out for you."

"And you didn't think your mom and dad ever did any of those things?"

"I can't imagine it. No, I don't believe I can."

"Annie I'd bet you ten thousand dollars your mom and dad have more fun with each other than you can imagine. Seven children and all those years of experience, I'll bet they know exactly how to enjoy each other."

"Morris, can you think of your Mom and Dad that way?"

"No, but I've seen snapshots of them together when they were younger, and I could tell they were crazy about each other. I can see them thoroughly enjoying each other. I think I can assume they've pleasured each other in all the ways we try to."

"Mom said I gather from what Morris said Christmas morning he knows what you went through with Don. I said yes mom Morris was the first person I could talk with about it. I didn't speak with the frankness I did with you. But yes, he knows toward the end of the marriage I was repeatedly forced and beaten."

"Is your mom going to tell Hester and Teresa what happened to you?"

"I don't know. We didn't talk further about it."

"You should encourage her to do so. They need to know."

***

It was late, but Annie didn't stop talking. Morris sensed it was important. He could see Annie was grappling with coming to terms with something between Connie and her, some adult mom daughter understanding. "Mom said a lot about commitment and how sooner or later if there were none our relationship would falter. I asked her what she thought of you. She never answered me. She went off on a tangent about you not being a Quaker.

"I said Mom can we drop the Quaker thing. Do you like him? And that's where it got weird. I think she was trying to give me back some of my own medicine for using language like a street prostitute. She answered saying yes, I like Morris, and he certainly likes me. I said, mom, what does that mean? She went on about how male and sensual you were. I couldn't imagine my mother talking like that about you, and I questioned it.

"She said Annie dear you opened the door. You told me in the crudest terms imaginable how you spent eight days in the hospital after emergency surgery to repair your bottom. You graphically described how it was torn by your husband. I said okay mom, enough. I get it, but what are you insinuating about Morris?

"She said he looks upon me as a woman. He's imagined me as his partner. I said, God above mom he would never, not in a million years. She said, yes dear, and he did so with Teresa, Hester and maybe even Temperance. She's no longer a child. Temperance looks just like I did when I was younger. I said, I'm sorry mom, but I don't believe for one second Morris would ever have a romantic interest much less a dalliance with any of my sisters and surely not with Temperance or you.

"She said, Annie, I didn't say he would do such a thing. I don't believe or think that. I'm saying he's looked upon us and imagined all the women in our house that way. I said, God above mom what's he done to suggest such an awful thing. She said nothing dear, and it's not an awful thing. He's a man, a very sexual one. You live with him, sleep with him. You must be aware of how graceful and sensual he is?

"I said, Mom, he's young, fit. He played baseball and hockey in high school. Morris was offered athletic scholarships at five schools. He still goes skating whenever he can, and I'm fully aware he appreciates women. More than any man I've ever known, but why do you believe he's entertaining such unholy thoughts and desires in your home?

"She said, Annie I didn't mean to suggest he's been anything, but polite, and well mannered. He's never been suggestive in any way, but Morris likes me. Proper Quaker wife or not it's renewing to be admired that way by someone as young and handsome as Morris, especially after seven children."

"I said, Mom, you don't believe Morris would have sex with my mother? Annie when you get home ask him to be honest about imagining the women of the house. I think his answers will surprise you. I believe he's had experience with a woman who's special to him and I can only assume it's you, dear. So, Professor Morris Stevens tell me what the hell she was talking about?"

"Only if you can imagine them as women and separate from being your sisters or your mother. Can you see them as just women?"

"I'll try."

"When I first meet a woman and if it's in a situation and a place that's informal and I have the time. I sometimes try imagining us as lovers and what that might be like. It's just playing in my head, not something I would ever try or put in motion, well almost never."

"Did you do that with me?"

"I told you the first time I met you I thought you were one of the most attractive interesting women I'd ever seen. I couldn't stop myself from imaging you in my bed. I wanted to make love to you."

"You did that to my whole family?"

"Well no. Not the men."

She shoved him saying, "You're awful. You were thinking about having sex with them?"

"Not in a specific way it's more about how they look, how they might kiss or react or what it might be like to be in bed touching them."

"That's having sex with them. Pretty much everything you can do with a woman."

"It's imaging. It's not illegal or anything real. When I saw you come in that first night at the Atkins's I sat straight up and looked at every square inch of you. I said to myself, wow! What a lovely, unusual, and beautiful woman."

"Then your very next thought of me was all those other things you just told me you thought about my mother and sisters?" He looked at her. She said, "Really Morris you took my clothes off, my sisters, my mom's?"

"Annie your mom's a lovely woman. With that smile you share, she's damn sexy. She has welcoming eyes, beautiful clear skin, and she knows by now what she's doing around a man. Having seven children has probably made her able to be looked on and handled without experiencing all that much embarrassment. I concluded if Connie loved her partner she'd be a remarkable lover."

"God above Morris she's my mother.

"I told you I will not talk about this if you can't see Connie as anything other than your mom."

"I'll try harder."

"Remember I just met your family for the first time and you know I like women. It's not a dirty rotten thing its pure admiration, and acknowledgment. It's curiosity and besides almost any woman can be a potential sex partner. We all know sex comes second after staying alive."

"Really Morris, my mother?"

"Annie come on what part of imagining has anything to do with reality. She's a marvelous, glorious woman, and I found her delightful. Don't tell me it never crossed your mind before it happened to wonder what you and I might be like together?"

"Mom asked me how we came to live together, so I told her. I explained how I got fed up with your niceness and told you I wanted to spend the night. Mom said Annie I don't need to know about this. And I said oh yes you very much do."

"So, you told your mother about our intimate relations?"

"No Morris I was trying to help her see our living together was about my trusting in my judgment about you. About me trying to get over what happened with Don and trying to understand and find out what normal is."

"Well, my dear I think your mother was trying in her Quaker way to tell you she was a sexual being and understood such matters. Connie was trying to take some of the starch out of all the propriety and correctness she pounded into you. Your mom felt awful about her lovely decent Quaker daughter being trapped in such a horrible situation. She recognized neither she nor your Quaker upbringing was of any help to you. Connie was telling you she enjoyed and acknowledged her own sexual desires. That it was okay. That said, Annie, the only thing I'm sure of is; it won't be safe for us to return to your ancestral home unless we're married."

THIRTY TWO

With the start of winter quarter, Annie and Morris settled into their lives as professors. Four months flew by during which he helped Annie dig up additional material and go through the arduous process of restructuring, rewriting, editing and turning her Ph.D. thesis into a book. She sent it off to the Anthropology Department's publishing house and crossed her fingers.

After some rewriting and revisions, in late April, Annie's book was published. It was resoundingly well received by the academic world. Annie was thrilled. She considered writing her thesis and completing her Doctorate while living with Don to have been a major accomplishment. Now she had a well-received published work and thought it one of the major triumphs of her life.

They would both have birthdays that summer. She would turn twenty-eight on June fifteenth, and Morris would be twenty-seven on July sixth. A lot of what they were dealing with and trying to sort out between them as a couple ran afoul of her upbringing. She was understanding and seeing her joys and wants and needs as being in direct conflict with much of her upbringing.

Morris found himself more and more appreciating her witty, tongue-in-cheek asides regarding her strict Quaker upbringing.

But Annie's inability to get past being embarrassed about sexual matters amused Morris to no end. He teased her about it and about his demure Quaker partner having a much more diverse and broader variety of sexual experiences than him. Morris grew to be pleased and thrilled with them as a couple. But try as he might he found himself with this nagging thing in his head about Hanna. Just the fact he thought about her and he thought maybe far too often was troubling.

Hanna was now a bona fide celebrity with articles written about her and her art in magazines and the New York Times. She made TV appearances on national talk shows. Hanna let him know about all of this with notes sent to him in her beautiful hand painted envelopes. Annie saved them all. Morris was pleased for her and her rapid almost phenomenal rise to the pinnacle of the New York fine art world

Hanna was selling paintings for unbelievable amounts of money, and he was thrilled to read about her or see her on TV. It was hard for him not to think of her and what might have been between them. He realized somewhere way inside she was something special unto herself and to him and if she belonged to anyone, it was to the world. But he knew Hanna would never share herself fully with a mortal man. Morris knew that would never happen. He didn't believe Hanna was made that way.

Morris felt he very much needed to tell Annie something about his relationship with Hanna. But he did not understand what his relationship with Hanna was, or how to go about telling Annie about it. He knew on some level his relationship with Hanna was significant and dynamic. That they meant a great deal to each other.

But Morris knew his feelings didn't matter because whatever it was with Hanna couldn't go anywhere. Even though Morris had no idea why he accepted that Hanna was the most amazing unbelievable sexual partner, he'd ever have. But that was not something Morris was prepared to put on Annie's plate. He had no way to explain why there was such a world of difference between making love with Hanna and making love with anyone else.

He also acknowledged those wonderful, incredible, unbelievable experiences only existed four separate times. They spent a grand total of fourteen days together. It was scattered over a year, and it wasn't like they lived together or had access to each other like he and Annie did. Still, he couldn't explain the joy, the transcendental ecstasy he and Hanna experienced together. Morris had no illusions about how powerful those times were. How much he enjoyed them, or how much he wished there was a way for them to share a life. However, he knew better.

He thought long and hard how his attraction to Hanna began and grew before all that sexuality ever happened. It was something different from what he and Annie shared, but it continued to be influential, significant, and perplexing. But for all of that, Morris knew in his heart and soul and separate from any conscious deliberation, he'd never have a life with Hanna. No family or children, none of the things he wanted, or any of the things that make up a loving marriage.

Hanna had her work it was her life what she loved. She did it with a passion and dedication close to obsession. Morris decided there wasn't anything to be said to Annie about Hanna. Annie was a beautiful, powerful, loving being more than willing and capable of supplying him with everything he could need. But Morris wrestled with his feelings for months over not understanding why he couldn't stop thinking of Hanna.

Morris knew full well he and Hanna would never marry and have children much less be a family. He decided having Hanna in his thoughts was the same as being in love with a devout nun or a married woman. She'd made her promise to another. Hanna married her creativity. It was time, long past time for him to accept it and let her go.

Spring quarter started, and Morris made his decision. He brought it up with Annie in late May. They'd both have this coming summer free, and he wanted them to marry and get on with having a future together. Morris felt it was time to make the commitment to each other. He firmly believed he'd put Hanna to rest or at least understood with their differences they could never have what he and Annie would. Hanna's life wasn't anything to do with or about the kinds of things Morris needed and wanted.

Sitting on their patio looking out across the lake with Annie snuggled up against his shoulder Morris said, "Annie we've been living together for almost six months and walking and talking for three before that. It's time to decide some things."

Sitting up she said, "I was so comfortable, does this have to be now?"

"Annie it's time. We need to get married, the balls in your court. You need to shit or get off the pot."

"Lovely Morris! What an endearing, extraordinary, and unforgettable way to ask a gal to marry."

"Annie you've known since before Christmas I've wanted to marry you. I know at least intellectually you've decided you're safe with me. We need to get on with making a life together."

"Morris, I believe we can make a marriage work. I do. We both have our feet on the ground. We're realistic."

"What does that mean Annie?"

"We're practical people; we deal with our lives and each other sensibly, realistically. We're true friends, we're comfortable together. I don't believe you have a secret life. We know better than to say or do things that can't be taken back. And yes, my dear Morris, I know you love me, and I believe I love you."

"I hear a big but in there."

"I have to be absolutely positively sure I'm not making this up."

"Annie?"

"I know way down deep I haven't been able to trust myself. I'm still struggling to be at ease sexually.

"Annie you're doing fine.

"It's not a conscious thing, but I know it's there. It's holding me back, and I'm not sure why, but I know it is."

"Annie, maybe you need to take a chance that things will be okay with us. Being married would make our living together and having sex legal. You know right and proper in our families and everyone else's eyes, but especially between you and your Quaker rule book."

"I suppose it could be. I know every time I think of my parent's I think by living with you I'm being wicked."

"Is that why you volunteered for that homeless shelter gig, so you had an honest excuse not to go back home over spring break?"

"No, I wanted to meet your parents and your brother and sister. I thought it was imperative for me to go with you and do that."

"Well, the only way to get over this living in sin thing I know of is to make this legal. Maybe then and with a little time, you'll allow yourself to think of cohabiting as a reasonable and proper thing. As a married woman, you'd have every spiritual, legal and religious right to enjoy sex with your husband."

"Maybe, I sure hope so."

"Annie, if we marry you can quit all this worrying about being a bad girl in the eyes of the world. I know at least intellectually you feel safe with me. We've had no trouble with making our wishes known. I think we've gotten the sex stuff straight between us."

"Okay.

"What's okay?"

"I'll marry you."

They got the license and made plans to marry on June twenty-seventh at a local justice of the peace. This was done with no announcement or fanfare to anyone, only wanting to make their cohabitation legal. She reminded him that in the eyes of her family they still wouldn't be considered married until there was a proper Quaker wedding. Morris agreed that a Quaker wedding in Philadelphia was needed.

Annie's educating him about what would be required of them to have such a wedding was accomplished over dinner. Morris said, "First things first. Before we go further, I need to call your parents and ask for their blessing. I hope even though I'm not a Quaker they'll be pleased. If so I'll ask them to help us with arranging our wedding at your family's meeting house in Philadelphia."

Morris's call was warmly received by Mrs. Taylor. Connie seemed as pleased as she could be. Both her parents seemed relieved when Annie told them they were getting married on June twenty-seventh, but still wanted to have a Quaker wedding back home.

Mr. Taylor was more reserved, but when speaking to Annie, he seemed very pleased about their news. Morris believed Nathan's reservation was because Morris had been and was still living in sin with his daughter. Morris thought this could be a sore spot with Nathan for some time to come. Maybe even past being officially Quaker married. Morris hoped, at some point, he might let himself get over it. The plan was to be married in Philadelphia at the family's Quaker meeting house before the fall quarter began. Morris was pleased and believed in his heart he and Annie would be terrific together.

THIRTY THREE

Knowing this could be trouble Morris let the oversized white envelope lay on his desk for a whole afternoon. He knew it was from Hanna she always embellished her envelopes with some of her art. He slit the top open and pulled the contents out. Morris held two sheets of paper and ten one-hundred-dollar bills. He read:

Hi,

It's me. Morris, I need your help, but just for one night, June seventh. I need you to sit with me because if you aren't there I'll wet myself or my head will explode. You've guided me through so much. You've always pointed me in the right direction. This time I need you to keep me from floating away.

I need your calm wisdom and your strength. I need to stay grounded because I don't think I've ever been so scared. This is far worse than prom or the night I called you about St. Joan. It's worse than being beat up. That was quick, but this will go on for hours.

He thought to himself Hanna you need me like a hole in the head you've been featured in Time magazine and the New York Times. You're the beautiful up and coming young artist who sells paintings for thousands and thousands of dollars. It goes on and on to infinity.

Morris, I've been nominated for both my set and lighting design for the musical "Forever." The voting members almost never give the award to a rookie or a foreigner. So, there's not much concern about me getting it, but I must be at the award ceremony. I swear if you aren't there to hold my hand I'll come undone and float away.

They tell me in recent times it's rare to get four exceptional shows in a season. The other designs nominated are unbelievably good, so the competition is fierce. I'm glad I don't have to be a judge. Just being nominated is such an honor; that was more than enough for me. Maria's up for director, and so is Meg Stanton the costume designer and Steve Nock for his choreography. If Maria wins, it'll be her fifth.

It's a huge deal, black tie and real dress up for the ladies. I sent the money because I'm asking, Morris, I'm begging. I know it's a lot of bother and expense, especially if you need to juggle your class schedules. We've got a hotel room reserved for you. Bring your tux. Call when you get to your hotel and have a room number. I'll have the ticket and instructions delivered right to your door.

Please, please come. I can't tell you how important it is to have you with me. And surprise, surprise Morris, this is one of the good times. But I'm scared to death about the whole thing. Henric and Maria have given me no choice just like mom about prom. I've got to be there.

Please Morris, please come.

---Hanna---

He told Annie that Hanna his family friend from long ago, the one who was afraid of her own shadow at her senior prom, the one who was nearly beaten to death when she was thought to be one-half of a gay couple. She wanted him to be there with her at the Tony Awards. He explained Hanna's need for him to be there to Annie in a way he thought she would accept and she did. He gave her Hanna's letter to read.

Annie said, "She sent the means you should go I'll bet you'll have the best seat in the house. It'll be fun for you. I'll tell everybody I know you're going to be there with her. Maybe we'll get to see you on TV. It'll be fun for everybody. Be sure and tell your mom and sister. They'll love it.

***

He went, and it was a hassle. The cabbie could only get him within six blocks of the theater, and he was on his own. He arrived at the theater breathless and fifteen minutes late. Morris had been in some big weddings and attended quite a few formal affairs at the University, but nothing even close to this.

He had the ticket and instructions, but he couldn't figure out where to enter the building. He asked several people before he found his way inside. The next thing he knew he was being escorted to his seat by a nicely dressed attractive young woman. She took one look at his ticket and began deferentially addressing him as Doctor Stevens.

As they got closer to the stage, he saw Maria, Henric, Erica and some others all clustered together. If Hanna hadn't been with them, he would not have recognized her. He gasped when he saw her. Standing there in a gorgeous floor length fitted silk dress she was stunning. Morris could see a long row of pearl buttons running down the back of her dress. They stretched from her neck to the swell of her hips.

There were ten or twelve of the same pearl buttons holding the full-length sleeves tight to her forearms. The dress was a radiant beautiful turquoise that perfectly matched her eyes. She was wearing a pearl necklace, red lipstick, and pearl teardrop earrings. She looked as if every lithe shapely bit of her had been sewn into that dress. Wearing that magical welcoming effervescent smile and with her short tousled white-blond hair, scarlet mouth, and those turquoise blue eyes he had to take a very deep breath. Hanna was stunning.

Hanna hugged him saying, "I'm so glad you're here I feel better already."

With his mouth against her ear, he said, "Hanna you look incredible."

"You like my costume? Erica and Maria, had it made for me."

"It's stunning Hanna and so are you." He shook hands with Henric and Erica surprised him kissing him on the cheek and gathering him in her arms she hugged him to her. Maria gave him a third big hug. His escort smiled and said, "Good luck tonight Doctor Stevens good luck to all of you."

It took him a few minutes to realize he was sitting close to the stage in an area reserved for the Tony nominees and finalist for this year's awards. Realizing he was part of Hanna's and Maria's entourage, Morris took the next few minutes to look around. He felt warm in his stomach and out of place. It was a spectacle like nothing he'd ever seen. Radio City Hall is a spectacular place, to begin with, and fill it with six thousand people dressed in their finest, and it was a sight to behold. There were TV cameras and celebrities everywhere, but the thing that astounded him most was the emotional power in that room.

When he was nine his uncle took him to a hydroelectric dam, he stood in that vast space on the floor with those giant turbines and never forgot it. They didn't make much noise. They hummed. No vibrating or shaking, but you could feel the power of them working in your whole body. This space was bigger, but here the power was in the air, everywhere around him.

With Maria sitting on the aisle to his left and Hanna on his right, Morris watched as the glittering song and dance specials of the evening marched on. They went one after another until they reached the point of announcing the winners for direction, scene design, costumes, and lighting. Maria didn't win, and he heard her mumble, "I wonder who I pissed off."

Morris felt Hanna take his hand. He didn't remember the words or when the winner was announced. He did remember his hand being almost crushed and Hanna saying, "Oh my god, I don't believe it." She jumped up. They all stood with her. She was kissing him and dancing between Maria and Henric and heading up the aisle to the stage. Morris sat down stunned and overwhelmed at feeling such joy for her.

He'd seen some excited people in his life but watching Hanna at that podium was just about the most fun he ever had. She wasn't shrieking or screaming, but she was as alive as anyone he'd ever seen. Her incredible otherworldly voice quieted that vast space to silence and with unreserved joy she began. "I can't believe it. You gave it to me. I won a Tony. This is so wonderful! Thank you, thank you, and thank you some more."

Hanna thanked Maria for her support and faith, the producer for giving her the opportunity, the lyrist and composer for all their input. She thanked the cast for their efforts and all the people who worked so hard on the production. She said, "Thank you, mom and dad, for loving me and putting up with me. And God bless Henric Olbermann and his wife Erica for their support and backing without which I would've never been able to be here."

"I especially need to thank my dear friend Morris Stevens who through his help, years and years of selfless support, and patient kindness got me here. She shouted Wow! Thank you, every one of you. It's truly, deeply appreciated." She was gone from the stage. She reappeared several minutes later taking her seat next to him.

He sensed her fighting to come to terms with her accomplishment and what it meant. Morris could tell she was in the middle of a massive adrenaline high and was about to burst with pride and joy. She took his hand, and they were announcing the award for best lighting design and Hanna Williston's name went everywhere throughout that cavernous auditorium.

Hanna with a look of total and complete surprise said, "Me! They gave me both?" This time she slowly got up hugged them and made her way to the podium. She stood there with tears streaming down her face and said, "You gave me both! I could hug every one of you. Thank you again! This is truly overwhelming! I'm such a novice and to be here and get these awards is unbelievably moving. I've already thanked everyone I can think of, and they told me we're running late. But I must take a moment to thank the set designer for giving me all that marvelous scenery to light."

Hanna waited through the laughter and plowed on. "I can't leave here without thanking my wonderful understanding friend Morris Stevens who taught me how to feel light with my hands and hold it in my heart. Thank you, Morris, and thank you one and all. Thank you from the bottom of my heart!"

There was a standing ovation for her. And why not, she was young, fresh, and so sincere. Not a single person in that room doubted her ability, her sincerity, or her gratitude. She was the future and a brilliant bright candle up on that stage. More than anything she was so genuine it touched everyone's, heart.

Morris would be told by his mother he looked very handsome on the TV and pleased for Hanna, especially when she hugged and kissed him. His mother also expressed being surprised at what an amazing, remarkable woman Hanna had become. "She left us all speechless, our little Hanna, what a marvelous thing it was for her and Annett and Robert."

***

Morris was in bed in the dark, but nowhere near sleep. He glanced over at the red symbols staring blankly back at him and registered 1:37. He rolled over thinking he heard tapping on his door and sat up listening. It was. He got out of bed threw on his extra-long Northwestern t-shirt and opened the door to Hanna's beautiful blue dress and fresh smiling face. "Can I come in?"

She went past him, past the bed, and sat in the little-stuffed chair. "Hanna, what's going on?"

"Why didn't you come to my party?"

"I didn't know where it was. I couldn't get within thirty feet of you, and I couldn't get a cab to save my life, so I walked back to the hotel. I waved at you and blew you a kiss to let you know I was going."

"I saw you leaving Morris. But I didn't get to talk to you or thank you for coming. You kept me sane; I didn't float away or wet myself. It was the third nicest thing you've ever done for me. Just having you there kept my feet on the ground. I still can't believe what's happened. Morris, I won a Tony."

"You won two Hanna, and I'm impressed."

"Nothing feels real or believable about this. Everything's so unreal. I need you more than ever. Can I stay? I need to be held and feel safe. I know you're real Morris."

"Hanna I'm getting married."

"Jesus Morris that was abrupt. Or was that no Hanna you can't stay?"

"Sorry it just popped out, but you needed to know.

"That's serious business for you?"

"It wasn't a decision made lightly."

"When?"

"The twenty-seventh of June."

"Don't ask because I won't come. It would kill me to witness that. Do you love her?"

"We're good for each other."

"That's not an answer! Do you love her like you love me?"

"Hanna I've never loved anything or anyone the way I've loved you, but you're already married. You don't date or marry mortals, and you don't make babies. You won two Tony Awards, and you sell paintings for hundreds of thousands of dollars. You've been featured in several national magazines, and the New York Times. You spoke eloquently; charmingly tonight on national TV in front of God knows how many millions of people.

"We're from different worlds Hanna, and sometimes the hardest thing to learn is to accept what's possible and what isn't. I'm just trying to do the best I can in my world, and you're obviously doing the best you can in yours. Unfortunately, they're not in the same universe."

"Morris I'm going to get undressed and get in your bed. Just give me my kiss. I need to be with you more than anything you can imagine."

Getting married or not he had no will or desire to even try not to be with Hanna. She was all he thought about for years, and he still thought about her. He never understood what they were to each other before their night and day together at her graduation party. Morris never recovered from that night or the others. Now it haunted him, and every time they were together since was even better. Coming to her he said, "You'll never get that dress off by yourself."

"Does that mean I get to stay?"

"Yes, Hanna that means I want you to stay."

"You won't regret it, I promise."

"No regrets Hanna, but you'll need my help to get out of that thing."

"I told Erica it was way too many buttons."

He came up behind her and began undoing the twenty-eight pearl buttons. When he finished, the dress was open all the way to her matching blue panties. "Hanna, you looked wonderful up on that stage. I think everyone in the theater fell in love with you and thanks for your words they were awfully nice." She turned to face him and then with the sleeves at last unbuttoned he helped her pull the dress up and over her head. He said, "Hanna you did it. It was all your hard work. What a tribute. Your peers, they all voted for you, your work."

She sat on the edge of the bed naked except for her blue panties. She said, "On the final rehearsal night I sat out in the house trying my best to believe I did that. I created it and lit it, I had lots of help getting it there, but it was my concept and my ability to figure out what to put up there. It was better than I ever imagined. I sat there trying to believe I created it, me. It's real. I did that." They got under the covers. He put his hand on her cheek, and she said, "I'm ready just get in me."

As he did Hanna, let out a long sighing groan, and he said, "I hope that's pleasure."

"Love me Morris, just love me."

His noon flight came and went. He didn't want to leave her. His lips were raw from kissing her, nothing of his worked. It didn't matter. He wanted her more than ever before. He didn't understand why or how but being with Hanna was so far beyond his puny brain's understanding. It was he thought like being moved to somewhere in heaven.

Hours later he was standing in front of her, silent, helping her into her dress. He methodically buttoned the twelve buttons on each of her sleeves. He turned her and started at the bottom buttoning the twenty-eight buttons. The whole time he was helping her into that dress it grew more and more weird. He was dressing a doll, getting it ready to go back in the display case. Morris was near tears, and he didn't understand what the hell was wrong with him. Why he was here. Why he was doing this. In silence, he kept doing her buttons. As he neared the top, she said, "Morris are you really getting married?"

"Yes, Hanna I am."

"Will you still help me?"

"Not this way. I won't be able to do this anymore."

"Morris, do you have anything with her even close to what you have with me?"

"No Hanna, I've never been with anyone who could take me where you do. I don't think I ever will. I don't believe it's possible."

"Then why are you doing this?"

"Hanna, I want a family and children and all that becomes."

"You're right I can't give you that, but please save a little space to help me if I need it."

"Hanna, I'm here for you. I came."

"Yes, Morris you've always been here for me."

"Hanna just ask, I'll be here for you."

"Thank you, Morris. Now give me a big hug. Say goodbye and get on your way."

All the way home on the airplane he tried his best to sort this out, make peace with Hanna, and what this thing between them was. However, he couldn't. Deep inside all he wanted was to be with her and to feel that way forever. He could do that, but it would be an empty hollow life, without children or any sense of family. He couldn't square being with Hanna and him wanting children and to be a family. It wasn't possible.

Annie wasn't pleased with him. He was five hours late. He called and left a message at the airport, but Annie wasn't about to drive back to Evanston and then back to the airport. So, she waited. She did smile and come to him when he arrived. They hugged, and he apologized.

He told her he was bone tired and asked if she would mind driving. He always drove. His request was a first and set her on edge. She didn't ask him if something was wrong preferring instead to cajole and tease him on the way home about how nice he looked on television. How all her friends, the faculty wives, and husbands, who watched with her, liked how surprised he looked when Hanna kissed him.

Her effort went by Morris because he hadn't seen himself on TV and couldn't remember much about what happened at the awards. When Annie asked, "Can you tell me how you teach someone to feel light with their hands and hold it in their heart?" He knew she was leery, jealous, and rightfully worried.

He said, "I shouldn't have gone. Hanna seemed so frail and afraid when she asked for my support, but as everyone discovered last night, Hanna's all grown up. She's in a league of her very own."

Annie said, "Your little friend was magical up there on stage receiving those awards. She was so refreshing and genuine; everybody watching with me wanted to hug her, and that unforgettable, enchanting voice amazed us all. I was so jealous. Her sets were magical, and what a presence, if I had that voice I'd know for sure you'd never leave me. She's stunning, her eyes, well, she's unbelievably beautiful. Her smile was otherworldly, utterly captivating. She got everything didn't she Morris?"

"Yes, she did. Are you jealous or afraid Annie?"

"Both!"

"I'm marrying you, Annie."

"Sorry, watching you on TV last night was seeing you in a very different world. When you missed your flight, I got worried, and you seem awfully sad. Did something happen?"

"Can we talk about this tomorrow? It was an overwhelming spectacle, and I'm not good at that. It was one gigantic hassle from start to finish. The whole thing seems like some unreal dream."

"Well you're still in one piece, and we're almost home."

"Annie? Thanks!"

"For?"

"For being wonderfully you, for loving me, and being such a powerful, enchanting part of my life."

Tired and spent as he was they made love. As always it was warm, comfortable, and pleasurable. Not in any way like being with Hanna. For all of Morris's emotional effort, brains, and intellectual ability he couldn't even begin to understand why. They didn't do anything differently than he did with any of his other partners including Annie. But Morris was mystified why being with Hanna was so overwhelming, so breathtakingly enthralling.

THIRTY FOUR

Organizing and getting their Quaker wedding to take place in Philadelphia turned into more work than he ever imagined. He soon discovered a couple wishing to have a Quaker wedding at a meeting house had a few hurdles to cross. To start the process, they had to mail a letter of intent to marry to the clerk of that meeting house. The clerk then read the letter at the next monthly meeting for business.

Those present appointed a three-member clearness committee who would discuss issues involved in marriage with the couple. Annie told him the process involved thoughtful questions, and careful listening all designed toward addressing potential difficulties along with reviewing and discussing the spiritual aspects of marriage.

Morris mumbled something about such a process although perhaps well-meaning had been of no help to Annie about ensuring the success of her first marriage. Mr. Taylor told Morris both he and Connie met with the members of the committee and gave their wholehearted approval of their proposed marriage. But despite her parent's wholehearted endorsement Annie and Morris were notified in writing by the committee they would be required to meet with them before they could approve the proposed marriage.

The reason given was Annie's previous unsuccessful marriage along with Morris not being a Quaker. Annie and Morris arranged the meeting flew to Philadelphia and stayed at her parent's home, and it was awkward. Even though they were now legally married, her parents asked them, quite nicely, if they would sleep in separate bedrooms while they were staying with them.

According to the family's traditional beliefs, they were still unmarried. Morris didn't expect this, but he wasn't surprised. Doing his best to go along, Morris said, "Of course." But, he was finding all this principled ritual tedious and trying. It wore on him.

Morris was surprised at how annoyed he found himself over their not being able to be together in bed talking things over. Morris also assumed their committee meeting would be nothing more than a complete waste of everyone's time, a rubber stamp kind of thing, another Quaker ritual to jump through. Reminding himself, he was doing all this for Annie and her relationship with her family

Morris put on his most charming smile for the meeting. His approach was cautious, but Morris was thinking, what could the committee members ask or want to understand that would prevent them from having a Quaker wedding? After all Morris reasoned, they'd been living together and were now legally married.

***

The meeting started with introductions and Morris was puzzled by the committee's makeup. There was an ordinary, but bright looking woman, Heather. She appeared to be a few years older than them, an older man of about sixty-five, Simon. The third, Ruth, was an attractive woman somewhere around forty and both Simon and Ruth worked hard to put them at ease. Heather seemed to Morris to be more of an observer. He thought she might be being groomed for the future, like a student teacher.

Simon and Ruth spent the first half hour probing both Morris and Annie about their understanding of marriage and the seriousness of the vows they would be making. They questioned Morris about his beliefs, experience, and the nature of his religious background. During this questioning, Heather watched both Morris and Annie with such intensity it made Morris uneasy. Trying to ignore his feelings and thinking this was all going well right up to the point Heather said, "And you're living together as man and wife?"

The question came at Morris as more of a statement of fact, but still an issue requiring an explanation. This was the kind of thing that Morris wanted to appear as not in any way threatened or defensive about. But before he could say anything Annie jumped right in, and said, "Heather we're already legally married."

Heather said, "If that be valid why are we talking about you being married at meeting?"

There was silence, and Morris broke it without a moment's hesitation. "Heather, we married in a civil ceremony with the two of us, a witness and a judge. It's important to both of us to be married in the presence of our families and friends and to ask for God's help. For that, we need your blessing."

Not smiling both Simon and Ruth at almost the same instance said "Good." Heather barely smiled. But Morris felt a change in the room. He was no longer sure of their standing with these people or why it appeared to have changed. But Morris no longer felt confident of the outcome. He felt on edge.

Heather looked at Annie and said, "It's been made known to us over the course of your previous marriage you were repeatedly beaten and sexually misused, and you left the marriage."

Morris sat there wondering, Jesus, really, how'd that get known? He said, "You're going there? You're going into Annie's first marriage? Morris looked at Annie trying his best to get some clue about what to do about this unexpected turn of events.

Annie quietly, unemotionally said, "Yes. That's correct."

Heather asked, "Have you received professional help or counseling for such treatment or are you trying to deal with the pain and trauma on your own?"

Morris about to say whoa people this is wrong when Annie said, "I've been seeing a woman counselor through the health services department at the University. She's a psychologist, a rape counselor."

Heather persisted, "Do you feel the counseling is helping? That you're making progress?"

"I do."

"Are you going to continue with the counseling after the marriage?"

"Yes."

Morris knew nothing of the counseling, and even though surprised by Annie's revelation he felt he needed to stop this. Trying to he said, "Heather do you really expect Annie to have to talk here about something that was the worst thing that's ever happened to her?"

Surprising him, Ruth jumped in saying, "Yes, we do Morris. You will live with the consequences of that marriage all the days of yours."

Heather looking directly at Morris said, "When I was in college, long before I married, I was beaten and raped by a man I was certain loved me. Such a traumatic thing is not something you recover from on your own. I've tried to imagine the consequences of Annie being continuously subjected to such treatment by her husband. I can only conclude it will affect everything about your marriage, specifically your ability to enjoy and benefit from a healthy loving sexual relationship with each other."

Morris trying to end this line of questioning said, "Honestly I have no complaints about Annie or our sex life."

Heather wouldn't let it go asking, "How about you Annie?"

Annie looked across at Heather, Simon, and Ruth and said, "I've occasionally struggled with having sex. I'm ashamed to admit I sometimes go along or even fake my feelings. My counselor and I are working hard to sort out my issues about it. I love Morris as completely and unconditionally as I possibly can. He feels the same toward me, and I believe with all my heart we'll have a fruitful and joyous marriage. My struggle centers more on not trusting myself to see others realistically, to feel sure I'm not making the same mistake I made about Don. It's not so much about the physical abuse."

Heather asked, "Have you spoken with the counselor about your ingrained Quaker issues surrounding pacifism? How you reacted to the violence, how you're coping with it."

Annie said, "We've spoken on such matters. It's a lot to explore and come to terms with. But she said she felt I was in good shape in that regard."

Heather said, "Annie I know this is difficult for both of you. I apologize for asking these questions, but I must. Quaker women brought up in homes with strict rules of appropriate behavior often have problems about submission. If they end up in a marriage with an abusive partner, they often submit to such treatment in silence accepting it as Gods will for them."

Annie said, "I've talked on these matters with my counselor. I don't think they are or will be an issue in my marriage to Morris."

Heather turned to Morris and asked, "Morris in light of what you've heard here today concerning Annie's disclosures how do you feel about entering into marriage with her?"

Morris delighted to have the chance to bring this to an end said, "All I can say is, I love Annie. Not because she's an unbelievable lover or is submissive and makes love whenever I want. I love Annie because she's a brilliant, kind, decent, and loving woman. Annie grew up in a large, loving Quaker family. She has more resilience, certitude, and inner strength than a mother lion. Together we are strong enough, mature enough, thoughtful enough, and dedicated enough to work through any problems we may encounter. I want her for a partner for the rest of my life, and I'd like to commit to that here at a Quaker meeting."

Simon rose reached across to Morris and shook his hand saying, "Thank you both for being so forthcoming with us. We know this was difficult for you. Now, I'll ask my fellow committee members, to say so if they have any objections to your marriage." They all said, "No," and Simon said, "Good, we'll appoint an oversight committee to help with and oversee the arrangements for the wedding meeting. They'll work with the family. Annie are you comfortable instructing Morris on the specifics of a marriage meeting?"

"Yes Simon, I remember it well."

"Good and God go with you. And if we don't see thee before the wedding the committee members will join with you, sitting on either side of you during your wedding meeting."

Morris ever so glad to be through this ordeal walked in silence to the car. When they got in the car to leave Annie said, "Are you terribly disappointed with me?"

"Good heavens Annie, whatever for?"

"For not telling you about the counseling. But mostly for sometimes faking my feelings and being dishonest about our lovemaking?"

"Annie the counseling was a surprise, but I think it's terrific a good thing. I was aware you were occasionally hesitant about going through with making love. I also felt sometimes you doctored your feelings about the lovemaking."

"You've never said a word."

"Annie after the way Don treated you I think it's remarkable you have any interest in sex with me or anyone else."

She slid across the seat and threw her arms around him. She said "Morris, I want to love you with all my heart and soul. But it's petrifying that I could be seeing you as I want and not as you are. It's not a conscious thing it's stuck in me. But I'm working on it. The counseling's helping, it's better."

"Annie, do you think getting married here with our families and all your friends will help you or is it going to reinforce what happened with Don?"

"I think being married in my Quaker tradition will make everything easier. I know we've married Morris, but my family won't accept us as married until we have a traditional Quaker wedding. This must seem insane to you, but it's my life, what I live with. This kind of thing is why I was afraid of telling you I was a Quaker."

"Annie, I understand. Why do you think I'm here doing this? I want to be married to you. I want your family to see us that way and all the rest of your Quaker world."

"Morris all I care about is having my family accept you as my husband. That in their eyes we're married."

"Annie from now on I want you to promise me you'll stop faking and trying to please me. I want you to say, Morris, can we stop? Or if you're not up for starting just say, can we not do this now. And Annie if you can would you go further and try to explain what's going on with you?"

"Morris, I almost always want to, but then my feelings will change. It's sort of like I'm a watering can with an unseen hole in the bottom, by the time I get to the garden the waters all run out."

"Annie, you need to trust me. You can say anything, talk about anything, or ask me anything. I'm in for as long as we'll have, and I'll never ever treat you like Don did."

***

When they got back to the house, both Nathan and Connie wanted to know how everything went.

Morris said, "Not all that well for Annie, but they gave us their permission to marry at a meeting, and they're appointing an oversight committee to help with the arrangements."

For the first time since he met him, Morris saw Nathan accepting and embracing him into his world. He was effusive, congratulating them both on their successful interview. Morris smelling something amiss asked, "Did you have doubts about the outcome? Is there something we should know?"

Nathan said, "When we were interviewed by the committee Ruth said neither Don nor Annie asked for a clearance committee to help them with their marital problems or their divorce. So, can you tell us what ended the marriage?"

Connie said, "I couldn't lie. I told them in the simplest terms of how you were treated. Hester asked me a series of questions, and I revealed more than I wanted. I finally told her I wasn't comfortable talking further about it. It was privileged personal information and not mine. Hester said you have my word. Nothing said here will be divulged to any others."

"Then she said, you've told us Annie's been keeping this to herself. She's been trying to deal with the degradation and humiliation without professional help. Now she wants to marry again. As a psychiatrist and regardless of the strength of a person's faith I don't see any way someone repeatedly subjected to that kind of brutality and humiliation will ever be all right without professional help

"Heather was concerned about you. Saying to us what happened to your daughter is a grave matter. Her marriage was a living nightmare, and it was perpetrated on her by the person who was meant to love and care for her. I'm not being dramatic there are no other words for it. Your daughter's married life was a nightmare of sexual torture."

"Hester went on, saying, Annie seeks to marry again and is asking for our blessing. I feel if she doesn't get professional help she'll carry that first marriage and all that mistrust, fear and revulsion into her second. You can both see how it might cause a problem with her ability to trust her new partner, or how it might interfere with them being able to fully enjoy each other.

"I said, Hester, they love each other we're both sure of that. Annie's an honest, forthright person I think anything further should be asked of her. Ruth said say no more we'll talk through these matters with the couple. They shook our hands, thanked us for coming, and for our honesty. We got in the car, and I started crying. Your father started crying, and we sat there in the car crying our hearts out."

Mr. Taylor embarrassed, said, "So yes Morris. We had some real trepidation over the outcome."

Morris said, "Hester's a psychiatrist? Here I thought because she appeared close to our age she was there as a trainee. I don't think I'll be making any further assumptions about your Quaker ways.

***

They returned to Evanston and let her parents take over making the bulk of the wedding arrangements. Annie explained what they were to do at their wedding meeting and rehearsed their vows with him. The wedding ceremony was as simple as could be. No best man, no bridesmaids, no flower girls, music, not even rings, just a wedding certificate which would be signed by everyone present. Morris asked, "Annie what about your dress isn't that going to take some thought?"

"Not much, it's a Quaker wedding, the second one for me, so no white wedding dress, and simplicity in all things."

"We've got to wear something we can't sit up there in front of everyone naked."

"We'll be fine. But since it's your first why don't you wear your cream linen suit."

"I might. It's a summer wedding; somebody ought to wear white, but a white suit on a guy at his own wedding that might be a touch much."

"Just don't wear black."

"You've got yours all figured out, haven't you? So, play nice and tell me."

"I'll be wearing a beige linen, floor-length dress with long sleeves; it's a fitted open neck sheath. You'll like it it's split on the right side to mid-thigh."

"Sounds racy."

"For a Quaker bride, it is. It's my way of getting even with Mom and Dad for spilling the beans about my first marriage. But mostly for having us staying in separate bedrooms even though we're married."

***

Annie and Morris entered the meeting room holding hands. They made their way to the front and sat in two chairs centered between the six already seated clearness and oversight committee members. They sat in silence facing the meeting, their families, and friends. The meeting began when Annie and Morris took their seats. The assembled sat silently waiting for the couple to stand and say their vows.

The only decision either needed to make about their wedding was when to rise and say their vows. They agreed whoever feels its time will squeeze the others hand as a signal to stand. It was further accepted whoever squeezes will say their vows first. Morris felt sure of himself, but still sensed Annie wasn't. He decided beforehand, if it killed him, he would wait for Annie to be the one to choose when to rise and say their vows. With the merest hint of a smile on his face, Morris sat eyes down, waiting.

They were seated for six or seven minutes, eight at the most when Annie squeezed his hand signaling it was time. As per their agreement, Annie spoke first. Standing facing each other Annie began. "Friends, in the presence of God and before these our families and friends, I take thee Morris, Baird Stevens to be my husband, promising with Divine assistance to be unto thee a loving and faithful wife so long as we both shall live."

Following in turn smiling, pleased beyond anything imaginable, Morris said his words. "Friends, in the presence of God and before these our families and friends, I take thee Annabelle, Annie Taylor to be my wife, promising with Divine assistance to be unto thee a loving and faithful husband so long as we both shall live."

Annie's father stood and came to them holding their mounted wedding certificate and had them sign. He turned facing the meeting and read the words written on it, then asked all present to sign it. Nathan handed it off, and it began making its way around the room. As they sat Morris glanced over at Annie and saw tears streaming down her face. Searching trying to locate his handkerchief and after some fumbling managed to hand it over. As the meeting once more returned to silence, Morris took Annie's hand in his giving it a heartfelt squeeze.

As explained in the little handout they prepared for the non-Quaker guests. In the Quaker tradition, there are no ministers; Quakers believe all are equal before God. This means everyone attending is considered an officiant. Once the vows were said, anyone who so chooses can rise and speak. Once Annie and

Morris said their vows there was little silence. The attendees stood one after another and expressed their praise, hopes, and best wishes for the couple.

Morris just wanted to take Annie in his arms and hold her tight, but he patiently waited while everyone did their praising, best wishing and congratulating. Finally, after a long four minutes of silence, Simon rose and shook hands with the couple and the other committee members. Signaling to everyone present the wedding meeting was concluded. Morris stood and took Annie in his arms and hugged her to him.

A Quaker wedding certificate is a simple document which states the couple's names, date, and time and place of their joining in marriage. Their words and vows said to one another are written on it by one who has a beautiful hand (In modern times most often a professional calligrapher). The signing of their wedding certificate by them and everyone present gives such a simple ceremony an incredible amount of meaning and power.

The couple can see the names of everyone, all their friends and loved ones who witnessed their commitment. Most couples frame the certificate and hang it where they can see it every day. With the words there for all to see the document is imbued with both the love of that day and the force of the obligation entered.

They served a light luncheon for their guests in a nearby hall, and the couple stayed until it was over. Annie, Morris and their parents along with all their brothers and sisters were having dinner at the Taylor's later that night. Annie and Morris planned to spend five days at a Catskills resort before returning home and were hoping to be on their way before noon the next morning.

Morris's parents and brother and sister were also leaving tomorrow. Annie and Morris had flown to San Francisco during spring break, so his mom; dad, brother, and sister got to spend time with Annie and get to know her. They were pleased they had done so and weren't all meeting each other the day before the wedding.

After staying and sharing their time with their guests and friends at the luncheon Annie and Morris arrived back at the Taylor's around four. The first thing Annie said was, "I'm getting into something more comfortable."

Morris said, "Me too."

Connie said, "Annie we've moved your things into the guest room."

Annie said, "Really?"

And Nathan said, "Annie thee are husband and wife."

THIRTY FIVE

Annie's and Morris's lives revolved around being professors. It wasn't just teaching but included lending help and guidance whenever they were called on to do so. They both formally and informally tried to help their university community when and wherever they could. On one occasion giving a young married couple and their child an upstairs room and their car to drive, they did this, so the husband would be able to complete his final quarter and receive his master's degree.

There were many long hours spent helping students with their master's and Ph.D. theses. Many nights it included having them join in with Annie and Morris along with their three live in graduate students at dinner. It was always more than a good meal. It became a time of acknowledgment, celebration, and understanding about just how joyous and rewarding the process of learning could be.

Morris roughed out a start on a second novel which was Annie's story. However, after about three months he put it away deciding he had much more to learn about Annie. Their marriage was changing him and Annie in ways Morris didn't understand but welcomed. Like a lovely green plant that puts out a few blossoms one day and then continues, putting out a prodigious profusion of unending color. Annie didn't stop, she just kept flowering.

She was flourishing and earning a reputation on campus as an outstanding teacher. She made her subjects dance with life. Word of her student's fondness for her, her dedication, and exceptional ability as a teacher quickly got around campus. Having published a well-received academic work the powers that be offered Annie tenure. The unexpected offer delighted her. It validated her and her work and was one of the biggest indirect compliments she ever received. She was genuinely surprised. Morris was not. Annie was an elegant, powerful woman. She taught with joyous passion and humor.

Her students loved her. The faculty loved her. Morris at first not able to imagine why the uproar over his wife's abilities sat in on three of her classes. He wanted to see for himself what all the enthusiasm was about. After doing so, he was even more surprised and delighted. At dinner, the night after his third appearance, she said, "Really, Morris you don't see enough of me you've resorting to auditing my classes?"

"I wanted to see for myself what all the student love was about."

"And?"

"You definitely have a gift."

"And?"

"And, I guess I'm hoping some of that loving enthusiasm and energy will spill over into our bedroom."

"Morris are thou complaining, pouting, whining, or are thee hoping?"

"Annie, please don't do that thee and thou thing, it reminds me of all those nights we spent in separate bedrooms at your parent's house."

"Well, thanks to mom you got to poke me on our wedding night."

"I thought about sending her a thank you note for making that possible. But from our smiles the next morning I think everyone in the house knew Annie had been thoroughly, extensively, and joyously poked."

"Morris, you are such a storyteller. That was the worst piece you'll ever have. I've never been so overwhelmed with joy. I kept alternating between grinning and crying every other minute. We didn't even finish. I remember you laughing."

"It was a great wedding night Annie. For the first time, we got to talk to each other naked in bed at your parent's house. I loved it. The idea, that everyone in the house thought we were up there in that room joining our two pieces of light together. It made me smile all the next day. And don't you dare tell them you were so pleased and happy you were crying? And never say I was as close to you as I've ever been and all I was doing was smiling and holding you."

"Don't worry Morris mums the word."

"I remember apologizing to you about half the drive to that resort. I did try to poke you even though right in the middle of it you again shed tears. Do you know how impossible it is to kiss somebody who's crying?"

"Come on Morris I wasn't that bad, I've never been so happy. We didn't need to make love."

"I tried because it was our official wedding night. I didn't want to disappoint."

"Morris, nothing about our wedding night was anything, but glorious. It was one of the best nights of my life. I knew whatever we faced would be together. I felt like a grown up with a whole life to look forward to with a person who loved me. I didn't need a poke. I felt fantastic and utterly gloriously fulfilled."

Grinning, Morris said, "That next morning we came into the kitchen, and everyone was gathered there waiting. I loved that Teresa and Hester kept looking at you. They were trying their best to see if there was something discernable about a bride fresh from her wedding night. They were looking for anything, anything at all noticeable or different. I could see the whole thing had them ensnared in a world of wonder and suspense."

"I saw it too, Morris. And even though it wasn't from love making the whole family could see how delighted I was. That night was the closest I've ever felt to anyone. And here we are three weeks into fall quarter. We've both been so busy taking care of our obligations it's now been to the day, fifteen days since we've done any poking?"

"Really Annie, that long I had no idea you kept track?"

She started around the table reaching for his hand.

"Annie, what are you doing it's not even dark out?"

She stopped and looking at him said, "Do you have something else in mind? Should we dry the dishes?"

The truth of the matter was Morris often had something else in mind, but he said, "No Annie you know I take a few minutes to change gears. The dishes will be just fine air drying."

They crawled in together and began as they always did kissing. Morris soon noticed Annie's kisses had a never experienced urgency. He felt with every fiber of his being she was enjoying the pleasure of it. For the first time, Annie was allowing him to see her wanting. He went along, kissing her neck and breast. She was holding him and pushing herself against his mouth letting him know in everything she did she wanted this.

He slid down her torso, and as he did, she opened her legs, and he was between them using his tongue. She pushed back against him, and he slipped his fingers inside. She was moving against him with surprising urgency. A few seconds later Annie said, "Get in me."

He pulled himself up and slipped inside her. They carried on kissing making love with their mouths, bodies, and hands every way they could. He grabbed her fanny with both hands and pushed into her as far as he would go. She rocked her hips up against him encouraging and matching him with all her heart and soul. After minutes of holding his weight off her, he kissed her lips and slipped off beside her.

He lay next to her silent trying hard to take in all of what just happened. This was an experience far, far from the Annie he'd been intimate with. Morris was delighted, fascinated, and afraid. He wanted more, and despite his fear of this being a one-time aberration, he began once again kissing her face and lips. She responded as before, kissing him back. Her tongue slipped between his lips, and they started.

They took much longer this time using every drop of loving enthusiasm and energy they had. Many, many long minutes later satiated and unable to move they lay beside each other in spent silence as the last of the sunset reflecting off the lake came in. The glow of the dying sun bathed the room spreading across the sheets and over their naked bodies.

Annie's skin was glistening with perspiration. She was beautiful. Bathed in that low warm light, her body young, firm, her lovely nipples still aroused, she looked every inch an Egyptian goddess. Laying there glowing in the almost darkness she was transformed into a most unexpected marvel. He knew he was about to fall asleep. It wasn't what he wanted. He struggled up supporting his head on his arm beside her. She was laying there, every bit as spent as him.

Morris thought of Hanna telling him of sitting in the auditorium on dress rehearsal night of Forever, trying to believe this thing in front of her eyes was a hundred times more than she ever dreamed possible. Morris understood. He knew what Hanna experienced.

"Morris? Seriously? You're thinking about trying again?"

"Give me five minutes and some help I'm pretty sure I can."

Rolling on her side facing away from him she said, "Maybe in the morning."

He curled up behind her and said, "I love you, Annie," and fell sound asleep.

He never asked her what changed, but all those previous times he spent being so cautious and careful were gone. Their lovemaking became a natural thing of pure joy. Morris couldn't believe what was taking place between them. She was responding with loving passion to whatever he did. It all seemed to be welcome, an enormous pleasure to her. What had been mellow and comfortable became exotic. They wanted each other all the time.

Months later Morris asked her what happened. Annie said, "Our first Christmas I asked my mother what she thought of you. She told me you could hide your feelings better than anyone she'd ever met and said I would never know you unless you let me in. You have Morris; you've been so honest with me about your feelings and so accepting of mine and me. You've taken me on, all of me, even the awful stuff. You don't judge you don't see my struggle to stay with Don as misguided or creepy even though I do. You accept me as I am, with all my crazy fears and feelings of shame, all my ever so ingrained prudish Quaker attitudes."

"Annie it's called decency."

"Somewhere deep inside me I believed, for real, you knew how to accept and hold me close, but I knew you'd always see me as a separate person. I knew you'd never ever try to own me, use me, or possess me like Don did. That misguided nightmare was behind me. I knew I was safe. I relaxed and just let myself be me, it's wonderful.

A year flew by. Morris and Annie established a teaching routine that included supporting their students especially their graduate students with study groups. Their home was awash in students. They spent two weeks before fall quarter began in Door County going to every little town, and place of interest. They were making love like honeymooners and upon their return, and despite her IUD, Annie found herself pregnant.

On Thanksgiving she said, "Morris, what we have together is heavenly. I feel so blessed and thankful. That I could feel like this, it's enthralling. Best of all we're getting a little girl out of all this loving pleasure. To be like this, to have such wonderful loving is the most seductive charming thing I've ever known. Given the state of birth control back then it's a small wonder my mother only has seven children."

THIRTY SIX

It was Saturday, June fourteenth the day before Annie's twenty-ninth birthday. Annie and Morris arrived at the hospital excited, but also experiencing butterflies about this new person soon to be a big part of their lives. Annie just wanted their daughter born so she could be normal once again.

She developed Preeclampsia the week before she was due which curtailed everything. As a precaution, Annie was confined to lying on her left side in bed and checking her blood pressure twice a day. She passed the time reading and tried not to be sad about being confined. Annie missed getting out with Morris and going on their walks. The bed rest went on for four days before labor started. They arrived at the hospital about two in the afternoon. As it was their first birth experience, they were a little apprehensive.

The birthing process kicked off with Morris having to make a big stink with a hospital administrator about him being allowed in the delivery room. Joyce said to him as a way of explanation, "Sorry about that I thought your being with Annie for the delivery had been agreed upon by everyone."

Morris asked, "Why do they have a rule about husbands not being in the delivery room?"

"Men have been kept out because the staff worries about the husband becoming a patient at just the wrong time. Possibly passing out and falling and getting injured. Witnessing their wives give birth is a big shock to most men."

Three hours later Morris asked why everything was taking forever, but he was assured this was normal. It was another four hours before Annie reached nine centimeters, and they were told the baby was presenting face up. Joyce told them if she didn't rotate into the correct birth position, they would perform a cesarean birth.

The baby must have heard the prognosis for minutes later Annie let out a big groan as the baby rotated. About ten minutes later a nurse with her hand between Annie's legs announced, "She's at ten. A short time after Annie started pushing everything unraveled.

One of the nurses said, "The heartbeat's erratic." Moments later he heard, "I've lost it." There was a flurry of activity. He heard Joyce say the baby's in the birth canal and something else to a nurse. The nurse left.

Moments later, Joyce, seated between Annie's legs said, "I think we're okay the heads crowning."

Moving to where he could see Morris saw their baby's head come out of Annie. There was a bluish white thing coiled many times around the baby's neck. Joyce's gloved fingers were tugging and pulling to work it loose. A few seconds later he saw Joyce clamp and begin cutting the cord from around their little girl's neck.

Joyce said something about cord stricture. Moments later he saw their blue splotchy white tiny little girl go into a cart the nurse who left earlier brought back with her. She didn't cry, but as she was whisked away, Morris saw her little arms moving.

Annie said, "Joyce what happened?" Seconds later trying to get up Annie yelled, "Oh my God! It burns."

Looking up Joyce said, "Annie?" Seconds later Annie twisting, whimpering, and gasping said, "I can't breathe."

Joyce had already stopped whatever she was doing between Annie's legs and come up next to her putting the stethoscope on her chest. Morris heard Joyce yell. "Sandy, get the Heparin tray. Mary grab a ventilator."

Annie almost crushed Morris's hand. Her nails dug in. He knew this was all wrong.

The nurse put the ventilator over Annie's nose and mouth and squeezed the bag. Joyce was setting up to give her an injection. Another nurse was counting and pushing on Annie's chest.

Wild-eyed Annie found Morris's eyes looked at him in desperation and began shaking. Annie's eyelids fluttered, closed. She stopped moving. Joyce shoving and rocking her shoulder was yelling, "Annie! Annie, can you hear me?" There was no response. She was still, bone white. Her lips were blue, and when he looked at her limp hand, he saw her finger tips and nails were blue. There was no motion, nothing.

Almost shouting Morris said, "What's happening?"

Joyce with her stethoscope on Annie's chest said, "I think it's an embolism."

From here on what took place was unclear. Morris heard his voice, "It's a hospital! For Christ sake, do something!"

Everyone was moving. He heard Joyce say, "I'm sorry Morris I don't, Annie's gone.

"What do you mean she's gone?

Standing just behind him with her eye's full of water Joyce put her hands on his shoulders and said, "It was massive. Morris, I'm so sorry, there was nothing I could--- do.

He heard his voice, the words, "She--- died? Annie's dead?" It was his voice he was sure, but the words were nonsense. Nothing to do with them he was sure. He collapsed inward and motionless still holding Annie's hand with both of his he sat there looking at her face trying to breathe, to think, to understand, the words.

Lots of things happened, and lots more words were said. They told Morris their baby died, but all he remembered was asking if Annie could have her baby with her, if they could be together. Morris stayed in the room on a straight-back chair while the nurses went about straightening up. He watched in silence as a nurse brought in their daughter. She carefully, placed her in the crook of Annie's arm. No one was speaking now. Morris stood beside them soundlessly, endlessly looking at their faces.

They were so still. Annie's freckles were gone sunk into the milky bluish whiteness. Their little girl had the same blue-white color. He stared at their faces trying to understand. Maybe if he could think. He wanted to scream at them to come back, he did, but not out loud.

Out in the hall, two hospital administrators were talking to him. He never heard a word. He nodded many times, and after a long time, he thought a lifetime later a woman came and drove him home. Morris thought it was John's wife Dee, but he couldn't remember anything about being in the car.

Robbie's wife was at the house when he got there. It was after midnight, and there were two women there with him. He was in a hazy awful place. No matter how hard he tried, he could neither understand nor believe this was real. He couldn't make any sense of what the women were saying to him. Unable to think, terrified and exhausted, he apologized, took off his shoes, and crawled still clothed into bed and passed out.

Daylight screamed through the big bedroom windows. Eyes open Morris was awake and dressed. Something was wrong, God awful wrong. It hit him like a baseball bat. Trying to understand he stopped breathing. The second day was more coherent. Morris was aware of things needing to be done. A funeral and something else, call Annie's parents, his sister. He tried hard, but Morris couldn't think of how to do any of this.

The hospital called that second day. The voice said the autopsies were completed, and the remains could be picked up. Remains, he started crying and couldn't stop. Never in his life had he experienced anything like this. A thing greater and more horrific than anything he could image or scare himself with. He'd been torn in half and was still alive; it never let up, subsided or lessened, it kept on and on. The shock of it stuck in him and made him sick. He looked at himself in the mirror, but he couldn't recognize what he was seeing, nor when touching his face, could he feel himself.

John Stanton and his wife Dee came that second day and John made the arrangements with a funeral home. Morris called her parents and tried to tell them of this, but he couldn't. He was telling Nathan so incoherently in desperation he handed the phone to John and wandered off overcome.

It was four days later, and he was even more lost than the first day. He tried to think about that day, but he couldn't remember. He could see their blue-white faces. On the third day, Morris was doing ordinary things. He put on clean clothes, made coffee, made the bed, and put away some of the food people brought. Morris couldn't sleep, and when he did, he didn't sleep for long. He couldn't get their faces out of his head.

It was the morning of the fourth day. He heard the doorbell and then the always more insistent heavy bronze door knocker. Dressed, but unshaven since that day Morris went to the door wondering the whole way, what now? Puzzled and annoyed he pulled the front door open wanting to say, please whoever you are go away. There on the wide brick stoop stood Mr. and Mrs. Taylor and all six of Annie's brothers and sisters. Morris stood motionless in the doorway.

This was so unexpected he couldn't fit it in his head. Connie seeing his confusion stepped forward and hugging him said, "We thought it important to come and be with thee."

In tears, he said, "Please, come in."

Mr. Taylor said, "We would've come sooner, but it took time to round everyone up."

It did not go unnoticed by any of them, Morris; his eyes full of water, appeared old, hollowed out. The women went into the kitchen. The boys stayed in the living room with Mr. Taylor and Morris. Mr. Taylor said, "Morris you don't look like you've been taking care of yourself?"

"I haven't slept much, and I forgot to shave. I can't believe this is real, that it happened. Both, it was so incredibly fast."

Nathan asked, "Do you have help?"

"Robbie's wife Karen and John Stanton's wife Dee have been here keeping me company and straightened up. Lots of our friends brought food. I don't know what to do. My sister's coming tomorrow; she said she could stay for a while."

"I'm so sorry about this; I know you're all busy with school and work. This must have taken a huge effort for you all to get here so soon, but I'm glad you came."

Franklin asked, "What about the rest of your family Morris?

"My parents are either in Amman Jordan or in transit. They're in the process of moving there. They were scheduled to arrive the day this happened. I don't even know where they're living, but they won't be coming back for a while. David's in San Francisco trying to finish up the house sale. Alice's been trying to contact Mom and Dad but has had no luck so far."

Mr. Taylor said, "Morris go shave and wash up. Then we can sit down, figure out what needs to happen, and help you make plans to get it done."

Morris said, "Robbie and John offered to help. They're knowledgeable about these matters."

Morris gave his and Annie's room to Mr. and Mrs. Taylor. The three boys went to one of the upstairs bedrooms the three girls went into another. They saved the study with its bathroom for Morris's sister, and Morris went into the third bedroom on a cot.

Later that afternoon they met with John, and Robbie James and their wives. Both men knew the area well and knowing the circumstances they sat with Nathan, Connie, and Morris helping with the details. Robbie explained there was a Friends meeting house in Evanston, but he knew it couldn't accommodate the number of people who would want to attend.

Nathan asked, "How many people should we expect?"

John said, "I think between five and six hundred maybe more. Annie was well known, and much loved. She had a gift, she was an extraordinary teacher."

Nathan said, "Our Annie, that many I had no idea."

Robbie said. "If it happened during the school year, we'd be trying to figure out how to accommodate and feed twice as many.

John said, "I hope you don't mind. I've taken some preliminary steps to have whatever kind of service you wish to take place here on campus at the Alice Millar Chapel. It's not a simple building, not a Quaker meeting house, but it's convenient, non-denominational, seats seven hundred, and the University's made it available.

After a few additional calls, they came to an agreement on everything. There would be a Quaker service using the Alice S. Millar Chapel as a meeting house. Annie and her daughter would be cremated together. The family planned to bring their ashes to Philadelphia where they would have a second service for Annie's friends and family. They would be interred in the Taylor family cemetery plot.

Morris wasn't any better but having her family with him kept him moving and doing. It was very much what he needed.

Between Connie and Nathan and the six children, they took care of everything. Under Connie's direction the boys took this on as an adventure of loving obligation. The girls just as lovingly helped with the food and they all helped with the upkeep of the house.

It was crowded and awkward for the children, but no one complained, not a single word. But Hester, the sister who looked like Annie, was a struggle for Morris. She touched his arm in the kitchen two days later, and when she said, you look much better today. It brought him to tears. She said, "I'm sorry Morris, my being here must be hard. I've never thought about how much Annie and I look alike until now."

Composing himself, he said, "It's all right Hester. I've never mixed you up."

The next day Morris took the whole family and his sister Alice to the campus and showed them where his and Annie's walking dates took place. He rolled it into a tour. Morris showed them the classrooms and lecture halls where Annie taught. He took them to Annie's office at the Anthropology Department and introduced them to her fellow professors and the staff. He showed them where they ate lunch together and where they liked to sit and talk when they first met. Her family seemed to find solace and comfort in seeing the places where Annie worked and lived.

Mr. and Mrs. Taylor and Morris sat up Friday night before the funeral and talked. He was surprised they both admitted even though they struggled with it they came to understand how important it was for Annie to live with Morris.

They told him how much it meant to them when Morris didn't just speak about Annie that first Christmas but talked to the whole family about their relationship. Mrs. Taylor asked him to tell her about the day at the hospital, and he told her as best he could. With tears in her eyes, Connie said she wished she had visited and could've seen them together in this beautiful house. She regretted not doing so. "I would've enjoyed seeing you here as a couple. Annie's letters were full of the terrific life you two were sharing and how much she was looking forward to your daughter."

THIRTY SEVEN

"Good morning, welcome, I'm Annie's, ah Professor Steven's, father, Nathan Taylor. Annie and her family are Quakers. I'm going to assume most of you are not and will be unfamiliar with our worship customs. So, before we begin, I'll briefly explain our beliefs and our service which we call a meeting. But before I do and since we're unknown to all of you, I would like to introduce Annie's family to you."

"First is Annie's mother Constance, whom almost everyone knows as Connie. And Annie's oldest brother Franklin, oldest sister Teresa, and middle sister Hester." When Hester stood and turned to face the assembly, there was an audible intake of air. Given the circumstances, Hester's appearance was disturbing. Hester flushed at the reaction, and Mr. Taylor said, "Yes, there can be little doubt Hester and Annie are sisters. Next, we have Pearce and then our two youngest Temperance and Obadiah." The family sat, and Mr. Taylor continued.

"We'll conduct Annie's service as we would back home at the family's Philadelphia meeting house. Our meetings last about an hour and are carried out in silence. Quakers are a simple spiritual group. There are no ministers or finery, nor are their scripture readings and generally no flowers, nor do we have choirs.

"The words Quaker and Friends are used interchangeably, and we come together at our meeting and sit in silent meditation. We believe all are equal in the eyes of God, so you are all officiates. If anyone feels moved to speak, he or she is encouraged to stand and do so. We call that ministering. Funeral worshipers offer prayers, memories, songs, readings, and any other expressions of love are welcome. Together, as a community Quakers share our love for the person who's died and in doing so hope as a group to provide comfort to all who mourn.

As a youngster I asked my mother why everyone came together and sat in silence. She said, to still your mind Nathan. It took me a while, but I eventually got it, and our core belief is simple. At the center of our Quaker faith is the concept of the Inner Light. That in every human soul, there is implanted an individual element of God's own spirit and divine energy. This part, known by early Quaker's as that of God in everyone, the seed of Christ, to Quakers is, in the words of John, 1:9, the true Light, which lights every person who cometh into the world.

"Quakers believe first-hand knowledge of God is only possible through that which is inwardly revealed to the individual person. This knowledge comes through the working of God's quickening Spirit. Broadly, the concept of the Inner Light is twofold. First, the Inner Light discerns between good and evil. It reveals both in human beings, and through its guidance, offers the alternative of choice.

"Second, the Inner Light opens the unity of all people to our consciousness. Friends believe the potential for good, and evil, are latent in everyone. As beloved children of God, all human beings are brothers and sisters. No matter how vast our differences of experience, of culture, appearance, or age, or even understanding we are one human family.

"Friends see it as their task to build a broader community throughout our world. Quakers do this by recognizing and affirming in each other the divine potential, the Seed, the Christ, the inner light within us all. We believe we must learn to deal with one another by affirming and nurturing the best we find in each other and we do this by answering that of God in everyone. In such a community Friends worship in silence only standing and speaking to witness to the sovereignty, compassion, and love of the God of their experience.

Nathan paused then continued, "There's always an element of mystery about love which people cannot fully penetrate. But we Quaker's are convinced love has a timeless quality and cannot be destroyed by death or limited by time and space. This conviction is underlined by the experience of Quaker worship, and by our awareness that the personality of Jesus has remained with us and was not diminished by his death. His life was based on his profound trust that God is love. Friends respond to this love. They experience heaven here and now and believe whatever lies beyond death must be for our good.

"Great sorrow is here today, more so for a loved one like Annie taken away in youth and in the strength of her days. But our thoughts and prayers should be those of great thankfulness for lives such as Annie's. Annie's life has truly borne witness to the enduring upholding power of Christ. We are gathered here to honor Annie's life and to experience God's presence. Because our meetings are conducted in silence and not in a scripted order, you'll need to know when it is over. To show the close of the service, I will ask my oldest son Franklin to join me here. We'll stand and shake hands and the hands of others nearby.

"You are encouraged to do likewise. Our shaking of hands will signal the funeral meeting is over. Ushers will not dismiss you; you are free to leave or come speak to the family or with the other friends of Annie gathered here. After the meeting, those of you who wish to do so are invited to share a light luncheon with us. It will be served from Parks Hall. The catering staff has assured us they can feed us all.

"The university has graciously provided this lovely spiritual place for us to all join and say goodbye. And knowing

Annie as I do, I want you to know she would be surprised, probably a little thrilled, but mostly profoundly humbled by the attention and love of so many. I know I am. We'll begin Annie's meeting when I take my seat."

Maybe five minutes of silence went by before an older woman stood and began speaking "I'm Margery Evans one of the more senior faculty wives here at Northwestern. I've known Annie since her first day at Northwestern. She stayed with us when she first arrived. Annie's helped me out on several occasions, but I want to speak today of one.

Last year I asked Annie to come with me while I attempted to offer support to a family who recently lost a child. Annie was closer in age to the couple, and I've known Annie to be exceptionally generous and caring with her students. I was sure she'd be a great help to both the young mother and me.

"When we arrived, we were met by Joan's husband a young man about Annie's age. He informed us Joan was lying on their bed in silence, inconsolable. This was the second day in a row, and he didn't know how to help her. We went into the bedroom. I introduced Annie while I was asking Joan a few questions trying to coach her into responding, but with no result. Annie took off her coat, pulled a chair up next to the bed took Joan's hand, and sat beside her. Neither spoke.

"The silence was painfully awkward for me. Joan looked right at us acknowledging us but didn't respond remaining silent. The silence grew more oppressive and powerful with every passing minute. Her husband stuck his head in and asked if we would like coffee or tea and I said I would. The heartbreak and pain in that room were palpable. Even though it was only maybe seven or eight minutes, I needed a break. I asked Annie if she wanted me to bring her anything she said, you go ahead Margery I'll sit with Joan.

"I was dreading going back into that room and took my time having my tea. When I returned, Annie was sitting on the bed cradling a sobbing Joan in her arms. Neither spoke, and I sat down in the chair next to them and stayed quiet. The silence now broken by Joan's crying wasn't the same. It wasn't unbearable, or even oppressive. It was cleansing and somehow even restorative. I didn't know Annie was a Quaker and went to silent meetings, but she was able to stay in that silence and help Joan. I couldn't, I didn't have the strength to be that close to all that pain.

"Annie got it. She understood Joan's need to be held and allowed to cry her heart out. I don't think Annie said more than a few words to Joan. Maybe hello when we first got there and call me if you'd like someone to sit with you when we left. We all knew she meant in silence would be okay. It was a remarkable thing for someone meeting another for the first time. God bless you Annie for your strength and understanding, but most of all for your kind loving ways. Bless you Annie and your baby girl. We're really going to miss you.

Thomas Edgerton, one of Annie's graduate students, stood and began explaining how he'd come to Annie telling her he had to drop out of school in the middle of his last quarter. He didn't want incompletes on his record and end up with F's. He wanted to know if Annie knew of anything he could do to avoid the incompletes.

"Annie asked, what's happened that you need to leave school. I told Annie, my wife; our seven-month-old daughter and I were losing our home. The bank sold it, and we hadn't been able to find another place we could afford anywhere even close to the campus. My car had broken down; it would be two weeks before I'd have enough money to get it repaired.

"We were down to twelve days to find a place to live. Getting back and forth to work and my classes was taking all my time. I saw no way around our predicament, but to drop out and move us home to live with my folks. Annie said Tom, let me talk with Morris and come see me tomorrow. The next thing I knew we were living upstairs in Annie's and Morris's house. I was driving Morris's car to work and back until mine was fixed.

"It was tight with all of us in one room, but thanks to Annie and Morris I graduated five weeks later at the end of the quarter. I have a good job and a nice life. It would've never happened without Annie's and Morris's gracious kindness. But there was so much more to living with Annie. She was terrific with our little girl and a true friend to my wife. There was such joy in their house I can still hear our little girl's laughter when she was in the highchair in the kitchen with Annie. Neither of us will ever be able to think of our time here without thinking of Annie and Morris. We'll carry them in our hearts forever."

Annie's students began to tell how much they enjoyed her classes. Some said they couldn't wait to get to her classes. They all said Annie made learning such a joy. Some talked about how much they appreciated her efforts to not only educate them but to put the world of people and cultures in human terms. Continually reiterating no matter what color, we were, or where we came from, we were in this together.

"Many of her graduate Students spoke about her devotion, help, and support. How Annie individually affected their lives, not only as a teacher, but as a woman and friend. They spoke of the tremendous sadness and anguish they felt upon learning of what happened to her and her baby."

"My name is Darlene, and you heard about me earlier when Mrs. Evans spoke of the young woman who lost her baby. I didn't know what an inner light was until today. Intimidating as this is I need to share with you what it meant to receive Annie's inner light. I'd been cheated, robbed of my child. I carried him for nine months and struggled giving birth to him. Seventeen days later Adam died during the night. Adam was loved, cherished, and irreplaceable, and he was gone from me, from us forever.

"I've never experienced such loss nor the anguish and hopelessness that went with it. I was inconsolable, abandoned by God, and angry that our beautiful little boy never had a chance. It was a cruel, mean thing for a loving God to let happen.

"Annie took off her coat pulled up a chair took my hand and sat with me. She was just there beside me. Annie had the kindest eyes and was such a presence. She just sat there in silence holding my hand. I don't know for twenty minutes, maybe thirty. I started crying. Annie took me in her arms and held me and let me sob my heart out. She never said a word. She just held me and let me cry and cry. John, my husband, bless his heart tried in every way he could to comfort me, but he was in so much pain himself we seemed to make each other worse.

"Perhaps time would've accomplished it, but that morning with Annie changed me. I was still engulfed in all the anger and pain, but I felt like someone accepted me and understood. There were no condolences; no words of empathy or kindness there were no words at all. Just Annie's loving acceptance of me. Annie shared an enormous amount of her inner light, and I hope I did in some small measure in thanks share some of mine. God bless you, Annie. May God hold and keep you and your daughter with as much love as you did me."

"My name's Steven Harrison, and I'm the spokesperson for our quartet. We're here to play for Annie, her baby, her family, for all of you." They stood one by one and introduced themselves. Steven continued, saying, "We want you all to know why playing here for Annie is so important to us. I was an undergraduate student in one of Annie's classes. Upon learning, she was an honest, impartial, but keen advisor. I told her of my desire to continue to graduate school.

"I asked her if she thought I was foolish to consider a graduate program in music. Everyone was encouraging me to do the smart thing and get my graduate degree in something more practical. We talked about practicalities, and she began sounding me out about my music.

"I told her there were four of us who got together three times a week to play and practice. We loved playing together and were serious. I explained getting a position with a major symphony was a tricky proposition because once hired musicians like Supreme Court justices stayed for life. Openings for posts are few and far between.

"Annie said, Steven, the whole time we've been talking the only time your eyes came alive was when you were talking about your quartet, your music. Annie suggested we find a suitable venue on campus and perform in public. She said there's something about doing something for a living that lets you know right away if it's what you should be doing. I said we're good, but nobody's ever heard of us. We couldn't charge people. Annie said, but you can do a series of free performances. Just pretend you're getting paid. The result will be the same.

"Our first concert was in a small space that seated a hundred and fifty. We had no idea how many people if any would attend, but we went ahead. We printed flyers giving the location, date, time and our music program and posted them around the university. Then we started praying someone besides us would be there.

"Annie announced our performance in every one of her graduate and undergraduate classes. She rounded up, I'm not kidding, twenty-two faculty wives and husbands and showed up front and center in the auditorium. Word got around, and it wasn't long before we had to move to a larger space at Lutkin Memorial Hall. The four of us are in the graduate school music program. We're looking forward to long and fruitful lives as professional musicians. We just wish with all our hearts Annie and her daughter could be with us. I can't imagine anything more awful or tragic than losing them.

"Our first piece was Annie's favorite. Chopin's Nocturne No. 2 from Nocturnes, Op. 27. The second is for you Annie and your baby girl." They concluded playing a haunting Brahms's lullaby that left that big room and all those people in it in heartbreaking silence.

Morris never understood why. He thought later it was the sudden starkness of the silence or the sun being hidden by clouds, and the sanctuary's rapid darkening. Morris could feel himself wanting to get up and run and to keep running until somewhere far away he'd collapse. But he was standing, turning, and hearing his voice.

"I'm Morris Stevens, Annie's husband, our little girl's father." Startled, realizing he was facing over seven hundred people he stopped. Every pew was packed. There were people everywhere; seventy or eighty were standing by the walls.

The sun broke through and the light pouring in through those huge stain glass windows washed over brightened and warmed everything. It was ethereal, glorious, and mixed him up. It was Annie in all her glory, beautiful, spiritual, and right there with him. The light overwhelmed him. He looked out upon that crowded light-filled space for many seconds before he spoke

"I had no idea Annie touched so many lives. She would be so amazed and pleased you've all come to say goodbye. He started again. They're both gone from me, from all of us, and hard as I try I can't comprehend what happened that day or why. But it did, I saw it all. Looking at you in that hospital even your wonderful freckles disappeared. I tried my best to talk to you. To call you back, but neither of you heard me. I think it was all in my head. It was so awfully quick.

"I want you to know Annie you were everything, everything I wish I could be. You and our little girl were the beginning. But I've found a place, it's inside me, a place where you can both be with me all my days." He paused for a moment and finished as if he were the only one there. "Annie, all that's left is your love. I swear Annie, I'll share it. I'll keep it with me always and do my best to make all your goodness and love part of me." His voice wavered. "God, I'll never understand why this happened, but please take care of them." Eyes filling with water he sat trying desperately not to come apart.

Morris hoped what just happened wasn't insanity. He knew full well he had no ability or words to explain how he felt. Morris didn't understand why he got up or spoke, or anything about what he thought he was trying to do. He hoped for Annie's sake what he said made sense. Morris didn't know if he said words or just imagined them. He wasn't sure.

Brian Robertson, one of Morris's graduate students, rose and said, "Morris it's not just Annie and your baby. I'm going to try to speak for every one of us who knew you. I say try because it scares the life out of me to be in front of this many people. It's not because I don't know what to say. I'm educated; you and Annie did everything you could to see to that. It's because of this awful thing that's happened. The reason there's so many of us here is you are special to us.

"You were only a few years older than your students, and you both accomplished so much and were so good at what you do. We all wanted to be like you. To be successful, find a partner, make a life like yours and Annie's. You were such an example. We'd see you together having lunch or walking, especially when Annie was pregnant. We all hoped to be like you. Losing Annie and your baby, there aren't any words that'll ever make it tolerable.

"Annie would say something humorous about being so hugely pregnant in her classes, and she'd do it with such loving humor. We all knew what your marriage and family meant to you. You told us in everything you did. Annie was the best teacher I've ever had. Even better than you Morris and I'm not saying that because she also happens to be a beautiful woman. Students would ask her all the time, Professor Stevens's where did you learn to teach like that?

"Annie didn't actually make it easy. She made it a wonderfully enjoyable, a very human experience. I had to get up and speak. We all talked about you two. All of us, all your students did. We admired you both and that two such remarkable people were married to each other just seemed to us lesser mortals an unbelievable amazing thing.

"Coming to your house for help, what can I say? It was like being asked to dinner at King Author's roundtable, to join the Supreme Court, and attend a Beatles concert all at the same time. This is heartbreaking to every one of us who know you. Our prayers are for Gods loving care for Annie and your baby girl, but for you to Morris."

Several of her fellow professors rose and spoke of Annie's care and concern, of her going to enormous lengths driving them all nuts to find answers to questions posed by not just her graduate students, but also her undergraduates. One and all they spoke of how she loved teaching, how she had the gift, and it showed in her classrooms and especially her students. How her enthusiasm and joy were infectious, and they each caught some of it making them not only better teachers, but more positive people.

It was now close to an hour and after a few more moments' twelve people stood one after another and introduced themselves. The last Christopher Watson said, "Annie's, been a supporter of ours since she first arrived at Northwestern. Our ensemble to a person is heartbroken about what's happened. All we could think of to do for Annie and her baby girl was to come here and sing and hope they hear us.

"The song we will sing to Annie and her baby girl is from the Largo part of Antonin Dvořák's New World Symphony. It was adapted into the spiritual-like song Goin' Home, by Dvořák's pupil William Arms Fisher. He wrote the lyrics in 1922. The arrangement is ours. When Annie first heard us sing this, she said afterward, Chris I'm so glad you insisted I come. It went straight to my heart.

"For you and your baby girl Annie, may God gather you in his arms." All eleven in unison using their voices began singing the orchestral introduction. With an incredible powerful lyrical baritone voice, Christopher started in singing the words. By twos and threes, others joined in some singing with Chris while others sang background as a choral orchestra.

Those beautiful, powerful voices rang clear throughout every nook and cranny of that vast sanctuary. Mixed with the glorious light pouring in through those remarkable stain glass windows it moved everyone. When it ended, there was weeping throughout that huge gathering. Before long, by ones and twos, threes and fives they all slipped into that ever-engulfing silence. A few moments later Mr. Taylor shaken, stood with watery eyes and began shaking hands with Franklin.

THIRTY EIGHT

Morris didn't go to Philadelphia for the second funeral. He spoke with Connie telling her he didn't believe he was ready to face staying in the guest room. Nor could he watch Annie and his daughter's ashes put in the ground. Morris hoped she and Nathan would understand. He said, "Connie if this seems improper or inappropriate, please say so. I'll come. I can stay somewhere else, I'll manage it, but I'm just lost. I don't think I can go through another funeral service."

Morris thought about her family a lot. He was deeply appreciative of their coming to him the way they did. Morris now saw Nathan and Connie, the whole family in a different way. They were in as much shock and pain as he and, yet they did everything they could to help him and make him whole again.

They did it in their loving, gentle Quaker way. He would never forget the week they spent with him and his sister. They all knew Morris's world ended in that hospital room. Everything that mattered was torn away. Morris's own family was scattered to the winds. His younger brother was living in a dorm at Stanford; his sister finished graduate school at the University of South Carolina and was living and working in Columbia. Morris's mother and father were halfway around the world in Amman Jordan.

However, Annie's family were together all safe in that big house in Philadelphia. Morris no longer understood his relationship with her family or what form it would take. He felt closest to Annie's mother, Connie. But that was mostly because of her smile, her kind ways, and what Annie told him of their talks with each other.

Nathan had surprised Morris with his gentle ability to help him keep moving and make progress, especially with the details of the funeral. Their time together was only a few visits, and this great shared sadness, but Morris felt loved by him. Nathan and Connie and all six of the children became special to him. Keeping them close was a way for him to hug Annie to him. Annie's and his baby's deaths took hold of Morris like nothing he'd ever experienced. It never stopped or eased up. It was an endless sorrow. He always thought of himself as strong. Nothing got to him not for long. He always kept going.

Morris experienced a lot of death when he was young. He witnessed a playmate, a little boy down the street be shot and killed when he was seven. When he was ten, he and his best friend found his mother just after her suicide. At twelve Ricky Strand, his friend from school and his baseball team drowned right in front of him and six other friends. His grandparents when he was thirteen. Four high school friends died in car accidents.

Death never seemed far away or gave him any time to prepare. Even after seeing Hanna with her head and face black after her beating and near death after her emergency surgery he righted himself. But this thing with Annie and his daughter just kept on and on, through every waking moment. It was he believed because he couldn't conceive of the absolute finality of it, that there would be no more of them, of her ever.

He couldn't sleep, and when he did, he couldn't stay asleep. He was close to exhaustion. Toward the end of that first month he would wake and have a few normal seconds. Then it would all be there, and he would need minutes to once again process it.

Annie was just there they were talking, laughing. He struggled to believe any of this was real or happened. When he no longer could, he'd recite the official version out loud. "Morris your daughter was deprived of oxygen by her own compressed cord. She was brain dead and died seven minutes after she was born.

"Annie died right in front of you of an amniotic fluid embolism. An event so rare only one of her doctors ever heard of it, Joyce didn't know what happened until the autopsy. It's real all right. You saw it with your own eyes. Losing Annie was way, way far beyond tears. It settled in him quietly, solidly and with purpose. Morris was losing the desire to continue.

Fortunately, his sister came back to be with him. Alice did everything she could to get him to care and heal. Alice was a godsend because she was relentless. She took Morris to stores, she made him buy new clothes, and get a new pair of shoes. Alice took him out to eat and to places where he'd have to interact with people. They walked on the campus and by the lake. Alice talked with him and took him back to their grand old lake home. She talked him through their younger lives fleshing out their many shared memories.

Alice reminded him of his struggle to complete his first book. Of how hard he worked keeping up with his coursework. How hard Annie worked to overcome her traumatic first marriage. She said, "Morris, life's not fair, it's hard work! She stressed how Annie would expect and want with all her heart for him to live life fully. Not just for him, but for her and their lost daughter. For Morris to keep alive all, they hoped and dreamed of. Annie would want him to share her love everywhere he could. It was the best way Morris could give her life the enduring meaning it deserved.

He was slowly accepting Annie's and his baby's deaths. He thought he should name her. She only lived a few minutes, but she was alive, he saw her little arms move. His little girl was a living person with a soul. She had a death certificate they put a name on it. Morris told them a name that night. It was one of the names he and Annie talked about, but he couldn't remember which one. So, in his mind, Morris named her Hope. He thought it could've been what he told them. It didn't matter. Hope was appropriate and something that would be easy. Nothing else about this was.

Alice left, weeks passed. At the start of fall quarter, Morris returned to the classroom. He was a good teacher. His students liked him and respected his fairness. Even though he was known as the taskmaster and a tough grader, there were no shortages of students for his classes. Morris loved his subjects. He loved his students, especially the interchanges between them. He felt a little awkward at first, but he soon got his legs under him. At least that part of his life was almost as before.

The package came to his office in the Humanities department. He knew by the enchanting children dancing playfully around the address it was from Hanna. The painting he unwrapped wasn't large maybe twenty by twenty-four inches. It was framed in a beautiful five-inch-wide black and gold ornate classical Renaissance frame. Just off center was a little black-haired girl perhaps three who'd been dancing her way through the mist. Eyes bright she was paused in an archway.

She was in a delicate lacy pristine sparkling white tutu, matching white shoes, a top, and tights of the palest pink, every bit the ballet dancer. She was elegant, vivacious and oh so confident. Yet with all of that, she was a little girl, an exquisite, beautiful child. She appeared to be somewhere between the real world and a mystical place where angels might go.

There was a black haired shadowy figure of a woman smiling in the background her dark eyes ever so carefully watching over the little girl. The little girl was looking right at him with the clearest blue eyes. She was brimming with life; obviously secure, happy, and well cared for. Seeing Annie and his lost daughter filled his heart with joy and at the same moment, a massive wave of sadness washed over him.

There was a note. Morris's eyes were so full of water he struggled to read it.

Dear Morris,

I'm so sorry such an awful thing has happened. I only found out a few weeks ago. Why didn't you call? I feel horrible about this. All the years of support and help you've given me. It was my turn.

Please, Morris, I hope with all my heart you know I'm here for you, I'm thinking of you every day and praying for you. Morris, I tried my very best to capture your lost loves. I did my best to give them life.

Thinking of you, Hanna

Morris thought to himself, no Hanna I can't, we'd end up making love like always. Only this time I'll never be able to deal with the guilt. It's better for both of us this way. Staring at the painting, he wondered long and hard how Hanna could capture Annie and his daughter, give them life. It was far beyond creative or imagining. She had given them not only life and joy, but such a lovely remarkable place to always be.

The little girl on the canvas was a living breathing being. She was alive there in all that paint with her mother. Annie would've loved this, and like him, she would've cried her heart out. A week later he sent Hanna a short note; it was all he could manage.

Dear Hanna,

The painting is the most helpful touching thing anyone has ever given me. Only you could have given Annie and our daughter life and such a marvelous place to always be. Thank you, Hanna! I'll treasure and keep it with me for as long as I live.

Thank you with all my heart, Morris

Toward the end of fall quarter, Morris appeared to everyone to be on his way to recovery and once more leading an everyday professor's life. He wasn't. His love of Annie and his daughter was in his heart like a red-hot ember that would not go out. He would often wake from a sound sleep and wonder where she was. Then it would be upon him like a ton of sludge pressing on him squeezing the very life from him. He would struggle and fight just to breathe.

His three graduate students returned in the fall, and they tried to keep up the meal preparations, but Morris couldn't do it. None of them could. They carried on trying, but it wasn't the same. At night if alone in the house he would yell just to break the silence. Sometimes he would dream of Annie so vividly he'd wake all hot and sweaty. His arms empty his mind clutching frantically at the formless wisps of a fading dream.

Every night for months and months, straight through Thanksgiving and Christmas, he worked on the book he started the first year they were together. It became Annie's story. What her life meant to him and everyone else. Five months after their deaths he finished it. He didn't know what to do with it. It was his understanding of all Annie went through in her short life. It spoke of her amazing transformation as a wife and professor. His shock and inability to understand what happened that awful day. It spoke of her family and growing up Quaker.

He wrote of her struggle to overcome her first husband's sadistic treatment. How she found her way to once again trust her judgment and love another. He wrote of her steadfast energy, her sense of humor and deep-seated goodness. Of Annie's constant sharing with others and of his admiration and gratitude for what she gave him in their Quaker marriage and it was one.

All of this became possible because Annie came to an understanding and made peace with her powerful inner light. With this knowledge, she made Morris more than he could ever hope to be on his own. It was a story of persevering love, not a love story. Annie's inner light was there in every chapter.

Writing the book allowed Morris to understand and accept Annie, his daughter, and their marriage, that his family, were gone from him forever. The book held all his tears for the lost life and promise of both Annie and their baby girl. All that remained was her love for him. When he told his sister about the book, she said, "I'd like to read it." So, Morris sent it to her.

Five weeks later a package arrived from his publisher. Inside was an edited copy of his manuscript along with a note and business card from a Mr. Keith Littleton. The note said after talking with your sister at some length and learning the book is based on the recent tragic events in your life. I thought I would forego bothering you and turned your manuscript over to my best editor, Doris Ivy; she's made a few she said sparse changes and would like you to read the proof and sign off on it if it's acceptable to you.

Keith said he'd like any rewrites completed as soon as Morris could. Keith was concerned if there were to be extensive changes it would hold up the publishing schedule. He wanted to get the book printed so he could begin sending it around and start working on the marketing.

His note concluded with: "Morris I don't get a book like yours often. I found myself, a grizzled New Yorker touched. I fell in love with Annie. It's a compelling, thoughtful story. Annie was indeed a gift, and I think everyone should have the opportunity to know her. Morris was shocked. He was yelling in his head, for Christ sake Alice, why? You didn't even ask. He didn't know whether to throw up or call his sister and yell.

Pacing, his thoughts racing, thinking to himself, it was private, Alice, and personal, incredibly personal. It was our life, our dreams. After a few moments of going back and forth, he settled down realizing you're right Alice! It's her life. It's Annie's story, her goodness, and decency.

But he could not re-read it. He wrote every word in tears. Just thinking of reliving it hurt horribly. He noted his acceptance and signed on the cover page and gave it to Janice the office secretary to repack and return. He thought no more of it and busied himself on working out a syllabus and lesson plans for a new graduate course John asked him to teach.

The book, "Abbreviated Lives," the publisher's title not his, changed his life. His academic works gave him position and credibility in the academic world. His previous novel was successful and a best seller for long enough to provide him with some campus notoriety. Because of the subject of his first novel, Morris's fellow professors gave him a kind of jealous grudging acknowledgment of achievement. But most considered books for general consumption trivial and not comparable in any way to the rigorous intellectual standards of Morris's academic works.

However, a runaway bestseller such as "Abbreviated Lives" was, well, a different thing altogether. It was deemed a work of art by the critics. It created a firestorm of change bringing Morris fame which he didn't want and fortune which was also problematic. Agents were talking to his publisher about buying the movie rights for sums of money he couldn't conceive of.

Morris was surprised and overwhelmed by the book's success. It hurt him terribly when he found himself getting rich off the story of Annie's short life. He wrote it for himself trying to see her. To understand her inner light, her love for life, and for him. Morris was okay with sharing Annie with others, but God above not to get rich.

He got a note from Hanna it helped him stop feeling so awkward about all the money pouring in. She said:

Dearest Morris,

It is such a joy to know a man who knows and understands what life, devotion, and loving kindness are. At the end of your book, I couldn't stop the tears. I cried for Annie, your baby, but mostly for you. I'm so sorry about what happened, but I'm glad you wrote about her. You were blessed to have lived with someone so remarkable in so many ways.

I got to know her and love her right along with you. It was a very unusual experience. I learned a great deal about you and Annie, about marriage, and love. Reading her story, you shone through the whole thing. Others wouldn't see you hiding there, but I did. You were there to me like a great set design.

When the curtain opened, you set the scene, the mood. Within seconds of us first taking it all in you faded into the background and never once interfered with Annie's story. You were there in the background throughout the story, subtlety shifting the scenery underlining the place and time for your actors. Morning, noon and the pleasant softness of evening you did it with the ever-flowing mood of light.

You never came forward or interceded, but you supported her with everything at your disposal. You let that marvelous woman have and hold that stage, and now it's hers forever, and you were subtle. We never saw your hand at work we just soaked it up as we read the words. I couldn't put it down, not even to eat or sleep. I read it right straight through, I've read it three times.

You are a beautiful, creative person Morris. It was a powerful lesson. I fell in love with Annie and your marriage, and I hope someday somehow, I can approach Annie's masterful understanding of love and family. I would be so pleased. It would be wonderful if I could come to have that kind of dedication and certainty. Morris if I ever do I'll consider myself complete.

Praying for you, Hanna

THIRTY NINE

Because his publisher insisted, and he was under contract to do so after spring quarter ended Morris began a book tour. It started with Morris doing three big venues, one in New York, and one in Los Angeles and another in Chicago. The rest of the tour, the low-key part was in smaller places like Omaha, St. Louis, Atlanta, Denver, Cincinnati, Phoenix, and Austin Texas. His last one was in Minneapolis. There were no morning shows and unlike the three big venues no evening lectures requiring him to speak to audiences of hundreds and stay afterward.

He quickly grew to dislike the airports and getting to and from the many flights. The hotels, restaurants, cabs, and cities, everything, even himself became monotonous gray wash water. By the time he reached the last stop, Minneapolis, the tour had gone on far too long. It was the most trying thing he'd ever done.

Morris couldn't wait for it to be over. Toward the end, he wished he'd never agreed to publish the book. It was a simple story of a well-educated young woman and her struggle to have an academic career, a loving marriage, and family. One about living a life dedicated to ceaseless trying to overcome, to courage, innate wholesome goodness, selflessness, and never giving up.

The only good thing the tour did was keep him out of his house and away from everything they worked so hard for and so instantly and painfully lost. He reminded himself of whose life it was, whose story it was, but he was weary and needed a break from talking about Annie and the book.

The book gained real traction among young people and women. He was pleased it was liked even admired, that the critics loved it. He thought like him the critics fell in love with Annie. The book and its continuing popularity gave him more than a little notoriety on campus. He was the darling of his fellow married professor's all of whom very much appreciated what he and Annie shared. But the tour did allow him to escape from the campus, the uproar, and his empty house.

Sitting at a table for hours a long line of people in front of him all of them with questions and comments about the book's characters. He answered politely and always said thank you for coming. Morris asked who this would be for and before he looked up, a voice said, "Robert and Annett Williston."

Morris stood and shocked, stuck out his hand saying, "Robert how nice to see you. How are you and Annett? My goodness, it's been a long time. You look terrific."

"We're doing well. Could you come to the house for dinner tonight? We need to talk with you."

"Is this to do with Hanna?"

"Yes. And you."

"Are you living in the same place?"

"We are. Will six thirty work, Morris?"

"Sure, and I'll be on time."

He drove the familiar roads and made the familiar turns, but somehow none of it looked the same. The Williston's house, freshly painted and landscaped looked better than ever. He pulled into the drive and knocked on the door. Annett opened the door. Close to her not hiding but using Annett as a shield was a little girl with coal black hair and startling turquoise blue eyes, Morris recognized the eyes the moment he saw them.

He dropped to her level and asked. "And who do we have here?"

The girl peeping out from behind Annett said, "Emily, who are you?"

"I'm Morris Emily. It's nice to meet you."

Dinner was kept interesting by Emily and her continual observations and questions to Morris. "Are you my mommy's special friend Morris? Are you special Morris?"

"Yes, Emily I am."

"Mommy told me you help her with her imporment things.

"I try when I can."

"Mommy told me you're why I'm here."

"Well, Emily I think that must have been the biggest most important thing I've ever done for mommy and you."

After their last exchange, Annett took Emily off for a bath and bed. Morris said, "Tell me about Emily and how you have her here with you."

"She yours Morris, Emily's your daughter."

"I assumed as much."

Robert said, "Hanna's going to be angry with me for doing this, but I can't stand it any longer. Hanna's in big trouble and I don't know what to do. She's slowly killing herself."

"When did this happen? The last time we saw each other Hanna was on top of the world?

"It was something to do with Henric and Erica, she wouldn't tell me what. She bought the building she's in from them even before the Tony awards, but something happened after she got that enormous price for that big painting. I still can't believe Hanna's art sells for that kind of money. I think the falling out was over money, and something about the work."

"Isn't she doing any theater work?"

"Something happened there too at just about the same time. Something about not fulfilling her contract, it was an awful mess. She ended up hiring a law firm and a bevy of lawyers. She wasn't happy about any of it, and she's done no theater work since. I'm worried sick about her. She's always too busy to talk to us. She'd never tell me the truth about what's going on, anyway. The only reason we know anything is she loves Emily with all her heart and soul. She's been coming every month for the past three years. She'd stay for a week just like clockwork. But she hasn't been here in three months."

"Why didn't Hanna tell me she was pregnant?"

"She said you married months before she realized she was pregnant. Hanna felt she'd already messed up your life enough. She told us she'd be a mother but could never be a wife. Hanna said I wouldn't know how and I've never wanted it."

Morris said, "She's always said that?

Robert said, "On the trip back here from New York to have Emily she told me about your relationship. Hanna told me you became lovers, and it was the most marvelous thing she ever experienced. Hanna told me she wasn't capable of being married and giving you what you needed. Hanna said she kept luring you back to her, she was using you and it was unfair.

"Hanna told me you came from the gods because you were the only person who always understood, helped her, and pointed her in the right direction. She told me she got everything, all her direction, her fame and fortune, everything came through you. She said she'd never given you anything back. Not once. She knew you wanted and needed a wife and family. But she wasn't that person and knew she never could be."

Morris said, "I don't know how, but I would've been a father to Emily."

"She knew you would, but she didn't want to interfere with your marriage or cause you or your wife any heartache about getting her pregnant. Hanna made us promise we wouldn't tell you about Emily. She wanted to set you free, so you could live the life you deserved. Hanna's never brought you up since our trip back here to have Emily. Well not until she read your book about Annie. That profoundly affected her. She was impressed with what you and Annie had. On her last visit, she said I think I've misplaced my whole life somewhere without even realizing what I was doing."

"Robert I'll go to New York. I'm sure she'll see me. At the least, I'll find out what's going on."

"Morris, you need to get her to come home. I won't stop worrying about her until she's here back home with us at least for a while. You're not going to like hearing this, but when Hanna stopped coming to see Emily or being forthcoming about what was going on. I hired a private investigator. The report he sent was chilling. What Hanna's been doing is unbelievable. That Hanna's behaving in such an aberrant frightening way has us both sick with worry. Annett's aged ten years since she saw the report. She's heartsick.

"We were planning to fly there with Emily and walk in on her. But given what I learned from the investigator I wasn't holding out much hope of getting Hanna home. When I read in the paper you were coming to Minneapolis, we thought you might be better at talking to her than us. Her behavior is completely out of character. I'm afraid the way she's carrying on she's either going to overdose or get herself killed. We're both feeling hopeless, and Emily asks about her every day."

Robert's description of her behavior was disconcerting, but not coming home to be with her daughter after being so faithful for three years scared Morris. It entered his mind Hanna could be working up the courage to do away herself. Morris flew to New York as soon as he could make arrangements.

***

Three days later Morris was sitting on the concrete floor at the door to Hanna's second floor living quarters. Hours and hours dragged by since the last of her crew went home. They passed him on the landing reminding him to be sure to close the outside door if he left before Hanna returned. For the last time that night he said to himself, give it five minutes more. Twenty minutes later Morris was getting up to leave when he heard the outside door open and voices in the stairwell below. Morris stopped moving.

"No, you're not coming up," it was Hanna's unmistakable sensual voice. It was soft, but understandable. The mans' wasn't. Muffled and slurred Morris couldn't understand what he was saying.

"That's all you ever want. Quit it, Steve, let go. Go home; I'm tired of this."

The man said something Morris couldn't make out. She said, "There's nothing to understand. I can't do this anymore. No, Steve, I don't need a fuck. It's meaningless."

The man said something, quite a lot, but he still couldn't understand him. With crystal clarity, he heard her, "The hell with the painting do you think you're the only gallery that'll work with me? Now leave before I say something we'll both regret."

Her voice was clear as a bell, "You're too stoned sweetie. You couldn't do anything even if you wanted to. Oh, for Christ sake put that thing back in your pants. No, I won't give you a blowjob. Now shoo, go on; and make sure the door shuts." The door abruptly closed, and he heard her say, "What a twit." He heard her footsteps slow and measured on the steps, and Morris gathered himself and stood. Hearing him, she stopped and said, "Is someone there?"

"It's Morris Hanna." There was a silence that lasted so long he almost repeated himself.

"God almighty, Morris, It's you? It's been forever. Come sit on the steps with me."

"Hanna I've been sitting on that concrete floor for hours. I'm stiff as a board. It's late. I'll come back tomorrow."

"No, come in. We can sit on something comfortable."

In the light of her living room seeing her his heart was breaking. She was still a Monarch Butterfly, but her wings were worn and tattered. All the perfect sharp-edged pristine brilliant orange and black colors were dulled, smudged. His magnificent Hanna looked translucent, worn out. Reading his eyes, she said, "I'm a mess Morris, and I'd sure like to believe you didn't hear the conversation in the stairwell."

"Sorry, I didn't cover my ears."

"That's pretty much my life."

"Who is he?"

"One of my gallery's owners."

"Are you important to each other?"

"Not in the way he thinks, but that's my fault. Sometimes when I do too much cocaine, I've let him love me, but no Morris he's just a man. We're not close."

"Tell me what happened between you and Henric?"

"I did a large painting, seven by ten feet and at the show's opening, there was a spontaneous bidding war, when it ended an avid collector, an older woman, Marion Haley, paid two-million-sixty-five thousand dollars for it. I stood there with my mouth hanging open.

"As hard as I tried, I couldn't believe it. That's when all the trouble started. The losing bidders went to Henric and Erica and begged them to have me do something similar for them. They offered to pay two million sight unseen for a similarly sized painting. At the time, I was doing a new Broadway show with Maria and a complete idiot of a producer.

"No one told me, but Maria and the producer got into a horrendous argument, and she quit. Then the writer quit, and the costume designer left. The show was in deep trouble, and the new director and fixer writer started adding and deleting scenes like they were changing socks. The show differed entirely from what it began life as. It had nothing to do with what I initially designed. They kept making changes, and I couldn't do it.

"It was the new director's first Broadway show. He was panicked, and so far in over his head, the show never stood a chance. It became complete madness. I left and refused to come back. The producer hired a second new director, two more writers, and a new costume designer. He replaced me with a new set and a new lighting designer. The show never opened."

"Sounds like the Titanic."

"There was some idiotic clause in the contract I signed that got overlooked. When the asshole found out I sold a painting for almost two million dollars he sued. The producer thought he could use me to cover some of his losses. He was a jackal and tied me up so completely I never had time to do the additional paintings. That guy made me so mad I ended up half crazy. I fought him with everything I could. He lost in court, but it was the biggest nastiest most drawn-out hassle of my whole life. It didn't do my art career any good either.

"He got personal and ugly and so did I. I was forced to subpoena people to testify about what was going on. It didn't win me any friends. He was an idiot and incompetent and spread shit all over me. But he's a producer, and everyone was terrified of crossing him, so most of it stuck. Not a single soul besides Maria voluntarily came forward to refute his claims. Hardly one nice thing in the theater world's been said about me since. It's a small community, and I've been tagged by his associates as a brilliant, but impossible offensive bitch to work with. One who doesn't honor obligations? I've done no theater work since."

"Wow! I'm really sorry."

"Enough of that stuff. It's good to see you Morris, but why are you here, now, today?"

"Hanna it's time to come home."

"That's nice, but where might that be Morris. Where would home be?"

"It's not here Hanna, and you know it.

"Is home at your beloved Northwestern?"

"Hanna don't be sarcastic you never were, and it doesn't suit you. It interferes with everything about you, your smile, and most of all your joy."

"Sorry! I've developed some serious anger issues I haven't been able to figure out let alone get over."

"For what it's worth Hanna I don't believe Northwestern is any longer home, but we need to find it.

"I thought I had."

"Hanna, we have a child a daughter. I think somehow, we all belong together. To be in each other's lives That's what I know."

She said, "I'm going to take a shower. Should I put on some coffee? There are soft drinks in the refrigerator."

"Go, I'm fine. Get cleaned up. Morris sat alone in Hanna's remarkable, fantastic space looking out through the twelve-foot-high windows at Manhattan glittering away in the darkness every bit the exotic, otherworldly beckoning place.

Morris sighed and suddenly felt old. He was unsure about being here or what he would say to her. She was different. Life wasn't kind. She came out of the shower wrapped in a blue terrycloth bathrobe and sat on the sofa next to him. She tucked her legs up under her and said, "Morris you look exhausted. Come to bed, you need to sleep."

"I don't have anything."

"Don't worry about it. Just get in bed."

He didn't argue and stripped off everything, but his underwear. He fell asleep almost the moment his head hit the pillow.

FORTY

Morris woke to the smell of fresh coffee and the sight of Hanna across the big open space in the kitchen area wrapped in that blue bathrobe. She brought him a cup of coffee and lay down on top of the covers next to him.

She asked, "When did you find out about Emily?"

"Three days ago. I went out to your parent's. Your mom answered the door, and Emily was peeking out from behind her. I dropped down and asked her what her name was. She said Emily, who are you? I knew the moment I saw those eyes and heard that voice whose she was. Other than hiding her somewhere your mom and dad didn't have much choice

"What were you doing in Minneapolis?"

"It was the last stop of my book tour. Your dad came to the book signing and cornered me. He invited me out to the house for dinner."

"They always thought you were special. Everything got better for Hanna when you showed up. So, which one spilled the beans?"

"I knew the minute I saw Emily she was yours. Knowing of your disdain for men and her raven black hair I suspected she was mine. Emily told me during dinner."

"So, how'd she manage that?"

"Emily was across the table from me asking questions, one of which was, are you mommy's special friend, are you special Morris? I said yes Emily that's me. She said mommy, told me you helped her with big imporment things. I said, Yes, I try to. Emily said mommy, told me you're why I'm here."

"Wow, I should know better. I'll have to be more careful about how I say things."

"She's bright, but I doubt she had any actual understanding of what her words meant.

"Don't kid yourself what I said stuck in her head. She understood special Morris had everything to do with her being here."

"Tell me about her."

"Emily's three. She'll be four February twenty-first, and she was born in Minneapolis nine months and two weeks to the day after the Tony Awards."

"Was that intentional Hanna?"

"I wish I could say yes, but I've never been more surprised in my whole life. I thought something else was wrong. When the doctor told me I was almost four months pregnant I must've said, I'm pregnant, me? Are you sure? I was so surprised I kept saying it, I must've said it a dozen times before I left his office."

"You told me you were using birth control."

"As my Doctor said when Emily was born, my birth control device was still there intact. That Emily entered the world with my IUD in her hand."

"Holy shit Hanna, Really?"

"No silly, it's just a cute way of making fun of a failed contraceptive method."

"Well, I no longer believe medicine's reliability is even close to all it's cracked up to be."

"Dad came out and drove me home. After Emily was born, I stayed with mom and dad for four months. Duty called, but

I've been going back, every month for five or six days, seven if I could manage it."

Morris said, "And for the past three months no visits from mom. Emily misses you. She told me to tell you; to please come see her. You've got your mother and father worried sick about you."

"So am I.

"Is something else going on? Are you drinking, is it drugs?

"I've done way too much cocaine, but I'm not a habitual drug user or drinker. I work every day. It doesn't matter anymore. I'm lost. I'm as empty as a person can be. My work is meaningless. There's nothing left Morris, not one damn thing."

"Hanna, please tell me you haven't been thinking about suicide?"

After some hesitation, Hanna said, "I've thought about it, but don't worry, Morris. There's not enough left for even that."

"Hanna don't think about it. Do not go down that road!

"I try not to."

"Well, how about this? With the help of your mom and dad I've got a plan for us, at least for a short time."

"I've always counted on my wise older man Morris for help."

"Pack up your paints, canvasses, tools, and brushes. Put everything in storage, rent this place. We go back to Minneapolis and live with your parents until we can figure out something workable for everybody. Your Mom and Dad begged me to bring you home. They want you back home with them and Emily. At least for a little while, until we can get things figured out.

"They actually said they want me back?"

"Hanna, they love you more than you can imagine. You're their bright shining star. We've all been following you, cheering, but you're fading. Everyone who cares about you is worried sick. Hanna, we're not kids anymore. You told them we were lovers; I was the father of your child. They know nothing's right with you, that you're in trouble. My wife and daughter died, and nothing's been right in my life since. I'm as lost as you."

"Morris, you wrote a best seller about her."

"Writing it kept me from going under."

"She was your love, Morris. She was incredible. Just reading about her I fell in love with her."

"She's dead Hanna. Annie and Hope are gone forever."

"The Love isn't."

"Hanna long before we were lovers we had this terrific bond and concern for each other. It started when we were teenagers. I don't know why it was so strong. I've never figured out what it was, but it's something we could start from." Morris heard the words coming from his mouth and tried hard to believe it was him saying them. For the first time since that awful day, there was a twinge of anticipation the barest hint of hope in his voice. He was mentioning possibilities which were new, genuine.

He was surprised. With the sudden loss of Annie and Hope, all sense of any kind of future evaporated. "Hanna I'm here because I care about you. We've had something special for a long time, from that first Fourth of July, the Thanksgiving dinner, the prom. I want a life that works for us, for you and Emily and me, one that works for all of us. Maybe even marriage."

She stiffened, snapped around, eyes blazing. "Really Morris! You think I'd let you put a ring on me? How about throwing in a dog collar and a fucking leash!"

Her sudden ferocity shocked him. He lashed back, "Christ almighty Hanna, what's with you? You wrote me a beautiful letter saying you read my book; fell in love with Annie and our marriage. What's with the rage and what's with my just mentioning marriage that so upsets you?"

"All of it, everything about it!"

"Okay, okay, I won't bring it up again, but for God's sake Hanna, we have a child. We've got to figure out something that works."

"It should've been me Morris, but I pushed you away. It's all on me, and it was deliberate. I read your book, but I know nothing about what Annie gave you. You're a tenured college professor at Northwestern one of the premier schools in the country, you've written four books. Two were best-selling novels. The one about Annie was magnificent, incredible. You loved her, and you married and made a life together. Morris, you have a life there and a home, you've got a real life with people around you who deeply care about you."

"Hanna I'm sorry I yelled, but when you snapped at me for just mentioning marriage, it really hurt. You scared me, but I won't bring it up again."

"I deserved it. I have no right to be making judgments about you and what happened to you, not after what I've done.

"Hanna the people from my novels lived in my house. I'm living there alone. The house is full of heartbreaking memories. I can't stand the emptiness of that place or my life there."

"It wasn't you Morris. I was angry at myself, I'll be honest, but it's a hard thing to do. Being with you, face to face it's become almost unbearable. I don't want you to know what I've done, but someone's bound to tell you. You'll find out. I'm sorry Morris, I'm about to hurt you, and once it's out, you won't want me as a friend much less a wife. I've ruined everything I've despoiled us, ruined everything we've been to each other."

"Hanna, you don't need to explain.

"Morris it's important. I can't hide this. It will change how you see and feel about me forever. You extended a hand you offered me more, and I pushed you away. I've done it over and over, and I just did it again. I've let dozens of men I hardly know fuck me and done it again and again. I go out get coked up and let who'll have me fuck me. I don't give a care about those men.

336

It's the emptiest most degrading self-centered disgusting life you could ever imagine. I don't date or want to marry or make babies. Well, I did, once."

"Hush! Hanna, I don't give a damn about your fornicating! You haven't crippled or killed anyone. You're the most amazing creative person I've ever met. We've loved each other some weird unknowable improbable way all our lives and we probably always will. So, I'm here for you, Hanna. I care.

"You were my magic Morris I'll give you that. No matter how many men I was with Not one's ever come even close to you."

"Hanna, I'm not talking about sex. We need to get this right between us. Married or not we need to learn, understand, and know one another so we can be Emily's parents."

"What are you saying, Morris? You want to start over, to go out with me, to date? You want a new beginning?"

"I'm asking you to help me figure out a way to have a life that works for you and me and Emily. I don't know what that life is, but it isn't this, and you know it."

"How would we do that? Emily doesn't know you. She barely knows me. She thinks of my mom and dad as her parents. We couldn't just whisk her away from them to Northwestern or anywhere else, she'd be traumatized."

"Hanna, I can't live there. That house is full of the people I loved, cared and wrote about. They're all dead, and the place is full of them. They're everywhere, it's overwhelming. I had three graduate students living upstairs, and it didn't help. They couldn't stand that Annie wasn't there. That she died. They left. The house is empty and so am I. Your parents invited me to stay with you and Emily at their house. To stay as long as it takes for us to get to know and be comfortable enough with each other to figure out what to do."

"Are you're telling me you'd give up Northwestern? You'd come back to Minneapolis and stay with me, us?"

"Yes, that's what I'm telling you."

"Why didn't you come all those years back? God almighty Morris you could've kept me flying high and safe. With you here, I would've never had even one of those crashes. You could've transferred to Columbia, I know you could've. I can't believe what's happened to us."

"Hanna, I couldn't go with you, not even to have what you gave me the night of your graduation party. Trust me, Hanna, given what's happened since it's the only thing I've ever wished could've been different."

"You married Morris.

"Yes, and I wanted what the people I wrote about in my first book had. What I grew up with. I knew I'd never find a lover like you. It wasn't possible. I didn't even try. I wanted what Annie, and I worked out between us. That kind of love came from a different place. Annie lost her life because of it."

"You can't blame yourself for what happened, it wasn't your fault."

"Maybe not, but if I'd figured out how to be with you or even what we were to each other, I doubt Annie and I would've married. She wouldn't have gotten pregnant, and she wouldn't be dead."

"From reading your book, my take was she was brilliant, brave, and you both believed you could make a wonderful life together. Morris, you promised each other you would. I read those words you said to each other. From your book, I felt at least between you and me you succeeded."

"Don't misunderstand me, Hanna. I loved Annie and being married to her. But it only came about because I gave up on you. I couldn't imagine how to have a family with you. Believe me, Hanna, I tried. You were already married to something else. You married your creativity, your art. I took the only path I could. Annie and I loved, but not like you, and I did. Annie and I shared kindness, companionship, loving support, warm comfortable sometimes thrilling sex, true friendship and caring deeply for and about each other. All the things we all need and want in our lives."

"Morris, you never ever once talked about marriage or even the possibility let alone asked me."

"Hanna you've forgotten your mantra. I don't date, I don't marry, and I don't do that thing that makes babies. I grew up with it. It was never any different. You were like some goddess soaring out into the stratosphere. It's been there since that afternoon in your room when I first saw your paintings. But that mantra's always been there.

"You're unique, special Hanna, and it's not just me. Your professors turned the whole department inside out bringing Maria in to launch your career. You won two Tony Awards on your first Broadway show. Nobody who saw you up on that stage will ever forget you. Your art is breathtaking. Henric saw you. He knew how special you are. You've sold millions of dollars of paintings, you're adorable and sincere. The TV cameras love you, and so does Time Magazine, Newsweek, and The New York Times. They all do, but most of all, The New Yorker Magazine and Dick Cavett.

"I never wanted to impede that, and I had no idea of how to be a part of it, nor did I know how to deal with being part of it. I worshiped you, but I knew there was no way for us to be married. It would've been between you and all that creativity. It would've never been right. You had no space for marriage, and you know it."

FORTY ONE

"Hanna, the night you won those Tony awards I was so pleased for you, I couldn't stop smiling for you. All I knew was how much I admired and loved you. Our times together were so otherworldly and unbelievably fantastic I wept just thinking about it. I didn't date because I knew there wasn't anyone who could take me where you did."

"What about Annie?"

"We loved each other, and we were good together. We were pleased with our life. We settled into our marriage and enjoyed helping and being with each other. I loved her, Hanna, and she loved me. I would've been happy until the day I died. But it wasn't meant to be, and she sure didn't deserve what happened. Hanna, what we have is different. You are the greatest most spectacular woman I've ever made love with. But if there's to be any hope of this working for you, me and Emily it will have to be about a lot more than heavenly sex.

"Wow! I don't know what to say, Morris. You helped me grow up. You've always been honest with me, but I never wanted to marry. I was too afraid. You were kind, and you always listened. You read between my lines and Morris, you were the only person in my life who understood what I was capable of and what it meant.

"I've known we loved each other since that day in my room when you first saw my paintings. I'm sorry Morris, but I was terrified of letting you see the real me. That first time we made love I'd no idea what to expect, but I had to know, and I knew it could only be with you. But that night and the next day left me terrified. It left me forever open to and longing for you.

"Had you asked I would've married you, but I wasn't capable of or able to give you any of what Annie did. It would've been a disaster. I think what you and Annie experienced, what you worked out, is what love is."

"You're right Hanna, but I believe with all my heart there's enough between us we can grow it into that kind of love."

"Morris, you've always helped me. Whenever I asked, you were there for me, and it was so one-sided. It started in high school and just kept on and on. When I was beaten, you came all that way to be with me. You brought that wonderful book and gave me hope. You kept checking on me making sure I was all right, always encouraging me. The night on the phone when you told me about the St. Joan production you saw with Michael was the night I became a set designer. It's still one of the best things I've ever done. Thanks to you I understood how to distill real. I now saw the reality in abstract, genuinely tidy and simple ways.

"I'll show you pictures of St. Joan. You'll be amazed when you see what your little talk spawned. When I met with Maria, she went through my renderings, and when she got to the end, she said, Professor Adams is right you are an unbelievable talent, Hanna. This is a brilliant way to do St. Joan. And Morris that was just one of so many one-sided exchanges you've had with me."

"I never felt it was one-sided Hanna, not in any way."

"But it was Morris."

"Hanna since I first met you you've always, always been special. The first time I saw your paintings was unbelievable;

it moved you to a whole different level of being. Just to know someone that accomplished, creative, and talented is extraordinary. Then to be loved like the night we first made love was and is the most otherworldly experience of my life."

"Morris you're right I know there's a lot more to marriage than making love. Your book was about that other. Annie will always be with you. You should treasure it and what you had together. And Morris, I have none of what Annie brought to you. You speak of my talent my creativity, but I don't feel I have any of what Annie did, of what she was, of what she gave you."

"Hanna, she made me what I am. Without thinking or trying in any way, Annie buffed and polished me until I glowed. She taught me to believe, and trust, and about faith, and to be okay with myself. It's because of her I'm as positive as I can be we can figure out that part. Hanna, I believe you've got to have faith in the goodness within you. Just trust and have faith in what I see in you."

"Morris, I don't think I've ever had any faith. I got up every morning raring to go, and I was having the time of my life, I didn't care or think about anything, but the work and getting it right. I'm self-centered and selfish, and it was heavenly Morris. Nothing got in my way. I didn't care about men, and even less about being married. But I had to find out why men and women are different. After that night and day with you at the St. James I knew, and I couldn't believe how I felt.

"I knew there would be no one else in my life. Not that way, not like you, but I was terrified you'd see me. I was so scared. If you knew me, how shallow, timid, selfish and afraid I was I knew I'd lose you. When I was working, I was safe, okay. But after our first time together I was as terrified as I've ever been. Those times at my studio when you visited, you were as important as my work. I couldn't let you in, I wanted to, but I couldn't. I knew I couldn't do both.

"The day after the Tony awards I wanted to beg, to scream, don't go, Morris, stay with me. But once again I pushed you away, and now, I'm as lost as I can be. I'm just working for money; its plain wrong, my hearts not in my work, it shows. My arts become a job my livelihood. I miss the theater and those wonderful, creative, interesting people. Most of all I miss Emily, I feel dreadful about abandoning her. I'm empty inside. There's nothing left, but ashes."

"Hanna, stop it!"

"No Morris I won't. I've hurt people. I let Maria go; we haven't talked since that awful fucking trial. She was the only one who stuck up for me. I wrecked my relationship with Henric and Erica. Look at my face Morris. I'm used and bitter. I'm no better than a street whore. It's got to hurt."

"What's that all about Hanna? It's so unlike you."

"I don't know. I tried to find my kiss, to feel what I felt with you. It's become the only thing in my life. My holy grail, but it's never that. Not even close."

"Hanna, your kiss was a stand-in for what we felt the night of your prom. I don't know what you experienced, but it was lots of surprising feelings for me and the nicest most special thank you I've ever received. When I hear you say my kiss, it's code for a wondrous warm moment in time, a lovely long ago safe heavenly place."

"I need that place, Morris."

There was a long moment of silence. Hanna said, "When I sent you the painting of the little girl, and you sent back that short note it broke my heart. I put everything left in me into that little girl and her mother. I bought Annie's book, so I'd have her likeness. It had been three years since we'd seen each other, and I knew in my soul from that short note our lives had been severed."

"You're there aren't you Hanna? You're going to kill yourself?"

"Yes, Morris, I am. I don't want to be here anymore."

"Come on Hanna this isn't you. You're strong, you're good, kind and decent, you're not like any of this.

"I'm an awful person Morris, I've lost or wrecked everything that ever mattered. I didn't know how to let you be close. You married another. It was too late for us. I had to let you go. When I learned about what happened, I reached out to you the only way I know with a painting. For once I wanted to comfort you, to be there for you. You sent me a five-line thank you. It broke my heart."

"Hanna, stop?"

"NO! Let me finish. My work's soulless and so am I. I read your book, and I knew with every page I could give no one what Annie could, I cried myself to sleep night after night, I felt like such a child. I understood your love, your marriage, but I didn't understand how to be that to another. I have none of what Annie did nor do I have any understanding of how she loved."

"Hanna, please, stop!"

"Damn it, no! Let me finish. I'm a continual one-night stand; I've stopped going home to see Emily. I despise what I've become, what I'm doing, but I can't stop, and I've nothing left and no hope; if I had a fragment of courage, any courage at all, I'd end it."

At that moment he thought to refute her words, of trying to make her see she could change things, that this was neither fixed nor hopeless. To tell her he adored her, and the painting of Hope and Annie more than Hanna would ever believe. That his five-line note was from his soul written in fear and all he could manage. Instead, he said, "Shush," and put his fingers over her mouth and just let her lay there in silence with her head on his shoulder.

A few moments later Hanna rolled against him snuggling her face against his. Whispering, she said, "I'm so ashamed of trying to find what you gave me with all those other men. Knowing I have, is it even possible? Can I ever be anything to you?"

"Hanna, stop! Just stop it."

"God above Morris I can't believe what an awful mess I've made of everything, I was so afraid."

"Of what Hanna?"

"Of you knowing who and what I was, of being obligated to you, of having to share my time or myself. I was afraid you would swallow me whole, and I've always loved you Morris, but I've been afraid since that first day in your boathouse. I never knew how to love you, and I don't have any idea now."

"Hanna I've always held you with open hands. Remember, let it grow wild."

"But if we married?"

"There'd be expectations, a commitment. Something both parties accept. They work hard, to be honest, and get that part straight. Like right now Hanna with all I am or will ever be, I need to be with you."

There was silence, and Hanna said, "I'm not sure I can."

"Hanna, it would mean everything."

"Morris, I'm disgusting how can you want to?"

"Hanna, I need to be with you. Please, for us, for me and what we had."

"I'll try. I will, but I think I'm going to cry."

"It's okay. You can cry. Crying's allowed."

Hanna smiled briefly, slipped off her robe and got under the covers. Morris kissed and held her, and soon enough feeling as they did years ago, in amazement they surrendered. They only stopped for food. They made love the whole day. Now in darkness, lying next to one another she asked, "Are you all used up?"

"Give me a little time and some help, I'll be ready."

"You want to keep going?"

"Don't you?

Reaching over and turning on her bedside lamp she said, "Yes Morris, I do. I've never had enough time with you. After all these years, it's the same magical heavenly thing. I've been such a fool. Nothing's different, it's like no times passed."

He said, "Hanna we both know this thing that happens between us isn't just sex.

Yes Morris, somehow, it's here for us like it's always been. I've never understood it, but even I know it's a whole world more than just sex. Smiling, obliviously feeling better she said, "Well there are things different, my tummies not as hard since I had Emily."

"Hanna it's so nice to see your smile."

"Thank you, kind sir."

"Hanna, I could be with you like this for days and days, I can't believe how I feel with you."

"I'm a self-centered fool, Morris, and I've been wearing blinders all these years. I've been so afraid, and I couldn't see it. I can't believe how stupid I've been. It's all there in your book. You're right about everything, and I can see it. If you're serious Morris, I'll do it."

"Do what Hanna?"

"Marry you.

"Really! You'll give this up and come live with your parents with Emily and me?"

"Everything I need is there. I've got to start over and Morris you don't get to change a thing. I'm the one who needs to change, and you're going to help me like you helped Annie."

"Hanna this won't be easy. Learning to be honest with another is scary hard work. There'll be a thousand times when you'll get mad and want to give up."

"But I won't Morris, I want this.

"It'll take time to work it out."

"Morris I'm sure I know what I need to do to make a life with you. I should've done it long ago, but I didn't know how. I've never understood my pushing you away. What my fear was, but I'm sick to death of being afraid. God above Morris I've always been terrified of letting you know me, but not anymore. Just tell me you believe we can have what you and Annie did? That I'm capable of that?"

"I'd never ask you to marry if I didn't believe it with my whole being. We owe this to each other to Emily. Hanna, we've got to try, and as hard as we can."

FORTY TWO

Watching Morris fixing breakfast in the morning she said, "I'll call Henric this afternoon and get things moving."

"You're still talking?"

"Not once since he caught Erica and I in bed together. But Henric told me when he sold me the building he wanted the first crack at it if I ever sold. I owe him that. It's been over two years, and they're still together. So, I'm sure all's been forgiven, or they've reached an understanding."

"So, who've you been selling your paintings through?"

"We'll talk about that later. It'll be part of recovering my sanity and getting back to being Hanna."

He took her by the chin and looking into her eyes said, "Convince me you no longer want to kill yourself?"

"I'm okay Morris, truly! I promised, and I won't lie to you."

Morris said, "You were there. You were going to, weren't you?"

"Morris, you beautiful man, I'm on the other side, I'm in the light. It's my life. All I've got, and I don't care what happens, I'm not afraid. Even if this blows up and I end up alone, I'll never go back into that place."

***

Hanna called and talked with Henric. He and Erica showed up the next day about ten. The meeting was cordial. It got even more so when Hanna said she'd sell the building back to him for what she paid him for it plus her remodeling expenses.

Henric was so pleased he offered to buy all the furnishings, pay for cleaning the place, Hanna's moving expenses, and just about anything else she wanted. Erica said little and looked uneasy. But she kept looking over at Hanna and then at Morris like she did during their first meeting in Minneapolis at the St. James. Morris could sense even though Erica was dealing with her concern for Hanna she was also trying to understand something about him.

At the entryway, as they were leaving Erica turned to Morris and taking his hand said, "Morris I read your book on language misinterpretation. You did a remarkably skillful job of helping us better understand such puzzling dilemmas. But your book about Annie that was unforgettable. I was so sorry about what happened, but I couldn't put it down. It meant a great deal. I fell in love with Annie, I felt like I knew her. I was overjoyed with the power of her life and her remarkable ability to share her love."

"Thank you, Erica; I'm glad it meant so much."

"I hope you keep writing. You tell a wonderful, meaningful story extraordinarily well. I insisted Henric read it. Two nights later I woke up next to him in bed to the sound of him crying his heart out. You're both an absolute wonder to both of us, and I hope with all my heart you'll find your way."

Erica's words twisted Morris all up inside. He was forced to feel Annie all mixed with Hanna. He was embarrassed and surprised by his conflicted feelings, but he said, "Thank you, we'll sure try."

Erica hugged Hanna and kissed her on the cheek and said, "Thank you, Hanna, thank you for everything." Henric shook Hanna's and Morris's hand, and they disappeared down the stairs. Morris would ask Hanna many months later, but he already knew her relationship with Erica was much more involved than just another of her coke-fueled sexual experiments. Hanna and Henric agreed to get together in two days with his attorney and complete the sale.

"Morris, I have to meet with my crew and tell them I'm closing up shop. I don't want you anywhere around for it."

"I'll stay in the living quarters unless you want to do it here in which case I'll hide out in the studio."

"It's going to be difficult. There'll be hurt feelings, maybe tears, and a lot of disappointment, maybe even some yelling. Mostly it will be sad for all of us, but especially for Maryanne and me. She's an incredible artist in her own right. Maryanne's been with me from the start, and we're close. She's the sister I never had."

Three days later they married in a civil ceremony with Maryanne as the sole witness. That night because Hanna read it in his book and she asked him to, they held hands and repeated those ever so simple Quaker wedding vows to each other.

They fell asleep holding each other. It was July twenty-second. Morris left the next morning returning to Evanston to meet with the realtors and tell John Stanton he was selling the house and resigning.

FORTY THREE

Morris hadn't seen or spoken to John since going out on the book tour ten weeks back. So, as soon as he got to his house, he went to the phone, called and set a time to meet John that afternoon. Looking around while hanging up the telephone Morris became aware of how empty and still his big old house was. His eyes were on the vase of flowers long dead he'd forgotten to throw out before leaving on the tour.

After his renters left Morris spent the last of spring quarter by himself. Dee and Karen, John and Robbie's wives and some of the other faculty wives took turns bringing him cut flowers. They'd come in get out some of Marion's beautiful vases arrange the flowers and put them in the living room and dining room. They would clean up and leave. Morris never knew who had been there. But Morris appreciated their concern and generous efforts to brighten his days. Seeing those fresh flowers always improved everything.

One morning Morris was there when Dee showed up with this enormous bouquet of delicate tiny white flowers and lacy greens. She put them in that elegant green vase on the high table behind the sofa in the living room. Dee said, "They won't last long, but they were so pristine and fresh I couldn't pass them up.

Morris said. "They're so delicate. What are they called?

Morris had never heard or seen Dee get upset. She shocked him when, she angrily said, "How could I be so stupid? What an idiot? The flowers are supposed to brighten your day I didn't even think about it. I'll go get something else."

"They're perfect, and you've put them in Marion's green vase, it's my favorite. Whatever's the matter with them?"

"They're called baby's breath Morris."

"They're beautiful Dee, and that's a perfect name for them."

That magnificent bouquet was now ten weeks later a lovely vase full of still intact branched, dead twigs. The hundreds and hundreds of white petals and tiny lacy green leaves had fallen undisturbed all around the vase in a perfect circle of brown. Seeing that elegant vase on the table encircled by all those curled up tiny brown petals; feeling the stillness, the silence, just being back in the house it overran him. Annie was everywhere in those quiet rooms.

Feeling himself sinking Morris spoke out, "I'm home, Annie, I'm back." He was moving through the rooms talking. "I have a daughter Annie. She's three and a half. I'm selling this place your home, and I've married Hanna. I know after the Tony awards you worried about her and what she meant. You had no need to worry Annie. I loved you so much. I still can't believe what happened to you, to Hope, to us. You're right! You knew there was more to Hanna, we had history, and I couldn't resist her. Please try not to be jealous. As God is my witness, I have and will always love you.

"I slept with Hanna the night of the Tony Awards, and I told her that was it, the last time. I was getting married, and I told her I would always help her, but I couldn't be with her that way ever again. She understood. She never, not once again called and asked me for help and Hanna never told me she had my child. I didn't know until about a month ago. Her name is Emily. She's beautiful. I know you'd love her."

Going in the kitchen still talking he said, "Annie we would've joyously spent our lives together with our children our family. I was so looking forward to everything about it. For yours and Hopes sake, I wish it had been an accident, and we'd all died together. I wouldn't feel so guilty about being alive, about Hanna or being blessed with Emily. I wouldn't worry about you thinking my love for you as lessened by my marrying Hanna. But we have nothing comparable to what you and I shared, not yet.

"Annie our lives and hopes were dashed to pieces, and I'm starting over. I'm going to share what you taught me about love, and yes, it's unfair, but please try not to feel bad. It's been a terrible struggle, but I've accepted you, and Hope are gone. But Annie our loves not, and I'll do my best to love Emily the way I would've loved Hope. I'll do it for both of you. Annie, we were living in heaven while you were here, and I can't bring you back. All I can do is share your love and try my best to believe you and Hope are somewhere safe and cared for.

"You were a living treasure, Annie. I'm keeping you both with me never doubt that. I promise you, Annie. Hanna and I will do our best to get it right, we promised each other, and we'll work just as hard as you and I did. He saw Annie standing in the kitchen, she was smiling at him. This was her place, Annie's home. Morris knew he had to let go. A little later he stepped out onto the wide brick entrance and closed and locked the door behind him. He felt a little braver about telling John he was leaving.

***

Morris took a seat across from John thinking of all he and Robbie had done for him. John, always glad to see Morris, wearing a warm smile, said, "What's so all-fired important we had to meet right away?"

"John there's no good way to say this. I've put the house up for sale. I'm leaving the University."

John was shocked; his face went slack. He sagged, disheartened to his core. Many seconds of silence went by before John said, "Jesus Morris why? What the hell's going on? You're a tenured full professor; you're a vital part of this place."

Morris felt awful. John's shock and sense of betrayal were everywhere in that office, but mostly on his face. It made Morris want to cry like a lost five-year-old. They talked for a long time. Morris told him of Hanna and how he came to have a daughter with her. He spared nothing telling him everything. John said, "Morris, I'm profoundly sorry about everything that's happened."

"I know you are, and it pains me to add to your sadness, but under the circumstances, it will be impossible for Hanna, Emily and me to be here."

John, his face a little closer to normal said, "I was planning to retire at the end of the next school year. It was all arranged stamped and approved. You were meant to take over as chairman of the Humanities Department. Morris, I know you won't believe what I'm about to say. But we all believed you and Annie would have provided an even stronger leadership role than either me and Dee or Albert and Marion."

"Wow! And you're right John. I don't feel Annie, and I were anywhere near as accomplished as you and Dee or Marion and Albert. You're talking about an enormous enduring legacy to fill. But I'm pleased to know you thought us that capable."

"I'm sick about this Morris. Losing Annie and your baby was a nightmare for you, for all of us. I didn't think last spring was the right time for talking about the future. I put it off. Once your book became such a huge success, and you left on the book tour we never had the chance to talk about the future. Now to lose you, well it's mind-numbing."

"Your news was a huge surprise, John.

"Why?"

"What you just told me was so unexpected, and we were both young, babies both of us."

"Robbie and I decided you were the future of the department. The powers that be were in unanimous agreement. We all felt the department couldn't be placed in more capable hands."

Morris's eyes filled with water. Wiping his eyes, Morris said, "I had no idea, what an honor."

"I'm disappointed that you're leaving. Actually, it's devastating Morris, but I wanted you to know how much we think of you."

"John, you told me once what Albert and Marion did for you. You said you owed them everything and could never repay them. I feel the same about you and Robbie, and I should've talked to you before I went on the tour. I knew then I didn't think I would be able to stay on. But I thought it prudent to wait until I completed the tour and see how I felt before saying anything

"You knew I wasn't keen on the promo tour. But toward the end of spring quarter, I couldn't wait to get away. Annie and our baby were everywhere. I couldn't think of one without thinking of the other. They were in the kitchen, in the bed, in our backyard, and everywhere I went on campus.

"All the joy in that house disappeared with Annie. The three boys living upstairs left. They couldn't stand her absence any more than I could. But they were sweet about it; they came to me together and told me how awful they felt, that they couldn't bear being there without her. They helped me clean the upstairs. We put clean sheets on the beds, and that was that. By two that afternoon, they hugged me each in turn and were gone."

"Morris, we were watching you, and you seemed to all of us to have settled back in. Your students were praising you to the heavens. We knew you were writing again. We all thought you were on the mend."

"Sorry John, I did my best to hide my despair. But I wasn't doing well.

"I should have insisted you go to health services and get help."

"I went, and it helped, but not enough to allow me to stay. John, I have no idea what the future will bring. But given everything I know, it can't be here, and I apologize for not talking to you sooner. I can't change what happened, but it's troublesome that what happened has messed up so many lives. Do you think it possible that Robbie might consider heading up the department for a while?

"Unless I can talk him out of it Robbie's leaving at the end of winter quarter. He and Karen are moving back to Vermont."

When they parted that afternoon, Morris left hoping he hadn't destroyed their relationship. Morris knew John was hurt, but Morris wanted to believe with all his heart John understood and accepted why neither he nor his new family could live here.

The next morning Morris had almost the same conversation with Robbie. Robbie was a little more accepting of Morris's situation and why he could no longer live here. He explained John's shock and unwillingness to accept Morris's leaving. Robbie said, "John's worked his whole academic life to make the Northwestern Humanities department what it is today. John believed he was passing it on to someone even more capable than him.

"Your leaving has squashed his plan and hopes for the department's future. You've left him with an enormous hole to fill. And I'm sorry Morris, but you're an exceptional, competent and brilliant person. Replacing you will be almost impossible. Settling for second best makes this more difficult for all of us. John will hold every candidate up to you, and he'll find them wanting."

After the Realtors left Morris locked up the house and caught a flight back to New York. He pitched in the next morning helping Hanna get her life's work packed and ready for the movers. It took five full days to get everything settled and prepared for the moving van

Hanna called Henric and told him they were leaving tomorrow, and she'd swing by and drop the keys off at the Gallery. When she hung up, she said, "We're having dinner with Erica and Henric at their apartment. We're spending the night as their guests.

"Jesus Hanna, how awkward will that be? Do you really want to leave New York with that taste in your mouth?"

It was a lovely evening. Morris was amazed a cuckolded husband, his wife, and her ex-lover, and her lover's new husband could spend such a warm, charming, friendly evening together. In the morning, Erica took them to the airport in her chauffeured car. Morris helped the driver with their bags and Erica holding Hanna in her arms said, "I love you, Hanna. I always will. But I want you to know all's right between us. Henric and I are so much better with each other because of it and you to Morris, with the help of your endearing book. Everything's been put right."

Hanna said, "I had no doubts, I was sure you'd be okay."

Letting go of Hanna Erica said, "Don't look back Hanna, love this man and build a life for your family. You are both such amazing creative people. I'll keep you both in my prayers. If you ever return to New York, please let us know and promise me you'll stay with us."

Morris saw way too much going on between Hanna and Erica. He also knew better than to ask or ever bring it up. Morris said, "Thank you Erica, and please be sure to tell Henric, thanks again. It was a lovely evening for all of us."

Hanna gave Erica a long hug. Morris grabbed their bags, and they went through the terminal doors.

FORTY FOUR

Robert, Annett, and Emily met them at the airport. Emily was as excited as she could be. When they reached the house, Morris pulled their bags from the trunk, and everyone headed for the entryway. As he went through the front door, he asked Robert, "Where will we be?"

Grabbing two of the bags Robert said, "Follow me. I remodeled the upstairs after Emily was born; this is going to work out nicely." Morris felt about as awkward as he ever had. He knocked up this lovely sweet man's jewel of a daughter married another and left him and Annett with the responsibility of his daughter. He was coming here to live with them and felt awful about everything her parents were forced to put up with.

Robert picking up on his unease said, "Morris when Hanna drove back with me to have her Baby she told me your whole history. I want you to know from the bottom of my heart you're welcome here. There's so much creativity and talent between you and so much pain and loss. You deserve to have some joy in your lives."

Morris said, "We've a good start. Emily's a joy, a treasure."

"It took a lot of courage for you to give up everything, to come back here and try and figure out your lives, if we can help just ask."

"Giving us a place to stay and the time to work on this together is a godsend. Emily will be safe and feel safe and thank God neither of us needs to worry about money. We're fortunate about that."

Robert said, "I know in my heart you'll work out a proper way to take care of Emily. This will be good for all of us."

Within three days of their arrival, it became apparent to both Hanna and Morris that Annett was struggling with what to tell her friends about her daughter and the man who came home with her. Annett's neighbors and acquaintances dropped by unannounced using one ridiculous excuse after another. Annett would introduce them, saying things like, "You remember my daughter, Hanna and this is Professor Morris Stevens."

Her friends just wanted to see them, to look at Morris and Hanna. After four days of this Annett announced she was inviting some of her closest friends for dinner. Annett reasoned her friends could get Hanna's and Morris's story straight from her wayward daughter's mouth. She was more than willing to let her friend's shoulder some of the burdens of dissimulating what was going on under the Williston's roof.

Annett's friends were aware Hanna was both a successful fine artist and a successful theatrical designer. Most everybody who knew the Williston's saw the Tony award ceremony and watched Hanna's appearances on television. Annett made sure of that.

Annett was proud of and pleased with her daughter's success. But renowned artist or not having a daughter who was an unwed mother living in her house with a man was another thing altogether. Even though she'd agreed to it, it was embarrassing. Annett cared about what others said and imagined the worst. Her friends and neighbors all knew the child living with the Williston's was Hanna's illegitimate daughter.

Her friends also knew the man now staying with them; Morris Stevens was a family friend of Hanna's and a best-selling author. They suspected he was Emily's father. Annett supposed the worst of whatever else was making the rounds about her daughter and her companion were stories made up from the lurid imaginations of bored housewives. The ultimate reality for Annett was they were rooming together in her house.

Not at all helpful to either Annett, Robert or Hanna was Morris arriving forty minutes late For Annett's well-planned dinner party. When Morris arrived, everyone was seated at the table passing the food. Morris spent the first few moments apologizing trying to set things right. He could see Annett was beside herself and Robert the always present peacemaker sought to help him out, saying, "I'm sure there's an explanation Annett. Give Morris a chance to tell us what happened."

"Minneapolis has changed a whole lot since I last lived here. I got turned around. The situation went downhill from there. It didn't help that the people I was to meet with were around the corner from where I understood we were to meet. We found each other. So, other than cutting it short, getting caught in traffic on the way home, and being late it wasn't a complete waste of time. But when did Minneapolis graduate to a big-time rush hour? I had no idea, and I apologize for being late and not getting to meet with you before dinner."

They'd been living here for five days, and this was the first-time Morris did something that upset Annett. Impatient with him and wanting to move this along Annett started the introductions saying, "Morris I'm sure you remember Steven and Sharon Costellano. On their right are Tony and Susan Benson. On their left are Craig and Laura Anderson and across from you are Howard and Jenny Evans. "I hope you remember them. They were good friends of your parents."

Morris thought, Annett what are you doing? Of course, I remember these people. They were mom and dad's best friends. I'd have to be brain dead to forget who they are. Boy, I've messed this up. This won't be fun for anyone. Howard recognizing Annett's distress said, "Morris it's been quite a while since we last talked. It was twelve years ago, at one of your parent's Christmas parties."

"I was an undergraduate. You were interested in my double major and wanted to know why I chose humanities and linguistics."

Annett continued, interrupting and explaining to Morris. "Next to your mother and father these are our oldest and dearest friends, and they all wanted the chance to see Hanna and meet her friend."

Hanna looking at her mother with unbelieving eyes, said, "My friend? We're married mother. Morris is my husband."

Annett said, "When? Hanna, why didn't you tell us?"

"I never thought about it, Morris and I talked it to death, I'm sorry, I assumed you knew. Anyway, all's right in the suburban world. You're not harboring an unmarried daughter or condoning her living in sin in your house. Honest mom, according to the state of New York we're one-hundred percent legal."

Even though her voice still held remnants of anger Morris could tell Annett had been relieved of a big troublesome worry. But, she still held back some. She said, "Hanna if you had been wearing your rings I would've known?"

Morris smiling said, "She wouldn't have it. She said, Morris I'll marry you, but you might as well try and put a dog collar on me as a ring on my finger. It's never ever going to happen, saved me a lot of time and money."

When Annett relaxed everyone else also breathed easier. Jenny Evans was laughing as she said, "Hanna I saw all of your interviews on the Dick Cavett show. He had that running observation he used in all your interviews. He'd say I see we still have no ring? We could all tell your charming sincerity, wonderful smile, and always lovely presence made him wonder why. Later, he would ask how it was possible that there wasn't someone, but there never was. Each time I thought to myself that's one solitary, independent young woman. Watching and listening to you I didn't feel you would ever find a man special enough to marry."

Hanna said, "What about you Jenny I see you're wearing a wedding ring and an engagement ring."

"Oh, I never minded rings. I knew the first time Howard, and I met it was forever. It never bothered me for the world to know. I thought it appropriate others see me as taken, that I was Howards no qualms, and with all my heart and soul. But listening to you on the Cavett show, the one about seven weeks after the Tony Awards, I knew you had another kind of fire. I could see it was crowding out everything else. What's it like having that much creative energy burning away inside you?"

"I never thought about it. I woke up early every morning raring to go, and I didn't want to go to bed at night. All I wanted was to keep going. It drove everybody around me crazy, there'd be a painting or set design in my head, and I wanted to get it out, to make it real. It wasn't a healthy way to be, but I accomplished a lot." Nodding toward Morris, Hanna said, "He's the same way about his writing."

Sharon said, "You're no longer designing or painting?"

"I lost the path. So, no, I'm taking a break and concentrating on Emily and our marriage, there's a lot to learn."

Jenny said, "Hanna I want you to know watching you the last time you were on the Cavett show I thought you were one of the most extraordinary young women I've ever encountered. The paintings they showed that night even on TV were as powerful and inspiring as anything I've ever seen. That painting, a girl in a blue dress with pearls, was the most sensual disturbing, beautiful thing I've ever seen."

Hanna said, "She was special; a little sad, but I kind of wish I still had that one."

Jenny said, "I hope for all of us you find that path again."

Hanna blushed and said, "Thank you, Ginny. Accepting compliments is hard for me. It makes me uncomfortable, then I get self-conscious; I never know what to say."

"Me either," Laura said. "But I've decided the best way for me is to simply smile and say thank you."

Jenny looked across at Morris and said, "Since we last saw you you've become quite the interesting person yourself. Let's see if I've got it straight. You have a Doctorate in Humanities, and you write serious, thoughtful academic works. Along the way, you've thrown in two best sellers. After the tragic loss of your wife and child, you've reconnected with and won the hand of this marvelous woman."

"That's me in a nutshell."

Jenny said, "Morris I'm so pleased to have the chance to get to know you as an adult. What a remarkable couple to be at dinner with. Your parents must be bursting with pride."

Morris said, "Thank you, Jenny that was very nice of you."

Laura asked, "Morris would you mind a personal question?"

"Not at all."

"I understand you were a full professor with tenure and owned your own home, a very nice one. Why didn't you keep your position and you and Hanna move to Evanston?"

"I met Emily for the first time about five weeks ago. Hanna and I've been involved in each other's lives as friends since high school, but we've never lived together or even dated. Emily never met me until just before we moved back here. Hanna came every month for a week or more, but still, they were visits. Annett and Robert raised Emily. We thought it would be traumatic for everybody to make a sudden change like moving to Evanston.

So, thanks to Annett and Robert we're all living here getting to know each other.

Laura said, "You're so young Morris, you already had tenure and at Northwestern. Isn't that what every academic strives for?

"Yes, it was an honor."

"And you gave it up?"

Hanna said, "Tell them, Morris. They want to understand why."

"There were over seven-hundred people at Annie's, my wife's funeral. Most of them are still there, part of the University. Annie was an amazing personality. She was a respected well-liked, much beloved Professor. At her funeral, many people alluded to us as a couple, to our marriage and our being an integral part of Northwestern campus life.

"I couldn't imagine what it might be like for Hanna and Emily and me to live with Annie's legacy everywhere around us. And I don't know if any of you've read my novels, but the characters were based on real people who lived in my house. The continual reminder of lives and dreams dashed to pieces and gone forever was overwhelming. I couldn't be there."

Mrs. Costellano said, "Given the situation living here with Robert and Annett seems a sensible solution."

Morris said, "Hanna was exhausted. Way too many twenty-hour days. She gave up her building, her studio, and home, her assistants, her friends and her whole business life in New York. We both felt we'd need time to recover and take over. Annett and Robert were kind enough to help us. It's been a workable way for us to work out the kinks. It's given me a chance to get to know Robert and Annett, and I will be forever grateful for what they've done for Emily and us."

Susan said, "Hanna have you given up painting altogether?

"I had three assistants, four apprentices, and six thousand square feet of studio space. I was painting every day for at least twelve hours often more. So, no, I'm no longer painting at that level."

Susan said, "Morris you gave up your whole way of life too? Do you miss it?"

"Yes and no. I miss my friends, my students and all that intellectual energy. But Hanna and Emily, well that's living every day with a big beautiful grown-up diamond and a fresh uncut stone we're all dying to polish and help shape. We know this will take time and a lot of effort, but I can tell you we're enjoying it."

FORTY FIVE

Hanna came with Morris to Evanston for the closing on the sale of his house. Morris wouldn't stay at the house with Hanna preferring instead to stay at a hotel. The next morning, they arrived at the house in a cab. Getting out and standing on the sidewalk in front of the house, Hanna said, "Really Morris, this was yours and Annie's?"

Almost as if he didn't believe it himself he said, "Yes, this was our home. This is where we lived."

"God almighty Morris it's a mansion."

Once inside Hanna began exploring. Going from one room to another, she was touching the furniture and looking over the many beautiful rugs. A short time later she returned to the living room where Morris was standing in front of the big windows looking out on Lake Michigan.

"Morris I'm so sorry, I had no idea, none. It's glorious. The furnishings, that library all those books. You're giving up everything you worked for, your whole life to be with us, aren't you?"

"Hanna, it wasn't meant to be. It's over, and it's Marion's and Annie's home. I have to let it go."

"This place is beautiful. It's so warm and welcoming, it has such dignity. This must be heartbreaking for you."

"Hanna, you've no idea how blessed I feel to have Emily. To be given a second chance with someone as special as you. It's an incredible kindness."

He got his car started and out of the garage. They came back the next morning to make sure all of Marion and Albert's books; their fifty-year collection was loaded on the truck and on its way to the university library. The moving van came later that morning. The movers boxed and loaded up the several hundred books Morris held aside along with a few of the furnishings and some of the household items the new owners didn't want.

Hanna picked up a framed photo of Annie along with their framed Quaker wedding certificate. She wrapped them in a blanket and put them in the trunk of his car to bring home with them. He took a last look around and locked the door. They drove to the realtor's office and signed the papers. Morris handed over the keys to the new owners and a great wave of sadness and relief passed through him. At that moment the doorway on this life closed forever. Morris would never again be able to be here as he once had.

Morris thought of Albert and Marion and all they endured and all they taught him. Of the many lives who were part of that house. Of Annie and all their many hopes and dreams. How living with her changed him, making him so much more capable. She gave him both real strength and loving understanding. He left the real estate office sad about all of what was lost, but with renewed hope for his new family and their future.

They returned to their hotel, showered, and changed in preparation for a farewell dinner that night at Dee and John's home. Hanna was meeting John, Dee, Robbie, and Karen for the first time. All four knew of Hanna having seen her on TV at different times. Knowing of Hanna began the night of the Tony Awards. Twenty faculty wives and husbands including John,

Dee, Robbie, and Karen got together at Annie's house. They made a party out of seeing Morris at the Tony award ceremony

They'd read about Hanna in "Time Magazine," "Newsweek," and "The New Yorker." Some of them read the "New York Times" articles. On the surface, they knew who and what she was. But Hanna in the flesh was something to behold. Rested and hopeful about her new life Hanna quickly regained her creative energy. It no longer manifested itself as raw, youthful efflorescent power. She was a sophisticated and worldly being who without doing a single thing was an amazing presence.

Hanna looked as fresh as a twenty-year-old. There were a few crinkles in the corners of her eyes, and her skin wasn't so babyish looking, but she needed no makeup. Sometimes she wore simple earrings, but that was the extent of her adornment. Most people have never encountered such a personal presence either male or female. It came to most as a shock.

It didn't matter if they knew of her or didn't. With her still graceful, lithe body, her lovely face holding those remarkable blue eyes, and a voice that just stopped everyone stone cold, people were awed by her. At grocery stores, gas stations, even airports, it didn't matter. Wherever they went, it was the same, people stopped, stared, and when that ever so genuine smile spread across her face people melted and wanted to hug her.

Finishing up helping Dee load the dishwasher and dry a few pots and pans Dee smiling at Morris, said, "I need to talk with you. We can leave Hanna to enthrall the others for a little longer. Walk out back with me. Outside in the garden, Dee said, "John's pretty much past the shock of losing you, and he's accepted the why. But it's been hard on him. He admired you both and your marriage; he had such hopes for your life here.

You couldn't know how heartbroken he was when Annie's life ended. I've never seen John so sad. You were special to him, both of you. The son and daughter every father hopes for. He saw your marriage to Annie as the crowning achievement of everything he hoped and wanted for you. He saw you and Annie as being able to become a living legacy at the University. John believed yours would be one even stronger, more influential and beloved than the one Marion and Albert built."

"Dee, I wasn't able to see either myself or Annie in that way. I believe Annie had that ability the potential, but I couldn't see it in myself even through John's and Robbie's eyes. I never felt to be anywhere near that accomplished. Marion and Albert, you and John are an institution unto yourselves, you are all such gracious caring people."

"Morris, it wasn't just Robbie and John, we all saw you that way. Didn't you hear what your students and fellow professors said about the two of you at Annie's funeral? You were already there?"

"She's gone, Dee. This life went with her. If I'm anything even close to what you're suggesting it came from living and learning from Annie, but it's gone forever. All that's left of us is for me to hold on to her inner light and spread her love everywhere I can."

"John's told me about you and Hanna, your history, about your daughter. Why you're together."

"Emily's been the easy part, she's terrific. But I've never understood Hanna's and my relationship. It was spread over many years. But we're struggling like two strangers meeting for the first time on their wedding day. But we're getting there."

"I'm glad you brought Hanna with you, and we could meet her. I think you're the luckiest man alive to have two such remarkable women in your life. Hanna and Annie are what we faculty wives call the magical people. They get Nobel prizes; they invent life-changing things. They write books and win Pulitzer Prizes, Tony Awards, and show us how to see the world in new ways. Hanna and Annie are remarkable, unforgettable people."

"Dee, I want to thank you for welcoming us to your home and having us to dinner. I did so want the four of you to meet Hanna and spend time with her. It was important, thank you."

"Morris, I have to confess. Annie had such a brilliant intellectual, very amusing loving way. She used it easily, but ever so enthusiastically to draw people to her. I came to love her more each day I knew her. Reading your book, I felt honored to have known you both. She was a most remarkable and loving person."

I've had nowhere near as much time with Hanna, but she's breathtaking Morris. She pulls you in and captures you with just her presence. Sitting next to her at the table I could feel her creative energy. It's like an aurora. Put that power together with her amazing voice and that terrific smile, and I was captivated. I wanted to hug her. Her paintings are astonishing, and Morris I know you won't like me saying this, but I've always wondered what it might be like to have dinner with Michelangelo or Rembrandt, to meet and talk with them."

"Dee, Michelangelo and Rembrandt were unbelievably creative beings."

"So is Hanna Morris, she's every bit as special."

FORTY SIX

After Morris's book about Annie was published, Connie Taylor wrote him the most amazing letter. Connie thanked him for sharing their love, their lives, and their marriage with the world, but mostly with Annie's family. She was amazed and delighted to know what her daughter fought through and what she became.

Morris saved Connie's letter and would take it out and re-read it. Doing so always left him refreshed almost elated. During the school year following Annie's death, Connie called several times and wrote to him. They began corresponding. Connie's were about what was going on with the family. His were asking after the children and Connie and Mr. Taylor.

Two weeks after Morris and Hanna returned from closing on the house Morris came to this time when he knew he needed to go to Annie's parents. He felt this enormous sense of obligation to tell them in person he'd remarried and why. It was an unsettling frightening prospect, but he felt he owed them nothing less.

The moment they learned of Annie's and their baby's deaths they rounded up everyone, dropped everything, put aside their personal pain, and put their lives on hold. They came and surrounded him with their caring kindness. They were marvelous people. He never forgot their love and support. How they helped him that awful week. He loved them, and they were a big important part of what and who he was.

He comprehended for the first time during that week what it meant to share your inner light with others. Annie had been doing it all along with him and everyone else. But Morse didn't understand it. Not until the family came and spent that week caring for him. That week changed Morris. The Taylor's gave him the courage and strength to begin to accept his loss. Annie and her family's loving nourishment, along with their compassionate understanding made it possible for him to love Hanna and unreservedly love Emily. They taught him how to look at Annett and Robert with clear, loving, thankful eyes.

Here it was a little more than a year and a few months after Annie and their baby's deaths, and he was remarried. By doing so, he no longer knew what he was to Connie and Nathan. Morris was struggling with what this would mean or do to his relationship with them. His apprehension about the Taylors steadily worsened because he included his relationship with Hanna and the night of the Tony Awards in Annie's story.

Morris knew anyone who read his book would know about Hanna. In the book, Morris described his knowing Hanna, and their relationship, to help the reader better understand Annie's love and devotion to her inner light. He tried to show his and Annie's marriage as something different and more understandable than his relationship with Hanna. He didn't try to define or interpret his relationship with Hanna, but let the reader try to figure it out. Morris couldn't.

Morris felt his sleeping with Hanna the night of the Tony awards was dishonest. An awful thing he'd done to Annie. Morris felt knowing of it had to have upset the Taylor's. Connie never mentioned it in their talks or letters. Morris believed he betrayed Annie when he slept with Hanna three weeks before they married. He thought surely the Taylor's must. Morris was coming here to tell them because of that night with Hanna he was the father of a three-and-a-half-year-old girl and had married her mother. He felt and expected the Taylor's would be shocked and very disappointed with him.

At the very least, he thought both Connie and Nathan would have serious doubts about continuing the relationship. But Morris knew no matter what the outcome, this had to be done by him, and in person. He liked Annie's whole family. Her sisters and brothers were patient and thoughtful. They kept him going with kindness and heartfelt consideration. They didn't complain once about losing a week of their lives, they stood by him.

Even if this would be the last time, he'd see Connie and Nathan he didn't want to lose their affection or their good will. He'd no idea what to expect, but they had to be told before they learned of it some other way. Morris felt no reason to be optimistic about their reactions. But he went ahead with the arrangements. He declined to stay at the house saying, "Connie you know from reading my book what our wedding night meant to Annie. If I stayed in that guest room, I'd be crying all night long."

Before he left Morris and Hanna talked for several hours about his visit to the Taylors. She suggested if he could part with it he give the painting she'd done for him of Annie and her daughter to the Taylors. He brought the painting with him but was unsure of what he would do.

He rented a car and drove out to the house arriving about eleven. Connie fixed a nice lunch for them. It was Saturday and Pierce, Temperance and Obadiah made him welcome greeting him with smiles and lots of questions. Temperance had become a beautiful young woman, and Obadiah like Pierce was now taller very much on his way to an exact likeness of his father.

Nathan said, "Morris Connie and I would like to take you to the family cemetery, so you will know where Annie and Hope are."

Morris said, "Is there a place where we could talk?"

Nathan said, "Woodlands Cemetery is a serene place. It's quiet. There are benches. It's a pleasant day, I'm sure we'll find a suitable spot."

They took separate cars because Morris told them it would give him more time before he had to get back and turn the car in before catching his flight home. Morris was afraid this would end badly. He didn't feel at all comfortable telling them his news from the back seat of their car. Morris felt riding back to the house with them to get his car could turn into an unbearable nightmare. So, he drove. Upon arriving and taking it in, Morris said, "This is lovely, it's beautiful but it doesn't appear to be like any of the Quaker Cemetery's I've seen."

Nathan said, "It isn't. Somewhere back around 1855, my great, great grandfather said I want a headstone for Mary, something I can pray over. We must bury her where our people won't speak against us for going against Quaker simplicity over a headstone. Our family members have been buried here ever since. Even though our markers are likely the simplest stones found here, we're all together."

They walked a short way from where they parked. He found his eyes drawn to a sheltered shaded place under the sprawling outstretched arms of an enormous old oak. The gravestones there were the same, a simple three-foot-high thin white marble stone with a notched arched top. Morris easily recognized the newest one and read the simple words:

Annabelle Annie Stevens
Beloved Daughter and Wife
June 15, 1941 ~ June 14, 1972
Daughter Hope
June 14, 1972

As he read the words, Morris's eyes filled with water. He covered his mouth holding the end of his fist against it. The tears came. Connie grabbed him up hugging him to her. She took his hand and led him to a pair of stone benches and sat him down. As Nathan sat next to Connie across from Morris, he asked, "What is it we need to speak of Morris?"

On that lovely peaceful late summer afternoon, they sat facing each other on two stone benches not far from Annie's and Hope's marker. Morris began by telling them how much they meant to him, how much he loved Annie. He warned them what he was about to say would be difficult for them. Connie said, "Morris we both read your book. We know and understand what you and Annie shared and how much your marriage meant to you. I wrote to you of our feelings on it.

Nathan said, "Truly Morris reading of your life together and what Annie accomplished helped tremendously with losing her. There was only one thing in your book that troubled me. It was your spending the night with the young woman who won the Tony awards. I understood your relationship even why it happened. But it wasn't right. You were living with Annie, and it occurred a few weeks before you married. If she'd known of it, I don't know if she would have married thee."

Morris said, "I've really struggled with what I did. I was too ashamed to ever tell Annie. And yes, if I told her and we hadn't married she wouldn't have gotten pregnant and died.

Believe me, if I could have one wish, just one. I would wish, even if not with me, for Annie and Hope to be alive and enjoying their lives somewhere on this earth."

Nathan said, "Morris, do not go into such a dark place. It's filled with if's, and's, but's, and maybe's. You both did the best you could. Your marriage may have been short, but while you had it, it was everything either of you ever hoped or dreamed of. Cherish your time together. Forgive yourself that transgression. Use all that love you and Annie shared as best you can."

"That was the only time I've ever been unfaithful. I would've lived all my days with Annie full of joy and never even considered such a thing. I apologize, but there's more I must tell you. The night of the Tony Awards the night Hanna and I spent together she became pregnant.

"Until three months ago I knew nothing of this. I'm the father of a little girl. She's three and a half, and her name is Emily. Hanna never contacted me or told me. She swore her parents to secrecy and never again asked for my help. Not wanting to interfere with our marriage or cause us any heartache she never again interacted with me, nor I with her."

Morris continued telling them of his and Hanna's relationship from the beginning right up through their civil marriage and moving in with her parents. Morris continued telling them even though they had known one another for a long time but in all the ways that mattered they were very much strangers to each other. It was like meeting for the first time on their wedding day. Connie and Nathan listened without expression, and when Morris finished Connie asked, "How is Emily doing with this?"

"I think Emily's very pleased about having both of us. She's bright and quick about things. I read to her almost every night, and it hasn't taken long for her to come to like and trust me."

Nathan said, "You are a very likable and kind man Morris. I knew the first day in the guest room. Annie had made a good choice this time.

Morris said, "You did nothing to let me in on that.

Nathan smiled and said, "Morris, you were living with my daughter outside of marriage. I was struggling with it. But I'll admit listening to your words Christmas morning I moved past most of my concerns. I thank you for them and Annie for her honesty with Connie about her marriage with Don. We came in a roundabout way to understand your living together was your only viable path to a marriage. So, whether you knew or not, I accepted it."

Connie said, "Morris I can't thank thee enough for immortalizing Annie with your words. It meant more than anything you could've ever done for us. Knowing her to be such a grown up and complete person from your wonderful book has made her premature passing a little more bearable for all of us. We've all read your book even Obadiah. Annie's gone from us, but Morris we all know she would want you to keep living and trying to do what's right. We would expect no less of either of you."

Nathan said, "Morris you were very much obligated to marry Hanna and take care of your little girl. I'm not saying that out of righteousness, but because misguided as Hanna was she's always loved you. Hanna bore your child and kept her and loved her. Don't apologize to us or anyone else for doing what you know to be right."

Connie said, "I'm sure you and Hanna can grow to love one another just like you and Annie did. Annie's gone from us, from you, but you'll have her love for as long as you live. Death doesn't end love. You'll come to draw on it and share it."

Nathan said, "Morris we want you to reconsider and have dinner with us and stay at the house tonight. Franklin, Teresa, and Hester are coming home to be here tomorrow to visit with thee. They'll be disappointed if they miss seeing thee." He stayed, and Connie put him up in Franklin's room.

All night he thought about what remarkable forgiving people the Taylor's were. He finally fell asleep hoping some of their gentle forgiving ways would rub off on him. The next day right after lunch he went to his car and got the painting. He explained upon learning of what happened to Annie and Hope his lifelong friend, Hanna Williston painted and sent him the painting along with a note. Hanna and I talked about this, and we believe your mom and dad, all of you should have it. I know such gilded fancy things aren't the Quaker way, but we would very much like you to have it.

Morris stood the painting on the counter against the wall and put Hanna's note with it. They were silent. No one said a word. Franklin stood and said, "That's the most beautiful thing I've ever seen. That little girl's alive." Morris glanced across at Connie and Nathan. Tears were streaming down their faces.

Temperance in her exuberant way said, "It's Annie, and Hope, isn't it?"

Heather and Theresa walked up to the painting and Heather said, "It's wonderful Morris, it's beautiful."

Connie said, "Morris are thee certain?"

Morris said, "They belong with you. I always have them with me. They're both right here," and he put his fist to his heart.

FORTY SEVEN

After three months of living with Robert and Annett Morris bought a classic barn still in excellent condition, it needed only a new roof and it came with an abandoned, dilapidated house that sat up on a hill looking out over a lake. He purchased the whole half section, three-hundred and twenty acres which included the entire hundred-and-eighty-six-acre lake.

The property was west of Minneapolis not far from the small town of Waconia. The house and barn were in a lovely spot surrounded on three sides by seven fifty-year-old big sprawling White Oaks. They took down the dilapidated house and built a modern, open, gracious five-bedroom home. They remodeled most of the barn into a painting studio for Hanna and the lower part into garages, a workshop, and storage areas. After several dozen trips to the site, the day after it was completed Morris, Hanna, and Emily moved in.

Between the two of them, they had sufficient resources to last for the rest of their lives. But at present they were more interested in their marriage, Emily, and being a family than being at all concerned about careers or working. Hanna did start painting again, and when summer faded, and it got colder, she painted in earnest.

The three of them shared their days. They would have breakfast and dinner together and sometimes lunch. They went for long walks in the woods or spent their days on the beach or at the nearby arboretum They always spent their evenings together. Hanna embraced this new life. Seldom did she get so wrapped up in a painting she didn't come to bed until morning.

Both Hanna and Morris balanced their lives better than before. Hanna put Emily, Morris, her marriage and herself before her painting and anything and everything else. They were enjoying this new life and their obscurity. The people in the little town where they shopped for groceries and other necessities now paid no more attention to them than any other young family.

It had been embarrassing at first. People would point them out and sometimes would appear with a book or a copy of a painting and ask to have it signed. But these were humble, modest people who treated them with kindness. Both Hanna and Morris found their modesty and sincerity touching.

Hanna's voice and cadence still stopped people in their tracks. When they were shopping people would come around aisle ends and displays to see who belonged to such a voice. Hanna would smile embarrassing and disarming them. But after a few months, they were no more of an oddity than anyone else in town. That fall, a small group of local high school teachers approached them and asked if they would speak to their classes. Hanna and Morris enjoyed this finding a surprising number of talented, capable students who eagerly participated, and Hanna soon became a regular.

Morris was writing. He began a book about an unusual young woman, one born with intelligence, a marvelous distinctive voice, a gift for drawing and a fertile creative mind. The young woman was fearful of others, reticent, and high school was difficult. She went through the trial and pain of being attacked and severely beaten. The young man with her died, and she struggled to learn to live with her feelings of being responsible for his death.

Her creative ability was astounding. So, overpowering and startling, as to be close to unbelievable. The people closest to her were amazed by her ability. The rest of the world settled for marveling at her paintings and enjoyed her always creative stage designs. After two months Morris put it aside remembering all too well what happened the last time he began writing about someone he loved.

Morris continued to exchange letters with Connie and Nathan. The day he left, both John Stanton and Robbie James asked him to keep them apprised of his new life. To let them know how Morris and his new family were getting along and what he was doing. He wrote to both John and Robbie explaining their lives and of their changing situation to both men.

It wasn't long before John and Robbie were encouraging him to take on an academic project. They suggested several topics they felt would be both a challenge and worthwhile. John offered to send a letter to the head of the University of Minnesota Humanities Department on Morris's behalf asking him to grant Morris research privileges. Not wishing to hurt the feelings of either John or Robbie Morris asked John to please do so.

***

Morris spent a spring morning helping Hanna straighten up and clean her studio. Hanna looking for something said, "Morris, have you seen my series of paintings of Emily, I could only find one. Thank God it was my favorite. There should be six more around here somewhere. I'm sure I rolled them up together."

"I sent them to Henric. I told him to keep the one he and Erica liked the best and to sell the other five."

"Morris! Why would you do that? I sold that building back to him for what I paid him for it, a third of what it was worth. I gave him two million dollars. Even his shyster lawyer couldn't believe the deal Henric was getting. He was worried about being accused of being part of a swindle. He kept asking me, Hanna do you understand what you're doing? Are you sure about this?"

"You gave him that great deal because your love affair with Erica almost destroyed their marriage. I know it broke the man's heart."

Hanna turned whiter than her hair then flushed dark red saying, "And who told you we had a love affair?"

"Hanna, I see what's in front of me even when I don't want to."

"Morris this is embarrassing, it's awful. I'm so sorry. It was hard enough telling you about carrying on with all those men. I'm still ashamed, but you knowing Erica and I had a love affair, that's truly awful. Is there a point in learning of all my debauchery when you'll walk away? I think the things I was doing were disgusting. I can't imagine what you think."

"Hanna why are you surprised, you already told me Henric caught you in bed together?"

"Loving someone is way different than a coked-up one-night stand. There were a lot of men, but they meant nothing. But Erica, Morris neither of us asked for or tried to make anything like that happen. It just did. Morris, being with Erica was the only time I've even come close to being with you."

"She was gentle, and I felt loved and safe. She felt the same for me. I knew it was wrong, but I needed her in my life. I couldn't have you, and I needed her warmth and love. When I knew you were out there and I could summon you, I was okay, but when you married, I knew you were gone from me forever. I wished you had died. You kind of did, except you married, which was worse. Because I knew you were alive, still there. I came apart, and I turned to Erica. It was a selfish thing, and I regret it."

"Hanna, you can't regret loving someone or being loved by another. Right or wrong, good or bad it makes you what you are. Annie taught me that much."

"The afternoon Henric walked in on us and caught us was the worse day of my life. Almost as awful as realizing because of me Frank Sweet died. Maria and I were naked and holding each other just gazing into each other's eyes. Henric knew the second he saw us it wasn't sex for fun or some aberrant cocaine dream. He knew it was serious. He collapsed in a chair right there in the bedroom. He said, my Erica and Hanna, unbelievable, the two most important people in the whole world. How could you do this? Erica how did this happen?"

"Erica pleaded with him to leave so we could get dressed. He kept saying, "Erica I don't understand. How did this happen? What did you need from me and why didn't you ask? God above woman you must know I love you more than anything or anyone in this whole fucking unforgiving world.

"She kept saying, it just happened Henric we didn't plan it, it just happened. He said you didn't have to act on it. I sat there exposed feeling just like I did when mom told me Dennis Sweet died. I wept and couldn't stop. It came from my soul. I knew he was right we didn't have to act on it. Having to face Henric, to see what I'd done to him, to his marriage, to Erica was horrible. Henric was so hurt, he couldn't stop his tears. When he left the room, Erica kept saying, I'm sorry Hanna, I'm so sorry. I hadn't seen either of them in two years, not until they came to talk about the building."

"That's why you were using a different Gallery, and everything fell apart?"

"All the awful things happened at the same time. I doubly hurt Henric and his business when I left. I couldn't face him. He had three clients lined up who agreed to spend two million each on a similar size painting. I never did the paintings."

Morris said, "How did you and Erica end up together? Never mind. It's none of my business."

"It is your business, Morris. Erica was like me. She doesn't like most men and keeps pretty much to herself. She was bringing clients by the studio and we started seeing a lot of each other. We hugged and kissed one afternoon, and I just let it happen. After we were found out Erica tried to call and talk a few times. That was about as awkward and uncomfortable for me as just finding out you've known all along I was in a serious lesbian relationship."

"You needed someone, Hanna. You didn't have me."

"Sorry Morris, I wish. But I already knew I lost you forever, and I loved her, and she loved me. I'm not a lesbian, and I can't explain how or why."

"You don't have to."

"I would like to believe you understand and can forgive me.

"I do."

"Have I hurt you all over again? I didn't care about any of those men, but I very much-loved Erica."

"Judging from what I saw the day they came over to talk about buying back the studio Erica was still struggling with her feelings for you.

"You noticed that?"

"She was close to tears."

"She was glad to see I was all right, there were lots of rumors."

"Hanna, I saw more than her being pleased you were all right."

"She wanted to talk about me being something more, and I had to tell her Erica if I were that way I'd be yours forever. But I'm not and cutting her off was the hardest thing I've ever done. I loved her, but nowhere near as much as she did me. At first, the sex was pleasant, sweet, and worked. But it wasn't anything like being with you. It slowly became mindless like cleaning my brushes, I was with her, but I was just doing it.

"I wish with all my heart I'd broken it off before Henric walked in on us. She told me later Henric suspected something was going on, that she was seeing someone, but in his wildest imaginations he never dreamed it was a woman much less me.

"Hanna, I thought you were nuts for accepting their invitation to dinner, for sure about us spending the night. But I'm glad you did. I believe it resolved a lot of things for all of us. I could tell Henric understood neither of you was a lesbian you needed each other, especially you."

Hanna said, "They're gracious people. When Erica said goodbye to us at the airport, I understood, and I felt better. I knew everything was all right between them."

"Henric sent me a note it came yesterday, and for him, it was surprisingly warm. I've got it right here; I'll read it:"

Dear Morris,

There was much excitement among our clients about once again having Hanna with us and seeing her work. Our clientele has one, and all made it clear we needed to get her back. All five of Hanna's paintings you sent sold opening night of the spring show. I kept one for us as you requested, and I've included an idea for a painting. Please, Morris, it's only if Hanna feels up to working on something of this nature. Should she, ask her to size it to seven by nine feet.

Either way, we'll welcome receiving anything she sends anytime she can. The same rates as before, thirty-five percent of any sale, we'll take care of everything including the packing and shipping costs. Morris Hanna's a phenomenal artist. Those paintings of Emily have an unimaginable power. We hung them on the north wall by themselves. The whole of our clientele just walked over to the far end of the gallery and stood there looking at them. No one spoke, they were speechless.

Those images of Emily were ethereal, and yet that wonderful little girl was so alive, she was the epitome of living joy. The way Hanna manages the paint and the luminosity; her color values are just incredible. It's hard to believe, but she's even more accomplished than before she left us. She keeps getting better and better. I struggle to imagine how great she'll become.

There are no gallery charges. Your generous gift more than covered everything. It was nice to learn things are going well. We both appreciated knowing how much you're enjoying your life together with Emily. Thank you, Morris, for sending the paintings and your warm letter, but more than anything, for being there for Hanna, do your best to care for her she's a remarkable creative being.

Kind regards, Henric.

"There's a check from the gallery in the top drawer of your desk made out to Hanna Williston Stevens for two-million-one hundred and twenty-thousand-dollars."

"Morris, you can't be serious."

"It says, proceeds from the sale of five Hanna Williston Steven's Emily paintings."

"That man knows how to market an Artist."

"He does, and he has an awesome talent he's working with. Oh, and before I forget, we're having company this weekend."

"My, my, Morris, now what have you done?"

"I tracked down Maria Carson and asked her to spend the weekend with us."

"She's coming?"

"Friday I'm stopping by the U of M and meeting with Professor Hamilton. I'll pick her up after that at the airport at three thirty. Maria's giving a series of seminars next week on directing to the MFA students. Maria said to tell you she's bringing her sense of humor. She wondered where you disappeared to and was surprised to learn you married, but not who the guy was. She was delighted and pleased we wanted to see her. Maria also had some amusing things to say about abandoning the ship of fools and forgetting to tell you. She also said she's got a show if you're interested."

"Well Morris my dear, since you've been messing with my life, how's your sense of humor?"

"Good, why?"

"I might be pregnant. Just a little."

Smiling Morris said, "We're getting old for that don't you think?"

"You are. I'm not."

"Okay, a little pregnant? Isn't that one of those yes or no things?" Hanna's glorious smile was unambiguous.

Lifting her right off her feet Morris said, "I'm okay with everything about us especially something that wonderful. Are you Hanna? Is living in the middle of nowhere all right and comfortable? Is being married working for you? Are you pleased with us, with this?"

"Morris, it was a choice. I wouldn't be pregnant if I weren't the most grateful, thankful, woman alive. I couldn't be more pleased, just keep helping me be honest and being you, and I swear to you I'll never stop smiling or loving you."

***

Dear Morris,

Just a quick note, I'll be unusually busy for the next few weeks, but I wanted to congratulate you on your excellent news. Do you know what you're having or are you planning to wait and see what shows up?

I hope my sending this poem is okay. I found it tucked in amongst Annie's things you sent. It was stuck inside one of her cards. There was a note saying, should anything ever happen to me please be sure my Morris gets this.

All our Love, Connie

Morris when I come to the end of the road
and the sun has set for me.
I want no rites in a gloom-filled room.
Why cry for a soul set free?
Miss me a little, but not too long
and not with your head bowed low.
Remember the love once shared.
Miss me but let me go.
For this is a journey we all must take
and each must go alone.
It's all part of the master's plan,
a step on the road to home.
When you are lonely and sick of heart
go to the places we know
and bury sorrow among the trees there.
Miss me, but please Morris let me go.

(Anonymous)
Morris you'll have my love forever, Annie

*****

ABOUT THE AUTHOR

Mr. Davis attended three grade schools, two Junior highs, three high schools and three universities. Not by choice and at the age of forty-six he finally earned his bachelor's degree. Richard is married has five children four grandchildren and four great grandchildren. Over his first working eighteen years he designed theatrical sets and the lighting for more than 280 professional productions.

The bulk of these were done at summer stock and regional repertory theaters scattered throughout the United States. He also designed for several colleges, civic opera and ballet companies and did set design work for industrial productions and movies.

His second eighteen years was spent in the trade show industry. He was president and founder of one of the first e-commerce design firms and owned a marine chandlery store and four related e-commerce businesses. Upon retirement he began writing as something to do that was more frustrating, demanding, and satisfying than working in the garden or cutting the grass.

www.ingramcontent.com/pod-product-compliance
Lightning Source LLC
Chambersburg PA
CBHW021429240626
47153CB00001B/84